Acclaim for
Pierce

"With its movie-like scenes, settings, characters, and action depicted so vividly, the novel is indeed a visual feast, yet it is also so much more. What's most significant about this novel is its relatability to anyone with a heart, to anyone who has lost someone, and to anyone who has had to grieve and move forward. Every man or woman can find something to connect to in the struggles and ultimate hope and triumph of Leo Vasari."

—Dr. Maura Gage Cavell,
Professor of English
and Director of the Honors Program
at Louisiana State University at Eunice

"*Pierce* by Roberto Ferrari is that rarest of debut novels—a riveting read with memorable characters whose fates the reader actually grows increasingly concerned about with each turned page. The novel's intricate plot twists slowly unravel a psychological drama . . . and a gay love story that brings an added dimension to the book's powerful narrative. With a particularly keen ear for realistic dialogue and insightful and sharply crafted characterizations, Ferrari has given us an important contemporary tale of loss, longing, love, and—ultimately—the cleansing power of forgiveness."

—Reed Massengill,
Author of *Portrait of a Racist, Self-Exposure,*
numerous other books, currently completing
Backstage Pass: The Men of Broadway Bares

NOTES FOR PROFESSIONAL LIBRARIANS AND LIBRARY USERS

This is an original book title published by Southern Tier Editions™, Harrington Park Press®, the trade division of The Haworth Press, Inc. Unless otherwise noted in specific chapters with attribution, materials in this book have not been previously published elsewhere in any format or language.

CONSERVATION AND PRESERVATION NOTES

All books published by The Haworth Press, Inc., and its imprints are printed on certified pH neutral, acid-free book grade paper. This paper meets the minimum requirements of American National Standard for Information Sciences-Permanence of Paper for Printed Material, ANSI Z39.48-1984.

DIGITAL OBJECT IDENTIFIER (DOI) LINKING

The Haworth Press is participating in reference linking for elements of our original books. (For more information on reference linking initiatives, please consult the CrossRef Web site at www.crossref.org.) When citing an element of this book such as a chapter, include the element's Digital Object Identifier (DOI) as the last item of the reference. A Digital Object Identifier is a persistent, authoritative, and unique identifier that a publisher assigns to each element of a book. Because of its persistence, DOIs will enable The Haworth Press and other publishers to link to the element referenced, and the link will not break over time. This will be a great resource in scholarly research.

Pierce

HARRINGTON PARK PRESS®
Southern Tier Editions™
Gay Men's Fiction

Elf Child by David M. Pierce

Huddle by Dan Boyle

The Man Pilot by James W. Ridout IV

Shadows of the Night: Queer Tales of the Uncanny and Unusual edited by Greg Herren

Van Allen's Ecstasy by Jim Tushinski

Beyond the Wind by Rob N. Hood

The Handsomest Man in the World by David Leddick

The Song of a Manchild by Durrell Owens

The Ice Sculptures: A Novel of Hollywood by Michael D. Craig

Between the Palms: A Collection of Gay Travel Erotica edited by Michael T. Luongo

Aura by Gary Glickman

Love Under Foot: An Erotic Celebration of Feet edited by Greg Wharton and M. Christian

The Tenth Man by E. William Podojil

Upon a Midnight Clear: Queer Christmas Tales edited by Greg Herren

Dryland's End by Felice Picano

Whose Eye Is on Which Sparrow? by Robert Taylor

Deep Water: A Sailor's Passage by E. M. Kahn

The Boys in the Brownstone by Kevin Scott

The Best of Both Worlds: Bisexual Erotica edited by Sage Vivant and M. Christian

Tales from the Levee by Martha Miller

Some Dance to Remember: A Memoir-Novel of San Francisco, 1970-1982 by Jack Fritscher

Confessions of a Male Nurse by Richard S. Ferri

The Millionaire of Love by David Leddick

Skip Macalester by J. E. Robinson

Chemistry by Lewis DeSimone

Going Down in La-La Land by Andy Zeffer

Friends, Lovers, and Roses by V. B. Clay

Beyond Machu by William Maltese

Seventy Times Seven by Salvatore Sapienza

Virginia Bedfellows by Gavin Morris

Planting Eli by Jeff Black

Death Trick: A Murder Mystery, A Donald Strachey Mystery by Richard Stevenson

Ice Blues: A Donald Strachey Mystery by Richard Stevenson

A Few Hints and Clews by Robert Taylor

Pierce by Roberto C. Ferrari

Pierce

Roberto C. Ferrari

Southern Tier Editions™
Harrington Park Press®
The Trade Division of The Haworth Press, Inc.
New York • London • Oxford

For more information on this book or to order, visit
http://www.haworthpress.com/store/product.asp?sku=5849

or call 1-800-HAWORTH (800-429-6784) in the United States and Canada
or (607) 722-5857 outside the United States and Canada

or contact orders@HaworthPress.com

Published by

Southern Tier Editions™, Harrington Park Press®, the trade division of The Haworth Press,
Inc., 10 Alice Street, Binghamton, NY 13904-1580.

PUBLISHER'S NOTES
The development, preparation, and publication of this work has been undertaken with great care.
However, the Publisher, employees, editors, and agents of The Haworth Press are not responsible
for any errors contained herein or for consequences that may ensue from use of materials or information contained in this work. The Haworth Press is committed to the dissemination of ideas and
information according to the highest standards of intellectual freedom and the free exchange of
ideas. Statements made and opinions expressed in this publication do not necessarily reflect the
views of the Publisher, Directors, management, or staff of The Haworth Press, Inc., or an en-
dorsement by them.

This is a work of fiction. Names, characters, places, and incidents either are the products of the
author's imagination or are used fictiously, and any resemblance to actual persons, living or
dead, business establishments, events, or locales is entirely coincidental.

Cover design by Jennifer M. Gaska.

Library of Congress Cataloging-in-Publication Data

Ferrari, Roberto C., 1970-
   Pierce / Roberto C. Ferrari.
      p. cm.
   ISBN-13: 978-1-56023-657-3 (pbk. : alk. paper)
   ISBN-10: 1-56023-657-4 (pbk. : alk. paper)
   1. Grief—Fiction. 2. Graduate students—Fiction. 3. Homosexuality—Fiction. I. Title.

PS3606.E737P54 2006
813'.6—dc22

                                                                        2006029899

For Nana

– ONE –

The burning in his throat from inhaling the joint between his lips was a taste he had never gotten used to. It was the acrid, sweet smoke that filled the air and his lungs, coursing upward through his nostrils, then downward through his entire body, that thrilled him. The taste, however, the dull irritant in his throat, he had never enjoyed all that much. Leo Vasari was celebrating his birthday. He would be twenty-nine in three days. He hated his birthday. Now, and every year thereafter probably. Aging itself would have been bad enough, but not enough to hate his birthday. It was because Matt had died one year ago on this night, April 28, three days before Leo's birthday.

It had been his ritual for one year now. On the twenty-eighth day of every month around ten-thirty at night he would sit on the swing in the screened front porch of the 1920's bungalow Matt and he owned in the Old Northeast area of St. Petersburg, Florida. He would drink a few Coronas until they numbed him, then smoke a joint. Like he had that night. Sometimes he would relive their last, angry words they had shouted at one another. If he were lucky, the beer and pot would make him drowsy and he would fall asleep on the porch swing. He'd imagine Matt wasn't pissed at him, that he just needed to drive to clear his head, and that when he woke up Matt would be there to greet him. They would apologize to each other. They would kiss to prove they were sorry. They would fuck to make up, then fall asleep spooning until the morning sun woke them in their bed.

He knew the dream would never come true. He had imagined it that night a year ago, because whenever there was craziness with Matt, it usually ended the way Leo's dream ended. April 28 played out differently, though. He wasn't woken by Matt, but by the police. They woke him during the night from his high-induced sleep, and he

Pierce
© 2007 by The Haworth Press, Inc. All rights reserved.
doi:10.1300/5849_01

groggily greeted them from the porch swing, stretching his muscles, aching from his contorted position on the wooden bench. He was bleary-eyed, but not so out of it that he didn't know they were police or there was marijuana around. He wondered if they could smell the residual pot in the air or on his breath, but they didn't seem to care.

"Excuse me, sir, is this the home of Matthew Pierce?"

Leo squinted his eyes, then rubbed them. There were two officers in dark blue on his front porch. The one who had spoken was a tall man with sideburns. His partner was a woman, her dark hair pulled into a ponytail, highlighting her chiseled face. Leo wondered if she was a lesbian. The male officer repeated the question.

Leo rubbed his temples, then nodded.

"Are you a relative, sir?"

He hesitated. He had heard this question before, on that one night when Leo had had to call 911 after what Matt had done to himself. Leo had to follow the ambulance because he couldn't ride with Matt. He heard it again at the emergency room, when they wouldn't let him in to see Matt, citing "family only." He now opened his mouth to speak, and cleared his throat. "We're roommates," he replied with a funny croak.

"We need to know the name of a relative we can contact. . ."

The male police officer's voice trailed off for Leo. As his vision cleared, he looked at the woman. He blinked his eyes, and it occurred to him that when he had said Matt was his roommate, she had stared at him. As he looked back at her, she glanced down, then back at him. It was a subtle acknowledgment. It made him relax. And then suddenly panic. "What happened to Matt?" he asked her.

She glanced up at her partner, who tried to repeat about a relative, but she saw Leo's fear and stepped forward. "What is your name, sir?" Her voice was firm, sympathetic.

He swallowed. His throat was raw, burning still. He cleared his throat again. He tried to stay calm. "Leo. Leo Vasari."

"Mr. Vasari, I'm sorry to have to tell you this, but your friend is dead. He was killed in an automobile accident a couple of hours ago." She paused a moment, then added, glancing down, "I'm sorry for your loss."

Her partner apparently realized they had been more than room-mates, because his tone changed when he spoke. He seemed uncomfortable. "Sir, would you like to give us the name of Mr. Pierce's closest relative, or would you like to contact them yourself?"

There were only two people: Matt's mother and sister. He needed to tell them. Somehow he conveyed this to the officers. The rest of the events from that night were a blur one year later, but Leo remembered that the officers came into the house with him. The woman even got him a glass of water. She commented about the disaster in the kitchen, but he didn't reply, and she didn't pursue. They stayed with him for a few more minutes. Before they left, he asked what had happened.

Matt had been driving his Mustang at a very high speed along I-275. At the construction zone after the Howard Frankland Bridge, just before the exits for WestShore Plaza and Tampa International Airport, he apparently lost control of his car and crashed full speed into a temporary cement median on the side of the road, where they were creating an estuary. There were skid marks. Rain had fallen earlier, making the oil-slicked roads dangerous. He had not been wearing a seat belt. The steering wheel crushed his sternum. He was thrown into the windshield. Leo could envision his body thrust forward, his screams echoing in a flash moment, the glass searing his beautiful face and body. The police told him he probably died instantly.

They asked Leo questions about the last time he had seen Matt.

"Before ten o'clock," he said.

They asked about Matt's state when he had left the house.

"He was fine," he lied.

"Was he taking any drugs or had he been drinking?"

The male officer had asked him that. He didn't respond immediately. He suspected Matt had gone to a bar for a few drinks. And there was no point in denying that there was alcohol and pot in the house. Still, he replied, "No."

They waited while he called Matt's mother Millie and his sister Theresa. They told him there would be an autopsy, which was normal

procedure. They gave him a number to call about the body. They
might be in touch again with more questions.

The officers left. He was alone. Now permanently. He sat on the
couch in the living room and stared. It was unreal. It wasn't right. He
thought he was dreaming still. He reached into the square ebony box
beside the couch and grabbed another joint. He went back to the
porch swing and smoked it, rocking himself to sleep, feeling the haze
of the smoke and the burning in his throat sedate him. He eventually
fell back to sleep, convinced it had all been a horrible nightmare. Matt
would be home soon, and they would make up, fuck, and sleep until
noon.

When he had opened his eyes a few hours later, the cooing of a
mourning dove waking him, he lay there for a moment, then stretched.
His first thought was to go look in on Matt in the bedroom, to sneak
up on him and fuck him with his morning hard-on. He lay back for a
moment pondering it, then remembered that he hadn't come home
yet. He hadn't woken him, apologized, and fucked. None of that had
happened. Leo suddenly jolted upright in the swing. Matt's Mustang
wasn't in the driveway. He remembered the officers, their description
of the accident. He realized in that moment Matt was dead, and it
hadn't been a dream or a bad trip.

Leo now woke up, after the twelfth time of performing the ritual,
to the sounds of the birds and the neighbors' cars revving. It was the
morning of April 29, 1999. He lay there silently on the swing, staring
up at the ceiling of the porch, the cracks in the whitewashed wood
staring back at him. He used his foot against the screen to rock himself, watching the rusty hooks holding the chains of the swing as they
whined from pressure. He imagined them crashing out of the ceiling,
wood and sawdust pouring on him, the roof following, crushing his
body, pulverizing it. He kicked against the screen harder, so that the
chains shrieked more loudly.

Nothing happened. He gradually slowed down and realized he had
to go on with his day like he always did. He had to get ready and go to
the university. He had been teaching three classes this semester. Today was his last one for the semester. He remembered he also had a

meeting, twice postponed, with his advisor about his dissertation. She would probably harp on him that he wasn't working on it. She had been sympathetic long enough, but he had to complete his work. He had to get off the swing. But he lay there, rocking. He even tried closing his eyes and going back to sleep. The sound of a truck distracted him. He heard the screeching of the brakes, the footsteps. He heard the knock on his screen porch door.

"Package for Leo Vasari?"

Leo turned his head to the side and stared at the UPS man. He hadn't spoken with an accent but he looked Latino. Through half-open eyes and dark screen Leo could see he had short dark hair, tanned skin, and a trimmed goatee. He was probably a year or two younger than Leo. His brown shirt was open a few buttons. Leo could see a small patch of hair in the middle of his chest. He was getting excited. He wouldn't mind getting fucked by him right now, right there, on the swing. It would feel pretty awesome. Matt and he had done it before. He was getting hard from the thought of it. But Leo couldn't get himself out of the swing.

"Can you leave the package on the steps?"

"I need you to sign for it. Sorry."

Leo sighed. "I know this is a lot to ask, but could you come in to me?"

The guy tried pulling on the door. It jiggled, but didn't move. "It's locked."

Leo scoffed. It was uncanny, the motivation that sometimes prevailed. He sat up. His head was groggy, so he yawned. He had come out the night before in a tank top and boxers. As he stretched, his cock got harder. He could feel it moving in his shorts. He walked toward the door, grabbing it. As he unlocked the screen door with his free hand, he noticed the guy watch him. The delivery man took one step back, then held it open as he handed Leo the electronic signing device. Leo scribbled his name on the pad, noticed the guy was staring at his crotch, then returned the pad to him. He was half unconscious of his actions, but he reached for the front of his shorts and started stroking on his cock. The UPS man was watching. It was like a scene from gay porn. He handed Leo his package. He took it with his free hand. "You don't want to come in or anything, do you? Some lemon-ade, perhaps?" Leo teased.

The guy grinned. "Um, thanks, but I'm on the clock. Deliveries to make."

Leo shrugged, pulling his hand off his shorts. "Your loss," he said like a bitch.

The guy pulled back and stared at Leo with a look of surprise. "Yeah, okay, whatever." The screen door slammed shut. The guy stepped down from the stairs, walked fast to his truck, and drove off. He never looked back.

Leo was still a horny queer. That hadn't changed, despite Matt's death. Leo was half tempted to go sit back on the swing again. Maybe jerk off. He was up though, so he had to get ready. He realized that he was starving too. He had left his front door open all night, letting air conditioned breezes escape the house, but he didn't care. He entered and shut the door behind him. He stared at his reflection in the foyer mirror. He looked awful. No wonder the UPS man didn't want to come in for lemonade.

Leo had thick, brown, wavy hair he had inherited from his Roman ancestors. He usually wore it short, but he hadn't gotten it cut in over two months, so it was tousled, skewed, and unwieldy. Sleeping on the swing had made it worse, adding two inches of fluff to his five-foot, eight-inch frame. He was pale from being indoors all the time. If he had the desire to go to the beach or work outside for a while, he knew he would tan quickly because of his Mediterranean blood. He pulled on the dark circle beneath his left eye to reveal bloodshot white around his mocha-brown iris. His pupils were a little dilated. He rubbed his hand over the rough bristles of his facial hair. He hadn't shaved in a few days, so he had thick stubble surrounding his thin pale lips. He rubbed his pronounced cheekbones. He had lost fifteen pounds over the past year. It was subtle weight loss, so not everyone had noticed, but he could see it in his reflection. Matt's mother, Mil-lie, had noticed. So had his own mother. Mothers comment on such things. But while his own mother begged for him to eat all the time and even showed up unexpectedly with her famous lasagna, Millie would sit back, take a drag on her cigarette, and say in her Brooklyn accent, "Don't eat. Starve yourself to death. That'll bring Matt back."

He continued into the house and looked at the package. Coincidentally, it was from Millicent Hunter's address in Clearwater. He found it odd. He was half curious to know what she was sending him. But only half curious. He tossed it onto the pile of other unread mail and magazines that was collapsing off the dining room table.

The house was a disaster. He used to be meticulous, almost a neat-freak with every object in its own place. Now, it seemed so unimportant to clean. Why bother? No one came to visit him, and he sure as hell wasn't bringing anyone home. He hadn't dusted in months. He had books from his studies scattered, half of them opened and piled on top of one another. An empty pizza box and used drinking glasses were tossed about the living room. Dirty and clean laundry were mixed on the couch and side chair. He didn't even know where the cordless phone was anymore. He shook his head in disgust, then went to the kitchen.

He ate a leftover bagel with cream cheese and drank black instant coffee. He showered, but he didn't bother shaving. He ran his fingers through his wet hair and put some gel in it, then threw on the first shirt that didn't smell from his closet. He realized it had a stain on the collar, but he ignored it. The department chair insisted they looked professional when they taught. Leo didn't bother. He prepared his briefcase, scouring around for papers he was supposed to have graded last night but didn't. He found some of them in the second bedroom that was the office, the rest on top of the television in the living room. It was frustrating, being forced to do things he didn't want to do. He hadn't always been like this. He used to love to teach.

He locked the door behind him and headed for his red Toyota Tercel in the driveway. He sped off toward the highway that would take him into Tampa. As he drove he was quiet. The radio had been on, but he turned it off. Most of the morning traffic had died down, but his class started at eleven and it was already after ten. He would probably be late. "Fuck 'em," he said aloud. He sat back and continued on his way.

He reached the Howard Frankland Bridge in about fifteen minutes. He sped across the bridge, glancing around occasionally at the bay that surrounded him on both sides, the waves capping not far from the edge of the bridge. The Florida sunshine in its cloudless sky was beautiful and blinding. Leo remembered when he had first moved from New Jersey, how everything had looked so bright and verdant, a proverbial postcard. He recalled especially how impressive the sky was, huge and cerulean blue, like a dome encasing a tropical paradise dotted only by a few puffy white clouds. Now, after more than ten years, Leo was accustomed to Florida. It hardly ever pleased him anymore. He knew he wasn't alone though; most residents were too busy to notice.

He was across the bridge in another five minutes, and it was here that he slowed down. Whenever he approached the end of the bridge, he would decelerate. There was usually a cop with a speed trap there, he would tell himself. Others usually slowed down too. The exits for the airport and the mall were coming up, and people weaved in and out of traffic here. He had to be careful too.

The construction between the end of the bridge and the exit had been taken down a few months ago, the estuary now complete. He breathed more heavily, taking quick glances outside his car. In the months just after the accident, passersby could see how it had happened. There were skid marks in the road that started in the left lane and coursed diagonally for about thirty feet toward the wall on the far right side. Hash marks and black metal scrapings scarred the temporary concrete median, situated among dump trucks, unplanted palm trees, and rolled up metal fencing. The median was gone now, and the tropical rains had washed away the skid marks. There was nothing but an estuary, with a high chain-link fence and flowering crepe myrtle to prevent people from bothering the spoonbills, herons, and sea turtles. Sometimes Leo thought about putting up one of those roadside memorial signs that dotted Florida streets and highways, where drunk and erratic drivers or their victims had died and loved ones grieved publicly by decorating them with flowers and stuffed animals. But there was no point in doing it. People always ignored what they had to say.

He shook his head quickly, then focused on his driving. He was in the exit-only lane. He sped and cut off two cars without his blinker. He heard the honking, but he ignored it. He kept driving, and arrived at the University of South Florida twenty minutes later.

After wasting an aggravating fifteen minutes trying to find a parking space, he hurried into the concrete building, bypassing college students of every age and size. He hurried upstairs to the English department. He had to filter through the main department to get to his office, which he detested, because he knew everyone would see him. He passed the secretary, who asked him for his final grades that were due tomorrow. He replied that he knew, but he swore to himself because he had only remembered the other day that the semester was over this week. He dumped his stuff in his office then hurried off to class to face their wrath, knowing he had to explain that he still hadn't finished their papers yet. He could only promise that he would get them graded that day. They could pick up the papers from the office secretary tomorrow. They groaned. One student cursed him out. He ignored them, and forced himself to wrap up their discussion of different writing styles they had learned about over the semester. Only three or four bothered responding. There was no final, and he was finished with them. He let them out ten minutes early, and wished them a good summer. No one replied.

He shared an office with another adjunct, Ms. Johnson. Her desk was always neat, her papers organized in piles. Her bookshelves were perfectly aligned with the thoughts of everyone from Bakhtin to Sedgwick. His desk was a disaster, with mountains of papers piled around him, everything from Norton anthologies to MLA handbooks tossed about like books at a rummage sale. His attempt to convince himself it was a sign of brilliance was unsuccessful. He hadn't been like this before. He used to be neat and organized like Ms. Johnson.

He sat in his chair and lay his head down on a pile of previous semester's papers. He moaned loudly. He wanted a joint or a drink. He wanted to go home. A throat cleared in the doorway, and he spun around abruptly. "What?" He did a double-take when he realized it was his advisor standing in the doorway. "Sorry, Dr. Palmer."

She leaned against the door frame, her arms folded before her. "Rough day?"

"You could say that."

She arched her eyebrows. "Well, I hate to be the bearer of bad news, but I'm about to make your day worse." She paused, giving him a moment to prepare. "Budget cuts. They're letting half of the adjuncts go. Your name is on the list."

Leo leaned back in his squeaky chair. "I suppose Johnson was kept on," he said, gesturing toward the neat desk.

Palmer looked away, then nodded slowly. "Look, Leo," she said, "it's for the summer only. They're having serious budget problems, thanks to our governor."

"Fine, I'll buy that, but I'm sure I was on the top ten list of adjuncts to be cut."

"You haven't exactly been the model teacher lately. In fact, you've been a royal pain in the ass." He looked back at her. He would have been more surprised had it not been true. "Come on, I'll buy you a cappuccino at the University Center." He hesitated a moment, then got up and followed her out of his office.

Palmer was shy of six feet, had spiky blond hair, and loved high heels and pink makeup a little too much. She was in her early fifties and had established a lurid academic career for herself in late Victorian literature, focusing primarily on the "New Woman" phenomenon of the fin de siècle. She had been a staunch feminist in the seventies and eighties, but her triumph for the past decade was lesbianism. Her fifth book, due out by Princeton in a few months, was on the three great literary lesbian Vs: Vernon Lee, Virginia Woolf, and Vita Sackville-West. Palmer was a popular professor, having taught at USF for about a decade. She was an inspiration to Leo for her academic drive, her queer and Victorian interests, and her up-front attitude. At least, she had been early on, when he had first decided to pursue his PhD.

"Dissertation?" she asked matter-of-factly while they sipped their watered-down cappuccinos, surrounded by the bustle of students studying, fraternizing, or goofing off. He stared at the dissolving froth in his cup. He knew this was coming. "Leo, you're joking, right?

You haven't done a thing on this in over six months." It actually was longer, but he hadn't told her that. "What the heck is going on with you?"

She knew his story. He had been open with her shortly after Matt's death, so she could understand why he had put things on hold at the time. He put the paper cup down. "Nothing," he answered.

"Nothing?"

"I mean it. There is absolutely nothing going on with me. I sit at home, and I drink or smoke. I move from room to room. I don't call anyone. I hardly ever eat, and when I do, I eat crap." He stared up at her. "Nothing is going on with me."

She put her cup down and sat back in her seat. "You need to talk to someone, a grief counselor or something."

"Why, so he can tell me what I already know? That I'm depressed?"

She shook her head. "Leo, I know it's been only a year, but you have to move on."

He glared at her. "Please, Dr. Palmer, no one understands what I've been through."

"Okay, fine. So what are you going to do about it?"

He shrugged, and looked away. He saw an adorable twenty-year-old on his cell phone staring at him, then smiling at him. Leo wanted to smile back, but a finger snapped in his face. "Hello? Leo, focus. What are you going to do about it?"

"I have no idea. Maybe the summer off is good for me. I should re-examine my life and figure out what's going on. A forty-day Christ-like hunger strike might do me some good." He picked up his cup again. The cappuccino was hardly palatable, but he drank more of it anyway.

She ignored his martyrdom and attitude. "You could work on your dissertation." She leaned back and folded her arms. "Did you apply for those grants I told you about?" He shook his head. Her frustration mounted. "Leo, you're starting to drive me crazy. You have to get on with this. You're about one-third of the way into your dissertation. The last I remember, you had already written your introduction and were into a chapter on *Lady Audley's Secret*. You have to continue. Don't quit now. And stop being so damned negative." She reached

out and shook his forearm. "Come on, I know you can do this." He
met her gaze. "Here," she continued, "let's get into this. Talk to me
about your dissertation."

He sighed, putting his cup back and stretching in his seat. "I really
don't—"

"Hush. Talk to me about it. Title. Clytemnestra something or
other, right?"

He responded as if he were reciting instructions for baking a pie.
"It's something like, 'The Clytemnestra Complex: Literary Murderer-
esses in the Mid-Victorian Period.'"

"Good title. It will probably change as you work on it, but tell me,
why *Lady Audley's Secret*? Why are you writing about this obscure
book from 1865? Who cares?"

He hesitated a moment before speaking. "1861. It was serialized
in 1861."

"So what?"

"Well, that's important because in some ways it connects to the social changes going on in England at the time." His tone started to
change. "The 1850s and 1860s were a time of prosperity for the English. Industrialism was increasing. There was a gradual change in art
and aesthetics. The middle class was rising in number and power. And
the role of women was changing as a result."

"Go on."

"Women were beginning to assert themselves, and demand rights
equal to men, socially and politically. For instance, new divorce laws
and education reforms for women went into effect in the 1850s. It's
not a coincidence that Mary Braddon wrote one of the first sensation-
alist novels at the time. It was considered shocking because it showed
the reader a new type of woman. She wasn't Patmore's angel in the
house. She wasn't idealized or perfect. She was a woman who had to
stand up for herself, defend herself." He paused. "She had to defend
what she wanted. Even if that meant killing for it."

Palmer nodded. "I see. So you think Braddon was advocating for
women to kill men in Victorian England?"

"No, of course not. Otherwise Queen Victoria probably would
have executed half of her prime ministers." Palmer chuckled, and Leo

grinned. "No, Lady Audley is in a desperate situation. She's a desperate woman. She has to find a way out. So she kills the man—or at least thinks she does—who loves her most, because his love is stopping her from her goal."

"Her goal is to be wealthy and secure. Isn't that selfish of her?"

"You can't put ethical value on her goal. It's irrelevant what we think, or her contemporaries thought, of her goal. The point is that she actually had a goal."

"So it really isn't about her being in a desperate situation. It's about her goal and his love."

Leo nodded. "Which is why Victoria didn't kill Gladstone."

"But she would have killed Albert?"

"If he had put her in a situation where she felt like she had no way out, and it prevented her from attaining her goals...perhaps." He drank the rest of his cappuccino, a feeling of accomplishment making him blush.

Palmer nodded. "Excellent," she said and winked.

He had to give her credit. She was good. They both laughed. "Okay, you got me, Dr. Palmer. Thank you."

"Leo, go to the library. Now. When was the last time you checked for new citations? Over a year ago, right? Get over there." As an afterthought, she asked, "Don't you have a relative who's a librarian?"

He hesitated a moment, then nodded. "Sort of. My ex–sister-in-law. She's a reference librarian here."

"So get her to help you. Unless you hate each other."

"No," he replied, although admittedly he wasn't too sure himself.

Palmer announced she had to get ready for her class that had its final that afternoon. She demanded he turn in some new citations by next week. "And I want to see a new draft of what you've written already, within two weeks. Hear me? Write this thing, before someone else steals your fantastic ideas! Like me!" He promised he would, she left, and he was alone again.

The boy on the cell phone was long gone now. Leo glanced around him. Students were studying for finals, drinking Cokes and coffees in anticipation of their exams. He didn't recognize any of them. For all he knew, he had taught half a dozen of them in the past year, but had no memory of them. It was all a blur. He could feel the depression like a wave starting to overwhelm him.

Palmer was right. He had to focus, get back on track with the dissertation. It was a distraction if nothing else. He needed it, especially today, this week, next week, this summer. He realized again that he didn't have a job for the summer. He wondered how he was going to pay for his car, the bills, or anything. At least the house was paid off. Matt's life insurance policy had taken care of that, their home improvement loan, and his funeral expenses. Leo almost hadn't gotten the money, however. The results of the autopsy toxicology report had shown elevated levels of alcohol in Matt's blood, but it was shy of the .08 limit. The insurance company then questioned whether Matt's death was a suicide, which also would have negated the policy, but since there was no evidence to support the theory, his death was declared an accident, both by the police and the insurance company.

Leo needed to figure out a way to pay for his daily expenses. He'd probably have to get another student loan. He rubbed the bridge of his nose. He had to stay focused on something good and positive, and get out of the depressive mode he was in. Worrying about bills wasn't going to help.

He had to do the research. He liked Palmer's drive. She had re-inspired him. Her brief conversation with him had enlivened a part of his brain that he thought was dead or dying. He enjoyed the intellectual repartee. That was what had drawn him into academia to begin with. The ideas, the inspirations. It made him feel better, even if just for a little while. He had to focus on his research, and that would help distract him from the depression. He only wished that he could do the research without seeing Theresa, his former sister-in-law.

Theoretically it was possible. The "virtual library" the university had spent almost two million dollars on was supposedly state of the art for everyone's research needs. He had seen it demonstrated by a young librarian over a year ago when he had brought his freshmen over for library research. It had impressed him only superficially, the never-ending sources of electronic information available at the touch of a few keys or mouse clicks. But he wasn't sure how to use it. Now he realized that if he had learned how to use it he could probably work on his dissertation from his home computer or even from somewhere else on campus and not have to see Theresa at all.

He didn't dislike her. It was awkwardness more than anything else. He hadn't spoken to her in about nine or ten months now. He still thought it was shitty how the whole divorce and everything had taken place so fast after Matt's death. He was sure it must have devastated Theresa.

Theresa and Leo were bound to each other by two men: George and Matt. Leo and George were brothers. Theresa and Matt were half-siblings, Theresa from Millie's first marriage, Matt from her second. Both of their families were also from the tri-state area. The Vasaris were from Paramus, New Jersey. Matt and his family were from Brooklyn, although they had had a summer cabin at a lake somewhere in New Jersey, but that had been years ago when Matt was a child.

Theresa and George had been married for about fifteen years when their divorce was finalized. Leo and Matt had been lovers for just over four years when he had died. It was almost incestuous, their whole relationship. What was the likelihood that two sets of siblings would partner up with one another? It was almost Victorian literary fantasy. And it had been somewhat magical, at least for Leo and Matt. Theresa and George's romance was another story entirely. And oddly, two siblings were now gone. Matt was dead, and George had run off back to New Jersey with some twenty-year-old, bleach-blonde Hooters waitress. That left Leo and Theresa.

They could have comforted each other, but they were never that close. Theresa wasn't emotional. She was missing that zest for life that flourished in Leo's Italian genes. Leo and George's mother, Rosa Vasari, said it was the blood of artists. She herself was an amateur artist, but her heightened sense of self came from being married to, in her mind, a descendant of the great Renaissance Vasari. It was proof enough for her that their family was destined for greatness. She had named her first son Giorgio after the artist, although never were two men more different: the first Giorgio Vasari had been a painter and biographer; the second Giorgio Vasari was a guido mechanic.

Theresa wasn't mousy. Leo had seen her stick up for herself against George through the years. She certainly wasn't a guido wife. Theresa had gotten her master's in library science from Columbia and chosen a career for herself as a reference librarian. Despite having been a student at USF for years, Leo had actually seen her at work only maybe a dozen times. And their interactions had been cordial, but certainly not friendly. Work was work for her, and during those hours he was a student like any other.

Her more conservative nature used to bother her brother Matt. He had been a sales manager at NationsBank. He had made a decent salary, thanks in part to his ability to sell big loans to anyone. He used to make great bonuses and had won a few outstanding service awards. At work, he was outgoing and personable, whereas Theresa was introspective and reserved. Matt was definitely the more positive of the two, although probably because it was mirrored at times with bouts of depression that only Leo saw. But he had seen none of that at first. Matt's power of persuasion had worked its charms on Leo early on. He swept Leo off his feet, seducing him when Leo was still uncertain whether he was even gay. He had experimented at the dorms and had gone to the nightclub Tracks in Ybor City a few times, but he was afraid to officially label himself.

Oddly, Matt and Leo wound up together because of Theresa and George. Matt had been living in Miami, not far from his mother Millie, and was transferred by NationsBank to their downtown tower in Tampa. When he had arrived he lived with his sister and George briefly, but wanted his own place as quickly as possible. It was coincidental that Leo was graduating with his bachelor's degree and he was trying to figure out a way not to move back home with his mother before starting graduate school in the fall. It was George of all people who suggested they become roommates.

Neither George nor Theresa knew at the time that Matt was gay. He had been straight-acting because the industry required it. Even Leo was uncertain Matt was gay at first. They met when Leo was invited to dinner during the first week Matt had moved to town. He saw Matt staring at him a little too much, and it made Leo self-conscious. He actually thought Matt was probably weird. His hyper attitude made him think maybe he was one of those neurotic people who challenged you by staring. And of course Leo was totally hot for him, especially the way his navy blue suit contrasted with his sandy-colored hair, cut military style, and accented his deep blue eyes.

Matt and George got along very well, which is another reason why Leo didn't suspect anything. His brother was completely homophobic, so he imagined there was no way Matt could be friends with him. Leo was a little nervous about the whole thing, but Matt wasn't terrifying to be around. And Leo was desperate not to live at home. They decided to find an apartment and see how it would work out. They found a two-bedroom apartment at the northern end of 4th Street in St. Petersburg, and they moved in. In less than a week, they were fucking and the second bedroom was an office.

Leo was getting excited thinking about those days once again. That was only about five years ago, but he could still feel Matt like he were around him at that moment. But the realization that Matt was gone overshadowed the physical sensations, and he lowered his head in despair. God, how he missed Matt. It was painful. People would talk about the feeling of emptiness when someone they love had died. He could understand that only too well now. Radclyffe Hall had written a lesbian-themed novel called *The Well of Loneliness*. That was what it was, an open vessel that couldn't be filled with anything. Leo drank Coronas and smoked pot, not to fill the vessel, but to try to make it permeable so the pain could drain away, at least temporarily. It was better than the nothingness that remained otherwise.

There was more to it though. There was guilt. He blamed himself for many things, but especially for their last fight. He knew he could have stopped him. He knew he could have done one or two things to make it better toward the end. All he had to do was not be friends with Millie, Matt and Theresa's mother. Had it been so difficult for Leo to do that for him?

Matt had been raving about this from the time his mother had first moved to Clearwater. At first, Leo thought Matt was jealous of the time Leo spent with Millie, that somehow he had a better relationship with his mother than Matt did. But he spoke horrible things about her almost daily, which hurt Leo because he thought Millie was great.

From the first time they had spoken, Leo had been amazed by her carefree, in-your-face attitude. One might think her rude or obnoxious, but to Leo she was free-thinking and unconcerned about what people thought of her. He admired her. And to Leo's great shock and delight, it turned out that they shared a common interest in Victorian literature, which was odd considering Millie's personality. Millie smoked, was a recovering alcoholic, and swore in a very un-Victorian manner. Millie and Leo had started their own informal reading discussion group, covering novelists and poets from Browning and Trollope to Tennyson and Gaskell. They would shop in secondhand and antiquarian bookstores throughout the Tampa Bay area looking for nineteenth-century publications. Leo was thrilled to have someone to share these conversations, and he suspected that Matt, despite his rage and odd behavior about his mother, was basically just jealous.

That night, one year ago, they had fought about Leo's upcoming birthday party. They were unpacking groceries. He noticed that Matt was upset and distracted, but Matt was silent about what was wrong. He knew he had to talk to him about the party though, so Leo mentioned he had invited Millie to the dinner they were planning. He knew Matt would be upset, but he didn't expect him to freak out the way he did. Matt started screaming and slamming cabinets and dishes. Their fight ended with a jar of sauce smashing against the wall, and Matt storming out of the house. Those were their last moments together.

Leo was sitting in his reverie for some time. He hadn't moved. Then someone asked him about borrowing the other chair, and the nightmare was over for the moment. He quickly got up and walked away. He tried to free his mind of everything. He had to focus on Palmer and his dissertation. He had to stop thinking about Matt and everything else.

He exited the University Center and walked across the campus in the now hot, blinding, afternoon sun toward the library. As he walked he squinted his eyes, forcing himself to focus on his research. He was on Braddon's *Lady Audley's Secret*. And then there was Wilkie Collins's *Armadale* to work on. He also had to focus on his primary research, the historical murderesses he had been researching, like Constance Kent and Adelaide Bartlett.

He focused on these things, and the words he would speak to Theresa. He wondered if she remembered it was the first anniversary of Matt's death. He even wondered if she would speak to him, or if she would perceive him as a monster like her ex-husband. He doubted that possibility. She might be cold or distant, but she didn't hate.

It occurred to him for the moment how oddly different Theresa, Matt, and Millie all were from one another. They were three points of a triangle: Millie, his outspoken, devoted friend; Matt, his seemingly bipolar dead lover; and Theresa, his angry, reserved ex–sister-in-law. They were unequal angles in a triad, and at the center was Leo trying to figure them out, unable to understand any of them fully.

He stepped through the two sets of automatic doors into the library. The cool air greeted him, and he was grateful for the moment for central air-conditioning in Florida. As he walked past the circulation desk and the elevators, it occurred to him that he didn't have his notes, papers, or anything. He stopped for a moment to consider what to do, then decided against needing them. He vaguely remembered that he could probably e-mail citations or articles to himself. Worst-case scenario, he could get paper and pencil from someone. Theresa maybe. That would be a good way to break the ice.

He took a quick deep breath as he pushed through the glass doors and entered the reference area. He hadn't been in the library in about a year, so he was startled to see computers everywhere. It took him a minute to adjust, and he tried to think of what he should do. He sat down at a computer station away from the reference desk. He glanced over and didn't recognize anyone there at first. He didn't know the librarians by name. Then he saw one man he had met a few times. He was a friend of Theresa's, but Leo couldn't think of his name. Leo turned back to the computer and opened Netscape. It opened to the virtual library home page, and he started to click for catalogs, articles, Internet resources, citation information. In less than three minutes he was totally frustrated and pushed back his chair. It was hopeless. He had no idea how to get to MLA, let alone anything else. He would need Theresa's help.

He got up from his chair and walked toward the reference desk. The librarians and staff were wearing name badges, so he glanced over and saw the man's: Charlie. He cleared his throat, speaking softly. "Um, Charlie, hi."

Charlie was a bald man in his late thirties. He flashed a smile at Leo, exclaiming, "Leo! My God, how good to see you!" He wasn't quiet at all. Two of the women librarians looked over inquisitively. "Where have you been? We haven't seen you around here in ages!"

Leo smiled back. He wasn't in the mood to flirt. He knew Charlie was gay, but now just didn't seem like the right time. Besides, Charlie was not his type. "Keeping busy. You know, teaching, research. Dissertation takes up a lot of my time."

"I bet." There was a silence, during which time Leo suspected Charlie was waiting for him to ask how he was. But he didn't. Charlie suddenly got serious. "I guess you're here because of Theresa."

"Um, yes, I was hoping to see her. I needed some—"

"She was a wreck after what happened."

He nodded in agreement. He wasn't sure what he meant at first. He could only think he was referring to Matt, or maybe even George. It bothered him slightly to think that Theresa had told Charlie these things, but maybe they were better friends than Leo thought. Charlie did seem to remember him right away. "Is she here?" he continued.

Charlie jerked his head back. "No, she left as soon as she heard the news." Leo didn't respond. "I thought you were coming to check on her. You don't know what's happened, do you?"

"No. Why? What happened?"

Charlie's hand went to his mouth in shock. "Oh, my God, it's her mother."

There was a pause. Leo was confused. "Millie? What happened?"

He shook his head slightly. "Oh, Leo, I'm so sorry about this. I thought you knew. She's in the hospital. Morton Plant in Clearwater, I think." After a pause, he leaned in and said more quietly, "Leo, I think she tried to kill herself."

– TWO –

Millicent Hunter was one of the fiercest women Leo had ever known. He had been drawn to her intensity from the minute he had first encountered her in November 1996. Matt and Leo had only recently bought their two-bedroom bungalow, after having lived in an apartment for two and a half years. Leo was home alone, studying for comprehensive exams. The phone rang. There was a short pause when he answered, then a voice said, "Matthew?"

Leo almost told the woman it was a wrong number. No one called Matt by his full name. "No, this is Leo. Matt's not here right now. Can I take a message?"

"Is that Leo like the ferocious lion or like the ingenious artist?"

Leo was unsure how to respond. The woman's voice was a little raspy and had a Brooklyn accent. He sensed she was middle-aged. He found himself grinning curiously. "Uh, like the artist, I guess." He went to the refrigerator and poured himself a Coke.

"Are you an artist?" she asked.

"More an academic than an artist."

"And you're not like a lion at all?"

Leo chuckled. "Well, I guess I can be at times." He drank the soda, still wondering who this woman was.

"You'd have to be to handle Matthew and keep my son happy."

Leo almost choked. "Mrs. Pierce?" he asked incredulously.

"Well, not anymore. I went back to my maiden name, Hunter." He heard her inhale a cigarette. "So how long have you and my son been screwing each other?"

Leo's mouth was agape. He put the glass down so that he wouldn't drop it. He was in utter shock. First, because Matt's mother knew they were lovers. Second, because until that phone call, it had never even dawned on Leo that Matt had a mother.

During the first few months, Matt and Leo had decided not to tell the family about their relationship. Matt said it was their own business what they did. Besides, it was both their opinions that George would probably kill them and Leo's mother would have a nervous breakdown. Theresa wouldn't have cared one way or the other. So they told no one. The fact that Matt's mother knew her son was gay shocked Leo. It certainly wasn't the response he would have expected.

But the odder notion was that Matt's mother was calling at all. Leo didn't know anything about her. He tried to think back to Theresa and George's wedding in New York in the early 1980s. No memory of a bride's mother, or brother, or in fact any family, came to him. It was strange he hadn't noticed it before. Even more bizarre was how both Matt and Theresa could choose not to speak about their mother.

"Leo, are you there?" she asked again.

"Yes, I'm sorry. I'm surprised that you're calling."

"You had no idea I existed, did you?"

"No, that's not it," he lied. "Matt talks about you. I'm just surprised that I've never spoken to you before."

"Well, that's going to change. Do me a favor and tell my son that I've moved to Clearwater. And that I expect to see him every once and a while."

She didn't hope to see him. She expected it. He liked her demanding tone.

"I'll be sure to tell him."

"Thank you, Leo. Here's my phone number." He wrote it down. "Tell him to call me. I hope that we can meet very soon. You seem like a very nice young man."

"Thank you, Ms.——"

"Millie," she interrupted. "Just call me Millie."

"Thanks, Millie. I'm looking forward to meeting you too. You seem very. . ." He wanted to say "nice" also, but he couldn't. She finished the sentence for him here too.

"I seem like a pushy old broad. Get used to it. I am." The phone went dead.

When Matt came home from work, Leo was cooking dinner. Matt ditched his jacket on the living room couch like always and was undoing his tie when he hugged Leo from behind. They kissed, and Matt grabbed a Corona from the refrigerator.

"You had a phone call today." Leo turned from the stove and leaned against the counter. "It was your mother."

Matt stared back at him. "What?" he said with a tone of anger to his voice.

"You know, you never told me you anything about your mother. I mean, obviously I knew she must have existed, but I guess I thought she was dead."

Matt continued undoing his tie and unbuttoning his shirt with one free hand. "She might as well be dead for all I care."

"She's your mother," Leo responded, startled by his remark. "How could you say that?"

Matt shook his head. "Just stay out of it, all right." He chugged the Corona.

Leo shrugged. "Okay, whatever. She left a phone number. She wants you to call her." Leo reached over to the counter and handed him the piece of paper.

There was silence for a moment, then Matt continued, "Look, there's bad blood between us, and I'm not in the mood to revisit it." He crumbled up the paper and tossed it into the open garbage in the corner of the kitchen. He didn't even seem to realize it was a local number, and Leo figured it was best not to mention that she had moved nearby.

"Your business, not mine," he replied. But as the night went on, during dinner, television, even later in bed, Leo couldn't help but wonder what had happened between them, and if there was a way he could make things better between them. If nothing else, he found himself intrigued to meet her.

Two and a half years later, Leo was standing in the same kitchen drinking a Corona himself, remembering that first encounter with Millie and Matt's reaction. It was after 6:00 p.m. After speaking with Charlie the librarian, he had completely lost interest in research and had gone home. He was dazed after hearing the news. Millie had tried to kill herself. It seemed incomprehensible, because he couldn't imagine what would possess her to do it.

Leo hadn't spoken to her since Christmas, so maybe things had become unruly for her. She seemed to have been doing fine back then. Maybe it was all a mistake. Maybe Charlie didn't understand what had happened. It was probably an accident. Leo didn't doubt Millie was in the hospital, but he doubted that she had attempted to commit suicide. Not Millie.

Leo swallowed down the last of his Corona and tossed the empty bottle into the garbage. It was piled high and overflowing, so that the empty bottle teetered on the edge of the trash. He reached over and took the bottle out, setting it on the floor beside the garbage can. He could smell week-old rotting leftovers. He turned away quickly. The kitchen table and counters were piled with more papers and leftover boxes of empty foods and filthy dishes. The whole thing disgusted him, but he was too focused on Millie for the moment to worry about it.

He had to know what was going on. He rummaged through his junk drawer and found his phone book. He reached for the phone and remembered the cordless was missing. He shook his head in aggravation, and got his cell phone from his briefcase. He looked up Theresa and George's old phone number and dialed. An operator came on announcing the number had been disconnected. He forgot that Theresa had sold the house. He needed her new number. He had to call his mother, she would know. He regretted his decision to call, but before he could change his mind, she answered during the second ring. *"Pronto?"* she asked, trilling in her best Italian accent.

"Mamma, it's Leo."

"Ah, Leonardo, *mio figlio!* How are you?"

Rosa Vasari had been born Rose Herschel in Queens, the daughter of a German-Jewish father. Marrying an Italian with a supposedly famous ancestral lineage had authorized her to do three things: change her name to Rosa, perfect the art of Italian cooking, and speak Italian as if she were an immigrant. Leo didn't have a problem with the first two, but the Italian language part was just strange. Leo's favorite moments were when she would slip into Italian and feign ignorance about the English language, which conveniently happened when she was caught in an awkward situation, like trying to use an expired coupon at the grocery store, or responding to a critic about her stilted painting technique. That was her other Italianism: she was an artist, thanks to the painting classes she took after his father had died fifteen years before.

"I'm fine, Mamma," he replied.

"Leonardo, *il tuo compleanno,* your birthday, is Saturday! You come for dinner?"

"*Sì,*" he replied, wondering why he amused her Italian habit. "Look, Mamma, I don't want to talk about this right now."

"What? You don't want me to celebrate your birthday? I cook for you and—"

"Mamma, stop!" he shouted. There was silence at the other end. He sighed deeply, then calmed himself. "I'm sorry. Look, this is important. I need Theresa's number."

"Theresa? Why do you need her number?"

He hesitated a moment and rubbed the bridge of his nose. He knew that she would carry on and tell everyone in her Italian-American Club about this. He dreaded the whole idea, but he needed to know about Millie. "I have to speak to her. I heard something today about Millie being in the hospital."

"Millicent is in the hospital?"

"Yes. I don't know anything yet, so I have to call her to find out. Do you have it?"

"*Sì,* of course!" She started to rummage through papers, not unlike Leo had a few minutes before. She sighed dramatically. "She was such a terrible mamma to her *bambini.*"

"She wasn't that bad. They had problems like all families do."

"No, *terribile.* Theresa told me. Did you know she abandoned them? Just tossed them to their *nonna* to take care of them!"

"How do you know all this?" Leo was taken aback, but not because it was news to him. Both Matt and Millie had given him their sides of the story. He just didn't realize his mother knew so much about their past.

"Ah, see, I pray to Sant'Antonio, and I find the number!" She recited it and he wrote it in his phone book, crossing out the old one beneath it.

He considered asking her again about what she had said, but then hesitated. What difference did it make now anyway? "*Grazie,* Mamma," he said.

"*Prego,*" she replied with a sigh.

He rolled his eyes. "I'll come to dinner for my birthday. About this time, okay?"

"Ah!" she exclaimed. "Why so late?"

"All right, five o'clock. I'll see you then. *Ciao,* Mamma!" He hung up the phone before she could reply, then took a deep breath and shook his head in relief.

He set the phone down, and waited to recover from the call. He opened another bottle of Corona. He drank it, wondering once again what he would say to Theresa. It was odd, how he was repeating this same thought from a few hours earlier, but it seemed a little easier now. It could have been the alcohol, but it was probably because he had something specific to ask her now. By the time he had finished the beer and set the empty bottle on the floor beside the other two, he had gathered enough strength to call her and not worry about what he was going to say.

He dialed the number on his cell phone. He heard it ring twice, then her voice mail picked up. He listened to her voice, and realized that it hadn't changed at all. She still sounded dull and uninteresting. "Hello, this is Theresa. Leave me a message at the tone." No "Have a great day!" or "I'll call you back as soon as I can!" Nothing like that.

He hung up. He decided to look for some food. He pulled out a frozen turkey dinner, then decided to have sirloin steak. He glanced back at the phone, then returned the food to the freezer. He picked up his cell phone and redialed. This time, when the tone passed, he spoke haltingly and with uncertainty.

"Hi, Theresa." He tried to sound pleasant. "This is Leo. I wanted to call and see how things were going. Um, could you give me a call back? Call my cell phone." He gave her the number, then hung up. He decided on the turkey. He microwaved it then plopped down on the couch between his laundry and magazines, setting dinner and a

Coke on the coffee table before him. He flipped on the television and channel-surfed while he ate.

It was after 7:00 p.m. now, and Theresa had not called. He rose from the couch, leaving his plate and glass behind, and went back to his cell phone in the kitchen. He redialed. The automated Theresa spoke in the same monotone voice. He left another message. "Theresa, hi, it's Leo again. Look, I hate to bug you, but I was in the library and I heard about Millie. I'm calling to see how she's doing. Please call me back. It doesn't matter what time it is."

Leo spent the next couple of hours watching nothing special on television. He called Theresa again. He picked up his plate and glass and put them in the sink among the rest of the dishes. He drank another beer. He called her three more times over the course of the evening, not always leaving messages, but each time he called, he become more agitated because she had not returned his call. Exasperated, he finally decided to go to bed. As he lay there, however, he tossed and couldn't sleep. Around 1:00 a.m. he finally yelled in aggravation and got out of bed. He went to get another beer, and discovered that he had drunk them all.

He paced through the house, his feet cool on the hardwood floor. It was dark in the house so he put on the lights in the living room. The eerie dank lighting from the torchiere lamps made his place look more gloomy at night. The mess everywhere didn't help. Somewhere beneath all the clothes was a black leather couch, and across the room, beside the television, was a matching side chair. The glass-top coffee table and end table were decorated with junk as well. Only the torchieres and the couple of paintings his mother had done stood out as being neat and orderly. The frameless paintings with their posed gold leaf, Italian trecento style oddly contrasted with the modern décor of metal halogen lamps and black-lacquered furnishings. Matt had liked Rosa's paintings more than Leo did, so there were quite a few hanging throughout the house.

He moved into the dining room and saw his briefcase. He remembered he had papers and grades to turn in. He had nothing else to do, so he pushed junk from one end of the dining table and started grading essays and assigning final grades with a calculator. He realized he had almost 150 essays to grade, as he had been one paper behind for each class. The thought intimidated him, but he had nothing else to do and he couldn't sleep, so he worked steadily through the night.

Occasionally he caught himself staring off. He was concerned about Millie. She was the closest thing he had to Matt and, despite that he had always hated his mother, she was Matt's mother and Leo loved her. He forced himself to focus on grading papers. He couldn't do anything about Millie. He had to wait for Theresa to call at this point.

He finished grading the last paper when he saw the morning sun come through the dining room window. He could sense that his eyes were bloodshot from all the reading and calculations he had been doing. He rubbed them. He was exhausted. Now he could fall asleep if he wanted to. He realized then that Theresa hadn't called him, and he grew angry.

He got up from the table. He picked up his cell phone and redialed one last time. All he had wanted was information and reassurance. There was no reason why she should ignore him like this. The phone rang once. He was ready for voice mail again when he heard a sleepy voice say, "Hello?"

He was startled for a brief moment. "Theresa? It's Leo."

She paused. "Oh. Leo."

"Did you get my messages?"

She yawned. "Um, yes. I got in late last night, too late to call. I was going to call you this morning."

He didn't believe her. He leaned against the countertop and folded his arms as he held the cell phone to his ear. She didn't say anything, and he was becoming more frustrated. "And? How's Millie?"

"She's in the hospital. She's stabilized."

"Theresa, what happened?"

"Look, Leo, I really don't want to talk about this right now. I've had a long night, and——"

"Theresa, please. You know how I feel about your mother. I'm concerned about her. I don't understand what happened. Your friend Charlie said she tried to kill herself."

He heard a stifled sigh. "She overdosed on Valium."

"Why was she on Valium?"

"Her doctor prescribed it for her." As an afterthought, it seemed, she added, "About a year ago."

He closed his eyes for a moment. "I'm sorry to hear that." There was silence for a few seconds. "She's at Morton Plant, right? I'd like to go see her."

"Yes, she's there, but I don't think that's a good idea."

"Why not? I'm friends with her. I'm practically her son."

Theresa's reply was harsh. "You are not her son." Leo was startled. He almost felt like he was her son. Son-in-law at least. He had taken her Christmas and birthday shopping because she didn't drive anymore and no one else would. He had gone book shopping with her more times than he could count. He knew her better than her own children did. Before he could reply, she continued in her usual monotone. "Leo, this doesn't concern you. It's a family matter. Don't bother getting involved." Before he could reply, she added, "I'm going back to sleep. I'll tell her you sent your regards." Dial tone.

Leo stood there for a few moments staring at the phone. He was shocked by Theresa's response. He had expected her to be stoic about her mother, but instead she seemed to outright shun him. It was almost like what Matt used to do. He didn't understand it. Why would Matt and now Theresa not want him involved in Millie's life? He already knew about her questionable past, how she had had a drinking problem, how she had abandoned her children to her own mother's care, how she had dragged her son off to Hollywood, Florida, against his will as a teenager after her mother had died, but none of that mattered to him. So she wasn't perfect. Big deal. Besides, he had heard it all mostly from Millie herself and it didn't change his feelings about her. And she was different now, a whole new person who didn't drink and who wanted to be with family.

He wondered then if maybe Millie was mad at Leo, and that's why Theresa didn't want him to go. He hadn't spoken to her in almost five months. If Leo was Millie's good friend, why hadn't he kept in touch with her or even visited her these past few months? His own demons had kept him away. It was no excuse, but it was all he had. He rubbed the bridge of his nose, feeling regret, and sadly lay the cell phone on the countertop.

When Matt had died, Millie had been there for him more than anyone else. She had insisted he sit beside her in the front row during the wake and funeral. She held his hand the whole time. He had stood beside her as they lowered his casket into the ground. He had rested his head on her shoulder and cried while the priest gave the eulogy.

He remembered especially, though, their conversation before they had left the funeral home for the cemetery. Millie was standing in front of the casket looking down at her son. He saw her hand near his chest. She pulled it away as Leo approached. Together, they stood alone, looking in the casket at the visage that had been her son and his lover. He thought she would be crying but her eyes were dry. Leo's eyes were swollen and bloodshot. She smiled sardonically, and held him close to her. She said, "They did an amazing job, didn't they? He looks beautiful. Like a blond Tom Cruise in *Top Gun,* right?"

He sniffled. "He doesn't look that good," he muttered, trying to follow her lead in being lighthearted, and she squeezed his hand in response. In actuality, he did look good. They had to do reconstructive work on his face because of the scarring from the windshield glass. His dark blond hair was neat and spiky with gel, like he usually wore it. His skin was pale, though, and his face glowed from the pink rouge they had put on his cheeks and lips to give him life.

"Why did he die?" he asked suddenly. "I don't get it. I just don't fucking get it!" His words choked in his throat.

"It was time," she said matter-of-factly.

He gazed at her, looking into her hazel eyes as she looked down at her son. Her face had lines by her mouth and forehead. But her eyes were dry. If he hadn't known her before, he'd think she was a horrible woman for not crying at her son's death. He knew she kept her emotions private, however, and she had done all her crying at home alone.

He disagreed with her though. "I don't believe God chooses people's time."

"Neither do I," she said. She met Leo's gaze. "I believe Matthew chose his time."

"What do you mean?"

"You know what I mean."

Leo swallowed and slowly shook his head. "He didn't. Don't say that."

She raised her hand in peace. "Leo, not now. Let's not discuss this. It's unimportant." Leo looked back at Matt's still form, disturbed by her words, but trying to calm himself. "Leo," Millie continued, "remember that I am here for you no matter what you need, okay? You're like another son to me." He nodded, and they embraced and kissed. She told him she would wait out front, and left him alone to say good-bye.

Her comment about Matt pinched at his mind. He didn't do this to himself. It had been an accident. There was no proof, no note or anything. Even the police had agreed. She was only thinking this because of that last time he was in the psychiatric ward. But that had been months beforehand, and he had been doing well in therapy since then.

Leo reached out with his hand and brushed his fingers against Matt's still face. He was frigid. He could feel the cold air of the air-conditioning blowing onto his hand and Matt's body. Leo moved the open palm of his hand down the front of his navy blue jacket. He liked the feel of the wool Alfani suit, one of their favorites that they had picked out together at Burdines. Leo's hand was shaking. He closed his eyes as he moved it down Matt's torso, over his frosty folded hands. He brushed the fingers, afraid to disturb them any more than that. He felt the buttons of the jacket beneath his fingers. He felt the smooth felt of the jacket's body. He moved lower, and he felt the padded bulge beneath his pants. He kept his hand there for a moment. He wanted to sense it once more. Just once. He could feel himself growing hard by the thought of Matt over him, filling him with his body as they rocked together as one.

But no more. It was over. He would feel it no more.

He opened his eyes, and stared back at Matt's sealed eyelids. He glanced down the length of his body one more time. He noticed then, inside his jacket, a piece of white paper. He almost hadn't seen it against the crisp white shirt. It hadn't been there earlier. He looked back at Matt's face, then at the piece of paper. There were a few photos in the casket, but no other mementos on the white satin bedding.

He reached down and lifted the paper from beneath his jacket, moving as if Matt had been sleeping and Leo didn't want to disturb him. It was an envelope thick with paper, and it said MOTHER on the front. It had been folded in half and had creases and smudges on it.

Someone from the funeral home called to him and said they had to leave. Leo didn't reply. He looked at the envelope, then back at Matt. He wasn't sure what it was. He had to leave though. The funeral home director came forward and leaned a hand on the upper door of the casket. "I'm sorry, Mr. Vasari. We really do have to leave."

Leo nodded and stepped back from the casket. The funeral director started to close the top, and Leo remembered then that he was still holding the envelope. "Wait," he said. The director looked at him inquisitively. But then Leo stepped further away and just nodded his head. Leo watched in slow motion as the top of the casket lowered, and Matt slipped away from the light. The director called to someone else to escort Leo from the room. Leo pocketed the envelope in his jacket, and left with the rest of the family for the cemetery.

One fucking year later, Leo was still in mourning and still questioning the significance of Matt's death. It haunted him. He could feel tears welling in his eyes and an emotional outburst rising. He missed that man so much it hurt like someone had ripped a hole in his chest and forgotten to sew it shut.

He had kept the note. He had never told anyone about it. And he had never read it. He almost had, returning home alone from the funeral, sitting on the couch in his grief getting drunk and stoned. He stopped himself from reading the letter only because he had eventually passed out, and when he awoke with a hangover he was too disturbed to deal with it. He put it in his office, in the rolltop computer desk, in a small drawer on the right side, safely tucked away.

He wouldn't read the letter. It was private, between Matt and Millie. He recalled that while Matt was in therapy he was writing letters to people, then throwing them out. This had to be one of those letters. He couldn't open it. Leo couldn't invade Matt's inner thoughts. Matt had never willingly shared much from his therapy, except that it was helping him learn not to cut himself, which was what they wanted more than anything.

It was all related to Millie somehow, the cutting and the depression. In the couple of counseling sessions that Leo had attended with Matt, it was brought to his attention that it was better for Matt not to have her in his life. There was no explanation why, just a resolution how to help make him better. Leo needed to be supportive by keeping her out of their lives.

After that first surprise phone call from Millie, Leo discovered that Matt and she had not spoken in over seven years. He had left his mother's house in Hollywood to live with a friend while he went to school, then worked in banking. He escalated quickly because of his good sales tactics. He had done it all without ever needing to see or speak to his mother, and had advanced quite well as a result. When Theresa had gone to Hollywood to help her mother recover from her alcoholism, Matt, who lived close by, did nothing. He didn't even visit her.

She had moved to Clearwater, and it was then that things began to get bad for Matt again. From the day of that first phone conversation with Millie two and a half years ago, Leo had known that Matt hated her. That became more and more apparent as time passed and Matt became angry, violent, or depressed whenever he was forced to interact with her. Leo had ignored it, thinking Matt needed to get over his issues, like Millie used to say, and had come up with various scenarios to bring the two of them together. And in the process he had only made things worse for his lover.

He could feel the guilt start to flood his being and tears formed in his eyes. He shook his head though. He had to block the thought and suppress the emotion, at least for now. He couldn't get more depressed than he already was. He had to understand why Millie would have tried to kill herself, and why now.

He realized that there was only one way he was going to find the answers. He had to visit her. This would have angered Matt and would annoy Theresa, but he had to see her. Only she could explain to him why she had tried to kill herself, and why on the anniversary of her son's death. It didn't make sense. If it were any other parent, he would have understood. But not Millie. She was tough. This wasn't her.

There was no other choice. He couldn't overwhelm Millie though, and he couldn't let Theresa know he was going. He would have to be discreet and patient. First, he had to see how Millie was doing. Then, he could ask the questions.

He got up and stretched. He caught his reflection in the mirror, and realized he looked horrible. It was one thing not to care about his personal appearance when it had to do with daily living, but he hesitated to see Millie like this.

Leo went into the master bathroom and took a long, hot shower. He scrubbed his body clean and washed his hair thoroughly. When he was finished, he stepped out of the shower and stood before the bathroom mirror dripping, his towel hanging from his hips. He wiped down the fog on the mirror, then shaved the days of scruff from his face. He dressed in a pair of jeans and found a clean, collared polo shirt he hadn't worn in some time. He threw some gel onto his thick tousled hair and let it go. It looked a little messy, but stylishly so. He actually smiled at his reflection, surprised by his own clean image, and then felt oddly silly for doing it.

He headed out the door, when he suddenly remembered his grades were due. He started to blow it off, then stopped himself as he was about to lock the front door. The school was in the complete opposite direction. Then again, it was too early to go to the hospital. He hated the thought of driving all the way back over to Tampa, but he knew he had to follow through on his obligation and turn in his grades for the students' sake. He sighed, then bolted back inside, shoved the papers and grades into his briefcase, and took it with him as he left.

– THREE –

The trip to the university, despite his initial hesitation, was to his advantage. He turned in all of his papers and grades, and the drive gave him easily an extra ninety minutes to think about what he was going to say to Millie when he saw her. He couldn't help but wonder what her situation would be like in the hospital. He knew she was in the psychiatric ward. That's where they had put Matt. Millie would have known this when she overdosed; she had signed Matt into the hospital.

He drove south on I-275 toward Clearwater and continued past the glass towers of the downtown Tampa cityscape, catching a glimpse of the unpretentious white concrete and green glass NationsBank building where Matt had worked the four years they were together. The building was nestled between the nameless, round, beige, office tower and the pyramidal-topped tower owned by a competitor bank. Six months before Matt had died they had promoted him to corporate sales. He was given a salary increase and an office on the tenth floor of the tower with an amazing view of the Hillsborough River and the gold minarets of the University of Tampa. That promotion had been a blessing, because a few months earlier they had almost fired Matt because of his poor attendance and bad attitude. They had rewarded him once his recovery had begun.

It wasn't attempted suicide that had led to his hospitalization, although at first that was what Leo had thought. The doctor knew better. Matt was a cutter. It was rare for a man to be a cutter, but it wasn't unheard of. Matt would use kitchen knives mostly. Leo had no idea when he did it. It never seemed to be when Leo was home. Leo always noticed it afterward, when they were in bed and he'd accidentally touch a new wound. Or he'd see Matt naked and ask about new red marks on his arms and chest. Matt's excuses seemed logical. He had cut himself when he tripped jogging down to Vinoy Park. He had cut himself on broken glass at the bar. He had cut himself in the yard pruning the bougainvillea. There was always a plausible answer. It had culminated that one night when Leo happened to be late getting home from his night class. He had found him in the bathroom covered with blood.

A car horn jolted the horrific image from Leo's mind. He rubbed his face with one hand quickly and shook his head. He had to clear the ghastly images out of his mind. He had tried to forget it all since it had happened, but he wasn't always successful.

He drove for some time, heading across the Courtney Campbell Causeway to Clearwater, and he hadn't resolved what to say to Millie. He was nervous about the encounter. Guilty, too, because he had neglected their friendship. She had been so good to him before and after Matt's death, and his reciprocation was to ignore her. He had to think of some good things that he could share with her. He thought to himself then that he should have gotten her a book. He could have stopped at that book store on Fletcher Avenue near the university. He was certain he easily could have found an old edition of Christina Rossetti, one of her favorite poets. It was too late now.

He was close to the hospital, and again he wondered what he would say to her. It occurred to him then that Theresa might be there. That could be a problem. He shook his head in anger. She had no right to stop him from seeing her. He loved Millie, probably more than both of her children put together. He had a right to see her.

He found a parking space easily enough, then walked toward the hospital. He entered the hospital foyer and was greeted by a cold burst of air. An elderly woman at the front desk stopped him, asking if he was visiting a patient. He said yes, then told the woman Millie's name. She sat at the information desk with another elderly woman. He watched her as she typed it into the computer. She was bent over the keyboard, staring through thick glasses at the monitor as she typed one letter at a time and stared at the screen after each tap to make sure she hadn't made an error. When she had finished, she hit the enter key forcefully, and leaned closer to the monitor. She pushed up her glasses and squinted. Leo pursed his lips and waited. "Hunter. Here it is. Hunter, Millicent. Room. . ." She trailed off for a moment. "Oh, dear," the woman said, almost in a whisper, "I see she's in the psychiatric division." She glanced up at Leo. "Are you family?"

"No, a very close friend."

"I'm sorry. You can't go up there."

"Why?"

"Immediate family only. Hospital rules," she replied smugly.

He scoffed. He had thought Theresa had made an effort to stop him. Now what was he supposed to do if the old biddy volunteer wouldn't even let him go up? He looked away in frustration and noticed the gift shop. He then looked over her head and saw the hospital floor directory. Millie would be on the sixth floor. He had an idea. "Can I send her something from the gift shop?"

"Certainly," she said. "Nothing with sharp edges though. They don't allow pointy objects up there. In case they injure themselves, you know." She sounded Hitchcockian.

He thanked her, then entered the gift shop. The sweet scent of roses and carnations overwhelmed him. They were too fragrant, and Millie would hate them. She preferred greens over florals. There was a rack of junk food near the door; odd, he thought it, for a hospital gift shop. But they had her favorite snack food: a bag of cheese doodles. The puffy ones, not the crunchy ones. Millie was particular about that. He grabbed the bag and headed for the register. He paid for his purchase, and said nothing about sending it to her room. Instead, he walked to the door and glanced outside before exiting. Both women at the front desk were occupied with new visitors. He noticed the security guard talking with a hospital administrator. Leo made a quick dart out of the gift shop and headed for the elevators around the corner, the bag of cheese doodles under his arm.

He caught his breath to stop his heart racing as he rode the elevator to the sixth floor. He laughed to himself about his own deceitfulness. He wasn't about to let stupid hospital rules prevent him from seeing her. When the elevator stopped, he alighted. He followed the red sign to the psychiatric ward. He felt positive about this visit, probably more so because he was being prevented from visiting her by Theresa and hospital rules, and he had beat them.

He turned another corner, and was greeted by a large set of double doors. They were painted blood red. Worse, they were sealed with a push-button combination lock. There was no way to get in except to ring the bell to the left of the doors by the intercom. He should have expected the locked doors. It was similar to when he would visit Matt at St. Anthony's. Except those doors had been Floridian peach like the rest of the hospital. Nothing stood out but the sign over those doors that told you where you were. Here, though, the doors were red and stood out along the white walls like a giant blood clot.

He rang the bell. A few seconds later, a muffled woman's voice responded. "I'm here to see Ms. Hunter," he told her.

There was silence for about ten seconds. Then, the voice said, "Sir, are you family?"

He didn't hesitate this time with his answer. He leaned in closer to the intercom speaker and said, "Yes. I'm her son."

Another pause. Then the voice said, "I don't have a son listed on her file."

Of course not. "Well, that's because I don't live here. I flew in this morning from. . ." He thought fast. ". . . Newark." No response. "I imagine my sister Theresa didn't put my name down because she didn't know I'd be here so quickly."

"Who is your sister?"

"Theresa Vasari."

"I have a Theresa listed, but her last name isn't Vasari."

Shit! She had gone back to her maiden name. "Sorry, I forgot. She got a divorce recently. It's Theresa Pierce."

There was another brief pause, then she asked, "Sir, what is your name?"

He was relieved for the moment. Now for his name. He swallowed to calm himself. "Matthew," he said, "Matthew Pierce." There was almost a biting sting on his tongue as he said the name, but even odder was hearing him say the name so formally, and identifying himself with his dead lover.

A few seconds later, the buzzer sounded and he heard a click. He took a deep breath of relief, stood taller, and entered. The woman who had been speaking to him through the intercom sat behind a glass window, which she slid open and smiled at him.

"Sorry about all that. Hospital rules."

"Not a problem. I understand."

She asked to see what he was holding, and he showed her the bag. "Mom's favorite," he added sheepishly.

"Sign in please." She handed him a clipboard with papers attached. He started to write his own name, then remembered he was supposed to be writing Matthew Pierce. His hand was shaking. He quickly wrote over the L with an M and continued signing his name. He suddenly panicked that she might ask for identification too, and he was relieved when she didn't. He hardly heard her when she buzzed him again and mentioned she would add his name to Millie's file.

He entered a hallway painted bright white and smelling strongly of citric disinfectant. There were closed white doors of offices on his left and right every ten feet or so, black name plates reading the names of various doctors or medical rooms. He heard whining voices behind one door, muffled cries behind another. The sanitized atmosphere was uncannily eerie, and it frightened him a little. He couldn't help but think back a year and a half ago to the first time he had ever entered such a space at St. Anthony's when Matt was there. His heart was pounding harder.

Leo entered the common room and looked around. The eeriness, he realized, was in his head, because as he looked around it wasn't that bad. The bright white was a bit overwhelming, but potted palm trees provided needed color. There were soft, comfortable gray couches and chairs, and oak tables with curved edges. Light gray industrial carpeting stretched throughout the room. There were about a dozen people in the room. One man stood at the nurse's station talking to them, his voice shaky but clear. A few were seated on couches reading. He noticed one woman sitting in a chair, staring at the wall before her. He thought he sensed her lips moving. Two other people were at a table doing a puzzle. It was more like a convalescent home than the psychiatric ward. Millie was nowhere in sight, though.

He went to the desk and asked for help. A red-headed girl in scrubs turned to him. He asked where he could find Millie Hunter, and she pointed to the windows off to the right of the common room. "You can't smoke indoors," she explained.

Leo chuckled. "Ah, I should have known." He thanked her and walked toward the glass door. On this side of the room was a wall of windows and the door that opened onto a courtyard reserved for smoking. It was a secret garden with brick walls at least nine feet high surrounding them, slits every six feet or so to allow light in but nothing out. The furniture was redwood, and various potted bushes and plants surrounded the patio. It actually looked comfortable, and it was quiet. He opened the door and stepped outside. The sun was hot as it was near noon, but being this high up in the building the air was cooler. There was a man smoking a pipe, pacing and mumbling to himself.

Millie was about fifteen feet before him. She had not heard him come outside. She was sitting sideways on the left side of a cushioned redwood sofa, her legs tucked under her. She wore her silver half-glasses. They complemented her short gray-blonde hair, although they probably made her look older than the sixtyish years she was. She stared off, looking at nothing in particular. She had been engrossed in reading a book that she now held so loosely in her right hand that it was about to fall from her grip. In her left hand she was holding her cigarette in the open air, her arm resting on the back of the sofa. The smoke was curling upward, and the ash on it was about a half inch long and slightly curving downward. Leo smiled at her ongoing habit. She would smoke a cigarette, always Marlboro Menthol, and inevitably wind up inhaling only half of it because the rest had burned away. Then after swearing with realization she'd light up a new cigarette and repeat the same pattern.

He took a few steps closer. "You're going to burn yourself if you don't flick that ash."

She glanced up unconsciously, adjusting her vision over the half-glasses, then jerked her head back, life returning to her quickly. "Oh, my God!" she exclaimed, pronouncing it like "Gawd" in the Brooklyn accent he loved to hear. She extinguished the cigarette in the ashtray on the table beside her and tossed the book aside. She jumped up and they moved toward each other and embraced. She kissed his cheek, and he could smell the sweet cigarette taste on her lips. It was oddly comforting.

"I can't believe it!" she said, holding him at arms-length. "What a surprise!"

He shrugged. "Oh, you know, I had nothing to do, so I thought I'd pop in and see how things were going. . . ."

"They're fabulous. Can't you tell? Don't you love my smoking room?" She twirled once as she spoke, her arms gesturing upwards. "Company is a little freaky," she added, gesturing with her thumb to the mumbling pipe smoker.

He chuckled. "Puffy cheese doodles!" he said with forced glee.

"Give me those!" She grabbed the bag from his hand and went back toward the seat. She waved him over to sit beside her and ripped open the bag. She moaned as she crunched into one. "It's like sex," she said. "No, better. Only your hands get messier. Of course, it's been so long since I've had sex I could have the two mixed up." She licked her fingers clean of their powdered cheese.

He laughed and shook his head. He wondered if she'd ever not surprise him with her candor. She offered him a cheese doodle, and he munched on one. She was acting giddy. Leo wondered if they had her on Prozac or something. She was a little too cheerful.

She leaned back against the seat and looked up at him, all the time munching away on cheese doodles. "You need a haircut," she mumbled.

"Yes, I know."

She rocked her head side to side for a few seconds. "I don't know. Maybe you should wear it long. Matthew probably would have liked it."

He forced a smile.

"How's it like on the outside?" she continued.

"Um, you're not in jail, you know. You've only been here. . .what? Twenty-four hours?"

She shrugged but didn't respond.

Leo looked down. He saw what she was reading and picked it up. It was a paperback with a Pre-Raphaelite painting on the cover. He stared at the title and looked up at her with surprise. "You're reading *Lady Audley's Secret?!*"

"They had it on the bookcase inside. It was that or *A Tale of Two Cities,* and I refuse to read that again. I saw the title and recognized it as one of the books you were working on." She munched away on another piece of puffed cheese. She waited until she had swallowed most of it, then asked, "How is your dissertation going?"

He scoffed. "Jeez, between you and Dr. Palmer!"

"Well, what do you expect? We want you to finish."

"I'm doing research and some writing, but it's slow going."

"Isn't that what you said the last time I saw you?"

If it had been any other close friend who had commented about their conversation the "last time" they had seen one another, and that "last time" had been almost six months beforehand, Leo would have believed they were being sarcastic to drive home a point. Millie was so straightforward, though, that he knew if she meant to say something like "Why haven't you spoken to me in six months?" she would have, without hesitation. She meant nothing by the last few words of her sentence. But that didn't mean he felt less guilty about the inference.

"This dissertation writing isn't easy," he commented.

"You're being negative. Matthew wouldn't like that. Knock it off."

He was getting uncomfortable talking about Matt. She talked about him so easily, as if he were just out to the store for milk. She had been like that ever since he had died. If Matt's death had anything to do with her overdose, her attitude didn't reveal it.

He glanced back down at the book. The Pre-Raphaelite painting was Dante Gabriel Rossetti's *Fazio's Mistress,* with the frizzy-red-haired Fanny Cornforth gazing into nothingness. He wondered if that was what Millie was like when she was contemplative or sad, a Rossettian woman staring into nothingness, pondering her own plight. She hardly ever cried. He had caught her in one of those moments when he had come out into the garden area and saw her on the sofa, unaware of anything around her. Her cigarette had been dangling in her hand, the book about to fall from her grip. She had been lost in her own sense of being, questioning, probably wondering what it all meant.

He gazed at her seriously. "What happened, Millie?" he asked.

She had reached into the bag again, but restrained herself and put the bag on the table. She used her fingernail to wipe her front teeth clean, then sucked her fingers dry. In the meantime, the other man walked from behind them and left the patio, mumbling as he passed them. After he had departed and they were alone, she leaned back against the sofa and shrugged. "It was an accident."

Leo attempted to hide his surprise, but was unsuccessful. "An accident?"

She nodded. "It's no big deal. It was an accident. I forgot how many pills I took earlier in the day and then took a few extra to go to bed."

He had hoped that it had been an accident, but somehow he knew she was lying. "And why were you taking Valium in the first place?"

This time she hesitated before replying. "I guess I was uptight or depressed or something."

"You guess?" he repeated. He put the book onto the table besides the bag. "I don't know, Millie. You're so matter-of-fact and proud of who you are, I find it hard to believe that you'd be depressed or that upset." He added as an afterthought, "At least depressed enough to accidentally take an overdose."

She glanced at him, in acknowledgment perhaps, then looked away. "We all get depressed, Leo. I'm getting old. I look like an old fart. I have no one to share my life with. Theresa and I don't have the best relationship. I mean, we're okay, but we're not running off together shopping at Dillard's."

"I don't think any of that is worth killing yourself over," he said.

"What do you know about it?" she asked. He had hurt her.

He hesitated before speaking. "It's because of Matt, isn't it?" he asked.

She looked away. "Yes, of course, that too." Her voice had an edge to it. Suddenly she jumped up from her seat and paced nearby.

He looked more closely at Millie. She did seem older, and perhaps less attractive in a way. Being here probably didn't help. He saw that her hair had lost much of its luster and was weak and limpid. Her hazel eyes were dull. She was wearing a worn red cardigan sweater over her white cotton blouse and off-white clamdiggers. She paced with her arms folded across her aging breasts and didn't speak again. Leo did see that she was upset and troubled, more than she ever had been before. There were newer wrinkles in her face, and she was slightly hunched forward. "Your timing was too coincidental to be anything but related to his death," he continued.

She stopped and turned. She reached down and grabbed another cigarette from her pack. She banged its head against the pack and stared at him. She lit a match so that the smell of sulfur ignited in the air. "You know they actually let me light the match myself, would you believe it?" She had changed the subject. "How do they know I'm not a pyromaniac?"

"Because there's no such thing as Old Lady Pyro."

She inhaled the cigarette. "Maybe I should burn down the plants out here and prove them wrong."

He raised an eyebrow in feigned shock. "Somehow I don't think you would do that."

"Why?"

"Because it's not like you."

She scoffed. "Oh, you are so naïve."

"Come on, Millie. I know you better than your own children do."

She exhaled deeply, her eyes opening wide. "Don't be so cocky, Leo. Really, what do you know about me?"

"Quite a bit, I think. We've had some in-depth conversations about our lives."

"Yeah, well, I never told you everything." She took another sharp puff of menthol and exhaled while she spoke. "Not everything is what it seems. We all have secrets, Leo. I do. Matthew did. Theresa does. Your mother even. The nurse at the desk. Even you, Leo."

"I don't have any secrets."

He knew he was lying, and that she was telling the truth. Everyone always had at least one secret they kept from others. It didn't matter if it was something cataclysmic that they had done in their lives, something emotional they couldn't deal with, or something stupid they were embarrassed to share. As she puffed away, a thought occurred to him. "What was Matthew's secret?"

She changed the subject again, too quickly. "How did you get in here anyway?"

He wanted to get back to Matthew's secret, and to why she had said it, but he knew she wouldn't go back. He would have to be patient. He leaned back against the cushions. "I lied. I told them I was your son. From Newark." She chuckled, and he was glad to see she found humor in his deception. "Look," he continued, "I'm not so much concerned about why you're here. I just want you to get help and go home soon. Do you feel any better?"

"Of course. I'm alive." Leo didn't respond to her attempt at humor. "You know the Florida Baker Act. I have to be here seventy-two hours, and the doctor encouraged me to sign myself in for another seventy-two hours for treatment. I'll be here for about a week."

"Like Matt," he finished for her. She nodded.

They stayed outside for a little while longer so that she could actually finish smoking an entire cigarette. The sun was getting hotter, so they moved inside carrying the book and cheese doodles, and sat in the common room with some of the strangers. Millie introduced Leo to two of the other people. It was uncanny, though, when she turned to them and said, "This is my son Matthew. From Newark." And when they exclaimed how sweet he was for coming all the way down to visit her, she tweaked his cheek and said, "I know! I'm such a lucky mother!"

They found a couch and continued to talk for some time. They caught up on old news. They chatted about Leo's family, his impending joblessness, and his dissertation. Leo was always amazed how even though she wasn't highly educated, she had world experience and could engage him in conversation about theories by Derrida and Barthes as long as he explained what they were about. She was a delight to speak to. It made it all the more difficult for him to understand why she was here. None of it made sense.

He visited with her for almost two hours. During that time, other visitors came and went. Doctors and patients moved from room to room down the white hallway. Eventually, the red-headed nurse announced that it was time for lunch, and a session with her doctor that afternoon. He was welcome to stay for lunch, but Leo thought it would be better if he left. They rose and he hugged her again, saying loud enough for the nurse to hear him, "Talk to you later, Mom." He started to go, then remembered something, so he turned back and whispered to her, "Don't tell Theresa I was here." ·

She said aloud, "Why not?" There was a slight panic in her voice.

Leo glanced at the nurse, who was standing waiting. "Could you give us a minute to say good-bye?" She nodded with a smile and left. He had his hand on Millie's arm. He looked back at her and said, "Theresa doesn't know I'm here."

She bit her lower lip. "I don't understand. How did you get here then?"

"I told you. I said I was—"

"No, I mean. . ." Then, she realized the truth. "Theresa doesn't want you here."

He shook his head. "No. And I don't know why." Millie fidgeted, her hands playing with the buttons on her sweater. "Are you all right?"

She nodded. "Yes, of course. I'm just surprised, that's all." She crossed her arms and held them tightly.

"Well, don't tell her I was here, or she'll get pissed off."

"No, of course not." They hugged and kissed cheeks again. "Can you come back?"

"Tomorrow. If that's all right?"

She nodded. "Yes, I'd like that very much."

He left her with a wave and walked toward the corridor. He took a quick glance back and she waved to him again.

She had been tense toward the end, when he had mentioned about Theresa not knowing he had come. It was a bit odd, and sad. Even more sad was for Leo to see her in this place. Still, he had to be positive. She had attempted suicide on the anniversary of her son's death, accidentally or not, but she had survived. She was bound to be distraught and look terrible. She was probably uncertain of her feelings right now.

She had talked about secrets. They all had them. He wondered what she was referring to. Once again he agreed that secrets were everywhere and in everyone's minds, but she seemed to imply there were things he didn't know about. There had to be something more going on with the whole situation. He'd go back the next day, his birthday, and spend more time with her. He'd have to take things one step at a time. It was more important right now that he had actually visited her.

Leo had a sense of peace about him. He left the hospital feeling lighter and realized he was smiling, just slightly, but it was there. He wasn't sure if it was a sense of accomplishment, or maybe feeling like he had done a good deed. Regardless, he was a little happy. It had definitely been a while. The feeling inspired him to do something different. He decided to stop at the Clearwater Mall food court for a late lunch, then wound up shopping at Burdines. He knew better than to spend money right now, but he felt like he deserved a treat, and bought a few Tommy Hilfiger shirts and other items that were marked down.

By the time he headed home, it was after 6:00 p.m. As he turned onto his street, he saw a UPS truck rambling past him, bouncing along with him on the historic brick-lined street. As it approached, he involuntarily checked to see who the driver was, and he swore for a moment that maybe it was the same driver from yesterday, but the truck had passed by too quickly for him to get a good look.

He parked his car, grabbed the Burdines bag and empty briefcase, and headed toward the front porch. There was a package for him laying on the top step against the screen door. He shifted everything to one hand and picked up the package. It was a package from Millie. Then he recalled that this wasn't the first package that she had sent him. There was another one, unopened, sitting on his dining room table. And she hadn't said a word to him about either of them when he had seen her that morning.

Leo went inside and dropped his bag and briefcase on the living room couch. He carried the package into the dining room and looked at the disastrous mess everywhere. The other one was resting on a paper hill of open and sealed mail. He picked it up, got a knife from the kitchen, and walked toward the living room to examine them both. Sitting on the couch, he sliced open the first package that had been sent. It was a book taped in bubble wrap. He ripped off the plastic and held in his hands the rare 1862 edition of Christina Rossetti's *The Goblin Market and Other Poems* that he had given her as a Christmas gift a year after he had met her. Leo and Matt had gone to New York for a Thanksgiving getaway in 1997 to celebrate his promotion after having been hospitalized. They had seen all the sites neither of them had visited since they were children, from the Statue of Liberty to the American Museum of Natural History, not to mention two shows on Broadway. Matt would have been content to relax the rest of the trip, but Leo had to visit the Strand Book Store.

He found the book misshelved behind other books. He was dumbfounded when he saw it, because he knew it should be in the rare book room. The binding had been designed by Rossetti's brother Dante Gabriel. He had also illustrated the main poem "Goblin Market" with a lesbian-like image of the two sisters asleep in an affectionate embrace. The book was worn out and beaten, almost a garage sale throwaway, but it was still a unique treasure. He had to buy it, and paid a high price for it, although he didn't tell Matt.

He gave it to Millie as a Christmas gift. She appreciated Rossetti's poetry more than he ever would, and she deserved it because they had become such good friends. He visited her at her double-wide mobile home on Christmas Eve morning, alone, and gave it to her as a gift. He never told Matt because it would have infuriated him and broken the rule of not involving Millie in their lives.

She was ecstatic over the gift. She made coffee in her black-and-white kitchen with red appliances, and spent the next two hours with him reading excerpts of "Goblin Market": the steady pulsating rhythmic beat of succulent plums and juicy pomegranates, horrifically enticing goblins, sisterly love. Rossetti was an unusual woman, Leo knew. She was reserved and religious, but wrote of experiences and emotions that didn't seem possible for such a proper Victorian lady. She was a dichotomy between what she could express and how she could live. She was smart and bold. She could see the world men lived in, and knew their excessive sense could undermine women's sensibility.

When he left her that Christmas Eve, she thanked him again for the wonderful gift and embraced him tightly. And now, he held the same gift in his hands again. There was no note. Just bubble wrap. It didn't make sense why she would send it to him. Then he wondered what was in the other package. He sliced it open and saw that it was thicker. Out came another bubble-wrapped book. The bubbles popped as he opened it, and he held a single volume from the Bonchurch edition of *Poems and Ballads* by Algernon Charles Swinburne, another of her favorite poets. This package startled him even more.

The original book had dated from 1866, but this edition was from 1925, one volume in the poet's official collected works. It wasn't rare, as almost every academic library had a copy of the whole set. Few individuals owned it, though. The dark blue cover was worn from handling. Leo opened the book. There was foxtailing on the inner covers, and he could see that the binding had snapped in one section from her constant reading and folding back of pages. His nose tickled from the musty smell of its pages.

Her copy was a gift from a Berkeley professor, an ex-lover from her California past. The book was one of the few possessions she brought back to New York with her when she returned after her mother had died. He had seen it on her bookcase the first time he had visited her mobile home, and she pounced on his interest. "Have you read Swinburne?" she asked with bated breath. He shook his head, and she pounded her heart. "Leo, you absolutely must read him. He's brilliant."

That afternoon, Millie and Leo spent hours talking about Swinburne and his poetry and life. She read poems like "Anactoria," "Faustine," and "The Hymn to Proserpine," feminine power exalted and eroticized, enthralling Millie as she read line by line. It was the first time he had ever heard Swinburne's poetry read aloud, and he was duly impressed by her passion. She kept this single volume of Swinburne's early poems proudly displayed on her bookcase. She thought him a genius, a literary Mozart. And like the composer he was undisciplined, wild, and erratic. He probably suffered from panic attacks and had attention deficit disorder. He drank excessively and was infatuated with flagellation, yet revolutionized English poetry by writing about feelings and desires without regard for social propriety. "We have so much in common," she said, referring to Swinburne.

So why send him this book too? He flipped through the pages, feeling the course edges brush against his thumb as they fluttered by. He saw a few pages folded down, and he opened to some of these. There were various words and phrases underlined in blue and black ink. He thought it odd that she would choose to damage one of her favorite books like this. In actuality, he couldn't understand any of it. It all seemed ridiculous that he was holding copies of what were obviously two of her most cherished books. But there was no note, no card, nothing to tell him what this was all about. It occurred to him that maybe it was supposed to be a gift, but wouldn't she have said something?

Unless there was no reason for her to say anything. It would have been obvious they were gifts had she actually died. She said the overdose had been an accident. Now he knew for a fact that she had been lying. He bit his lower lip in despair. Deep inside, he realized he had been hoping that it had been an accident.

He sat back on the couch and stared at the two books, one in each hand. He shook his head in disappointment and confusion, then put both on the coffee table. He picked up the bubble wrap and began to pop the bubbles without thinking. He stared at the two books, wondering why, about so many things. After a few minutes he realized all the bubbles were burst and he had no answers. He suddenly tossed all the leftover packing and bubble wrap onto the floor.

He looked around and saw he was surrounded by stuff. His tables were laden with junk. His couch had laundry strewn over it. Books and papers were everywhere. He knew there were similar piles in the dining room and kitchen. He hated what it looked like. Leo had been the neat freak, always yelling at Matt to clean his dishes and throw the garbage out. It looked like Leo had died and left Matt to fend for himself.

He jumped off the couch and picked up all the bubble wrap and packaging. He carried it into the kitchen. His intention was to throw it all in the garbage, but that was overflowing with rancid trash. He set the packaging down and reached under his sink for a plastic bag. He opened it wide, then dumped the packaging. From there, he started to move in a frenzy, cleaning the house.

He could feel the excitement of a Leo he thought long gone creeping back. He used to be able to clean the entire house—bathrooms too—in under 100 minutes. He was energized, so he sorted through the trash and dumped it outside, washed all the dishes throughout every room, picked up his laundry and refolded clothes that had been clean but dumped in a pile two weeks earlier. He put his clothes away, tackled the bedroom, and gathered dirty laundry into a hamper. On the way back into the living room, he laughed as he looked at the couch. The cordless telephone was nestled between the cushions where the clothes had been. He replaced it on the charger on the kitchen wall. He moved about the house like this for hours until he had cleaned the entire house. Finally, exhausted, he fell onto the couch, ate, and fell asleep.

– FOUR –

The disastrous family reunion dinner, as Leo called it afterward, had taken place a week before Christmas 1996, about a month after that first phone call from Millie. Leo had spoken to her two other times on the phone since then, but they had not met. Leo arranged things with Theresa despite her hesitation. At the time he truly believed a reunion would be good, and he wanted to meet Millie.

He didn't tell Matt that she would be there. If he had, Matt never would have come. He decided to let it be a surprise reunion. In his naivete, Leo envisioned an Oprah Winfrey scene, where long-lost parents were reunited with their children and everyone forgave without malice, especially at Christmastime. If Matt would give her a chance, everything would work out fine.

When they walked into George and Theresa's house, Matt was his usual lighthearted self. They had not decorated much for Christmas, although a small tree with lights and a few ornaments stood in the corner of the living room. The house smelled of baked potatoes and a roast. Matt was carrying a bottle of red wine and extended it to George as he shook his hand, then kissed his sister's cheek. As she moved to the side, though, Leo saw him freeze when Millie came into view. She spoke with her arms crossed, a cigarette dangling from one hand. "Hello, Matthew, how are you?"

He didn't respond. Instead, he glanced at Theresa, but she had stepped away. He glanced at George, who shrugged hopelessly. Then, he turned and glared at Leo, but he said nothing. Leo was uncertain what to do. He knew it was going to be awkward, but there was an anger that flared in Matt's face that frightened him. Leo's only thought for the moment was escape. He darted around his boyfriend and went right to Millie. He shook her hand, and introduced himself.

Pierce
doi:10.1300/5849_04

52

His first impressions had been determined by their three phone calls so far. She was still heavily New Yorkish. A little obnoxious. Bold. Outspoken. He had no idea what she looked like. Neither Matt nor Theresa had family photos. His impression of her physically was not disappointing or surprising. She seemed ordinary enough, not extravagant or distinctive. But a sense of strength emanated from her despite her ordinariness. Her hair was blonde-gray, and she wore it short, almost pixie-style. Her cigarettes were near her at all times, and she had quickly disregarded her daughter's request for no smoking in the house. She expressed great pleasure at finally meeting Leo.

No one spoke after that. It was quiet until the microwave beeped and Theresa asked everyone to sit. Millie extinguished her cigarette in a little ashtray she had found. George sat at the head of the table, Theresa and Millie on one side, Matt and Leo on the other, brother and sister across from each other. Dinner was quiet. Matt played with his food. He gulped down his glass of cabernet. He wouldn't look at anyone. Leo eyed him closely every few minutes. His stomach was fluttering, and he himself was having difficulty eating. As he looked around the table, he saw that everyone was feeling the same way. Leo felt obligated to break the ice, so he asked Theresa how the library was. That started a brief conversation. He glanced at Millie a few times and saw her watching him. He thought he saw her smile, as if acknowledging what he was doing. She picked up on his cue, and told Theresa how delicious the pot roast was. She asked where she had learned to make it. Theresa hesitated before responding, then said, "Grandmother taught me. She used to make this. You don't remember?"

Millie faltered a response. "Of course I remember." Her tone had an edge to it. "It tastes different from hers." As an afterthought, she said softly, "I didn't know you knew how to cook it, that's all."

For a moment, Matt glared at Leo. Leo could almost sense his words, pointing out to him yet again that his mother was a cold-hearted bitch who couldn't even remember her own mother's most popular dish. Leo looked away and tried to divert attention once again. He commented also that the dinner was delicious.

Millie continued speaking. "Theresa was always a wonderful cook. And Matthew used to bake desserts. Do you still make that chocolate cheesecake?" she asked him.

He didn't respond. Instead, Leo asked, "Matt bakes?" He was surprised to hear this, because Matt never cooked a thing at home.

"I thought he was going to be a professional bakery chef for a while. He wanted to go to that cooking school at the Art Institute of Fort Lauderdale. He used to get all creative with one of those bags to decorate cakes with. I had this one friend who thought his cheesecake—"

Matt dropped his fork on the plate with a loud clatter that stopped his mother in midsentence. He glared at her. "Don't." It was the first word he had said to her in years.

Millie wasn't intimidated. "Don't what? I can't talk about your baking?"

"Just. . .don't!"

Her mood suddenly changed from polite to pissed off. She pointed her fork at him. "You know what, you've got a problem. I'm trying to be nice here and have a civil conversation, and you can't even accept a compliment from me!"

Matt's face was red. Leo was uncertain what to do, but he watched as Millie stabbed her fork into another piece of meat and went to eat it, then threw the fork down so that it clattered as well.

"Seven years it's been," she said. "Seven fucking years, and you still won't even speak to me!" No one said a word.

She folded her arms across her chest and stared diagonally across the table at him. "You haven't changed, have you? You're still the same cocky little brat that lived with me in the Hollywood trailer park. I sure as hell hope you don't treat your boyfriend the same way you treat me, or I'd tell him to dump your ass!"

When she said "boyfriend" she glanced very subtly toward Leo. Leo could only respond by closing his eyes and sitting back. He heard Theresa groan. Then, George spoke up, and it was the response that Leo had always dreaded.

"Boyfriend? You two are homos?" George asked, his mouth full, in true guido style.

Leo looked at his brother and came out to him for the first time. "Yes, George, we're gay."

George was holding in midair his fork with pot roast and potato on it. "No fucking way! I hang out with Matt all the time. He goes with me to the games and shit!"

"George, being gay has nothing to do with liking sports. Just because I hate football doesn't mean—"

He snorted. "I ain't talking about you. You always acted like a little girl."

Leo's mouth hung open. He glanced over at Matt for support, but he stared off.

"George," Theresa finally said, "you're acting ignorant."

"You knew about this?" he asked.

"What is there to know? They're gay. So what?"

"This is bullshit! I'm not eating with a bunch of faggots!" He threw his fork down, pushed himself out from the table, and grabbed his car keys. "I'm eating dinner at Hooters with the real men." The screen door slammed behind him as he left. They heard his truck drive away.

There was a pause before Millie finally spoke. "I'm sorry," she said. Leo could sense that she was genuine in her apology. He could understand and had already forgiven her. She had no idea.

A chuckle, however, came from Matt. "Sorry? You're sorry?" he asked, his face twisted in sarcastic glee. "What a fucking joke!"

"I am sorry, Matthew. I had no idea George didn't know."

Matt started laughing. "You're a piece of work, Mother, you know that? You aren't even here thirty minutes and look what you did! You ruined my relationship with my brother-in-law in a single swoop. You're unfuckingbelievable!"

"Matt," Leo interjected, "she didn't mean it. She didn't know."

Matt suddenly spun and spat his anger at Leo. "And you! Who the fuck do you think you are to do this to me?" His face was flushed red and his eyes flared like a bull's. "What was this, some kind of joke to you? I told you I wanted nothing to do with this woman! Fucking asshole!" He shoved himself out from the table so forcefully the whole table shifted on the tile floor and Millie and Theresa jerked back in their chairs.

Matt followed George's lead and tore out of the house. The screen door slammed again. Leo jumped up and went to go after him, but Millie stopped him. "Leave him alone!" she ordered.

He was startled, but he stopped. He didn't think it was right for him to let Matt run off like that, but he wasn't sure if chasing him down was smart either. They heard his Mustang squeal away. Leo wanted to kick himself. The reunion had been a disaster. He never should have done this. He stepped back to the table, gripping the back of his chair for support.

He gazed at Theresa more closely and was surprised to see what he could only consider to be latent fury. Her neck was red, and she seemed to be breathing heavy. She stared at her mother, and Millie threw her hands up in the air. "What? I said I'm sorry. You should have told me that jerk husband of yours was homophobic!" Theresa shook her head in disgust. She stood quickly, grabbed dishes, and carried them into the kitchen. They heard tap water rush in the sink and pots and pans clanging.

Millie looked up at him, her arms crossed. "You all right?"

He nodded, then shook his head. It wasn't worth trying to hide it. "This sucks. I thought this was going to be a smashing success."

"Smashing, yes. Success . . . I've seen better." He didn't laugh. "Leo, you did a good thing. Don't beat yourself up over it. My son hasn't spoken to me in seven years. He's not going to suddenly welcome me with open arms no matter who would have tried to bring us together."

"I don't understand it. Why hasn't he spoken to you?"

She rolled her eyes. "Good God, where do I start?" She reached for her cigarette pack and lit up. She gestured for him to sit and he did. She took a long drag on her menthol cigarette and exhaled broadly. Normally, the sweetened tobacco smoke hovering around the table might have bothered Leo a little. But he ignored it to listen to her. Her commanding aura settled him somehow.

"My son hates me," she began. She sat back in the chair and crossed her arms so that her cigarette hand was still hovering over the table near the ashtray. "I assume you know that his father left us." Leo nodded. "What else do you know?" she asked.

Matt had been reticent about his past over the first two and a half years of their relationship. Only since Millie's phone call had Leo gotten him to open up a bit. "I know that his father left when he was, I guess, eight or—"

"He was going to be six."

Leo nodded. "And he mentioned about some lake in New Jersey—"

"Cranberry Lake," she interrupted again.

"Yes, that's it," he replied. "You spent summers there when he was very young." She didn't say anything. He noticed that she was watching him intently, and that her cigarette ash was burning and getting larger. "After his father left, Theresa and he were raised by their grandmother until she died about five years later. Then you came and took him to Florida." He shrugged his shoulders. "That's it, I guess. He lived with you in Hollywood until he moved out on his own."

The ash kept increasing on her cigarette, but she was oblivious to it. "Nothing else?" she asked.

"Not really. Not that I can think of right now."

The ash suddenly fell into the ashtray, and she scolded herself. "Damn it, I always lose cigarettes that way." She extinguished what was left, patting the butt into the ashtray as she directed her attention back to Leo. "He never told you about me?"

"No," he admitted.

"You didn't even know I was alive until I called, did you?"

He hesitated to respond. Then he realized it really was irrelevant trying to keep watching what he said. "No, I didn't know. I mean, I figured you must exist. I never heard Theresa say you were dead."

"But she didn't say I was alive either."

He nodded in agreement. "Did you go to Theresa and George's wedding?"

"No," she replied, then added, "and neither did Matthew."

"Why not?"

She lit another cigarette. "What makes you think we were invited?" Leo found that odd, but didn't respond. "I have two children, Leo. One wishes I wasn't around, the other wishes I was dead."

"Why do you say that? Theresa must be glad you're here. You get along all right." Millie raised an eyebrow. "So then why did you move

here if you don't think your children want you?" He found himself relaxing and able to speak openly with her.

She exhaled while she spoke. "Because I don't drive anymore, and
public transportation in south Florida sucks." As an afterthought, she
added, "And I wanted to see them."

"Why now all of a sudden?"

She shrugged. "It's just time."

"That's it?"

She nodded. "That's it." She took another drag.

Leo pondered her reason for a moment. "Well, Theresa doesn't
seem to be too resentful in my opinion. She obviously helped you
move here." Millie acquiesced with a nod. "Why does Matt hate you?"

She squared her jaw. "My son hates me because I was a terrible
mother. I took off on him when he was a child and didn't come back
for five years. Then I reappeared and dragged him off to Florida when
he hardly knew me. I drank pretty heavily. I had a few boyfriends
when he lived with me. He didn't like any of them. Made my life hell
in the process. We fought all the time when he was a teenager."

"There must be more to it than that."

"Why? You don't think that's enough to stop us from speaking?"
She puffed on her cigarette some more.

"For seven years? No, I don't think so. Unless there's more to the
story."

She extinguished her cigarette roughly into the ashtray. "You're an
inquisitive young man, Leo." She leaned forward with her hands on
the table. "Yes, there's more. There's always more." She took a breath
before continuing. "Matthew. . .has had problems."

This surprised him. "What problems?"

"Dealing with things. Emotional problems."

He eyed her quizzically. "I don't get that sense from him at all.
He's got it totally together. He has an amazing job, our relationship is
going great."

She nodded slowly. "That's wonderful. I'm glad he's doing so well
now."

"Why, what happened to him?"

"He hasn't told you?"

He shook his head. "Nothing more than I mentioned to you. I mean, he gets depressed every once and a while, but that's it."

"Then let's leave it at that. What's done is done."

"Well, what do you mean? I think I have a right to know."

"Yes, you do. But not from me, the mother he hates and doesn't speak to."

"But if he won't tell me—"

"Then you're not supposed to know. Besides, it's like I said. What's done is done. There's no point in going back. Look, I've moved beyond the past and I'm looking forward to at least becoming somewhat friendly with my children." Millie got up and gathered dishes. Leo rose and did the same. While they worked, Millie spoke to him again. Her voice, however, had changed, and she seemed shyer. "Leo, now I want to ask you something about Matthew." She stopped clearing the dishes. "What does he remember from Cranberry Lake?"

He shrugged. "I don't know. I can't imagine too much if he was so young."

"Leo, I have to know." She added as an explanation, "To better understand him, to recall things from days in our lives before he hated me."

"Matt really only mentioned it to me one time. I know you lived in Brooklyn, and you had a summer cabin at this lake." Millie's nod encouraged him. "He told me about the fun stuff he remembers, like fishing with his father a few times, swimming, things like that."

"Anything else?" she asked, glancing away.

Nothing else came to his mind right away. Then, "Well, it's not related to the lake, but when we were moving to our house a few months ago, I was getting rid of stuffed animals and he told me about this stuffed animal he had lost when he was young."

"What?" she asked. Her face paled.

"I think it was a teddy bear." Her mouth opened but she didn't speak. "He remembers that it was his favorite stuffed animal, but that's it as far as I know."

She shook her head in disbelief. "He actually remembers Teddy Pierce?"

Leo pointed toward her. "Yes! That was it. Teddy Pierce."

"I can't believe he remembers it," she muttered, almost to herself. "It was a simple teddy bear, less than a foot high. It was all brown except for the belly and inner ears that were white. It had plastic eyes and a little tongue that stuck out." She seemed to be gazing into the past.

"How did he lose it?"

She glanced back at him, her reverie interrupted. "I guess he lost it at the summer house the last time we were there." She fidgeted with the dishes again. "He didn't tell you anything else about the lake or the cabin?"

He shrugged his shoulders. "I don't know, Millie. It's like I told you. He hasn't really spoken much about his past."

"Maybe he thinks like I do. What's done is done. No point in reliving it."

"I guess." It seemed odd to him that she kept asking about the lake, however. "Is there something specific you think he might have told me?"

She hesitated before replying. "That last summer at the lake. . .it was the last time Matthew ever saw his father."

Leo was about to respond, but was interrupted by Theresa, who had entered drying her hands on a dish towel. "Mother," she said cautiously. They turned toward her. "What are you talking about?" she asked.

Leo responded before she could. "About Matt when he was a child."

Millie continued. "Remember Teddy Pierce?"

"No," she said coldly. "Mother, would you help me with the dishes?"

Millie lifted the plates higher to show she was helping. Leo and she followed her into the kitchen. "We were talking about Cranberry Lake too," Leo said to her, "where you had that summer cabin. That must have been an exciting thing to do every summer."

Theresa grabbed the dishes out of Leo's hands. "I hated that place," she said.

"That's funny," Millie replied, with an edge to her voice. "I remember you loving it, especially when Jack would show up, take you fishing, things like that."

"Mother," she said sharply, "help me with the dishes." She turned quickly to Leo with a forced smile. "Thanks, Leo. We'll just put these inside, and then I'll drive you home."

Leo was startled by the change in the atmosphere of their conversation, but he didn't argue. A few minutes later, Theresa drove first Millie and then Leo back home. When he got there, Matt's car wasn't back yet.

At this point in time, they had just moved into their house a few months beforehand and were still working on it. The front lawn was stripped bare of plants, except for overgrown bougainvillea climbing a small rickety white picket fence that ran around the front lawn. They were planning on landscaping with palm trees and ixoras. The house needed a fresh coat of paint. Leo walked up the steps and entered the front porch. The door creaked then slammed behind him. The porch swing they ordered would be coming soon. He was looking forward to that. He unlocked the door with his keys, then went inside. He turned on the new halogen torchiere lamps they had bought, and the room lit up with an eerie glow that Leo wasn't crazy about. The hardwood floors had recently been buffed, and their new contemporary living and dining room furniture was set in place. The men working on the new kitchen had stopped for the holidays and would return soon. He walked into their bedroom with its remnant pieces of furniture and changed into a pair of sweatpants and sweatshirt. He went back into the living room, turned on the television, then sat on the couch. He watched nothing in particular until he heard the Mustang pull up in the driveway sometime later. He quickly shut off the television. He clutched a couch pillow in his lap and waited. He could feel his stomach growing queasy.

The porch door squeaked open and slammed shut. Matt tried to use his key to open the front door, then discovered it was unlocked already. He came inside, and saw Leo sitting on the couch. He walked past him without speaking.

"I'm sorry," Leo said. Matt stopped near the hallway toward the bedrooms. He turned slowly. Leo could see that he was drawn in the face and had bloodshot eyes. He had been drinking. "I didn't know it was going to be such a disaster," he apologized.

"I told you I didn't want to have anything to do with her." He didn't yell, but he was pissed.

"I was trying to do something good." He paused a moment, then asked, "Where did you go?"

"I drove around for a while, then stopped for a few drinks at the Golden Arrow." Leo grimaced. He hated that dive gay bar near the dog track. Matt stood there for a few more seconds. "I'm going to bed," he finally said. He turned and was about to walk away, when Leo stopped him again.

"Do you know why she moved here?"

He turned slowly. "I really don't care."

"She's trying to make amends. She wants to get to know her son as an adult."

"I think she's a little late for that. She can't change the past."

"I don't understand why you haven't spoken to her all these years."

"And I don't want to talk about it!" He walked away.

Despite his angst, Leo couldn't give up. He tossed the pillow aside and followed him into the bedroom. Matt pulled off his sweater and jeans and hurled them into a ball in the corner with the rest of the dirty laundry. "You're going to have to talk about it eventually, you know."

"Why? What's done is done."

Leo was startled. He had spoken those words in the past at times. And he had heard Millie use the same phrase tonight. But it hadn't struck him until that moment when Matt said it again that they were probably more alike than they would ever admit. He couldn't tell Matt that though. Instead, he said, "She's here now, and she wants to get to know you."

Matt flung off his underwear and walked naked toward their bathroom. Leo had to look away not to be distracted. Matt easily turned him on. The only hair on his body was in his armpits and in his groin. It was darker in color, but blended with the dirty blond hair on his head. He didn't work out anymore like he used to when he lived in Miami, but the contours of his body revealed a nicely developed torso. Only light pink scars marred his beautiful form, scars Leo knew only to be removed lesions or other things from his undetermined past.

Leo waited until he heard the shower running, then followed him into the bathroom. "It couldn't possibly hurt to talk to her, could it?" he asked the shower curtain. "Would you do it for me at least?" There was no response but the sound of the water.

Frustrated, Leo turned and walked to the bed. He got undressed. They always slept naked. He got under the covers to wait for Matt. He lay his head on the pillow, more and more angry and disgusted both with himself and with Matt. He had no explanation for anything, and could think of nothing to make things better. Matt finally came out of the shower. He walked back into the bedroom naked, his hair still damp. Leo glanced at him, and could feel himself getting excited as always. Matt got into bed beside him. Leo rolled over to look at him. "Matt, come on," he urged one last time.

He finally turned his head to meet his gaze. "She really said she wants to get to know me as an adult?"

"Yes," he said. Leo knew that he was lying a little, but if it helped, there was nothing wrong with a fib.

Matt sighed. "All right, I'll see her every once and a while." He raised a finger into Leo's face. "But I'm telling you right now that I'm doing this because you're asking me to. I'm not happy about this at all."

"Matt, I just want you to try, okay? Meet her halfway, maybe?"

He responded by rolling onto his side away from Leo and turning off the lamp beside him without saying another word. Leo rolled onto his side away from him, his moment of accomplishment diminished by the cold response. He looked at the framed photograph on the nightstand of the two of them smiling, having fun at their friend Doug's party, then shut off the light and went to sleep.

The next morning after opening Millie's packages, Leo awoke with his eyes gazing upon the same framed photograph on his nightstand. It had not been moved from this spot since the day they had moved in. It was there every morning when Leo woke up and every night when he went to bed. He reached out with his hand to touch it, as if Matt's smiling face were real and not simply a pictographic memory. He lay in bed for a few more minutes, then forced himself up. Only the thought of seeing Millie at the hospital again made him want to be awake on this day of all days, his birthday.

He showered and put on a pair of jeans and one of the new shirts he had bought. He gelled his hair and brushed his teeth. He was ready to go visit Millie. On his way out, he looked around the clean house and was impressed by his accomplishments. He grabbed his wallet, cell phone, and keys, and headed out the door. He drove to a local Dunkin Donuts for coffee and a cruller, then headed to the hospital.

He was halfway there when he realized that he felt refreshed, and, oddly, happy. It couldn't be the coffee, good as it was. It was a very strange sensation. He knew it was Millie. Seeing her again had up-lifted his spirits. Despite all the questions about what had happened with her, he was glad that he had seen her again and she had not rejected him, especially after he had disregarded her over the past year. He knew why he had done it. It hurt too much to see her. Being with her after Matt's death had made him feel like he was betraying Matt somehow. It was so different from the early days when he freely went out of his way to go out with her, to take her book shopping and for lunch or coffee.

Leo was on US 19. Saturday morning traffic was light, so it wasn't too bad of a drive to the hospital. By the time he had parked his car, it was after ten-thirty. He headed into the hospital and walked right up to the sign-in desk. He didn't hesitate this time and said he was Matthew Pierce going to visit his mother. He rode the elevator, fol-lowed the arrows, approached the blood red doors with confidence, and rang the bell. The orderly was a man this morning, and Leo voiced his entrance through the speaker. They buzzed him in, and he signed in again without hesitation as Matt.

He didn't see anyone he recognized in the common area. He glanced onto the patio, but didn't see anyone there either. He went to the desk and saw the red-headed nurse from the day before come from the back office area. He asked where Millie was.

"She's in her room with someone at the moment."

"Oh, her doctor?" Leo asked curiously.

"No. The police."

Leo's head jerked back. "Police?"

She acknowledged his surprise. "Or a detective. I'm sorry. I thought it was okay. He seemed to know about her and since it was a suicide attempt. . ."

"It's all right," he reassured her. He realized he had overreacted as well. It seemed logical what she was saying. "Where is her room?"

"Turn here. Third door on your right."

Leo thanked her, then headed in that direction. As he approached, he heard a man say with strength, ". . . not going to get rid of me. I'm going to find out what happened, whether you like it or not."

"Get the fuck out of here!" he heard her yell in response.

"Taking more pills isn't going to change anything."

Leo entered. "What's going on?" The man turned quickly. He was about six feet in height with broad shoulders. His auburn hair was parted on the side and he had a thick mustache and eyebrows to match. His cheeks were scarred with pox. He wore a dark suit without a tie. Leo took in his appearance, and he had the vaguest sensation he had seen him before, but he couldn't think where.

The man didn't respond to Leo's question. Instead, he turned back to Millie, who was pacing near the window with her arms crossed over her chest, and spoke to her. "This isn't over, not until I know what happened." With that, he pushed his way past Leo and left the room. Leo wanted to go after him, but Millie called to him not to.

He went to her instead. She was enraged, her arms crossed as she violently rubbed her forearms. Her face was red. She quickly stopped and hurried to the nightstand and lit a cigarette. He knew she wasn't supposed to smoke indoors, but saying anything would only exacerbate her. The cigarette seemed to help. She calmed down and her face returned to its normal color. Leo waited another minute, then asked her, "Are you all right?" She nodded, then exhaled smoke with her breath. "Who was that?"

"Forget about him."

"I don't think I can. What was with the attitude? That's how he's supposed to help?"

"What? Help how?" She seemed genuinely confused. He could swear there was a moment of panic on her face.

"With the attempted suicide," he replied.

She seemed distracted, then nodded and continued smoking. "Oh, yeah, I know. He's an asshole."

"He was here about your overdose, wasn't he?"

"Yes, of course," she said forcefully.

He could sense she was lying, but he wasn't sure how to pursue the situation. "You should file a complaint."

She hesitated, then nodded, mumbling she would. She extinguished her cigarette into a paper cup filled with water and hurried over to him. "Forget the whole thing, all right?" She reached out her arms and they embraced.

She sat up on the bed and motioned for him to sit in the chair beside her. She asked him what day it was, and he told her. She suddenly looked back at him and exclaimed, "Holy shit! It's your birthday, isn't it?"

He laughed aloud. "Yes, it is!"

She leaned forward to hug him again. "Happy birthday! I would have gotten you a gift," she added as they separated, "but I figured you probably had a popsicle-stick picture frame already, and they wouldn't let me make you anything with material that might cause me to injure myself." They laughed aloud together, and Leo felt comforted that she seemed better.

Her room wasn't terribly disturbing. The walls were a light gray, with the same industrial gray carpeting from the main reception area coursing throughout the floor. She shared her room with another bed, but for the moment she was alone. There were two televisions across the room hovering above them, much like in other hospitals. Her bed was covered in a light pink comforter draped over the sides. It wasn't uncomfortable.

Their conversation had lulled for a few minutes. Leo realized she was probably starting to think of the detective from the morning, so he tried to think of something to say, even though he really wanted to know more about what was going on. He mentioned to her about his plans for the night. "I'm going to my mother's tonight. She's probably making her famous lasagna."

She nodded. "I remember that lasagna. It was fantastic. She made me some after Matthew's funeral."

He winced still from the way she could say it so easily. He didn't understand her nonchalance. It occurred to him in a brief moment that he might never understand. He could only be sympathetic to her plight and feel badly about the things that they had done to one another. It was quiet for a few moments. He finally broke the silence by taking a risk. "I got your books." She looked away. "Why did you send them to me?"

She looked off for the moment out the window. "I knew you'd ask me about that soon enough. When I woke up and realized I was still alive, after I panicked and was able to think more clearly in the hospital, I knew that you would ask me that question." She looked at him and spoke matter-of-factly. "I'm not supposed to be here, Leo. I'm supposed to be dead. If my husband Jack had had his way, I would have died almost thirty years ago. Shit, I should have died ten years ago from all my drinking. I was supposed to have died this week. I wasn't supposed to have to answer that question."

"But I don't understand all of this. I mean, if you were trying to killing yourself—"

"Leo, there are no 'ifs' about it. I was committing suicide."

He hesitated before continuing. "You wanted to give away some of your prized possessions?" She didn't respond. "If you wanted me to have them, why didn't you give them to me in person?"

"You wouldn't have taken them."

It was true. "But you would have tried to force them on me."

"How could I force you to take them, when I never saw you anymore?"

He was shocked that she had said it, because he wasn't expecting her to. Yet, in a way, it was what Leo was waiting for this whole time. The enormous, overwhelming guilt of having visited her only once or twice over the past year. He had been in pain, but he had caused her more pain with his selfish disregard for her feelings. She had offered him friendship and support. They could have healed together. Instead, he had rejected her in favor of isolation, never once taking into consideration how she felt.

"You don't want them?" she asked suddenly, with more force, distracting him.

"What?"

"The books. You don't want them?"

"Of course, if you want me to have them. I love them. I'm trying to understand why."

She shifted positions on the bed and crossed her arms before her. "Don't try to understand. There is so much more going on here that you will never understand."

He started to reply, to question what she was referring to, to ask for more information. As he responded he only barely noticed that Millie's eyes had shifted to the doorway and a look of panic blanched her face. He thought for a second the detective had returned, when he heard a woman's voice he recognized.

"What are you doing here?!"

It was Theresa.

Leo stood quickly and turned to face her. Her pale face was flushed beneath her shoulder-length light brown hair.

Leo glanced down at Millie. She sighed and looked away. He turned back to his ex–sister-in-law. "Theresa, I'm sorry. I wanted to visit Millie."

"I told you to stay away."

The red-headed nurse appeared in the doorway. She stared right at Leo and said, "I'm sorry, Mr. Pierce, but I had to tell her—"

"Mr. Pierce?" she yelled, interrupting her and glaring at him. "You told them you were Matthew? I cannot believe you!"

The nurse seemed startled. "Mr. Pierce?" she asked again.

Theresa turned on her. "He isn't Mr. Pierce! My brother died a year ago."

The woman looked quizzically at Leo. He didn't respond. She seemed disappointed and shook her head. "I'm sorry, sir, you'll have to leave."

None of them moved, but then Theresa pushed in front of him and stood beside her mother's bed. She turned back to Leo. "Get out of here before I have you thrown out. You have no right to be here."

"I do have a right! Matt and I were lovers, and Millie is my closest friend."

"Yes, you were lovers," she mimicked. "And you were friends with my mother. But you're not family. Leave, or I'm having them call security."

Leo was speechless. He'd never seen her like this, but then again he had never had a confrontation with her before. "Look, I don't understand what the big deal is. I'm not doing anything to hurt her. We've been fine."

"I told you to stay out of this," Theresa hissed, and the nurse attempted to intervene.

Leo started to protest, but then Millie suddenly shrilled, "Oh, for Christ's sake!" They all stopped talking, and Millie looked at all of them, shaking her head. Finally she looked at Leo. "Do me a favor and just go."

"What?" he asked in surprise.

"I'm serious. Just go. There's no point in making this worse. I'll talk to you soon."

Leo was crushed. He felt defeated, looking at all of them, but he could say nothing. Millie gestured for him to go by nodding. She seemed as aggravated as he was with the whole situation, but he was very hurt by the fact that he was being sent away.

He walked out of the room with a heavy feeling in his chest. As he left, he thought he heard Millie say to Theresa, "Was that necessary?" He didn't hear a response. He left the psychiatric ward and the solid red doors slammed tightly behind him. He walked to the elevator and pushed the button. When it arrived, he was the only one inside. He pressed the button for the ground floor, then leaned against the wall of the elevator and closed his eyes tightly. He leaned his head back against the wall and fought to control the guilt, sadness, and anger welling behind his eyelids. Happy fucking birthday.

– FIVE –

On a beautiful springlike day in February 1997, two months after the disastrous family reunion dinner, Leo had taken Millie on a book-buying trip to Tampa. They were now eating a late lunch in Hyde Park. The café had recently opened and was decorated with New Orleans–style wrought iron and marble-top tables, the sounds of Louis Armstrong and Kenny G piping through speakers both inside and out. They sat outdoors to enjoy the incredible day. Millie raved over her jambalaya, while Leo regretted having ordered a ham and cheese po'boy. Millie smiled and laughed when she was with Leo, and it made him feel badly that Matt was missing out on knowing his mother. Since agreeing to see her "every once and a while," Matt had done so just one time, when they had all gone to see the rerelease of the movie *Fargo*.

Through the amber lenses of his sunglasses, Leo watched Millie enjoy her lunch. She wore large round sunglasses herself, probably purchased at Wal-Mart for next to nothing. They looked cheap, but for some reason complimented her appearance. She was wearing a pale green blouse and khaki clamdiggers. Theresa had taken her recently to get a haircut and dye-job, so her hair was more blonde now than usual and made her look younger and fresh. As he gazed at her he found himself thinking about her life. His growing friendship with her was based on their mutual Victorian interests, but aside from that he knew little about her. In some ways it was like Matt, although he soon discovered she shared little of his reticence.

He held his sandwich aloft as he asked her, "Were you always like this?"

She arched her head, looking at him suspiciously. "What do you mean by 'this'?"

Pierce
© 2007 by The Haworth Press, Inc. All rights reserved.
doi:10.1300/5849_05

"You know, outspoken, determined, expressing your opinion—".

"Whether it's wanted or not," she interrupted, savoring a piece of jambalaya pork.

He chuckled. "Yes. Like that. You must have been a nightmare child."

"Hardly. I was Ms. Goody Two-Shoes." His eyebrow raised in surprise. "I was," she continued. "It was repulsive." She was almost finished with lunch and drank the ginger ale she had ordered. "My mother raised me to be a good girl. Obedient. Docile. Domestic. She didn't even want me to read. She used to take my books away from me because it would make me too smart and I'd never find a husband. The only rebellious thing I did when I was growing up was read. My father used to let me read. He would sneak home books for me, things like *The Secret Garden* and *Alice in Wonderland*."

"That's so strange. Nowadays, children hardly ever read, and your mother tried to take the books away from you." Leo picked at the french fries on his plate and started poking his fork into the po'boy, eating the salty ham slices. "What happened to him?"

She paused a moment, as if remembering. "He got sick. When I got married the first time, I didn't even know he had cancer. They didn't tell me. He was strong for my wedding though. Then, a few months later, he died." She was pensive. She sighed. "It was awful. I thought getting pregnant would make things better. Not that I vocalized it that way, obviously. All I knew was that I was so lonely without my father, and suddenly I wanted to have a baby. I got pregnant with Theresa, and the next thing I knew, I was divorced." She ate the last bites of her lunch.

"He just left you?"

She nodded. "He was terrified."

"Of what?"

She shrugged. "Children? Me? Kennedy? Castro?"

"Castro?"

"Oh, he was obsessed with communist plots. It was like I had married McCarthy. He thought the world was spiraling downhill and he didn't want to bring children into it." She paused a moment. "It's sad, when I think about it. He literally was the boy next door. Well, at least, the boy a few doors down from there. We went to school together. There was nothing about him that would leave you to believe he was going to get paranoid and walk out on me." She mused. "Larry Murphy. There's a person I've worked hard to forget over the years."

He made an apologetic face. "I'm sorry."

She waved a hand. "Please, it's all right. Larry isn't going to mess up my life anymore. Maybe I should have listened to him. I let myself get pregnant, and I did it for the wrong reasons. I probably never should have had Theresa or Matthew. Lord knows I've been a terrible mother."

"Don't say that about yourself."

She scoffed. "Leo, there's no need to sugarcoat things. I got pregnant with Theresa for selfish reasons and then brought her into a madhouse situation with Jack Pierce. And Matthew. . ." She shook her head. "I screwed that kid up big time." She looked at Leo through her dark, round lenses. "If I had known then what I know now, I never would have gotten married or had children."

Leo was disappointed to hear her speak this way. He wanted to remind her that she did love her children, despite the way things had turned out. And he wanted to remind her that they had loved her back as well, except he wasn't sure that was the case, so he said neither. Instead, he remarked, "If you had changed the course of your life, then you and I wouldn't have met and we wouldn't be having this conversation."

She smirked. "Oh, so something good did come out of my terrible decisions?"

"Exactly!"

"Well, I'll drink to that," she said, raising her glass of ginger ale.

Leo raised his own glass of iced tea and clinked glasses with her. They drank through their straws and set their glasses down. Leo was done playing with his lunch and set his fork down. He looked back up at Millie. "Do you wish you had been a grandmother?"

He saw her face stiffen. "That's a sore subject. Let's not talk about that." Leo regretted his question, seeing she was visibly upset. She sat back in her chair and crossed her arms over her breasts. She continued reminiscing, not wanting to change the pleasurable mood they had been having. "You know," she said, "going back to Larry. . .the funniest part of that whole thing with him leaving me was that my mother was more devastated than I was. I realized that I didn't love him. I mean, don't get me wrong, he was attractive and even pretty good in bed, but I didn't seem to click with him, if you know what I mean. My mother, though, was crazy. She went to his parents' house to apologize for my being an awful wife and making him leave me." Leo's shock was apparently evident. "I know! Can you imagine?" she exclaimed. "Anyway, she also tried to find out where he was, and they claimed to know nothing. The next thing we know, they moved away, we heard to the Pittsburgh area, but we never knew for sure. I think she felt like she had failed as a mother. Everyone in the neighborhood knew I was pregnant and had been dumped by my husband. I think everyone was sympathetic toward me except for my mother." She sighed. "It was probably the worst thing for me to do in that situation, but I moved in with her. I had nowhere else to go. I wound up filing for divorce, and then I had Theresa while I was living with my mother."

"No one ever found him?" he asked.

She shook her head. While she continued speaking, she reached in her bag. "I heard about two years later through mutual friends that Larry wound up in some religious commune in Montana or somewhere like that. He never contested the divorce, and he never made an attempt to see Theresa. I never knew what happened to him after that." She lit up a cigarette and raised her head to exhale. Despite her cheap sunglasses and plain attire, she carried an odd air of sophistication that Leo admired.

"You mean he's never seen her?" he asked.

"Not as far as I know. I asked her recently if she ever tried to find him. She glared at me and said, 'Why?'" Leo nodded in acknowledgment. As an afterthought, perhaps to add a pleasant note to the conversation, she added, "I named Theresa for my father, Terrence Hunter." She smiled. "I think he would have been proud and loved her very much."

The server cleared their table, and they decided to hold off on dessert. The afternoon sun was beating down on them, making it too hot for coffee. The server returned with the check, and Leo gave her his credit card, insisting lunch was his treat. As he signed the slip, Leo asked Millie, "What happened then?"

"Let's see. I lived with my mother, and argued with her constantly because she kept pushing me to get married again so that Theresa and I had someone to support us." She shifted positions in her chair, but kept her arms crossed and smoked her menthol cigarette. "Instead, I decided to go to college during the day to become a schoolteacher. I worked nights cleaning offices to earn money. I got my bachelor's degree in education from CCNY and taught sixth grade for about two years." She puffed. "It was a brief career stint. It ended when I married Jack Pierce."

"Why did you marry him?"

"He was very polite, and he adored Theresa," she said mockingly. "My mother pushed me into it. She kept insisting I marry him. She enjoyed pointing out how much money his family had and how good it would be for Theresa. I was hardly able to support us on my teacher's salary, and I had to get out of my mother's house. So I gave in. We got married. I got pregnant again. And then all hell broke loose."

"Why? What happened?"

She shook her head. "I don't want to talk about him," she replied, her tone hard-edged. She was silent for a few moments. The ash grew on her cigarette.

Leo realized he had struck a nerve, yet something in him made him push a little harder. "What was Matt's father like?" She didn't respond. "Obviously he must have been a good father to Matt, taking him fishing when he was very young and all that."

She threw the cigarette onto the ground. Her head snapped back at him. "That man was a fucking bastard," she seethed. She had apparently spoken louder than she realized. Two ladies at another table grew quiet and stared at them, but Millie ignored them. "He treated us like we were garbage!"

Leo was startled by her response. He hadn't seen her react this emotionally before. "I'm sorry," he muttered. "I didn't know."

She was still enraged and slammed the table with her fist. "Matthew has these stupid romantic ideas that his father was some wonderful man. Hardly. He hit Matthew from the time he was a baby. He'd hit him for stupid stuff all children do, like crying, for Christ's sake! And when I tried to stop him, he'd hit me too."

Leo's mouth was dry. "I had no idea." He really was shocked. Matt had given him nothing to suggest this was the same man. He drank more of his iced tea to wet his throat. "I guess Theresa must have experienced the same thing then."

She scoffed. "Oh, no. Not Theresa. Not his fucking little princess. She got whatever she wanted. She idolized him. It was sick what he—" She stopped herself. She turned away quickly, catching her breath. After a moment, she spoke more softly, but there was a slight tremor in her voice. "Look, I'm glad he's gone. Matthew didn't need him. None of us did." She lit another cigarette from the pack on the table.

He was hesitant to ask anymore questions, but Leo had to know one last thing. "What happened to him?"

"He left us, just like my first husband did. That last summer we were at the cabin." She spoke into the air, not looking at Leo. "He took off one night and we never heard from him again."

The idea that she had had two husbands walk out on her seemed incredible. "He never tried to contact any of you?" Leo asked.

She shook her head. "Besides, he's dead now," she said firmly, her eyes shifting away. "I found out from some friend of ours that he died a few years ago." She stood up suddenly. "Can we go? I'm done."

He followed her as they left the restaurant and walked back to his car. They waited while she finished smoking her cigarette. "You know," she spoke more calmly now, "I was a total mess after the whole thing with Jack leaving. I had to get away. I couldn't take it. That's why I dropped my children off at my mother's. I knew they were better off with her than me."

Leo knew there was more to that part of the story, from Matt's point of view. He had finally told Leo that she had left them with their grandmother, kissed them good-bye, then drove off into the night promising to be right back. They didn't see her again for five years. In the beginning they would speak to her on the phone every once and a while and get regular cards or letters in the mail. Then it was only on holidays and on their birthdays. Then she missed Theresa's birthday one year. And then Matt's. Then, there was nothing.

"So where did you go?" he asked.

She exhaled upward into the sky, relaxing again, pondering a time of freedom in her life. "I moved to San Francisco first, then went to Los Angeles and San Diego, then back to San Francisco. That's where I discovered the seventies, free love, Swinburne, and indulged in alcohol and weed like there was no tomorrow. It was fucking amazing." She paused, puffing on her cigarette. "Then one day Theresa called me out of the blue and told me my mother had died. It was a shock to me. It sounds cruel, but I had forgotten that I had been a daughter, a wife, and a mother. And I loved it. For the first time I was me, Millie Hunter, not Miss Hunter or Mrs. Murphy or Mrs. Pierce." She peered back at Leo through her sunglasses. "When my mother died, it all rushed back to me. I had to go back to New York, back to my whole reality that I had learned to forget. I wasn't going to stay though. I decided I needed to go somewhere else to start all over. Theresa was at Columbia on a scholarship and had met George, so I wasn't worried about her. I grabbed Matthew—against his will, I'm sure you know—and we moved to Florida, where one of my friends lived." She finished smoking her cigarette and tossed it on the ground. She opened the car door and stepped inside. She was done talking apparently, so Leo did the same, and they drove home.

He was thinking of good past times with Millie. After being thrown out of the hospital by Theresa, Leo spent the afternoon of his birthday on the porch swing drinking Coronas he had bought on the way home and smoking a joint he had gotten from the ebony box. He ignored the neighbors mowing their lawns and the cars pouncing by on the brick street. He heard children shouting and a dog barking. He reacted to none of the sounds. A mourning dove landed with a coo outside the porch. He flicked his finger against the screen, scaring it away. He tasted the burning hemp scorch his throat with the acrid fire he hated. His eyes were half closed, and he could see the afternoon sun in a bright haze. Now high, through the smoke, he recalled other sensations and images that weren't always accurate, but were haunting. Things he often tried to forget.

He saw a woman's gloved hand pat him and try to embrace him. He could feel her polyester dress against his eyes and smell her heady Enjoli perfume, her tucking as she cried and trying to rock him as if he were a child. He hovered near the casket. Suddenly there were wails that made him shudder. He looked behind him. People were in the room. He saw George, newly married, wearing black pinstripe, bored and hanging with friends. He saw his young mother caterwauling in the front row in black silk and a veiled hat comforted by her sisters, lace handkerchiefs fluttering to wipe away tears. He turned back, and the casket was open. He could see only the dark brown suit of his father's paunch. He couldn't see a face. He could smell incense, and he looked up at the beautifully youthful Father Tortone making the sign of the cross. He stared right at Leo, penetrating to his core. He knew what he had done. He smiled devilishly, winked at him, making his adolescent self feel both guilt and excitement at the same time. The wailing continued, and he shuddered. He could feel his own terror. Not from the corpse, but from the wailing. The women in their black costumes intoned like a Euripidean chorus, his mother a Hecuba, pointing to the casket and suffering from the pangs of Priam's heart attack. Father Tortone intoned an amen, and she rose steadily. She reached out toward the casket, hurled herself on it, dowsing his faceless father with tears and wails. The chorus rushed to save her, pulling her off. She fainted. George laughed. Leo ran away.

It was tragicomedy. He was giggling. He was crying. He had to stop. It was a terrible thought. He sucked on the joint one last time, and held it in his lungs so that it scorched his larynx and made his cheeks burn and lungs stretch. He finally choked it out and laughter followed. He was running still, from his father, his mother, his brother. And the nightmare began that wouldn't leave him for years. His father rising in his coffin and waving his arms in disgust, shouting foul language for what he saw and knew about his son. They were nightmares he had had over and over.

He was a freshman, only fourteen. Sophomore Tony Zambreno used to flirt with him, flashing winks and smiles in the hallways when no one else noticed. Then one day they saw each other between gym classes changing in the locker rooms, Zambreno wearing white cotton briefs that glowed against his olive Italian skin. He was on the wrestling team and had a body to match. He scratched at his sculpted bare chest and blindly circled one of his dark nipples. He wanted tutoring in English from Leo. He followed him home one day, into the house, into his bedroom, leaving the door ajar in case they heard anything. Leo went to get books, but there was no time for that. Zambreno grabbed at his crotch and he was hard instantly. He kissed him and opened his pants, forcing Leo's hand inside. He moaned while he led him on, kissing him with his tongue, pushing him to his knees, telling him to suck him. He didn't waste a moment. He glanced up at Zambreno, and he could see almond-shaped eyes encouraging him. He hardly had time to look at the enormous dark mushroom head before Zambreno shoved it in his mouth. He choked as Zambreno entered and moved his hips back and forth. He grabbed the back of Leo's head and pushed it so that now he was doing the action. Leo used his tongue and tasted sweet juices he never had before. "Fuckin' awesome," was all he heard.

They never heard the footsteps. They never realized anyone was there, until it was too late, and Leo's father entered yelling, "What the fuck?" and Zambreno had pulled out violently, pushing him away, zipping up and grabbing his jacket, racing out before Leo could even react to anything but his father hovering over him, his thick Italian hand wailing down on the side of his head, sending him backward into the wall. He cried like a baby. His father reached down and shook him, called him filthy names, slapped him across the head twice. The stinging stayed there even after his father left and slammed the door shut. Leo was forbidden dinner. He was forbidden to speak to anyone. He never spoke to his father again. He had a heart attack and died three days later.

He had no idea how long he was on the porch swing. It was probably a few hours. His eyes were closed. The lawn mowers had stopped. The children had quieted down, although he heard the little girl in pigtails and her father across the street. He heard a cooing and the light pitter-patter of feet that he knew was another mourning dove outside his porch, entertaining itself with his misery. When he opened his eyes, the screen door and the greenery outside were sideways and hazy. The wood of the swing was imbedded into the side of his head and it hurt. He blinked a few times to adjust to the slanted world and the brilliant sun through the Spanish moss draped trees and overgrown bougain-villea that surrounded his house.

He heard his telephone ring. It took him a moment to focus. He could hear through his open front door the answering machine pick up the call. *"Buon compleanno!"* he heard his mother exclaim. "Happy birthday! You have thirty years now! Or, no, I forget, it's twenty-nine! I'm calling to remind you to come to your party tonight." Leo groaned and shut his eyes. He had managed to forget. "I'm making the lasagna you like. And meatballs." Even that was not tempting him at the moment. He was actually starving, but the thought of in-dulging in dinner with his mother was too much at the moment. "I see you at five o'clock. *Ciao, figlio."* It was supposed to be at six. Why couldn't she remember these things?

He forced himself to sit up. He rubbed his temples. The grogginess was dissipating, the clarity of the moment, his mother's voice, ringing through the daze. He realized despairingly that it had only been a few hours beforehand that he had visited Millie and been thrown out by Theresa. He yawned. He dragged his feet into the house, then headed to the kitchen to munch on something. As he walked past the dining room table, he saw the two poetry books Millie had sent him.

Leo wanted to see Millie again. Maybe he could check with Theresa and plead with her to let him go. Or he could try sneaking up there again. It seemed unlikely that either would work. He shook his head in frustration as he continued into the kitchen. His stomach was grumbling. He hadn't eaten since breakfast. He checked the clock and saw that it was after four o'clock already. He groaned, and opened the refrigerator. It was virtually empty; he would have to go food shop-ping soon. He drank more of the flat cola, then rummaged through the cabinets until he found a bag of potato chips. He gorged on them.

He could see Millie sitting on her hospital bed and the look of sur-prise that overcame her when Theresa walked in behind him unex-pectedly. He thought also of how happy she had been to see him when he had visited her the day before. He thought about the detective too. She had been pissed off at him. The image of the detective came back to him in a mental flash. It occurred to him once again that the man looked familiar. He could see his face in his mind's eye. Not looking directly at him, but in profile, facing away from him. He couldn't think why.

He was still coming down off of his high, gorging on chips and soda. He was seriously tempted not to show up for dinner. Maybe go out instead, get drunk, then get fucked by a massive cock. Something a little more exciting for his birthday than dinner at his mother's. He sighed, tossed the empty bag of chips into the garbage, drank the rest of the soda, and headed for the shower to get ready for dinner.

– SIX –

Leo hadn't realized his mother was actually throwing him a party, so he was shocked to see middle-aged and elderly guests, all members of the Italian-American Club, in her house. He had met some of them in the past, but couldn't remember all of their names, so his mother made her rounds, reintroducing her son to the guests. He received wishes of *buon compleanno* for his birthday from everyone, and was handed a plastic cup of red wine. As the food was laid out, Leo realized his mother had outdone herself yet again. Everything smelled delicious, and he found himself anxious to dive into her famous lasagna with its homemade meat sauce. She had cooked two enormous trays of it, and had also made pasta primavera, meatballs stuffed with mozzarella cheese, chicken piccata, and had prepared a large salad. She had even baked her own loaves of bread. Everyone praised the magnificence of her cooking.

As the evening progressed, arias by Verdi and Puccini filled the air, some from the stereo sung by Pavarotti, others from the guests themselves. There was laughter and howling, arguing and scolding, and through it all Leo spied his mother more than once glowing with pride at her accomplishments. He had forgotten it was his own birthday party until it was time for espresso and a sheet cake appeared to the strains of "Happy Birthday" sung half in English, half in Italian.

By the time the last guests had left, it was almost 11:00 p.m. Leo shut off the music and it was notably silent. He sat in a dining room chair to rest and assumed his mother would do the same. Without stopping, though, Rosa picked up numerous dishes and carried them into the kitchen to start cleaning. He could hear the water rushing at full force and dishes clanging. He glanced around, wanting only to relax, but knew he had to help her or she'd never forgive him. He picked

Pierce
© 2007 by The Haworth Press, Inc. All rights reserved.
doi:10.1300/5849_06

up the giant bowl of leftover salad and headed for the kitchen. He placed it next to the other dirty dishes.

Rosa Vasari was about five feet, six inches in height. She had a pearlike figure and large sagging breasts. She had turned sixty a few months beforehand, but she fought the aging process by dying her hair a shade of brown similar to Leo's. She wore it in a thick wavy frizz that truly had no style. She wore makeup that was outdated: aqua eye shadow and bright red, clownlike lipstick. He had tried once to take her for a makeover, but she resisted, arguing that his father had always liked her this way. It was a shame because Rosa wasn't unattractive. She simply needed updating.

Her hands were in yellow rubber gloves as she vigorously scrubbed dishes in scalding hot water. He didn't understand why she did things the hard way. She had a dishwasher right beside her and she had fed a house full of people that night. Any sane person would use the dishwasher without thinking about it. His mother simply refused, telling him once it was a waste of money and water.

He brought in the rest of the dirty dishes from the dining room. As she washed, he put away some of the leftover food, and she told him to take home the lasagna, chicken, and meatballs. He agreed, knowing he needed food at home and savored every bite of her cooking. He got a dish towel and moved to the other side of her. He lifted a dish from the drain and could feel the heat permeating the plate and the towel. She must be scalding herself, but she refused to stop.

"You did an amazing job with the cooking," he said.

She shrugged. "The meatballs were no good."

He didn't argue with her false modesty. "You didn't have to throw a party like that. I really would have preferred something simpler."

She turned her head with anger, her faux accent flaring. "Ah, that's the thank you I get for planning a beautiful party and for cooking all that food!"

"No, Mamma, I'm overwhelmed. I think it's fantastic. I said you didn't have to do all of that." She scowled. "I'm serious. I love what you did. *Molte grazie,* Mamma." She seemed satisfied and turned back to her washing. Leo rolled his eyes and continued drying. Neither spoke for the next few minutes. He dried every pot, pan, dish, and glass as she set them to the side, and it seemed everything was getting hotter and hotter. She seemed not to notice at all.

When she spoke again, her voice was soft and barely audible over the running water. He had to ask her to repeat herself. Leo had to strain to hear her. He thought he heard her accent slipping.

"It's not good, for a man your age." She paused, then spoke forcefully with her accent again, "You need someone to take care of you. It's not good to be alone. I should know, how your father died and left me alone, God rest his soul." She made the sign of the cross and kissed her hot wet fingertips through the yellow rubber as she offered them to the heavens.

"You're serious, aren't you?" Leo put the dish down and stared at his mother.

She shrugged, continuing to wash the dishes. "Of course I'm serious! A nice Italian girl would do you good."

"Mamma . . ." he intimated.

"Or . . . a nice Italian boy." She suddenly flailed a soapy wooden spoon at him. "But only if he can cook as good as your Mamma!" She eyed him up and down. "You need to gain some weight. You're too skinny!"

He wasn't sure if he should be offended or laugh out loud. Before he could do either, the phone on the wall behind him rang. He turned toward it and answered. He heard a male voice at the other end, and it jarred him for a moment because it sounded like his father. "Leo?" It was George.

Leo hadn't spoken to his brother since Christmas, and only then it had been a one-minute conversation because his mother had forced the phone on him. He was shocked to hear how much his voice sounded like their father's. The enhanced New Jersey guido accent told him that his brother had easily adjusted to life back in the Garden State.

"What's going on?" Leo replied forcefully.

"Uh, nothing." There was an awkward pause. "Ma there?"

He should have expected that his brother hadn't called to wish him happy birthday. He had no clue apparently. "Hold on," he said. He turned toward Rosa. "It's for you."

"Who is it?" she asked. He told her, then handed her the phone as she smiled and dried her rubber gloved hands. She took the phone from him and exclaimed into the receiver, *"Giorgio, mio figlio!* Why you no call your Mamma more?"

Leo dried a few more dishes, vigorously at first, ignoring their conversation. Finally he stopped and went into the living room. He crashed on his mother's overstuffed floral white wicker sofa, gazing around the room at the angels and saints that surrounded him. His mother's artistry was pandemic, covering every available space of wall in the living room like a Victorian art gallery. Her years as an artist had resulted in various sized oils on canvas and watercolors on paper. He remembered back when he was seventeen and she had proudly displayed her first runny watercolor. He responded by asking what it was. "An angel!" she exclaimed, hurt. He was shocked. He thought it was Olivia Newton-John in a Xanadu headband and jumpsuit.

She continued with her classes though, and Leo was glad to say that she did improve over time. He could recall as a teenager how much his house smelled like oil paint and how much it used to bother him. As an adult he could appreciate the hard work she did. Yet, sitting in the room surrounded by these figures was unnerving and overwhelming. It was like being in a church, minus the wicker furniture.

Oddly enough, Matt had liked her work. He had been fascinated by her obsessively religious subjects. Matt told Rosa, and it turned out to be exactly what he needed to say to get her to like him. She started giving them new paintings every month or so until Leo had to tell her to stop because they had nowhere to hang them. He now had about a dozen of them hung around his house and at least as many stored in the office closet.

He could look throughout her living room and easily distinguish her early work from her more recent work. He didn't need to be an art critic to see how gradually over time her angels and saints became more realistic. One quirk seemed to be that her palette choices through the years matched trends in interior decorating. In the late eighties, all of her angels wore mauve and ivory. By the early nineties, they wore magnificent teal robes and had peach-colored hair. The other oddity was how their faces had modified from comic-strip characters into portraits. She was painting people in her life. Around the living room he recognized two of his aunts in one picture, and a couple from the party in two separate paintings. And then there was the picture of his father.

He rose from the sofa and moved closer to it. She kept this one particular painting in the center of the living room wall across from the sofa for her to admire, it seemed. It was large for his mother's oeuvre, nearly three feet by five feet, done in oils. She had painted it from a photograph taken sometime before his death.

The figure was a large saintly man, almost an oxymoron of a Renaissance angel. His face was harshly saccharine, his garments pearl gray, his wings off-white tinted silver. He didn't wear a halo, but in his hands he held a wrench and a hammer. He had been a mechanic like George, and Leo had no idea if mechanics used wrenches or hammers so the reality of the tools was lost on him. But the face haunted him. It was his father in profile, a rugged face with permanent stubble dabbed on a double chin. He could still sense the sharp chin stubble pressing into his own soft baby face when his father used to hug him ages ago. The figure's eyes were downtrodden, his mouth turned low. Unlike so many of her other angels and saints that were full of glee, this figure seemed lost in his own existence, looking for something or someone off the canvas that was unidentifiable. He had asked his mother once what he was looking at. As she answered, her eyes teared and she replied in her Italianate tongue, *"Nessuno."*

No one.

He used to imagine it was probably himself.

He hated this painting.

He had no idea how long he stood there looking at her work, but finally his mother's voice got louder and he realized their phone conversation was over. She came out of the kitchen with a cheery demeanor. Obviously speaking to George had pleased her, but how that was possible was beyond Leo's imagination. "Giorgio wished you *buon compleanno.*" He knew she was lying, but he didn't say anything. She came forward and he realized that she was holding something behind her back. They moved to the sofa and she sat beside him. She handed him a present with two packages wrapped in peach-colored paper tied together with frilly organza ribbons. "You didn't have to get me any-thing," he said almost robotically.

"Ah!" she exclaimed with a hand gesture. "It's your birthday!"

He took it from her. It was heavier than usual. He could sense by the shape of the one package that it was yet another painting. He un-wrapped the ribbons and paper, and she took them from him to reuse on some future gift. He opened the one box, and sure enough, a framed watercolor greeted him. It was not unlike a few others hang-ing in his own house already. "It's beautiful," he said with forced glee.

Rosa grinned in response. "For your office at school!" He hadn't told her he had been laid off for the summer and that he would have no office for a while.

He moved on to the other gift. It was heavier than most gifts he had ever received from her. He unwrapped the paper and started to throw it aside, until she grabbed this too and folded it neatly beside her. The gift was wrapped in tissue paper. It was only then that he realized it was a book. He was intrigued. She had never given him a book before. He ripped open the tissue, and in his lap was a brand new edition of the 792-page *Johns Hopkins Guide to Literary Theory and Criticism*. He jerked his head back in surprise. Palmer had mentioned that he needed to improve his understanding of literary theory. This was something he truly needed. "Mamma, this is fantastic!" He reached over right away and kissed her on the cheek. "How did you know to get me this?"

Her answer surprised him even more. "Millicent told me."

"What? Millie? When?"

She looked down into her hands clasped tightly together. "I phoned her, a few weeks ago. I wanted to get you something different, some-thing special for your future." She looked up at him. "I know you have been so sad. I wanted to do something nice for you." Leo smiled in ap-preciation. He was genuinely grateful for the gift and for her taking the time to find out what he needed. He noticed then that she was crying. "Leonardo, I'm afraid for you. I want you to be happy. I don't want you to be alone." She wiped at her eye. "Your *papà*, he was a good man." Leo looked away, involuntarily toward the painting, then averted his gaze from there. "He was good to me and you and Giorgio.

I was so sad when he died. I didn't know what to do. But I had my children to help me. You have no one. And you have been so sad since Matteo died. I want for you to be happy."

Leo was touched and they embraced. She sobbed lightly on his collar. He could take only a moment of this, and he separated from her. "*Grazie,* Mamma!" She smiled through her tears. "I'll be all right," he assured her, uncertain himself if this were true.

She sighed and wiped at her tears. Her mascara was running. Suddenly, almost as if it were an afterthought or she were convincing herself of something, she said, "I'm not jealous of Millicent." He noticed that her accent was slipping again.

He eyed her suspiciously, in a teasing way. "Mamma?"

"Okay, maybe a little. But it's because you're close to her."

"Mamma, I became good friends with Millie because of our interests. You're my mother. We're going to have a different type of relationship."

"I know, I know," she said, "just ignore me. I'm acting like a silly old woman." She dried her eyes. "How was she when you saw her?"

He shrugged, glad she had asked. "She's fine, I guess, considering the situation." He thought about Millie lying in her bed that moment, probably exasperated and wanting only to be home in her own bed.

"Millicent is a good woman." Suddenly, Rosa's accent flared back as her hand waved in the air toward Leo. "But you know she wasn't always so good before."

Leo rolled his eyes, disappointed in her change of being. Why did she have to ruin the mood? And why always with that stupid accent? He chose this time to ignore her remark and asked instead, "How was she when you spoke to her?"

"Like her usual self."

"She didn't sound. . .weird?"

She shook her head. "No."

"Nothing that would make you believe she was. . .upset maybe?"

"No," she repeated.

Her simple answers made him realize this wasn't the conversation she wanted. He sat back on the sofa and crossed his arms. "Okay, tell me when was she bad."

"Before," she said quickly, setting herself comfortably for a revealing talk. "When Giorgio and Theresa married. You know she didn't come to the wedding."

"Yes, I know about that. She wasn't invited, from what I understand."

She scoffed. "She was a drunk!"

"That doesn't excuse why she wasn't invited to her daughter's wedding."

She disregarded him. "She would have been drunk during the whole wedding. It's better she wasn't there. And the way she abandoned them when they were children!"

"Mamma, her husband had left her. She needed to refocus on her own life, get herself together."

"They had no father, and then no mother. It's very sad."

"So how did you ever hear about all of this anyway? From Theresa, I guess?"

"*Sì*. When she was in the hospital."

Leo thought about this, and looked at his mother curiously. "When was Theresa in the hospital?"

"Before we moved to Florida."

Leo was confused. "I don't remember Theresa ever going into the hospital."

She fidgeted with her hands, then rose unexpectedly. "You want more birthday cake?"

"Mamma, get back here." She stopped, then looked back at him. "What happened?"

She sat beside him again, gazed around as if there spies in their midst, then gushed with her gossip. "They didn't want to tell you. It was the summer you were at the camp."

Leo remembered the summer she was referring to. It was after his sixteenth birthday, and he and a friend from high school had taken jobs at a camp for children. It was a nightmare entertaining them all summer and doing things like camping outdoors, but he had fond memories of one hunky camp counselor.

"Why was she in the hospital?" he asked.

"She had a miscarriage."

"I didn't know Theresa had been pregnant."

His mother nodded sadly. "She said they had tried and tried, but there was little chance it would work. The doctor told her she couldn't carry to birth. She was very depressed afterward. She had to go to the hospital."

"Wait a minute. Theresa was in the hospital for the miscarriage, right?" Rosa didn't respond but gazed at him suggestively, encouraging him to guess. He suddenly realized what she had meant. "Theresa tried to kill herself, didn't she?"

Rosa responded excitedly, "And Millicent never visited! I stayed with her every day. It was *terribile*. Dirty. Rude nurses. Crazy people everywhere!" She shuddered dramatically. Leo knew it probably wasn't as bad as she was making it seem, although his memories of Matt at St. Anthony's haunted him in a flash.

"How long was she there?"

"Two weeks."

"What did she do?"

Rosa sighed. She gestured with her hands. "She cut her wrists. But Giorgio found her right away, *grazie Dio!* I stayed with her every day. But Millicent never came."

Millie not being at her daughter's side during Theresa's suicide attempt wasn't his issue at the moment. What freaked him out more was that Theresa and Matt had both used knives on themselves. Neither Matt nor Millie had ever told him about Theresa's suicide attempt. Millie and Matt lived in Florida by that time. Was it possible that they never knew? "Mamma, did Theresa tell her mother?"

She shrugged. *"Non lo so."*

"Then you don't know for a fact if Millie knew about Theresa. Did George say that they had told her?"

"No."

"Then it's possible she never knew anything, so you can't blame Millie for that."

His mother seemed at a loss for words, and she faltered, exclaiming, "She would have known if she wasn't drunk and ignoring her daughter!" She jumped up and cleaned papers and garbage from the party.

Her attempt at bad-mouthing Millie didn't succeed, and in turn Leo couldn't help but defend Millie by letting his mother know about her daughter-in-law. "You know Theresa isn't so innocent, Mamma. She freaked out on me this morning. She was screaming at me and threw me out of the hospital. All I was trying to do was visit Millie, and she had me thrown out when she saw me there."

Rosa didn't respond. She walked toward the kitchen and asked brusquely, "You want cappuccino?" He had no choice but to follow her inside.

When Leo arrived home at nearly 1:00 a.m., he was laden with gifts and leftover food. He put the food in the refrigerator, then entered his office to put the literary criticism guide on his bookcase beside his Webster's dictionary and critical texts by Foucault and Paglia. He had to shift some of Matt's old business books to another shelf to make room. He then searched for a place to put the painting. The office was painted sky blue with light oak furniture. The rolltop computer desk with its matching Windsor-style desk chair stood out as the focal point beside the one window in the room. There were two teal and peach angel pictures in the office, plus one large oil of an angel he vaguely recognized as his long-deceased grandmother. There were other morphed relatives and strangers scattered throughout the rest of the house. Leo looked back at the new one he held in his hands and knew where it was going. He opened the closet door.

He squatted and thumbed through them to place the latest one in the right location size-wise. He found a spot and slipped it into place. He was putting them all back when one caught his eye. He instinctively knew which it was even before he pulled it out. He hesitated to do so, but he succumbed. He sat down and removed it from the closet.

It was a portrait of Matt and him. After Matt had complimented Rosa on her artistry, she declared her intention to paint them a picture. Leo was glad it didn't appear right away, and in fact had hoped that she had forgotten about it, but she wound up giving it to them as her housewarming gift. The oil painting depicted both of them as saints and was framed in simple, straight-lined gilded wood. It was

16 × 20 in size. He held it in his hands. In the lamplight of the room, Leo gazed upon their reflection.

They were surrounded by a pale blue sky that gave off an iridescent glow. The figure of Leo stood on the left. He was wearing a brown cloak like that of a Franciscan priest. His head was crowned with a gold halo above his dark hair, and emblazoned on his cloak in a gold that matched the halo was the head of a lion. His eyes were larger than he would have liked. He didn't think it resembled him at all, but Matt had disagreed.

The figure to the right was more startling. He was naked, but for the white cloak that covered his hips. His face was rounded, and he had spots of pink on the upper cheekbones. His short blond hair was spiked, and his blue eyes gazed into the distance. There was a white gold halo shining from behind his neck. His arms were stretched upward and tied to a tree branch behind him. The portrait was quite life-like in its representation of Matt, at least to Leo's eye. Perhaps his cheekbones weren't so pronounced, but it was Matt. It was even sexy, in a way. But for the arrows and blood.

His mother always included objects that helped to identify who the subjects were, much like artists centuries ago had used symbols to help people identify saints. For instance, she had painted in Leo's right hand a book representing his schooling. On the ground near Matt's foot was a sack of money symbolizing his banking. Between them was an old-fashioned set of keys, the keys to their house, Rosa had said. The picture was somewhat creative with its symbolism, including what she had used to identify their names. Whereas a lion's head adorned Leo's cloak, Matt's torso was penetrated by three arrows, their feathered ends protruding from his body. Blood dripped from each of them.

When they asked about the connection, she seemed so surprised that they could not figure it out. "The arrows, they pierce his body. Like Saint Sebastian. Pierce. His name!" They said they got it, but she wasn't convinced, so she lectured them about spiritual piercings, Saint Teresa, the Sacred Heart of Jesus, and the martyrdom of Saint Sebastian himself. Leo thought the money bag would have sufficed; Saint Matthew had been a money man, hadn't he? But Leo let her ramble on, and when she had finished her explanation, they praised the ingeniousness of it all and promised to hang it up right over the sofa. Instead, after Rosa left, Matt said, "This is fucked up. I don't ever want to see this again." And so he didn't. They never hung it. It wound up in the closet with the others.

Leo hadn't looked at it in some time. He stared at the arrows piercing his lover and the blood dripping down his chest. The symbolism was surreal and subconscious, almost foreshadowing events no one could have ever known. Leo touched the face that was Matt's and he imagined his cool, smooth skin against his fingers once more. But the moment passed, and all he could feel was the rough texture of dried oil paint. He returned the painting to the closet with a shiver.

He left the room, turning off the lights behind him, and went into the kitchen for something to drink before going to bed. He had taken a bottle of cola from his mother's, so he poured himself a glass and sat at the kitchen table. He yawned loudly. He tried to think about anything else, but it didn't work. The painting was in his mind, followed by another image of Matt with blood on his body. He shut his eyes tightly to block it out, but all he saw was more red on the underside of his eyelids. He opened his eyes quickly, and in the fluorescent kitchen lighting, he could still see the red, now on the wall before him. He had cleaned the whole wall area by the window and the cabinets numerous times, but one year later a ghostly sheen of red remained.

Even before Leo had gotten home with the groceries on that particular night, Matt had been angry. Leo hadn't helped the situation by egging him on about his own birthday dinner and Millie. It was like he had been testing him, because he was sick of Matt's attitude about the whole thing. Leo had been pissed off himself. Matt had been in therapy at that point for about six months and he seemed to be doing better. In the meantime, Leo kept away from Millie, he did not bring her up, did not have her to dinner, and disassociated her from their lives. But he found the whole thing absurd. She was his mother, not some strange acquaintance. He tried to be patient and wait until the day he could come out of the shadows about Millie and bring her back into their lives. It never seemed like it was going to happen though, and he still had no idea why Matt hated her.

On his way home from the grocery store that evening Leo had contemplated the best way to broach the subject with Matt about Millie and his birthday dinner. He wanted her there with the rest of his family. He decided he would say it outright, and fuck the consequences once and for all. Matt would just have to deal with it.

He made that final decision in his car, turning down their street as it rumbled on the brick pavement. He had to wait a moment for the car in front of their house to pull away before he could pull into the driveway. His determination was distracting him, but he was angry because the other driver seemed to take his time pulling away. Leo glanced at him with a nasty look and shook his head in disgust. The man never looked at him and simply drove off.

Leo pulled into the driveway, beeped the horn to get Matt to help him, popped the trunk, and started unloading groceries. Matt didn't come outside, but Leo knew he was home because his Mustang was in the driveway and the front door was open. Sighing in disgust, he grabbed five bags from the trunk. He let the screen porch door slam hard and stormed inside. He called out. The television was on, but Matt wasn't there. Leo put the bags in the kitchen, then went back to the car and got the rest of them.

He was making his third and final trip back from the car into the kitchen when Matt walked toward him and they met in the living room. Matt was white and his eyes were bloodshot and swollen. He was coming from the hallway, so Leo wondered if he had been sick in the bathroom. He asked him if he was all right. Matt stared down at the hardwood floor, then up at the television. He said nothing. "Uh, hello?" Leo repeated, with a slight edge to his voice. "You all right, or what?" Matt looked up at him and muttered a response. "What?" Leo asked.

"I said I'm fine," Matt replied forcefully.

It was then that Leo noticed Matt was furious. He was seething. He could see that unstable flare in his eyes that he had seen only a few times, one of them being the night of the disastrous reunion dinner. Frankly, he wasn't in the mood for it. Matt was pissed off again, God knew about what. Millie probably had made the mistake of calling their house looking for Leo, or something tragic like that. Rather than

be sympathetic, Leo was over it. "Okay, then," he replied sarcastically, and carried the rest of the bags into the kitchen.

He was putting groceries away when a few minutes later Matt
came in behind him. He grabbed a Corona from the refrigerator. He
stared off into nothingness. Leo asked him, "Are you going to help me
or what?"

Matt glared at him, then drank his beer.

"What am I, your fucking slave now?" Leo slammed at him verbally, banging canned vegetables onto the countertop.

"Look, don't start with me, all right."

"Oh, excuse me. Obviously you're in a mood." Without thinking,
he added, "again."

He regretted it instantly. He had said he would be there for him
and would always be understanding. He had been patient and caring
for a long time now. But it was getting to be too much. There was
only so much unappreciated sacrificing that he could make without
exploding. But he looked up apologetically. "I'm sorry. I didn't mean
that."

Matt seemed to relax a little and nodded in acknowledgment.
"I'm . . . trying to deal with something, okay?" He chugged down the
beer.

Leo had stopped putting the one bag of groceries away and stood
facing him. "Do you want to talk about it?"

He shook his head. "You can't help me."

Leo sighed with frustration. "Matt, someone has to help you.
When did you speak to Dr. Tate last?"

"Two weeks ago, I guess."

"Maybe you should go back. You need to speak to him, apparently."

"He can't help me with this one. No one can." He emptied the bottle.

"Well, you could try me, you know. You don't tell me anything.
I'm supposed to be your boyfriend, your partner. I am the one who
got you to the hospital that night."

"Don't remind me."

"I think you need to be reminded. You have a tendency to forget me sometimes, that I'm supposed to be there for you. You don't tell me shit about anything, and I—"

"Look, Jesus Christ, stop it!" Matt yelled.

Matt walked past Leo toward the garbage and tossed the bottle inside. The clanging of the bottle against the rest of garbage inside was the only noise either of them heard. Matt then moved closer to Leo and put his hands on his forearms. He looked oddly beautiful to Leo in that moment, a distraught pale figure with bloodshot eyes, a face pleading for help, uncertain where to turn. It almost made Leo cry.

"I don't need your help right now," Matt continued. "I don't need anyone's help. I just have to figure some stuff out." Leo said nothing. Matt came closer and gave him a kiss. Leo responded, but he wasn't satisfied. It was a light kiss, nothing serious or flirtatious or sensual. A kiss of reassurance, a peace offering maybe. Matt then moved past Leo and grabbed a bag to start unpacking it.

His instinct told him to shut up and let it drop. His gut told him not to bring it up because it would make matters worse. But he was sick of making sacrifices. He waited a few more minutes, using the time to gather up his nerves, all the while unpacking another bag. He finally said, "I have to talk to you about my birthday dinner."

"What about it?" Matt replied casually.

"You know we're having people come over, right?"

"Yeah. You told me already. I'm going to pick up the cake that morning."

"You know who's coming?"

"It'll be me, you, your mom obviously. A few friends. I guess George and Theresa."

Leo hesitated a moment before continuing. He spoke firmly. "I'm inviting Millie."

"What?"

"You heard me."

Matt shook his head. "No, you're not."

"Yes, I am."

Matt exhaled fiercely. He continued unpacking the bag he was working on, dropping glass jars and cans on the shelves in the cabinet with bangs and slamming the cabinet doors shut. "Why?" he asked with anger.

"You know why. I'm friends with her. I like her a lot. She's the only person in this family who understands what I'm doing with my life."

"Oh, I know. We're all so fucking stupid compared to super smart Millie!" he mocked.

"Give me a break. That's not what I meant."

He looked at Leo. His eyes were flaring again. He was holding in his hands the jar of sauce.

"I don't want her here," he said.

"Well, I do. It's my birthday, and I'm going to invite her."

"No, you're not!" he yelled.

It caught Leo off guard, and he felt his heart pounding harder. Matt's face was red and his fury increasing. Leo wasn't going to back down. Not this time. "Yes, I am, so deal with it."

Matt exploded in anger. "What are you trying to do? Drive me insane?! I told you I hate that woman! I don't want her here! I'm in therapy because of that fucking woman!"

"Oh, please! I still have no clue what you're in therapy for, but you keep insisting it's because you hate your mother! How do I know that? You never tell me anything. I want her here for my birthday dinner. I don't understand what your problem is. I mean, my God, Matt, she's your mother!"

It was as if it were in slow motion, the jar of sauce flying at Leo. And even though Leo ducked to the side when the jar hurled from Matt's hand toward the wall, Leo didn't realize what had happened until the jar smashed against the wall behind him into a multitude of musical notes, glass and sauce an explosion of fireworks. Splashes of red hit Leo, splattering him like blood.

"What are you, fucking nuts!?" Leo screamed at Matt, his own emotions shrieking out of him, his body shaking at the violent outburst thrown at him.

"I hate my mother! She's a fucking bitch!" Matt yelled back, his face contorted and enraged, splashes of red on his face and body as well. "Stop being friends with her! You have no fucking clue what she's capable of or what she's done!"

He stormed out of the kitchen. Leo heard his heavy footsteps on the hardwood floor as he went into the office. Then, a few moments later, he heard him grab his keys from the front hallway. The front door and the porch screen door slammed wildly behind him. The screeching brakes of his Mustang followed him down the street.

He didn't clean up the mess. He didn't put away any more groceries. Instead, he cursed Matt out for everything, for his stupidity, for his arrogance and ignorance, for his pride and anger. He was furious. And looking back one year later, replaying the events as he had so many times in his mind, Leo blamed himself for making Matt more crazy and angry that night. He should have trusted his instincts and let him be. Of all the moments to have chosen to have a full confrontation and to make a demand for his own emotional needs, that night was probably the worst time to do it. The image of Matt striking the cement median flashed in Leo's mind, his body flying through the windshield, glass piercing his beautiful face and torso. He had driven him to it.

No. He couldn't believe it. He couldn't accept that he was responsible for Matt's death. He didn't tell him to get into his car and go speeding into the night. Matt had chosen that on his own. And it had been hours later when the accident happened. He would have had time to calm down. Besides, the roads were slick from the tropical rains they were having. The roads were dangerous. That's what the officers said to him. It was an accident. It wasn't his fault. It wasn't even Matt's fault. It was all an accident.

He looked away from the faded red stain on the wall. He drank the rest of his soda, then went to their bedroom. He fell into the bed and lay on his side. He gazed at the framed photograph on the nightstand. It was a comfortably casual portrait, and Leo's favorite photo of the two of them. Matt was sitting in a chair and Leo was bending forward from behind him. Their faces were beside each other, Matt's right arm reaching upward and capturing Leo's head in a caressing bond. His face was turned slightly, his lips brushing his cheek with a kiss. They were both smiling when the picture was taken, because it was one of those rare moments when all was right and they had each other forever. He kissed Matt's face, put the photo back, and shut off the light.

Grabbing a pillow, he clutched it tightly to his stomach and inhaled the down. It was one year later, and all he wanted to do in that moment was smell Matt's scent, to bring him back, maybe for one last moment. Time had made the smell fade, but he could recall his faint scent, a combination of earthy-minty tones from his favorite cologne and his naturally sweet-salty perspiration that drove him wild. He inhaled the pillows deeply, and he believed he could sense his smell, ever so delicately, deep in the recesses of the pillow. He clutched it tightly to his face and licked the downy threads, kissing them, pretending it was Matt one last time. He fell asleep with his tears wetting the pillow in his arms in a silent cry for comfort and peace.

– SEVEN –

Leo woke up after 10:00 a.m. The sunshine glared through the slats of the vertical blinds on the one window to his side. He didn't move right away. The pillow was still clutched in his arms, his face imprinted on it. Now it tasted like dried thread and rough quilted cloth, and he disengaged himself from it. He could smell his own tears and see the wet stains they had left. He rolled onto his back to release the pressure of his morning hard-on. He lay there for a few minutes doing nothing, then masturbated. It didn't suffice. He wished he had someone to fuck with.

He went into the shower, then ate cold leftover chicken piccata and a piece of Italian bread for breakfast. The sparseness of food reminded him that he needed to go food shopping. He drove to the Publix supermarket in the Northeast Park Shopping Center just off of 38th Avenue and 4th Street. He parked and walked toward the store, then noticed that the hair salon at the end of the strip mall was open. Half an hour later, he was amazed how a haircut made him look more like a normal human being and not some shaggy dog. He went food shopping. By the time he put away the groceries at home, it was after twelve-thirty. He ate something light for lunch, grabbed a notebook and pen, and headed to the library in Tampa to do research. With help from a graduate assistant at the reference desk, he found new resources in books and journals. As he worked, a thought occurred to him. He entered the term "women" first with Swinburne then Rossetti in MLA. He was surprised by what he found. He decided to talk to Palmer about these citations.

Pierce
© 2007 by The Haworth Press, Inc. All rights reserved.
doi:10.1300/5849_07

By the time he left the library with photocopies and printouts, it was after 6:00 p.m. When he got home, he dropped his papers in his office, sat down for more leftovers, and read the help-wanted section of the newspaper he had picked up that morning. When next he glanced at the VCR clock it said it was almost 8:00 p.m. He was bored and restless. He had had a productive day. He was entitled to wind down. He decided to do something he hadn't in a while: go out. He headed for Sunday T-dance at the Suncoast Resort. If he were lucky, he could get drink and sex in one place and hardly spend a dime.

He wasn't sure what it would be like at the resort. He hadn't been there in a while now. In fact, he hardly went out at all anymore. It always made him feel even more lonely than when he used to go with Matt. The few close friends Matt and he had had through the years had all dissipated or moved on to other lovers and friends. A few tried to stay in touch. He was to blame for those broken relationships. Millie wasn't the only friend he had disengaged from after Matt's death.

He parked his car behind the resort like everyone else, and made his way between two peach-colored hotel buildings to the outdoor tiki bar. It was much more active than he anticipated. Music from the dance club was piped throughout the resort. People were in the pool tossing a ball around and a drag queen and her backup dancer were performing on a makeshift stage nearby. Some people shopped in the stores that ran around the perimeter of the ground level of the resort, while others walked along the upper promenades, peering into hotel room windows or gesturing to other guys along the way with eye twitches and strokes of their shorts. He found himself half tempted to go up there, or to go in the pool, or to go shopping, but he knew he wouldn't do any of these things. Instead, he headed right for the tiki bar. He ordered a Corona and downed it in the first ten minutes he was there. He ordered a second Corona and was almost finished with it when he heard a voice on the other side of the bar that sounded familiar.

He looked over at the guy. He had on a tight white tank top that revealed a small but firm chest. A tiny patch of dark hair peeked over the top of the shirt. He had darker skin, gelled black hair, and a neatly trimmed goatee. He wasn't sure where he recognized him from, but he was a hottie. Leo finished his beer and kept glancing over at him. He was with a Nellie friend who had a hand clinging to his arm. After a few moments his friend hit him lightly on the arm, then went inside pouting. The guy ordered from the bartender. As he was waiting, he looked over and saw Leo gazing at him. Leo turned his eyes away quickly, then looked back. The guy returned his gaze, then looked away himself. When he returned his gaze, this time Leo forced himself to look back. He suddenly acknowledged Leo with a nod and smile.

Neither of them seemed certain what to do, so neither moved. Finally, the guy got his two drinks: a Heineken and a cosmopolitan. The Coronas had quickly worked into Leo's system and made him a little more brave. He put his bottle down and waved him over. The guy hesitated and glanced off to where his friend had gone. Then, he picked up the drinks, and came toward Leo. "Hey, what's up?" he asked.

"Not much," Leo responded.

The guy picked up the beer and drank from it. Somehow it made Leo like him better. "Cosmo is for your lady friend, I guess," he said.

"My . . . uh . . . boyfriend," he replied hesitatingly, "yes."

Leo nodded. "Going out long?"

"Few weeks."

"Good for you." Leo's tone was a bit rude. His thought for a hookup was deflating.

The guy shrugged. "Seems a lot longer."

Leo kept nodding. "Good luck then. Sounds like you'll need it."

The guy put his drink down and scoffed. "Are you this bitchy all the time?"

Leo looked at him curiously. He shrugged, thinking he was flirting. "I guess."

The guy chuckled, shaking his head and taking a swig from his beer. "You have no idea who I am, do you?"

They did know each other, and it frightened Leo that he couldn't place him. He wondered if he was a former student, or someone from Matt's job that he had met at a company party.

The guy shook his head. "You're the guy who I delivered the package to the other day. You didn't want to get off your porch swing."

Leo's eyes widened in shock, and he closed them just as quickly to hide his embarrassment. It was the UPS guy. He wanted to die. He realized this was one of those moments when he either had to be humble and apologize, or chalk it up and move on. Leo went with the latter option. "Yeah, you know, rough night. I was pretty damn lazy that morning."

"And horny," he added. He sipped more of his Heineken.

Leo could see the guy smirking at the corners of his mouth. Leo was flushing. He tried to fight off the embarrassment, unsuccessfully, then reverted to his former option. "Look, I'm sorry about that. It was morning, you know the bit."

"Yeah, well it doesn't matter. It wasn't that. I liked that part. It was your attitude that pissed me off."

Leo remembered he had blown the guy off. It was a complete farce, of course, because it was Leo's loss, not the guy's. He gazed into his empty bottle before him and started peeling at the label. He wanted to apologize again. The guy would never get it though, the night he had been through. He said nothing.

"Work on the attitude," he said. "Next time, you might get lucky with that lemonade." He winked, picked up his drinks, and walked off.

As soon as he was alone again, Leo left the bar. He felt humiliated, unsatisfied, and disgusted with himself. He drove through the south side of St. Petersburg, and he thought he caught a drug deal on a corner near 22nd Avenue. It reminded him that he needed more pot. His contact was another adjunct in the English department. Leo didn't trust getting his pot from someone else, so even though he was craving it, he resisted in favor of calling his contact when he got home or the next day.

He drove back to his house in a somber mood. The beer had worked into his system, but not enough to satiate him or make him go back to sleep. He was hungry again for some reason, this time for something fattening, greasy, and unhealthy. He saw a Pizza Hut and ordered a thin-crust with pepperoni and a bottle of soda to go.

Once he was home, he dropped the pizza on the coffee table and switched on the television. He went to the kitchen to get ice for the soda. He was pouring himself a glass when he noticed his answering machine light was blinking. He pressed the button and the electronic voice told him he had two messages. He was surprised and wondered who could have called him in the past hour or so since he had gone out. The time of the first message made him realize these calls had come much earlier and he hadn't noticed them until now.

The first call surprised him and he groaned to himself in frustration when he heard her voice. "Leo, it's Dr. Palmer. I haven't heard back from you in a couple of days. I want to know what's going on with your research and how you're doing." Leo was glad he had done some work that day, so at least he could tell her that. He had written nothing over the past few days though, and he recalled that she wanted a draft soon. "Also, I have to tell you," she continued with an almost lighthearted tone, "that your favorite officemate resigned this weekend. She apparently decided to join her fiancée at Vanderbilt. Which means . . . I think I can swing you a teaching job. Call me." She rattled off her telephone number at home. Leo wrote down her number fast on a piece of paper he got from the drawer. He appreciated what she was going to do for him and that he actually might have a job for the summer. He picked up the cordless phone and got ready to dial even though he knew it was late, when the next message came on and stopped him from dialing.

"Hello, Mr. Vasari." The voice was that of a professional woman with an English accent. "This is Dr. Bauer from Morton Plant Hospital. I'm phoning regarding a patient of mine, Millicent Hunter. I would like to speak to you about Millie. I understand that her son and you were . . ." he could hear her pause, "well, I guess lovers would suffice, or partners if you prefer." She resorted to her professional tone. "Would you be so kind as to ring me here at hospital tomorrow? Thank you." She left the number and hung up.

He had to replay the message to make sure he had heard it correctly. He wrote that number on the same sheet of paper. Leo was uncertain what to make of it. His first thought was that Millie must have asked for him, which was why the doctor was calling. Millie obviously wanted to see him again and could only do it with her doctor's help. Then it occurred to him that Dr. Bauer hadn't said anything about him actually visiting. She had only asked him to call her. No other explanation. He really had no idea why she wanted to speak to him, he now realized. Maybe it was the complete opposite of what he was thinking. Maybe she was calling to make sure Leo didn't see Millie again, especially after the stunt he had pulled saying he was her son, breaking rules to get in.

He glanced at the microwave clock and saw it was 10:24. He swore in frustration. It was too late to make any phone calls at this point. He'd have to wait until the morning. Now he regretted going out at all. If he had stayed home, he would have gotten these messages earlier and could have returned the phone calls right away. And he wouldn't have humiliated himself with the UPS driver.

He returned to the living room, ate his cold pizza and drank a Corona instead of the cola he had intended to drink, then went to bed. He had a restless night of sleep. His mind kept wandering to this Dr. Bauer and what she had to say about Millie. This was coupled by his concerns over the teaching potential. Palmer had said she might be able to get him something. It wasn't definite. When he finally woke up the next morning, he was groggy. He had breakfast food in his kitchen for a change, so he made ham and eggs with a toasted bagel and put on a pot of Maxwell House. The smell of the fresh-brewed coffee did wonders to refresh him. He used to make breakfasts like this every weekend for Matt and him, and it still felt odd doing it for himself.

By the time he had eaten and caught the morning news, it was after 9:00 a.m. He saw the sheet of paper with the two phone numbers on it. Dr. Palmer and Dr. Bauer. Oddly, the thought of calling either of them left a flutter of nervousness in his stomach. He wanted to have something positive to say to his professor and was hoping he had the teaching position, but he had not called her back right away so maybe it was gone already. And then there was this Dr. Bauer. He had no idea what she would say to him. He picked up the telephone and dialed Palmer first.

He was surprised that he had apparently woken her up. He assumed she was one of those up-at-dawn professors who wrote their twenty plus books before they had had their morning coffee. She was pleased he had called, however, and quickly asked him about the progress on his dissertation. He told her about the research he had done, but lied a little when he told her he was writing. He discussed with her the idea of incorporating Swinburne and Rossetti poetry into the dissertation. "They published their first works during the 1860s too, and I see some parallels to my topic," he explained. She told him to write something up on it for her to read. Finally, he asked, "About the teaching position. . ."

"Oh, yes, that. . ."

He felt let down. "What, Johnson changed her mind already?"

"No, she's definitely going. I'm pretty sure I can get you at least one class for the first summer session, if you want it. It starts tomorrow, Tuesdays and Thursdays at 9:00 a.m."

"God, yes," he replied. "I need the money."

"Great! Let me see what I can do. But you owe me, Vasari. Work on that dissertation."

"Yes, Ma'am." He thanked her, and had to admit that he was glad he had her on his side. It was a tremendous sense of relief that he might have a class to teach. But she was not kidding. He would owe her. He made a commitment to himself to work on the dissertation.

The relief was short-lived though as he found himself anticipating calling Dr. Bauer. He rationalized to himself that he should probably take a shower and get dressed since it was still too early to call the hospital. When he stepped back into the kitchen, it was 9:56 on the microwave clock and he decided to call. He lifted the cordless phone and, with a deep breath, dialed the number. An operator answered after the second ring. He asked for Dr. Bauer and he was transferred. The phone rang three times, and a British-accented voice said, "This is Dr. Bauer."

Leo cleared his throat. "Good morning, Dr. Bauer. This is Leo Vasari." There was no response. "From yesterday. You phoned me." Silence. "About Millie Hunter."

"Oh, yes, of course, Mr. Vasari. I'm sorry. I just walked in."

Pleasant enough. He felt more at ease. "Well, I got your message, so I'm returning your call like you asked." He heard her rustling papers. "How is she?" he asked.

"I would say she's recovering well."

"I feel very bad about what happened. I didn't know she was suffering so much."

She surprised him by ignoring him and instead asking him a question that took him off guard. "I understand you visited Millie on Saturday and there was an altercation."

He swallowed. "Did Theresa tell you that?"

"Actually, no. I first learned of it from the staff. Then I spoke with Millie and she told me who you were."

He sighed. "I apologize about what happened. I was just visiting her, Dr. Bauer, because she and I are close friends. I never intended—"

"No, I understand that, Mr. Vasari. I know it seems silly, hospital rules about family only. Mind you, masquerading as her son wasn't the smartest solution. Someone could have found you out."

"I'm sorry, Dr. Bauer. All I wanted to do was visit her."

"I easily could have added you to the visitation list had I known that you might come."

He was caught off guard again. "I didn't realize that."

"No, of course not. I'd have thought that Millie or her daughter might have mentioned you would visit, that's all."

He closed his eyes for a moment, realizing he had to accept responsibility for this. "It's my fault, Doctor. I haven't been the best of friends to Millie in some time. She probably didn't think I would visit even if I had found out, which I suspect I wouldn't have had I not heard about it from someone else." She didn't respond, but seemed engrossed in her file. Seeing how the conversation was not going bad, he ventured a step further. "Dr. Bauer, you don't think I could visit her now, do you?"

There was a momentary pause, then the woman replied, "Actually, I had something more than a visit in mind, if you are amenable to it."

"Oh," he muttered. "What?"

"I was wondering if perhaps you could come to our session today."

Leo was taken aback. "Me? Why?" he asked.

"I believe that having you present might assist Millie in her recovery."

"How so?"

She paused a moment before replying. "She speaks very highly of you. You apparently played an important role in her life these past few years. Your having been in a relationship with her son made quite a difference to her, it seems. And, considering that her son has passed on, I imagine you might be able to help in her recovery."

"I'm not sure what I can do, but of course I would be willing to help."

"Excellent. I'd like to ask you a few questions first, if that's all right. Some background information, that sort of thing." He agreed. "How did Millie react to your relationship when she first found out about it?"

"Fine. She was the only one who really knew at first and never had any issues with it. She shocked me with how up front she was about the whole thing."

"And you felt comfortable with Millie?"

"Completely. It was almost weird. We found out we had certain things in common, things I don't think she ever had with Matt or Theresa."

"Did Matthew get along with his mother?"

"Hardly," he replied. "Matt hated her."

"Do you know why?"

He hesitated a moment before responding. "Actually, Dr. Bauer, no, I don't know. I wish I did. I have a few suspicions based on things I've heard from both of them, but I don't know for sure. He would never discuss it with me. In fact, they both had a tendency to want to push things from the past into the past and keep them there."

"Millie's son died in a car accident . . ." She jostled her papers. ". . . a year ago?"

He swallowed. "Yes."

She was silent for a moment, taking notes it seemed. Then, she continued without breaking her train of thought. "How would you say she handled his death?"

That was a tough question. He wasn't sure how to answer it. He thought all along she had handled it well. Maybe too well. But then he had found out she had been on Valium, and now the suicide attempt. "I don't know," he replied. "Not well, I guess."

She seemed satisfied with his answer. She continued jotting a few notes, then spoke quickly again. "Is three o'clock all right?"

He agreed. "What about Theresa?"

"I will inform Millie and her daughter of my decision. It is for Millie's recovery that I believe you should be here, so I'm sure Theresa will agree."

Leo didn't think so, but he didn't say that. "I'll be there," he said.

He hung up the phone with a sigh of relief and clapped his hands together in excitement like a little child. He was going to teach and see Millie again! He couldn't help but feel like it was going to be a good day.

– EIGHT –

Almost a year after Millie had made that first phone call and spoken to Leo, he was giving his students their final exam and had taken his own final for a summer class on 1890s British literature with Dr. Palmer. It was August 1997. He went out for drinks with classmates afterward, and didn't get home until after eleven-thirty that night. He knew Matt would have given up on waiting for him for dinner. In reality, he half expected that Matt was out drinking himself. Leo was tired and wanted to go to bed. He pulled in the driveway and parked next to Matt's Mustang. He was surprised that Matt was home. The porch light was off, though, and the house was dark. It looked as if the house was deserted.

Leo grabbed his briefcase and books and headed inside. The door was open, and the cool air conditioning was escaping into the sticky humid night. He closed the door behind him and called to Matt, but there was no answer. He peeked in the dark kitchen, turning lights on. He started to get perturbed. Had Matt gotten so drunk that he had passed out and left the door wide open? He put his briefcase and books in the office.

He heard whispering. It was soft at first. He wasn't even sure he had heard it. He stopped, looking about him inquisitively. He heard it again. It was a muffled whisper. It had to be Matt, he realized. He felt a strange sensation overcome him, almost a panic, wondering if Matt was in bed with someone else. He crossed the hallway to their bedroom. He turned on the light, but he could see that no one was there.

He turned and called Matt's name again. No answer. His heart was starting to beat harder, his emotions confused and concerned. He could hear the whispering still. As he walked back down the hallway,

Pierce
© 2007 by The Haworth Press, Inc. All rights reserved.
doi:10.1300/5849_08

he saw the light under the main bathroom door. He listened against the door and realized Matt was inside. He could hear the whispering more clearly, but he didn't know what he was saying. He knocked softly. "Hey, Matt? You okay?" There was no response, so he knocked again. He opened the door.

The shimmering white bathroom with its bright lights blinded Leo for a moment as he came from the dark hallway. He stepped in, and he saw red in random splotches, which was odd because there was nothing red in their bleached bathroom. He looked down and saw Matt sitting on the floor between the bathtub and the vanity, resting against the wall below the window. His legs were sprawled out before him and his upper body was arched forward slightly. He was wearing only his briefs, but what was once white was stained in blood. There were smears of blood in the bathroom, starting at the sink and vanity, drags of it on the mirror, the walls, the shower curtain. But the worst of it was on the white tile floor and on Matt's pale skin.

He took in all of the horror in one rapid instant. He hurried to him, but felt his foot slip, so he slowed his pace, not wanting to startle Matt either. As he approached, he heard him whispering. In Matt's right hand he held a paring knife and he was randomly gashing into his left arm over and over, cutting into wounds that had already been slashed and opening scabs from the supposed shrub and glass scratches that had begun to heal and were now oozing. There were cuts on his arms and chest. It was impossible to know where he had sliced himself, because the blood was seeping in many places. His face was stained from his bloody hands rubbing against his eyes.

Leo was shaking as he came closer. He crouched down and moved closer to Matt, his hands stretched out before him to help and to defend if necessary. He swallowed to calm his nerves, and spoke softly to Matt. "It's all right, Matt," he whispered. "Give me the knife." His voice was quivering.

Matt's head was jerking and he still muttered nothingness. Matt wasn't responding. Leo moved quickly, and grabbed the knife from him. Matt's hand kept trying to cut himself, but now at least the blade was in Leo's hand. He took a quick breath, then reached with his hands, and cupped Matt's face in them. He turned his face up to look at him, and Matt's eyes were glazed with tears and blood, the whites bloodshot. He could sense the faint odor of alcohol on his breath. His mutters grew more quiet. He seemed to be focusing on Leo then. "Matt," he said more firmly, trying hard not to cry himself, "it's okay. I'm here."

"I'm sorry," he said, his voice childlike. "I didn't mean to go in there. I'm sorry!" he yelled more loudly, then started to cry. Leo moved forward more. He embraced Matt, pressing his body against his, the blood seeping into his own clothes. Matt cried against his shoulder, apologizing in his childlike voice. Leo rocked Matt a little, afraid to press him too hard in case he injured him more. He reassured Matt it was okay.

His voice started to change, and Leo pulled back. He wiped his eyes with a clean patch of his shirt, and he saw Matt focusing through his own tears. He glanced up at Leo, apologizing still, but more softly now, his own voice returning.

Then, a horrific scream of acknowledgment pealed from Matt's mouth and jerked Leo backward. It shattered Leo's own sense of peace that he was starting to feel at that moment, and he saw that Matt was aware of himself. He screamed, "Oh, my God! Oh, fuck! Oh, fuck!" His tears were back, but they were tears of pain and anguish, as he looked down at his own body and saw the wounds around him. He screamed aloud, and this time when Leo tried to reach out to him, Matt pushed him away. He screamed and slid to the floor, then curled into a fetal position where he wailed.

Leo's whole body was shaking. He rushed to the phone in the office and dialed 911. When the operator asked him the emergency, Leo could only mutter, "He's cut himself. All over."

After seeing the whole scene before him, Leo's first thought had been that he had been attacked, but he knew that couldn't be the case because of the knife in his own hand. Then he thought it had been an accident. The thought that it had been a suicide attempt was out of the question. It had to have been an accident.

He had to follow the ambulance to the hospital. They took him to St. Anthony's Hospital. Nobody would let Leo see Matt or answer his questions about how he was. It was immediate family only, even though he was able to provide all of the information they needed about his insurance. He waited in the emergency room while they worked on him, and eventually called Millie and Theresa.

They came together. They were frantic. Leo was wearing blood-stained clothes. He told them how he had come home, and what he saw, and how he tried to help him. He told them about all the blood and the cuts. Millie spoke first and surprised Leo with words she probably never meant to say. "Jesus Christ, I can't believe he did this again."

Leo blinked through misty eyes. "What did you say?" he asked. Neither of them replied, but they looked at one another. "He's done this before?" he asked them, his own fear coming through, the fact that this hadn't been an accident after all. They didn't answer him. Leo wiped at his eyes. He saw Millie cover her face with her hands and shake her head. No one spoke. The paging of a doctor over the loud-speaker was the only sound permeating their space.

"How is he?" Theresa asked.

Leo shook his head. "They won't tell me. They keep saying 'immediate family only.'"

Millie groaned in aggravation. "Theresa, go speak to them," she ordered. Theresa hesitated, then walked to the desk. Millie yelled to a nurse and asked her for scrubs, pointing to Leo's clothes. She returned with them rather quickly, about the same time Theresa saw a doctor come out from the ER. Leo wanted to go to the doctor, but Millie held him back. She encouraged him to change, following him to the men's room.

He repeated the question she hadn't answered before. "He did this before?"

Millie hesitated, then nodded. "He was sixteen."

"Millie, how could this happen? I don't understand any of this!" He choked up.

"I don't know, Leo. I guess I fucked him up raising him. At least, that's what he'll say, I'm sure." She handed him the scrubs. He turned, then stopped and looked back at her. He saw her hands rubbing her face, shaking her head. She looked up again and startled him. "Get changed. I'll tell you more when you come out."

He washed himself and changed quickly. He looked at the discarded clothes with Matt's blood on them. It was disturbing, and the flash of what he had seen rushed back to him. He threw the clothes out. When he stepped back into the waiting room again, the doctor was speaking to Millie and Theresa and he joined them.

Matt had eight cuts on his arms and five more on his chest. Fortunately, none were fatal. He needed stitches for the deeper ones, and he would have scarring. Leo realized for the first time that the scars on his body all these years hadn't been from accidents or skin lesion surgeries. It made him shiver. How could he cut himself? Leo couldn't comprehend it. And how could he not have noticed the cuts on Matt and believed his lame excuses that they were from shrubs or broken glass? He wanted to kick himself. How could Leo, a scholar, a teacher, a researcher, have missed what was happening right in front of him?

The doctor asked questions, and despite Millie and Theresa being blood relatives, they deferred his questions to Leo because he could answer them best. The doctor needed to know if he did this often. He told him no, not that he knew. He didn't mention about the supposed falls or the bushes. No, he hadn't been depressed, no more than usual. Angry maybe. Yes, he had missed more work than usual.

Millie suddenly turned to the doctor and spoke. "Look, this has happened before," she said, as if it explained everything. "But it was over ten years ago," she added.

The doctor nodded slowly, then said he was going to call the psychiatric ward. He would have to be treated properly. He knew a specialist in the field. "What field?" Leo asked, dumbfounded.

"Cutting, self-mutilating," the doctor said matter-of-factly. "It's my understanding that it's not as common among men, so this is an unusual case, but I'm sure Dr. Tate will do his best to help him." He walked away.

Leo didn't respond. He didn't know what to say. A cold wave overcame him, and he had to walk or he would pass out. He heard Millie behind him complain that she needed a cigarette. As she walked past him outside, he followed her, taking quick breaths to steady himself. They stood outside the sliding doors in the darkness. It was muggy, the air thick with humidity. They could feel a cold rush from the air-conditioning every time the automatic sliding doors opened. Millie lit up a menthol and exhaled. She turned the pack toward Leo. "You want one?" He shook his head, confused. She knew he didn't smoke. "It might take the edge off," she added. She inhaled and cool minty smoke filtered around their heads. He appreciated the offer, but he would have preferred a Corona or a joint instead. She puffed on her cigarette, taking a long drag so that the end burned brightly. "Leo," she continued, "I know what you're going through. I know how it feels, what you saw."

"Millie, it was a nightmare," he replied. He could see vividly in his mind the bright white bathroom and Matt on the floor with blood seeping everywhere. "I can't stop thinking about it." He shook his head to try to push away the image. "I want to know what happened the last time."

The ash was already extending and she had yet to flick it off. "Matthew and I were living with this guy, Bob something-or-other." As she moved her hand, the ash fell. She dropped the cigarette and squashed it with her shoe. "It was after dinner, and Bob and I were watching TV. I had this craving for ice cream, I think. Matthew and I had had another fight at dinner, so I guess I felt bad and wanted to make up for the fight. He wouldn't answer me when I called. I went to his room, and there he was, lying on the floor of his bedroom passed out. He had a kitchen knife with him, and he was bleeding on the floor. He wouldn't respond to me. I noticed there were cuts on different parts of his arm. I panicked. Bob and I carried him into the car and rushed him to the hospital."

"I never knew that had happened before. He never told me."

She nodded, then folded her arms. "I told you when we first met that my son had emotional problems."

Leo scoffed. "I didn't know you meant like this."

She paused before speaking again. "Look, Leo, don't be surprised if they check him into the psychiatric ward. That's what they did to him when I found him. They assumed he was trying to kill himself. They'll probably do the same here, so be prepared."

"But he didn't try to kill himself," he argued, then wondered, "did he?"

She shrugged in response. "I have no idea, Leo."

They walked back inside, and Theresa was coming toward them. She said the doctor had come out and said they could go see him. They headed toward the inner door when a nurse stopped them. "I'm sorry, only two of you can go in at a time."

Millie, Theresa, and Leo all said that they would stay, although none of them wanted to. The nurse suddenly asked who they all were, and Millie responded without hesitation, "I'm his mother, this is his sister, and this is his boyfriend."

There was a moment of uncomfortable silence. The nurse replied, "Immediate family only. The two of you can go in." She pointed toward Millie and Theresa.

"He needs to go in," Millie said, pointing toward Leo.

"No, it's okay," Leo said, feeling isolated. "I'll wait."

"Bullshit. You're entitled to go in."

"Mother, could we not make a scene?" Theresa asked excitedly. "Please, let's go in fast, see how he is, then let Leo know. I'm sure if we talk to the doctor, he'll let him in."

Millie glanced at Leo. He slowly nodded in agreement. "Tell him I love him." Tears welled in his eyes.

She came forward and kissed him. "It'll be all right." She squeezed his arm. "If anyone can pull through this, Matthew can, and it will be because of you."

He watched as Millie and Theresa hurried through the doors and entered the inner sanctum of the ER. The doors shut behind them. He was left alone, unable to do a single thing. The nurse muttered an apology but he ignored her and sat down. He could do nothing now but wait. He closed his eyes, and he could feel his heart aching. He struggled to forget the blood on the bleached tiles.

The red double doors of the psychiatric ward at Morton Plant Hospital, which he stood before now, still intimidated him, but this time Leo knew he was welcome without having to lie. He rang the buzzer, and when he gave his own name they let him in. He looked at the names before him, but Theresa's wasn't listed. He felt relieved. He could speak to Millie for a few minutes freely. He passed into the hallway and stopped at the main desk. A new nurse told him Millie was on the patio.

When he stepped outside from the air-conditioned common room the heat was intense. Millie seemed oblivious to it though. He was surprised to see her sitting as she had been the first day he had visited, in the same redwood bench reading *Lady Audley's Secret*. Her silver half-glasses rested on her face, and a half-burned cigarette dangled from her other hand. It was almost déjà vu. He walked forward and said, "I can't believe you're reading that trashy novel!"

This time, she glanced at him over her half-glasses. "Ah, the devoted son-in-law returns," she replied, then puffed away on the last of her cigarette and extinguished it.

"I didn't realize I was devoted."

"Considering my choice of sons-in-law, trust me, you're the devoted one." She got up and opened her arms. He embraced her and kissed her on the cheek. "You know," she gestured to the book still in her one hand, "this book isn't that bad. It kind of drags at points, like many Victorian novels, but it's interesting. The mystery is a little obvious though. I mean, you know she did it."

He grinned. "Did she though?"

She raised an eyebrow. "Oh?" she acknowledged. "Okay, now I'm intrigued."

They sat on the sofa, and he didn't hesitate to speak because he knew Theresa would be arriving soon. "I'm very glad that your doctor is allowing me to visit."

"I am too." She reached out and squeezed his hand.

"Theresa must be pissed." She shrugged in response. "What's her deal? You do want me to visit, right?"

"Yes, of course. I think she's being overprotective."

"But what could I do to hurt you?"

"Don't worry about it. Dr. Bauer thinks you're harmless. That's all I care about."

"How are you anyway?"

"Fabulous," she mimicked.

He smirked. "I'm serious."

"I am doing fine. I hope to God I'm out of here in a few days. I have a roommate now, and she's driving me crazy!" They talked about his birthday party and he thanked her for recommending the gift to his mother. Then, out of nowhere, it seemed, she asked him, "Are you dating anyone yet? Or at least sleeping with someone?"

"Uh, no," he replied, caught off guard. "Why are you asking me that?"

She shrugged. "I don't know. There's something about you. Besides, you've been alone for too long."

"Oh, please, don't you start too."

"Hey, you need to meet someone." She was gazing at him, and her demeanor started to change, as if she were reading his unspoken thoughts. "Wait a minute. You are seeing someone, aren't you?"

"No!" But a face was coming back to him, with a goatee.

"Then you at least met someone." He was speechless. "Spill it, buster!" she said.

He sighed. "It's nothing. I swear." He hesitated, feeling himself redden in the face. "Okay, so I have the hots for the UPS guy who delivered your books to me."

Her eyes widened in excitement. "You had sex with the UPS guy?!"

"No!" he exclaimed.

"But you want to," she prompted.

He laughed. "All right, yes, I want to. But it's not going to happen. I ruined the whole thing already."

"You spoke to him?"

"Yes, but I was rude to him that first day, and made an ass out of myself the next time I saw him. Besides, he has a boyfriend."

"What does he look like?" she mused.

He was grinning and flushing. "Latin, I think. Dark skin. Black hair. Goatee."

She raised a hand. "Stop right there! He's gorgeous! What's his name?"

He laughed in embarrassment. "I have no idea. Look, I told you, nothing is going on, so let's drop it."

She shrugged and grinned. "Okay, it's your business. I'll leave you alone. But maybe I should send you another package. . ."

He laughed. Millie lit another cigarette. As he watched her, he remembered that just a few days ago he had had so many questions to ask her. Now, he could hardly think of what to say. Surprisingly, the question that came out of his mouth even startled him. "Has that detective been back to see you?"

She froze and stared at him. "What detective?"

"The one in your room the last time I came to see you."

She pulled the cigarette out of her mouth. She seemed distracted with her response. "No, not since then." She glanced up at him quickly. "You haven't seen him, have you?"

"Me? No. Why would I see him?" Leo answered.

"I don't know. Maybe something about Matthew."

"I don't understand. What does he want?"

Before she could respond, the nurse from the desk told Millie that Dr. Bauer was ready for her session. Millie jumped up and grabbed her stuff. As he followed her, he realized that being interrupted had been more of a saving moment for her than mere coincidence. She was purposely not telling him about the detective.

He followed Millie down the white hallway to the fourth door on the left. It was open, and the nurse guided them in, then returned to her station. Leo glanced at the door as they entered and saw a sign had been slid in that said "In Session." Standing just inside the doorway was who he presumed to be Dr. Bauer. She quickly put out her hand and shook his hand in a firm shake. She was an inch or so taller than Leo with a small frame. She had a mass of frizzy graying black hair, and was probably in her late forties. She wore black plastic-frame glasses that were styled in what Leo would classify as nerdy, but with her high cheekbones and stylishly floppy hair, it made her look more trendy than square. She spoke with her English accent as she introduced herself and smiled politely. "I'm so glad you could come, Mr. Vasari."

"Leo, please," he replied, delighted to meet her.

He turned and entered the room. It had a soft smell of lavender and baby powder. The room was small but intimate, with the same steel gray carpeting as the patients' rooms, although a throw rug of brighter colors added flavor to the floor. The walls were painted sunshine yellow, and potted plants dotted the corners. A glass-top desk was in one area, and Dr. Bauer's diplomas and certifications hung on the wall nearby. The other walls were decorated with Impressionist prints in delicate pastels. The two overstuffed, pale blue side chairs were accompanied by a matching print sofa. Seated on the left side of the sofa was Theresa, her mousy hair in a ponytail, her face gazing off to her left at the wall as she rested her chin in her hand. She was wearing a free-flowing dress and Birkenstocks. She looked a little dowdy. Millie sat beside her daughter, putting her book, eyeglasses, and cigarettes on the table before them. Dr. Bauer gestured Leo to the chair on Millie's right, and she sat across from Millie. Leo cleared his throat, and said, "Hello, Theresa."

She glanced over at him. "Leo," she replied.

Dr. Bauer looked at Leo, presumably to see his reaction, and Leo smiled sheepishly. Dr. Bauer took this as a cue to begin. She leaned forward and put her hands together as if in prayer, but gestured them toward the three of them. "I'm very glad we've all agreed to meet. We're here to help Millie sort out her feelings, so that she can begin her recovery. I hope that everyone will feel free to be open and honest about how they feel. This is a safe zone, all right? Nothing said here will leave this room. And everyone will respect one another's true feelings and not judge them. Are we all okay with this?"

Leo said, "Sure."

Millie replied, "Yes, Doc."

Theresa folded her arms before her chest and sighed. "Yes, of course. That's fine."

Dr. Bauer turned her attention to Theresa first. "Theresa, why are you angry that Leo is here?" Leo was impressed. She didn't waste any time.

"I'm not angry."

"I think you are. Your body language says so. You had been sitting comfortably until he came into the room, and then you shifted toward the wall."

She sighed. "It's not anger."

"Then what is it?"

She hesitated, glancing at Leo quickly. "All right, maybe I am angry he's here. But what does how I feel have to do with this?"

"Your mother's recovery is my focus. If the two people closest to her cannot get along, your mother is going to suffer for it." Theresa looked away again. Dr. Bauer continued. "You were married to Leo's brother, weren't you?"

Theresa fidgeted. "Yes."

"And how did that end?"

"Terribly."

"Do you blame Leo for the failure of your marriage?"

"No, of course not. He had nothing to do with it. George ran off with some bimbo. If anything, Leo's always been the better brother."

"Thank you," Leo said instinctively, then glad he had.

Theresa met his gaze. "You're welcome." She paused before continuing. "Leo, I'm not angry at you. I didn't want you to come because I was afraid for my mother. I didn't want anyone to disturb her."

"It's all right, Theresa. I understand."

She pursed her lips. "And, I guess, I thought it was cruel of you to avoid my mother after Matt's death. You were supposed to be her friend."

Leo had somehow anticipated this. He sighed. "I'm not surprised you're mad, although to be honest, I thought that Millie would be more angry at me, not you. I feel like I let Millie down. I didn't continue our friendship as strongly as I used to. After Matt died," he found himself pausing, "it was so difficult."

Millie waved her hand and grimaced. "Leo, don't be ridiculous. I knew you would need time to recuperate. You guys loved each other a lot."

"But I feel so bad. You were good to me, listening to me whenever I had any issues or worries, even when Matt died, and instead of going to you, I ran the other way." He felt a catch in his throat. "I was afraid to be near you because it made me think about Matt, and it made me feel guilty because of how he felt about our friendship."

She reached out with her hand and rubbed his knee. "I understand," she said. Millie then turned toward Dr. Bauer and announced proudly, "See, Doc, we're all cured. No more bad feelings. When do I go home?"

Dr. Bauer eyed her seriously. "We're hardly finished, Millie. We've only begun."

Millie fell back against the sofa. "I figured as much."

"Millie, how do you feel right now?"

She looked at the doctor from her relaxed position. "You mean, other than frustrated? I feel fine. I've been feeling fine for a while now."

"I'm not asking about the recent past. How do you feel right now?"

She shrugged. "Happy. Satisfied maybe. Satisfied that the ice has been broken between these two."

Dr. Bauer nodded. "Excellent. And how did you feel when you tried to kill yourself?"

Leo turned quickly to Millie to see how she would answer. Her response startled him.

"I told you it was an accident," she said matter-of-factly.

"Was it?"

"Yes, of course it was. I didn't want to kill myself."

Dr. Bauer leaned her head in slightly. "They pumped—was it over a dozen?—Valium from your stomach. That was an accident?"

Millie held firm. "Yes. It was an accident. I didn't take them all at once."

"It was the anniversary of your son's death. That didn't have anything to do with it?"

"No," she replied forcefully.

There was silence in the room. Leo was confused. She had already told him that she had meant to kill herself. "Then why did you send me the books?" he asked innocently.

She didn't turn her head or even glance at him. She blinked and looked downward. Theresa spoke in her place. "What books?" She didn't respond. "Which books did you send to Leo?" Millie looked up toward Dr. Bauer and stared directly at her, as if to challenge her. Leo glanced back at the doctor, and was surprised to see her not backing down.

"They were two books of poetry," he said. "Swinburne and Rossetti. I gave her the Rossetti book two Christmases ago. The Swinburne book was her own. She sent them UPS last week."

"You sent him two of your favorite books," Dr. Bauer said, her focus exclusively on Millie. Millie backed down slightly, grabbing her cigarettes and fumbling with the package. "Millie, you know you cannot smoke in here."

"I need a cigarette," she said, and continued trying to light up.

"Put down the cigarette," Dr. Bauer said more forcefully, her accent strong and determined. Millie fumbled with it still. "Millie," she commanded. Her eyes glanced up at her. "Now. Put it down."

Millie complied and threw the cigarette down with the lighter. Leo was shocked.

"Thank you," Dr. Bauer said politely. Without batting an eyelash, she continued with her questions. "Why did you send Leo your books?"

"Because I thought he would like them."

"You gave away things that were important to you. Did you give away other things?"

Theresa spoke up. "She gave me some of her favorite videos."

"I said you could borrow them," she snapped back.

Dr. Bauer nodded slowly. "Millie, giving things away is a classic sign of suicide. Did you give anyone else anything?"

She scoffed. "No. Proves your theory wrong, doesn't it?"

Dr. Bauer was unphased by her attitude. "Why did you take those pills, Millie?"

The seconds passed quietly as Millie contemplated how to answer. Leo watched as she crossed her arms in frustration. She seemed trapped. He had never seen her like this. She finally spoke, with anger in her voice. "All right, so I took the pills on purpose."

Even though he knew this already, Leo found it eerie to hear her admit it so forcefully. He didn't understand, though, why she had been lying about it still. He glanced at Theresa. She was looking down into her lap.

"You didn't want to die though, did you, Millie? You said before you didn't mean to kill yourself."

"I lied."

Theresa raised her head. "Mother," she said, "don't say that. You're being ridiculous."

"No, I'm not. I did try to kill myself."

"Mother, stop. Dr. Bauer, she must be lying. She did it for the attention, isn't that what you mean?"

"Oh, please, Theresa. I didn't need to overdose to get attention."

"Then why," Dr. Bauer said, "did you try to kill yourself?"

"Isn't it obvious? You said it yourself already. The anniversary of my son's death." She spoke with a flourish, as if the point to be proven was the doctor's, not Millie's.

"Do you feel guilt over his death?"

"Yes."

"You feel as if you didn't get a chance to say everything you needed to?"

"Yes."

Leo listened to the questions and simple answers, still surprised to see how fast all of the information was coming out. Almost too fast.

"What would you say to him, right now, if he were standing before you?"

"I would say," Millie replied grandiloquently, "'Matthew, my son, I love you so much and I never meant to hurt you, and I'm completely to blame for fucking up your entire life, and for turning you into somebody who cut himself because his mother abandoned him and treated you like shit for years. I was a terrible mother and I deserve your hatred!'" She fell back into the couch again, her arms crossed, her face downtrodden.

Dr. Bauer didn't reply. She sat back in her chair with her hands pressed together brought to her lips as if to kiss the tips of her fingers. Dr. Bauer nodded. She was smug. She had made a breakthrough.

And Leo was pissed. He was angry at the doctor for her superior attitude and cockiness. He was angry at Millie, because he knew her better than this psychiatrist. Millie was lying. She never would have said those things to Matt. Worse, she had taken the memory of her son and mocked all of his years of problems and emotional issues, simply because she couldn't face up to what she had done to him. He was amazed at his own anger at her. He never knew in all of these years that he could be this angry at her, as angry as Matt had been because he couldn't deal with the same woman sitting before him now.

He realized Dr. Bauer was speaking. "I'm pleased with our session. I think we've made some excellent headway here." Leo tried not to gag. "Let's not continue with this much emotional turbulence for the moment. I suggest you spend a few more minutes speaking out on the patio or someplace else. Millie, you may have that cigarette now, outside of course."

They started to get up, but Leo remained seated. He was looking down at the glass-top table, staring at the vivid reds and yellows of the throw rug below. He wanted to say different things to her at that moment, but he controlled his tone as he spoke. "May I ask Millie a question?"

"Yes, of course, Leo," Dr. Bauer said. They sat again.

He didn't look up at her. His mind raced with questions. He chose to pinpoint her on the one she hadn't answered from before. "You never did tell me who that detective was."

"That's actually a good question, Leo. Millie hasn't told me either. I've stopped him from visiting her, though, because he upset her so much."

Leo looked up at Millie. "Who is he?"

Millie glanced at Theresa, who met her gaze briefly, then looked away. Millie looked at him. "It's really not important who he is."

"Then why did you ask if he had visited me?"

She swallowed. He could see Theresa looking back with interest now.

"Millie," Dr. Bauer said, "I need to know about him also. What does he want?"

Millie hesitated a moment, then looked at the doctor. "He works for me." She blinked. "Or, at least, he used to. I hired him. To find Jack, my ex-husband. I had always wondered what had happened to Jack, so I hired the detective to find him."

"You told me Jack was dead," Leo said. "It was . . ." he thought quickly ". . . like two years ago, you said you found out he was dead."

She met his gaze. "Yes, I know. Who do you think told me he was dead?" She turned away, then looked back at him. "He's been coming to see me for payment. I don't have money for him."

Leo glanced at Theresa, but she was looking down at the table. Her hands were on her handbag resting in her lap. He couldn't sense her feelings. She was always so difficult to read.

"Millie," Dr. Bauer said, "why didn't you tell me this?"

"I didn't want to. It's no big deal."

Millie was gazing at Leo now. She softened a bit, looking at him, sensing his anger and knowing why. "Leo, you know I loved Matthew. No matter what happened between us, I have always loved him."

He was still angry with her for mocking Matt's personal issues, but he knew that she was hurting too in this moment, and she hadn't meant to do that. She certainly hadn't meant to hurt Leo either. As he had never meant to hurt her over the past year. She had often asked him about Matt whenever they were together, and she always made it known to Leo that she would be willing to meet him halfway if he would give her a chance. She did love him. He nodded to her. His anger slowly dissipated.

Dr. Bauer arranged for them to meet the next day at the same time, but then told Millie she wanted to talk to her alone for the hour beforehand. They all agreed. Theresa was the first to get up. She kissed her mother and said good-bye to Leo and the doctor, and left the room. Leo accompanied Millie to the patio where she smoked a cigarette and he chatted with her for a few more minutes. When he left, he felt relieved. But he hoped that Millie wouldn't try to blind Dr. Bauer with half-truths and expect Theresa and him to support them.

He was stepping off of the elevator into the main lobby and heading toward the exit when he heard his name called. He turned and saw Theresa waiting for him near the information desk. "Can I speak to you for a minute?" she asked.

"Of course," he replied. They walked into the parking lot together. Dark clouds were starting to cover the sun. A rumble of thunder announced an impending storm. "Millie seems like she's doing all right," he said.

"I guess. Her spirits are up. I think you're partly responsible for that. She really does care about you."

"And I care about her. I just want to help Millie."

"I know." There was a flash of lightning behind Theresa's head, followed by another rumble and a rare cool breeze. The storm was getting closer. "Leo, did you think she really tried to kill herself?"

"At first I didn't think so. She told me it was an accident, and I believed her, but when I confronted her about the books, she told me the truth." He paused. "Theresa, why did she start taking the Valium?"

"Leo, I was as surprised as you to hear she was taking them. She did it shortly after Matt was killed, I guess. She only told me because I found them in her bathroom."

"It didn't worry you that she was taking them?"

"No, I thought about taking something myself, especially when your brother took off." The wind gusted around them. "You know, I thought she did it for the attention, not because she wanted to kill herself. With everything going on in my life, I thought she was trying to pull something to get me to pay more attention to her. I knew you hadn't been to see her either, so I figured she did it to spite us."

He wondered for a moment if that was why Theresa herself had once tried to commit suicide. He didn't ask her though. She didn't know that he knew. Instead, he replied, "You believe she would do that?"

She rolled her eyes. "Oh, yes. You don't know my mother as well as you may think you do."

He didn't agree, but he said nothing.

Another crack of lightning striking distracted them. Theresa said, "I better go before the storm starts."

He agreed, and they walked in separate directions. She suddenly called to him again. "That detective," she yelled. "Has he been to see you?"

"No, why? Has he seen you?"

"Yes," she replied.

"I guess he's desperate to get paid," he yelled back.

She didn't respond to his statement, but instead yelled back, "If he does see you, don't believe anything he says, Leo. He's a liar."

She jumped into her car and drove off. Leo stood in his place, wondering why she had asked him the same question Millie had. Did the detective expect Leo to pay for his services now?

The rain started to fall in quick heavy drops, distracting Leo and sending him racing to his car. He had gotten behind the wheel and shut his door just as the rain pelted down. A lightning bolt flashed across the dark sky and the thunder rumbled loudly a second later. The Florida tropical thunderstorm season had begun.

– NINE –

Either because he felt as if he needed a reward or he was experiencing an emotional release from the session, Leo took a swig from the second Corona he had been drinking during two-for-one happy hour at Lost and Found. The gay bar was located on Roosevelt Boulevard not far from the St. Petersburg-Clearwater airport. It was more or less on his way home from Morton Plant Hospital. He had not been here in some time. In the early years of their relationship, Matt and he would come by for happy hour or to see the drag queens perform their sappy lounge acts. Leo recognized the bleached-blond queen serving at that moment as the same bartender from years ago. In fact, the place itself looked the same. Colored streamers hung from the ceiling and mirrors reflected the disco lights flashing in the room. The aquarium was still off to the side. He swore he even recognized the same black and silver angel fish. The place hadn't changed in the least bit. It was sad, yet reassuring.

The disk jockey was playing various pop tunes, mostly upbeat, but Leo only half-listened. His thoughts were on the day. Only when someone asked if he had a light did he realize how crowded the bar had become. He looked over at one guy's watch and saw it was around 7:00 p.m. Cigarette smoke was rising in pockets around the bar. There were about thirty people in groups. He didn't recall the bar ever being this busy on a Monday.

He hadn't eaten since earlier in the day, so the beers gave him a buzz. He'd finish this beer, he decided, then make his way home to eat and rest. He was teaching tomorrow morning. On his way there he had used his cell phone to check his messages at home. Palmer had called with news that she had gotten him the job. He was grateful she had been able to help him. He couldn't let her down.

Pierce
doi:10.1300/5849_09

The bartender appeared before him and slapped down a shot glass filled with a clear liquid. A minty smell reached Leo's nose. He looked up in surprise. "What's this?"

"It's a gift," the bartender replied, chewing a wad of gum.

"Thanks, but you don't have to—"

"It's not from me, honey." He pointed diagonally across the bar where a group of guys raised their cocktails and saluted him. Two holding cosmopolitans winked, two others were laughing, and a fifth seemed to be hiding.

No one had ever bought him a drink before, and he was embarrassed. He pushed it toward the bartender and said, "If you don't mind, take it back to them. I don't want it."

"Tell them yourself," he said, then moved to fill another person's order.

Leo looked over at them and saw them giggling hysterically. He tried in that moment not to seem insensitive or unappreciative, but the last thing he wanted was to hang out with a bunch of hackling, drunk, queens. He raised the shot in their direction, and they seemed as if they were about to join him in a toast. Then, he smiled and shook his head, putting it back on the bar. He shrugged to apologize. They seemed horrified and quickly turned their back on him, apparently pissed at his lack of hospitality, or waste of a good drink. They all tittered at the one who had been hiding. Leo turned his attention back to his Corona and drank it faster. He wanted to leave as quickly as possible.

He saw over the bottle the one who had been hidden come out from behind his friends and walk down the end of the bar. He was heading toward Leo. As the person came closer through the smoke and bad lighting, Leo choked. He grabbed a napkin and covered his mouth. He forced himself to swallow the beer as it burnt his throat, and he tried to compose himself. The UPS guy was coming right toward him.

His goatee seemed newly trimmed and his hair perfectly gelled. He was wearing a T-shirt and jeans, and even in that simple outfit he looked hot. Leo had no idea what was going to happen, but he realized that he would have to stay put. He was dreading this, though, because from the behavior of the guy's friends, it was obvious that his reputation had already reached their ears. He glanced at them, and they were all staring at Leo.

"How's it going?" the guy asked. He put out a hand.

Leo hesitated, then shook it, and was surprised to feel the strength in the grip. He remembered what he had looked like in a tank top the day beforehand and knew he had a nice build, probably from the physical labor of moving all those heavy boxes. "All right," he muttered back. He could feel his stomach fluttering.

"My friends wanted to buy you the shot," he explained.

"Thank them for me, but I've had enough to drink. I was on my way home."

The guy nodded. There was an awkward silence. Leo took another swig of his beer and glanced around nervously as the guy said, "My name is Armando, by the way."

He cleared his throat. "I'm Leo," he managed to reply.

"Yes, I remember. Leo Vasari."

"You know my last name?"

"My job, remember?"

Leo nodded, an overwhelming sense of stupidity flowing through him at that moment.

"So," Armando continued, "I haven't seen you around here before. This is pretty far from your neighborhood."

"I was in Clearwater, taking care of something. I thought I'd stop by for a drink. I used to come here a few years ago when my boyfriend and I lived closer." Armando nodded in acknowledgment. Leo glanced at the shot glass and looked back at him. "You might as well drink the shot or your friends will be upset they wasted their money."

"Yeah, I guess so." He lifted the shot and was about to down it, then proffered it toward Leo. Leo raised his beer bottle and they chinked glass in an unspoken toast. Leo swallowed a large gulp of beer to calm his stomach and nerves, and Armando downed the shot in a quick swig. His face twisted in a grimace. "I hate schnapps."

Leo chuckled. "Nasty stuff."

"Tell me about it. I need a beer." He raised a hand to get the bartender's attention.

"Heineken," Leo said, "right?"

Armando glanced back at him and smiled. "How'd you know?"

"You weren't drinking the cosmo yesterday at the resort."

Armando got the bartender's attention and waited for his drink. Leo glanced over at Armando's friends and saw them giggling. It was disturbing. He waited until Armando had drunk some of the beer when he asked him, "Which one of them is your boyfriend?"

Armando smacked his lips before replying. "Actually, none of them. We broke up last night." Leo found himself pleased to hear that. "Where's your boyfriend?" Armando asked innocently.

Leo glanced down at his beer before replying. He'd been asked this question before, but not in a situation like this, where he was meeting someone new. "He . . . passed away," he replied, unable to say the D-word.

"I'm sorry to hear that." Armando looked away awkwardly.

Leo panicked for the moment, wanting to clarify things. It was sad and pathetic, but to Leo there still seemed a need among gay men to explain that a lover who had died didn't always mean it was from AIDS. "He was killed in a car accident, a year ago," he said.

"Oh, my God, that's horrible. I really am sorry."

Leo nodded in acknowledgment. They both glanced over at Armando's friends. They were still giggling and pointing. Somehow, though, the moment of excitement and nervousness had passed and Leo and Armando had entered a more somber state of mind. Neither spoke. Leo finished the last of his beer, then stood off his barstool. He was dizzy from the beer and the company, so he took a quick deep breath to get his balance. He put his hand out and waited for Armando to shake it. "I need to get going, Armando."

He looked back at him and shook his hand. "Okay. Bye, Leo."

"Thank your friends for the shot."

"Sure, no problem." Suddenly, Armando caught his arm. He had a solid grip. "Hey, Leo, if you're not doing anything tomorrow night, they do karaoke here on Tuesdays."

"Karaoke?" he said, trying to stifle his laughter.

"Yeah, it's hokey, I know, but we have fun. Why don't you come join us?"

Leo glanced back at Armando's friends, then back at Armando. "I don't know. I'll see." He said good night and left. As he walked down the side of the bar, he took another deep breath and kept his balance as he passed Armando's friends. He glanced up at them with a grin, and acknowledged them by saying "Ladies," to which one or two giggled and another called him a bitch. He ignored them and left the bar, an odd feeling of satisfaction and nervousness bubbling within him.

Armando filled Leo's dreams with a sexual potency he hadn't experienced in a long time. He woke up during the night highly aroused and jerked off in bed to his dreams of the hot Latino and him fucking on top of the bar as the disco ball and pulsating lights pounded off the walls and their sweaty bodies. He slept soundly after that.

Early the next morning, he sat at his computer working through Swinburne and Rossetti, writing about five new pages about how their poems could be incorporated into his thesis on the "Clytemnestra Complex." He also put together a syllabus for his class. On his way out the door, he stopped and looked at himself in the foyer mirror. His hair was neat, he was clean-shaven, and he was even wearing a tie. He looked like a successful man. He was on the road before 8:00 a.m., and weaved through rush hour morning traffic across the bridge into Tampa. He was anxious to get to school early, but found himself decelerating as he passed the spot between the end of the bridge and the exit for the mall and airport. He peered at the estuary where it had happened. He wondered if he'd ever be able to drive past this area without slowing down.

He continued on to school. His class was Tuesdays and Thursdays from 9:00 a.m. to noon. His first class that morning went surprisingly well. They even had a decent discussion on Faulkner's "A Rose for Emily." Sophocles's *Oedipus the King* was coming up, so he'd have to do some homework for that himself. On the way to his office, he picked up two joints from his contact who was teaching the same summer term as he. He also stopped by Palmer's office and presented her with his five pages and new citations. Her surprise at his progress was evident.

From USF Leo went straight to the hospital to participate in the next scheduled session with Millie and Theresa. It was after 3:00 p.m.

as he made it into Dr. Bauer's office and greeted everyone with apologies for being late. They were waiting for him and even Theresa gave him a small smile when he entered. Dr. Bauer was the first to comment on his attitude. "You seem like you've had a good day."

"He's wearing a tie again," Millie commented.

"I was given a class to teach at the last minute," he announced proudly. "And my research is going well for a change. I'm actually looking forward to going home and writing for a change."

"Excellent," Dr. Bauer said.

"Oh, please," Millie said, "you had sex with the UPS guy."

Leo was speechless. "No!" he protested with a laugh. Although he certainly had to admit to himself the idea had its merits.

"You're seeing someone?" Theresa asked. He could sense something in her voice. Disappointment? Surprise? He couldn't tell.

"No, I'm not seeing anyone."

"But he wants to screw this guy," Millie continued.

"Mother!" Theresa said, shaking her head in dismay. Millie was grinning broadly though, tickled to death that she was embarrassing Leo.

"So tell us about him," Dr. Bauer said.

Leo turned back to face her. He thought she was joking, but he realized from her hands clasped prayerlike, her eyes peering at him through her glasses, that she was serious. "I don't think so," he said. "I don't want to talk about this."

"Why not?" she asked.

"Because there's nothing to talk about. Yes, I'm attracted to this guy, but I don't want to talk about him." He saw them all staring at him. "All right, so we met up accidentally yesterday, and he wants me to meet him and his friends tonight."

"You're going, right?" Millie asked.

"I don't know. I haven't decided yet."

"Oh, please, just go. You need to get it on with this guy."

"Mother, you are so embarrassing!" Theresa exclaimed.

"Okay," Leo replied, "enough talking about me please!"

"May I ask you, though," Dr. Bauer said, "if you have dated anyone else since Matthew died?"

He swallowed. "No."

"It's been difficult to move on, hasn't it?"

His excitement was dissipating rapidly. "Yes." She was about to ask him another question, when he interrupted, his hand raised. "Look, I'm not here to talk about me. We're here for Millie, remember? My personal relationships aren't why we're here."

"As I said yesterday, your happiness and well-being are related to Millie's recovery."

"I understand that, but I'm not comfortable talking about my sex life with everyone, so I prefer we drop it."

"All right. There is a reason in a way why I'm bringing this up, though. As you both know, Millie and I met for the past hour and we discussed a few things regarding her relationship with her son that I think we should talk about."

Leo was becoming very uncomfortable. The atmosphere in the room had become quite serious, and his elation was deflated. He sat back in the chair forcefully. He reminded himself it was to help Millie. He would comply.

"Yesterday," she continued, "Millie mentioned that Matthew was a cutter. I'd like to talk about that and how it affected all of your lives. Millie, why don't you start and tell Theresa and Leo what you told me a little while ago, about how you felt that night when Leo called you and told you he had found Matthew in the bathroom?"

Leo closed his eyes to calm himself. He didn't want to discuss this.

He could hear Millie answer, with more courage in her own feelings. He wondered if she had been prepped. "I was disappointed," she said. "I really thought he was beyond all this. He had done great with his life. I was disappointed that he had failed again. He had been so strong, and I couldn't believe that he had failed again."

"Matt did not fail," Leo interrupted without thinking. He opened his eyes and saw Millie sitting back against the sofa with her arms folded across her chest. She looked at him. "Matt's problem was a build up of stress and anxiety over everything. We know already that it happened when you had moved to Clearwater. That's when it all started." He turned toward Dr. Bauer. "We already discussed that during one of our sessions with Matt when he was in the hospital. Millie walked out." He could sense his own anger steadily increasing as a memory of a past therapy session flashed in his mind. Two days in a row and he was angry at Millie, and never once before in the past couple of years since he had met her had he been mad at her.

"Leo's right," she agreed. "I walked out during the session. I wasn't about to sit around and subject myself to accusations because he couldn't handle his own life."

Leo was grateful at least she was being honest and not denying the truth.

"You weren't surprised by his actions, though, were you, Millie?" Dr. Bauer asked.

"No. I wasn't surprised to hear that he had done it again. I was surprised that it had happened with Leo, because Leo was the best thing that had ever happened to him."

"Did you think it was safe to come back into his life?"

Millie shrugged. "I guess. When I heard that they were in this relationship, I guess I thought it wouldn't hurt for me to try to reunite with him."

"How did you find out about their relationship?"

Theresa responded. "I told her. Mother had told me she wanted to move closer to me and she was worried about how Matt would react. I told her about how well he and Leo were doing, and I encouraged her to take it slowly with him."

"Millie, do you accept responsibility for doing things that might have caused your son great pain, that he would revert back to his old behavior?"

Leo gazed at her as she considered her response. He thought about her reply from the day before, and it occurred to him that perhaps Dr. Bauer had been more aware of Millie's faked confession than he believed. He watched as Millie nodded her head slowly and exhaled. "Okay, I'll accept that maybe I did things that screwed him up. But I never dreamed that he would try to kill himself."

Leo fumed silently. Matt had not tried to kill himself.

"Theresa," Dr. Bauer said, turning her attention toward her, "how did you react to the news that same night?"

"I was shocked. I knew that he had been in the hospital before, but I thought it was some adolescent attention thing. I couldn't believe he had tried to kill himself."

"Why does everyone keep saying Matt tried to kill himself?" Leo shouted. He turned his attentions toward Dr. Bauer. "You know about cutting, right? People who cut themselves are doing it to release pain, not to cause more pain."

"Yes, Leo," Dr. Bauer said, "that's true. But self-mutilators can go too far."

Leo squirmed. He hated the word *self-mutilators*. It made Matt seem like a monster. "I understand that. But Matt didn't try to kill himself."

Millie spoke. "What about his car accident?"

Leo turned toward her. "What about it?" He didn't want her to say it. He couldn't believe she still thought this.

"He purposely caused that accident."

"Don't say that!" Leo yelled. There was an anguish rising from his stomach, through his chest, into his throat and face. He could feel his eyes watering. "That crash was an accident! The police said so! Besides, how would you know, you hadn't seen him in weeks at that point!"

"I did—" she started, but then stopped herself.

"What?" he said, but she only shook her head. He was too upset to question her further about this. The pain was pounding in his body, and he struggled not to cry. He glanced at Theresa and saw her sitting there with her hands on her purse in her lap like an innocent schoolmarm who knew nothing of the world. It infuriated him, knowing she had her own secrets. She was sitting there smug, like the innocent child. He vented his anger toward her suddenly. Without thinking, he said to Millie, "You're wrong about the car accident and the cutting, Millie. Matt wasn't your suicidal child. She was."

He regretted his words as soon as they were spoken. He didn't know if Millie was aware of Theresa's suicide attempt, and he knew it wasn't his place to be the one to reveal it. But his anguish over the thought of Matt cutting himself and purposely crashing his car had overwhelmed him. It was too late though. He had opened his mouth.

He looked at them and saw Theresa sitting in the same position she had been a few moments beforehand. Her hands clutched tightly the purse in her lap.

Millie sat upright in the sofa and gave him a confused look. She glanced at Dr. Bauer, then Theresa, then back at him. "Leo, what are you talking about?" He didn't respond. "Theresa, what is he talking about?"

Dr. Bauer encouraged her. "Theresa? Is there something you'd like to say?"

She didn't reply at first. She clutched her purse more tightly. He could see her knuckles and fingers turning bright pink. She slowly took a deep breath and looked up at Leo. "I had no idea you even knew," she said. She didn't seem angry at him. He had a difficult time reading her, so he was uncertain how she felt at that moment. She released her hold on the purse.

Millie's face revealed her surprise. "I don't understand. What happened?"

She spoke frankly. "I cut my wrists." Millie grabbed Theresa's forearms and turned them over roughly. She traced with her finger lightly over the scars now almost faded. "I was very lucky," Theresa continued. "I did what most people do, and I screwed up by cutting the wrong way. George found me, and took me to the hospital."

"When did this happen?" Millie asked. He could sense frustration in her voice.

She shrugged. "Fifteen years ago? Something like that."

"Oh, for Christ's sake, Theresa! Why didn't you tell me?" She threw Theresa's arms away from her and jumped up from the sofa. She paced to Theresa's left.

"You were in Florida. You had your own problems. Matt was giving you trouble."

"You should have told me! I would have come to you!"

Theresa looked up at her mother and spoke bluntly. "No, you wouldn't have. Anytime I ever spoke to you, you were intoxicated. If I had called you, you'd probably have been too drunk to even know what I had said." Her words created a dense silence.

Millie stopped pacing, and squatted before her daughter. She didn't seem troubled by her daughter's accusation, but Leo knew that she must be hurting. "Why did you do this?"

She looked away from her mother. "I had a miscarriage."

Millie jerked back, startled. "You were pregnant?" Theresa nodded jerkily. "But I thought. . ." Millie glanced nervously at Leo, then focused back on Theresa. "I thought you weren't able to conceive."

Tears started to fall slowly from Theresa's eyes. She reached into her bag and pulled out a tissue and wiped her eyes. Leo felt terrible for having said anything. He watched with a heavy heart as Theresa spoke for the first time about her own pain. She swallowed hard and wiped at her nose. "I know," Theresa choked. "We tried so many times and it worked. It was like a miracle! I couldn't believe it. I was so happy. But I couldn't carry it. I had a miscarriage in the fourth month." She sobbed into her tissues.

"But you never even told me you were pregnant!"

"I was too afraid. I didn't tell anyone. I even made George promise not to tell Rosa I was pregnant. I wanted to wait until I knew it would be okay."

Millie covered her face with her hands and exhaled deeply. She reached out and took her daughter's hands in her own. "I am so sorry I wasn't there for you. I would have helped you. You know that, don't you? I would have done anything for you. I love you, and I would have done anything to protect you."

Theresa didn't respond, but sobbed into her tissues. Mother and daughter hugged and Millie kissed her daughter's forehead. Then, he heard Millie whisper to her, "That bastard did this to you, but he's gone now and can't hurt us anymore." Leo glanced over at Dr. Bauer, but she didn't seem concerned by these final words. He disregarded them himself. He assumed she was referring to George, and he couldn't be bothered if Millie hated him that much. He left them silently without saying a word.

It rained sporadically while Leo drove home, but no serious storms had passed over central St. Petersburg that day, so the afternoon sun was hot late into the afternoon. When he arrived at his house, he put his briefcase and books into his office. He dressed in a tank top and workout shorts. He had to get out. He was restless and needed to zone out. He grabbed one of the two joints he had bought earlier that day, and headed into the backyard.

The shed was a rusting metal building he wanted to tear down but needed to keep. It was packed with junk and tools he hardly ever used. The lawnmower had to be moved out to get around inside, so he did this. He pulled out his bicycle, resting quietly against a second unused one. His was aging with rust and the tires were nearly flat. The second one was in better shape, but he didn't dare touch it. He hopped on his own and rode around to the front of the house, heading down his street. The bumps from the bricks ached his ass, but he ignored the pain. The street changed to a regular paved road as he turned right onto Beach Drive.

Within minutes, he had cut through North Shore Park and passed by the municipal swimming pool. He rode onto Bayshore Drive and peddled furiously on another brick street. He continued toward the Renaissance Vinoy hotel, the old neo-Mediterranean complex that had been restored and painted hot pink then expanded to take over a city block in size. He rode around it along the seawall of Tampa Bay. He passed a few local Rollerbladers and retired walkers. Some smiled at him as he peddled past, but he ignored them. Passing the hotel, he headed for Vinoy Park with its myriad Greco-style statues dotting the walkways. He reached the neoclassical Museum of Fine Arts and turned left down 2nd Avenue, taking it toward the bay.

The paved street and its sidewalks stopped at the six-story upside-down pyramidal structure known as The Pier. It had been here forever, or so it seemed to Leo, but only in the past couple of years had it gone through a complete renovation along with the rest of this district. It was a popular tourist attraction again, with a night club on the roof, a Spanish restaurant, and tourist trap shops. A turquoise trolley clanged past him. He raced past a few straggling cars. Two black children were fishing off of the cement wall. He raced to the very end of The Pier, riding to the back, where he could lean his bicycle against a cement post and walk down onto the wooden fishing pier that creaked under his feet.

He found a quiet spot by himself where a brown pelican rested at one end. He sat with his legs dangling over the murky water below. He lit the joint. He inhaled it deeply, savoring the burning sensation in his throat and the smoky cannabis in his lungs and head. It soothed him almost instantly as he struggled to release the pain of the day.

He hated the session they had had. He felt sore and vulnerable. It had been a year since Matt's death, and he seemed to be the only one who had a difficult time talking about it. Millie and Theresa were fine discussing it. He didn't understand how that was possible. He couldn't help but question their affection for Matt as compared to his. He had to have loved him more.

As he inhaled again, he realized the absurdity of his own thought. You couldn't compare love like it was fluid in a measuring cup. Everyone's love was different and couldn't be evaluated one against the other. He was holding on so tightly to the memory of his lover that to have people speak about him, dead, was like they were wrenching him away from Leo.

He detested that they had deflated his exuberance that morning. Millie had been right. To a certain extent, the teaching and research had been productive and had invigorated him. But it was the thought of Armando that had charged him all day. And then they had cornered Leo about him. He didn't want to let thoughts of Armando go too. He suddenly hated Dr. Bauer and her psychological bullshit. He puffed on the joint so that he inhaled the smoke through his nostrils and down his throat. He was feeling lightheaded but relaxed.

He wished he hadn't opened his mouth during the session. Maybe it was good that Theresa's secret had come out, but it wasn't Leo's place to have revealed it. What made him the messenger? He was no one special in this equation. Theresa had been right. He was the outsider, the Pierce-in-law. He wasn't the son or the brother. Yet, it seemed as if he were playing Matt's role now. They were a triangle that had him equilaterally opposed to Millie and Theresa. He had replaced Matt in that family dynamic. And this wasn't the only triangular relationship he had been in with them. There had been Millie, Matt, and him in another triangle, one that had been emotionally disturbing for the apex of that triangle, definitely not equilateral for him.

Leo's mind wandered, and he realized he was thinking now of relationships in terms of Hegel and Sedgwick, and his head pounded. He shook it, then rubbed it to let it go.

Voices of children were getting louder around him. He sensed them coming onto the fishing pier and felt the wooden planks wobble and shake beneath him from their steps. He glanced at them with their fishing poles and fishing net. They were laughing loudly. They made the pelican fly away. He turned back to look across the water toward Tampa with the towers of the downtown business district like tiny blocks in the distance. The sun was setting behind him, The Pier blocking it from warming his neck. The eastern sky was a dull bluish-gray spotted with purple. Someone might think it was beautiful. Leo thought it looked like a giant bruise. He imagined the sunset behind him in bright pink and pale blue colors, but he didn't turn around.

The kids were coming closer, and they talked softly now, heading toward him. He looked at them. The taller of the two pointed toward him with his one hand, the other holding the fishing net over his shoulder. "You got a doobie? Can we have some?"

They had to be no more than ten and twelve years old. Leo was startled by their bravery, but obviously they weren't new to drugs. It made him sad for the moment, then sick. He realized he was still holding the lit joint in his fingers. He closed his eyes for the moment to regain his composure. He glanced down at the joint and quickly flicked it into the water. "Sorry, guys. All gone," he said.

"Aw, man, you fucking suck! Wasting good shit!" The other called him an asshole. They stormed off to the other side of the wooden pier, purposely stomping their feet so that the pier rocked. Glad he had been smart enough not to encourage their habit, he stood up and took a deep breath. He was high, but he focused on the darkening sky. He waited a few more minutes until the sky grew darker and the purple diminished to a dull iron gray. Then, he turned and left. He hopped on his bicycle and headed back around The Pier for home.

Halfway down the road, he realized he was having a difficult time keeping steady and almost hit a couple walking toward him. He stopped and got off the bicycle to walk it. The setting sun warmed him. Its blinding rays reached around the buildings of downtown St.

Petersburg. He moved slowly and gradually the sun fell faster than he was walking. It was twilight. The streetlamps flickered on.

He had reached the corner of 2nd Avenue, just before the art museum. On the corner stood the outdoor public toilets. He thought about peeing and put his bicycle against the railing. He looked up and saw a burly guy, darkly tanned, wearing a tank top and biking shorts, just hanging around. He didn't think anything of him at first, then realized the guy was touching his package in his skintight shorts. The guy made a quick jerking motion with his head toward the restroom.

Leo hesitated. The pot had made him horny, and he was surprised to feel himself responding. He wouldn't mind getting a little right then and there. Even if the restroom was disgusting. Even if the guy was disgusting. He took a sharp breath and headed up the ramp. The guy walked into the restroom.

Then, Leo stopped. His hard-on was swelling, but a thought suddenly crossed his mind. It was probably only about seven o'clock or so. If he went home, ate something, and got ready, he could still make it for karaoke. He smiled to himself, turned around, and hopped on his bicycle. As he peddled away, he saw the guy step out from the restroom and give him a look of confusion, but Leo ignored him. He was determined to make the end of his night be as good as the morning had been.

– TEN –

Walking up the short ramp to the bar, Leo could hear music penetrating the cinderblocks. He felt nervous. He wondered if Armando would show up. He opened the door and stepped inside. His first impression was exactly what he dreaded it would be: drunk gay guys laughing their asses off at an overweight fag hag singing a Whitney Houston ballad terribly off-key. He would have found it funny too, he realized, if it wasn't so awful.

The room wasn't large, but there were about forty people crowding around the bar, hovering near the karaoke equipment, and playing darts in the corner. Cigarette smoke wafted like a layer of air above the heads of the people. He peered through the groups in the amber-pink lighting but didn't see Armando anywhere. He suddenly wondered if he had been set up somehow. He calmed himself down. They were probably just late.

He squeezed up to the bar and waited until a bartender he didn't recognize finally asked him what he wanted. He ordered his usual Corona. He was just taking a swallow when a voice called to him from the other end of the bar. "Leo? Is that you?" he heard.

Leo looked down and tried to figure out who had called him. He saw hands waving. As the person came toward him, he recognized Doug Donovan, a friend of Matt's and his. They had not seen each other since the previous summer, and that had been on one of Leo's rare excursions out after Matt's death. Prior to that, the last time he had seen him had been at Matt's funeral. Matt and he used to be regulars at Doug's frequent parties.

Tonight, Doug was sipping through a thin straw his usual bourbon and Coke. He was wearing torn jeans and a leather vest with a chain linked across his bare chest. Both of his ears were pierced with silver

Pierce
© 2007 by The Haworth Press, Inc. All rights reserved.
doi:10.1300/5849_10

loops. Doug was close to forty now, and his graying hair complimented his looks. Leo knew he was kind-hearted, and regretted that
he had not kept in touch. After the funeral, Doug had made attempts
to get Leo out, but Leo had pulled away from Doug too.

When Doug got to him, they hugged each other warmly. Leo felt
liquor lips kiss him on the cheek. He apologized for having been such
a terrible friend, but Doug rolled his eyes at him. "Please, whatever.
Don't worry about it. After my mother died, I was a mess for like two
years, so I totally understand. How are you doing though?" He
sucked on his straw.

Leo shrugged. "Hanging in there, I guess. Trying to move on." He
glanced around the bar again unsuccessfully. "What's new with you?"

He flashed open the vest. "I have matching nipple jewelry now."
The last time he had seen him out, he had had his left nipple newly
pierced. Now both were, and Leo realized the silver link chain was attached to the nipple rings.

Leo chuckled. "That's fucked up."

"Pull on the chain." Leo hesitated. "Do it!" he ordered. Leo grabbed
the chain and pulled. He watched Doug's eyes roll up into his head
and his body shiver. "It's like heaven," he said, licking his lips.

"You're messed up," Leo said laughing. It was good to see him
again.

A heavyset queen started crooning "Somewhere Over the Rain-
bow" from the karaoke station, and Leo acknowledged unconsciously
that he was on key at least. He glanced around the bar again, and
thought he saw a cosmo or two being poured. He thought he recognized two of Armando's friends getting their drinks, so maybe he was
here. He didn't see him though.

There was silence for a few seconds as Doug sipped from his drink.
Leo wondered what else they had to talk about. It was almost frightening how a close friend from the past could return like this and instead of finding things to catch up on, they had nothing to say at all.
They both opened their mouths and started speaking at the same
time, then laughed. "You first," Doug said.

"I was going to ask if you were still seeing that guy from last year."

"Simon? That basket case? Please, we're in a relationship for like nine months, and suddenly he decides that he's a top and doesn't want to be fucked anymore. So you know that was a complete waste of my time, because you know I'm exclusively a top!" He sipped hard on his drink.

Leo nodded laughingly. "Uh-huh. Right, exclusive top."

"Shut up, you!" he said, giving Leo a light smack across his face.

In the minute or so they had been talking, other people entered the bar. Leo looked up and saw the back of a head that he thought he recognized. He saw the guy look around the bar, but not at him, then head toward the cosmo queens. When he got there, Leo saw it was Armando, and his stomach fluttered. He took a gulp of his beer, then realized Doug was snapping fingers in his face. "Uh, hello?"

"Sorry."

Doug turned and saw where he was looking. "Oh, okay, I get it now. He's a hottie. I've seen him here a few times."

"Do you know him?"

"No, but I'd love to. Looks like he's got some yummy boy butt going on."

Leo laughed. "He's not really a boy. He's in his late twenties, I think."

"Please, at my age, anyone under thirty-five is a boy." He sipped on his drink, then glanced back at Leo. "Wait a minute. You couldn't possibly have guessed his age from here. Do you know him?"

"No." Leo took another swig of his beer.

"You liar. You do so."

Leo grinned sheepishly. "Let's just say that we've met and I'd like to get to know him better."

"What's his name?"

"Armando."

"Sexy name. Did you fuck yet?"

"No! Why does everyone think that?"

"Because we're gay. So did you know Armando was going to be here tonight?"

"Well, he told me to meet him here." Leo gulped down the last of his beer forcefully.

Doug could only nod with a grin. "Then you better go talk to him."

Leo shook his head. "No, just wait. Let it happen naturally."

"Nothing happens naturally, Leo. Let's wave him over." He raised his arm and was about to call out his name, when Leo smacked him in the head and made him stop. He yelped in false pain, then laughed. "All right. I have to go take a piss. I'll be back."

Doug took his drink with him and headed down the bar. He moved toward the doorway leading to the restrooms. Suddenly, he stopped and winked at Leo, who watched in horror as Doug walked up to Armando and his friends and tapped Armando on the shoulder. They talked for a few seconds, then Doug pointed in Leo's direction. Armando turned toward him and smiled, and Doug gave Armando a peck on the cheek and disappeared waving behind him. Leo was mortified.

Armando came down the bar toward Leo holding a Heineken. He was wearing a polo shirt and jeans. Leo felt a little underdressed suddenly, wearing only a boring T-shirt. He glanced down at Armando's package, and he was pleased to see the jeans framed it well. Leo quickly ordered another beer, and when he turned back, Armando was standing before him.

"How's it going?" he asked.

Leo nodded. "Good. You?"

"Excellent," he replied.

Leo paid for his beer and took a swallow. He felt silly, like he was suffering from first date syndrome. Armando squeezed beside him and leaned against the bar. He drank from his beer. Leo leaned in slightly and said, "I'm sorry about my friend bugging you."

He laughed. "Don't worry about it. I'm glad he showed me where you were." As an afterthought, he said, "I wasn't sure if you'd show up."

Leo shrugged. "Karaoke isn't my thing, but I figured I'd check it out. It can't be that bad." As if on cue, the drunk fag hag started howling "I Will Always Love You." Leo and Armando looked at each other with horrified looks. "I take that back." They both laughed.

As the song screeched on for the next couple of minutes, they tried to ignore her and carry on a conversation but were unsuccessful. Finally, she stopped singing, and people applauded and booed simultaneously. She insisted on singing another song, and "How Will I Know" started. Leo was in utter shock and knew his dismay was apparent on his face. Armando spoke to him laughingly. Leo asked him what he said one more time, and he moved closer to Leo so that he was only a few inches away from his head. He caught the smell of an exotic cologne that he didn't recognize. He liked it. "Do you want to get out of here?" Armando asked.

Leo nodded forcefully. "Yes, please. Thank you." They downed their beers. They were getting ready to leave, when Leo asked, "What about your friends?"

"They'll be all right. What about your friend?"

Leo looked back at the far end of the bar and saw Doug toasting him with a fresh cocktail. He was getting friendly with Armando's cosmo girls. One of them was pulling on his chain. Doug motioned for them to toast as well, and bourbon and Coke and four cosmos lifted in the air. Doug waved, and they left.

In typical Florida fashion, as soon as they stepped outside the muggy dampness of the night hit them. They heard the girl squeal through the wall, and Leo had to put his hands to his ears. "My God, she sucks!"

"She's here every week," Armando said laughing.

"Can't they throw her out?"

"She's comic relief. People love her."

"Yeah, well, I don't find that funny at all."

Armando shrugged. "You get used to her." He added quickly, "Are you hungry? I didn't have time to eat dinner."

Leo had eaten something, but he didn't tell him that. At least it would be a place where they could sit down and talk. Armando suggested they go to a local twenty-four-hour family restaurant a short distance down Roosevelt Boulevard. They took separate cars even though they probably could have walked. Armando drove an older, white, four-door Hyundai, a sharp contrast to the brown truck Leo had already identified with him.

Leo had never been to this restaurant, although he had driven by it many times in the past. It was unimpressive on the outside, but indoors it was like stepping back in time. It resembled a 1950s diner with turquoise booths, pink walls, and terrazzo tables. The chrome shone and the lights were bright. Elvis Presley sang through the restaurant from mini jukeboxes at each table. A plump waitress in a turquoise and pink uniform and too much makeup, her badge on her breast reading "Suzie," told them to seat themselves. She handed them menus and took their drink orders. They both ordered beers again.

There were only about a dozen people in the restaurant, most sitting on the smoking side. They looked at their menus. Suzie brought them their drinks and put the wrong bottles in front of each of them. When they switched them, she said innocently to Armando in her Pinellas Park twang, "Oh, I thought for sure you was the Corona boy." They were about to order when a voice called from the smoking side and Suzie said she would come back to take their order.

They both chuckled at the spectacle. Then, Leo remarked, "That was rather inappropriate of her though," referring to her comment about the beer.

Armando shrugged. "Stereotypes. The curse of being a Latino. We drink only Corona or tequila. Being Cuban is the same as being Mexican or Puerto Rican. We all know how to salsa. We all have big dicks. . . ."

Leo smirked. "Oh, I see. And I suppose only the last stereotype is accurate."

Armando raised his eyebrows and drank from his beer in response, his lips forming a grin around the lip of the bottle.

"Sorry, boys," Suzie said, returning. "Assholes over there've been bitching at me all night. And Tula and Jamie both called out sick. I hate them bitches. So what'll it be?"

Armando ordered a pork barbecue sandwich and fries, and Leo ordered a Caesar salad with grilled chicken. After Suzie took their menus and left, Leo asked, "So what other stereotype is true in your case?" Armando eyed him suggestively with a flirtatious grin. Leo reddened against his will. "I was referring to whether you were Cuban."

"Half-Cuban, half-Venezuelan. I'm totally American though. I was born in Orlando. My mother's family is Cuban. They came over with the whole Castro thing. The family used to manufacture cigars, but they lost everything when they fled the country."

"And your father?"

"My father was a successful Venezuelan businessman, so I'm told. I never knew him. He got my mother pregnant and took off without marrying her."

"That's scandalous."

"It was, especially for my mother's family. Her parents threw her out, but after I was born they took her back in. I think it helped with my grandfather because she gave me their family name. She named me after my great-grandfather, Armando Sedilla, the guy who started their cigar business." He drank some of the Heineken.

Armando was very interesting. It was embarrassing to think how Leo had first met him and insulted him. Leo drank his Corona. "How did you wind up in St. Petersburg?"

"I went to the Poynter Institute in St. Petersburg for journalism. They have a great program. I got a scholarship." He went on to explain that he did freelance work, but was at UPS to pay the bills. "I live with my aunt over in Feather Sound." He paused. "Listen to me babbling. I'm supposed to be the reporter, not the interview subject. What about you? What's your story?"

Leo was enjoying listening to someone else's story. He had stopped thinking about things in his own life for a change. He wondered how to answer Armando's question. His life has been in total chaos for over a year now, and the latest events weren't making things better or easier. He wondered if he should tell Armando about some of what was going on in his life, then thought better of it. "I moved here from New Jersey. I'm teaching, at USF in Tampa."

"You teach college? How old are you?"

"Twenty-nine," he replied. He could have mentioned about his birthday, but held off.

"You look much younger than that."

Leo glanced at him with a surprised look. Instead of commenting, he asked back, "How old are you?" He downed the last of his Corona.

"I'll be twenty-seven in a few months. I took my time going through college," he explained. He glanced down sheepishly, then said, "Actually, I suck at math. I had to repeat math classes a few times." He continued quickly, "What do you teach?"

"English." Leo hesitated a moment, then added, "I'm working on my PhD." He started tearing at the label on the Corona bottle.

Armando nodded slowly. "Now that's impressive. So not only are you good-looking, but you're brainy too." He proceeded to drink the rest of his beer, and Leo could see that he was getting red in the face. He sensed it of himself as well. Suzie returning with their food saved him from having to reply. She bitched about the customers and her fellow waitresses again. They chuckled after she left. Armando dove into his sandwich, and Leo picked at his salad, finding himself with little appetite. He realized he was queasy from excited nervousness.

Armando started to fire off questions about Leo's dissertation, his studies, and his teaching, almost like an interview or an article subject. But Leo noticed that Armando was actually listening and trying to get to know him better. After a few minutes of this, Leo asked Armando about his freelance work.

"I write mostly entertainment pieces, movie and music reviews. Over the past year, I started writing about the Latino experience. I've got an irregular column in the *Weekly Planet*. 'Latino Living' by A. J. Sedilla."

"I don't read that paper very much." He added flirtatiously, "I will now though."

Armando laughed. They continued eating. When they were done, Suzie returned to clean up. She asked if they wanted another round of beers, and Leo was going to have one, but then Armando said he had better not because he was driving. Leo was impressed by his sense of responsibility. He turned down another beer himself, giving the same reasons, although he was craving a fourth. Leo felt himself comfortable with Armando, and they seemed to be getting along pretty well. He was definitely attracted to him. He wondered what Matt would think of Armando, not to mention Leo out with him.

The thought of Matt in that moment made him feel weird suddenly, as if a weight had landed on his chest. It apparently showed on his face.

"Are you all right?" Armando asked. "You look like you zoned out somewhere."

He couldn't explain to him how he felt at that moment. He tried to figure out what it was. Guilt? Grief? "My mind wanders sometimes."

"Do you want to go?"

Leo nodded, and they got out of the booth. They paid Suzie, splitting the bill. They stepped outside. As they walked toward their cars parked beside each other, Leo found his mind wandering back to Matt again, and now it annoyed him. He felt like his entire evening was being ruined by his own thoughts. He realized Armando was talking to him, and he hadn't heard him, so he focused on him as a diversion. He asked him to repeat his last sentence.

"I asked if you wanted to go back to the bar or do something else."

"I do not want to go back to the bar."

Armando laughed. He looked at his watch. "I guess you're right. Whitney is probably still doing another set."

Leo laughed, envisioning the awful fag hag. "No, I definitely don't want to go back there. Can we just hang out here for a while?"

"Sure," Armando replied, although it seemed by his tone that this had surprised him. "Let's get in my car. We can put the air on so we don't sweat to death." Armando unlocked his Hyundai and hopped behind the wheel. Leo opened the passenger side door and waited while Armando tossed things off the front seat into the back. "Sorry, my car is a mess."

Leo settled into the passenger seat and shut the door. Armando started the car and turned on the air-conditioning. He reached over to adjust the vents, and his hand casually brushed against Leo's thigh. He reacted almost instantly. Armando didn't seem to notice, though, which Leo thought was a good thing. "So, uh, why did you and your boyfriend break up?" he asked.

"Too much drama," Armando said. "He and his friends are a bit much for me."

"Is that the cosmo set?"

"Yeah, pretty much so. I'm good friends with one of them, but not the rest."

"They seemed to encourage buying me that shot last night."

Armando got uncomfortable. "Let's not go there. That was awk-ward."

"I can imagine."

"Well, probably not." He looked quickly at him, and said, "They didn't order it to get us to meet. They ordered it because I made the mistake of pointing you out as the guy who had. . .um. . .you know, that morning. . ."

Leo shut his eyes and turned away. "Say no more."

There was silence. "Shit," Armando said. "I'm sorry. I shouldn't have told you. The thing is, after they sent the drink over, I had to come talk to you. I felt really bad."

"It's okay," Leo said, opening his eyes and staring forward. "You didn't have to come over to apologize for them. Probably better if you hadn't." He was amazed at how quickly he was feeling stupid and pa-thetic. "Besides, I guess I deserved it. I was an asshole to you that morning. I regretted it afterward."

"No, Leo, you don't understand," he said. He put his hand on Leo's left shoulder and rubbed it. "I'm glad that they bought you that drink, even if they did it for other reasons, because I did want to talk to you." He reached upward with his hand and rubbed the back of Leo's head. He slowly maneuvered Leo's head so that he had to look at him. Armando eyes were gazing back with a serious look to them.

"Leo, I'm not joking. That morning, I know it was awkward, and I admit I got pissed because you blew me off. But I was really into you. I thought you were adorable. You were half awake and you had this natural look to you. No pretensions. And you had that morning hard-on." He grinned. Leo glanced away, embarrassed, but turned back. Armando was still stroking the back of his head. It soothed Leo. "I couldn't stop thinking about you the rest of the day. When another package came for you, I hoped I'd see you again, but you weren't there. Then when I saw you on Sunday, I was with my ex. You acted silly with me, so I knew you were embarrassed, and I wanted to talk to you longer, but I saw him waiting for me in the shadows, so I had to go. You have no idea how glad I am that they bought you that shot last night."

Leo listened to him, watched as he spoke with what seemed like genuine words, and saw that his eyes looked serious and intent on what he was saying. It was very sweet. Or total bullshit. He was going to say as much, and opened his mouth to speak, but suddenly Armando moved closer and pulled Leo's head toward him. Their lips met and Leo could feel the goatee rubbing against his face and his lips pressing against his own. The physical connection was both startling and pleasurable. He loved the tingling feeling against his face and reached out with his own arms to touch Armando's hair and neck. They kissed softly at first, then harder, and Armando pushed them closer together, so that they were separated only by the emergency brake.

Armando kept one hand on the back of Leo's head and reached down with the other across his chest, downward, reaching into his lap, pressing his hand against Leo's cock, swollen in his jeans. Leo was startled by how fast he was moving, but he did the same, and was startled to feel that Armando's cock was hard already, stretched off to the left side in his jeans. Armando moaned as soon as Leo touched his cock and started squeezing it. Armando reciprocated by doing the same. Armando pushed his tongue into Leo's mouth, and he welcomed it, licking it with his own, then pushing it into Armando's. He continued to moan and Leo reveled in the sensations pulsating through his body. He hadn't felt this intensity in a very long time.

There was suddenly banging on the windows of the car, from all sides it seemed, and they quickly broke apart, their hearts pounding. A bunch of kids laughed hysterically as they headed into the restaurant. They pointed and found themselves highly amused by their own antics. Armando and Leo looked at each and laughed. Leo was extremely grateful they were joking and hadn't caused a scene or actually hurt them. They weren't exactly in a gay-friendly neighborhood. "I think we better get out of here," Leo said.

Armando nodded. "I'd like to keep. . .'talking'. . .if you want to."

Leo chuckled. "Yes, definitely. Where do you want to go?"

"I don't know. We can't go to my place. My aunt's home."

"You can come to my place." Armando reached out with his left hand, caressed Leo's face, and nodded. Leo kissed him. Armando moaned loudly, and Leo laughed. "I assume you know how to get there?" Armando nodded. Leo kissed him one more time, then repositioned his cock as he opened the door. He got into his car and looked at Armando watching him from the driver seat of his own car. Leo buckled up, turned on the ignition, backed out of his space, and headed toward the stop sign. He looked in the rearview mirror, waited for him to appear, and he did. He watched as Armando licked his lips sensually. Leo laughed, feeling a tingle through his body. He was looking forward to this night. As he made a right-hand turn onto Roosevelt and drove toward the highway, he glanced back in his rearview mirror every couple of seconds and found himself pleasantly shocked to see that Armando was actually following him home.

He forced himself to focus on these good feelings. He loved what was happening. Yet, try as he might, one thought had troubled him from the second he had said it, and he fought desperately not to let it frighten him. He had never had anyone else back to their house before. For years, that couch, that porch swing, that queen-size bed, even that dining room table . . . only Matt and Leo had fucked on them. They had lived with all of this stuff and in that same house. No one else had been there.

"Damn it, Matt," he said aloud. "You're gone. I have to move on with my life." He didn't sound convincing. He didn't feel reassured. But as he turned onto the highway, he glanced into the rearview mirror again and saw Armando was still behind him, following him to the house. He remembered the kissing, the feeling of Armando's lips pressing against his, the goatee brushing against Leo's own smooth face. He was growing hard again. He talked himself out of the lack of reassurance. It was his house, damn it, and Matt was gone. He was going to have sex with Armando there no matter what. He glanced back in the mirror one more time, but he didn't see him, and he panicked for a moment. Then, the white Hyundai peeked out from behind another car and appeared right behind him. He sighed in relief, and headed toward his house in a more determined state of mind.

They arrived there about fifteen minutes later, having driven probably faster than they should have. Leo pulled his Tercel into the driveway and stepped out of the car while Armando pulled up and parked behind him. Leo found himself silently grateful he hadn't parked in the empty spot beside him.

Armando got out of his car and shut his door. He came forward and they leaned against Leo's car for a moment. Because Leo lived closer to the bay, there was a cooler breeze here then in the area where they had left. The tall palm trees and maples drenched in Spanish moss rustled in the light wind. Otherwise the street was quiet. "This is a beautiful neighborhood," Armando commented.

Neither of them spoke for a moment, then Armando moved in front of Leo. He reached out with his arms and embraced him close. They kissed. Leo felt his tongue penetrating his mouth and it enthralled him. "Come inside?" he asked suggestively.

"Oh, yeah," Armando replied.

He extracted himself from beneath Armando, forcing their bodies to rub together, cock against cock. Leo was looking forward to having some of that. He took his hand and led him up the brick steps where they had first met only about a week beforehand in that rather awkward moment. He opened the screen door of the patio and they walked toward the house door.

As Leo fumbled with his keys, he heard Armando shuffle his feet and felt him step away. "What?" he said, turning toward him. He saw Armando staring off in the direction of the porch swing, and for a moment, Leo wasn't sure what the problem was. Armando looked surprised. He heard then the creaking of the swing moving. A lit cigarette glowed in the dark.

Leo stepped backward slightly. "Who's there?" Leo asked, a mix of fear and anger disturbing him.

The person stood, dropped his cigarette, and stepped on it with a rotating twist. He came forward so that the porch light illuminated him. He was tall, with straight short hair. His curved mustache was what clicked for Leo. "Lovely night, isn't it, Leo?" he said. It was the detective from Millie's hospital room.

"What are you doing here?" Leo asked more in shock than anything else. Theresa's and Millie's questions to him about the man suddenly came back to him.

"We have to talk," he said.

"Leo," Armando said, "who is this guy?"

Leo scoffed. "He's a detective, believe it or not," he said.

"Private investigator, actually." He stretched out a hand. "And you are?"

Armando ignored the hand. "Look, mister," Armando said, "I think you should leave."

Leo nodded to the man. "He's right. Get off my porch."

"But we need to talk, Leo."

"We have nothing to talk about. I've been warned about you already."

"Warned?" he asked in response.

"Yes. You're not getting any money out of me, so just leave." Leo unlocked his door, then pushed it open. Before entering with Armando, he turned back toward the detective. "I said to get out of here. I'll call the police if you don't leave now."

Leo stepped inside and flipped on the light switch so that the living room glowed with the eerie lamp lights he had grown accustomed to. He took Armando's hand and had him follow him inside. They heard the heavy footsteps behind them, however, and the investigator, rather than leave, said from the doorway, "I'm not here about money, Leo. I'm here about the truth."

Leo turned. "What truth?"

"The truth about what happened to your boyfriend's father."

Now Leo was confused. It occurred to him then that the man was twisting the truth. It was a stall tactic to get him to pay up. "I don't know what you're talking about."

"You don't? Matthew did."

Leo didn't respond. He could see the detective eyeing him, knowing that he had struck a nerve. Leo wasn't sure what this was about, but he was making a reference to Matt that bothered him. Armando interrupted his thoughts. "Um, Leo, maybe this is a bad time." The reference to Leo's boyfriend had affected him. "Maybe I should go."

Leo turned back to him. "No, I don't want you to go. This asshole is leaving."

The man stepped into the house. "No, actually, I think your friend here needs to leave. We have a few things to talk about."

Leo was amazed by the man's audacity. He didn't respond. Armando grabbed Leo's arm and pulled him further inside the house. Leo focused on Armando, but kept glancing back at the man blocking the doorway.

"Leo, do you have any idea what this guy wants?"

Leo looked at him. "Supposedly money for some work he did for . . ." he couldn't think of the right word to describe Millie ". . . someone I know."

"Can I ask you a question without getting you upset?" Leo nodded. "Is Matthew your boyfriend, the one who was killed?"

Leo glanced back at the detective. He hadn't moved from the doorway. It was amazing how much he filled its frame. Leo looked back at Armando. "Yes," he replied with a sigh.

"Do you think you can trust this guy? Do you think he'll try to hurt you or anything."

He didn't trust him, but he didn't think he would hurt him, despite his towering size. And, he hated to admit it, but the private investigator had piqued his interest. He shook his head at Armando. "No, I don't think he's going to hurt me."

Armando nodded. "All right. It seems like he has to speak to you about something important. Just talk to him for a while. Give me your phone number and I'll call you in about a half hour to check up on you. Okay?" He took his cell phone out of his back pocket and programmed Leo's number in. Leo was trying to focus on Armando, but he was glaring back at the detective. Armando suddenly had both hands on the sides of his face. Leo turned to look back at him. Armando kissed him on the lips, less passionately now, more comforting and reassuring. "I'll call you soon."

Leo nodded. "You're definitely coming back?"

"Hell yes. If you want me too." Leo nodded. Armando kissed him again, then headed toward the front door. The investigator stepped aside to let Armando pass. He stopped at the door and looked back at Leo. "I'll talk to you in a half hour."

"Have a good night," the detective said pleasantly to Armando.

He didn't reply. He walked away. Leo heard the screen door slam shut behind him and his car start. Only once he had left did the detective turn his attention back to Leo and come further inside, shutting the door behind him. "You don't mind if I make myself comfortable?" he said, sitting himself down on the side chair across from the sofa. Leo stepped back into the room and flopped on the sofa across from him. The detective seemed at ease as he leaned back in the chair. "He seemed like a nice young man. I'm sure he'll be back and you can do . . . what you gay people do on dates."

Leo didn't respond. The detective started to light up another cigarette. "Don't smoke in my house," he told him. He probably would have allowed Millie to smoke in the house, and only Millie. There was no way this man was going to.

The man stopped himself from lighting up, then feigned surprise. "Oh, right, you must only smoke your pot on the porch then?" Leo stared back at him, perturbed and caught at the same time. "You left remnants in the ashtray outside," he explained, like a good PI would. "Can I at least have a drink? Soda maybe?" he asked.

Leo was disgusted with his attitude. He could see the guy speaking to Millie and Theresa like this. Theresa probably would have had a difficult time getting rid of him and probably would have been polite and gotten him a drink. Millie would have taken out a rifle and threatened him with it to make him leave. He, on the other hand, was probably somewhere in between. "Look, I don't know who the hell you are—"

"Oh, my apologies. Name's Frank Harrigan." He proffered his hand suddenly. "I guess we haven't been properly introduced."

Leo ignored his comment and his hand. "As I was saying, I don't know who you are, but you have no right to show up on my front porch like this. I already told you that you're not getting any money from me, so you might as well leave."

He put his arm down. "Yes, you did mention that. I'm a little confused about that. I'm not here for any money. I don't know where you got that idea from." Leo didn't respond. Suddenly, his face lit up. "Oh, I suppose your friend Millie said something like that. Is that how she explained me to you? What else did she say?"

Leo was unsure whether he should answer. There was a connection to Millie, though, so he figured even if the man was lying, he should play along, at least for now. Perhaps then he'd leave and he could get on with his date with Armando. "She said you were coming around looking for money for services rendered."

"'Services rendered'?" he mocked. "And what services would those be?"

"She said she hired you to find her ex-husband Jack Pierce."

Harrigan started to laugh, an exaggerated guffaw of sorts. "Ingenious of her actually. Somewhat the truth, but not entirely."

"What is that supposed to mean?"

"I know exactly where Jack Pierce is. He's in a cemetery in Brooklyn."

Leo felt as if Harrigan was trying to surprise him, but it did not work. "I know he's dead. You're the one who told her."

He guffawed. "Oh, that's good. She's shrewd, that woman." He leaned forward and stared into Leo's face with a devious smile. "I didn't have to tell your dear friend Millie. She's known for quite some time that her husband has been dead."

"What are you talking about?"

"Jack Pierce has been dead since . . . oh, I'd say, 1975, although he was buried about three years ago when they found his body."

"That's impossible!" Leo yelled. "How could Millie have know that? And Matt would have known that his father had been dead for, what? Almost fifteen years."

"Not if she didn't tell him."

"That's bullshit. You've got a lot of nerve coming around here lying like this just to get me to pay for work you did for her."

"Leo, Millie never hired me."

"She said she. . ." His voice trailed off.

He shook his head. "I was hired by a relative of Jack Pierce's to find out what happened because the police had given up on the whole thing. I've been doing this since about five months after they found his body."

"What do you mean. . .found his body?"

"In Cranberry Lake, New Jersey, three years ago. All they found were some skeletal remains, of course, considering he'd been in the water for over twenty years."

Leo looked away, shaking his head. "This is ridiculous. You're lying."

"Sorry, but it's the truth. She knows a lot more about Matthew's father, and his death, than she ever let on."

Leo thought about what Theresa had said to him, that he was a liar. "You don't know what Millie knows. You don't know anything for sure. He disappeared, that's all anyone knows."

He sat back, then raised his arms in a mini expression of self-defeat. "Well, I guess you may be somewhat right there. But that's why I'm in Florida. It took me a while to find Millicent Pierce, and then she took off. I caught up with her again, though, living in Clearwater under her maiden name. She keeps telling me the same story, that she knows nothing. So does her daughter, by the way, but her I believe. I figured at this point, if anyone might know something, it would be you."

"What are you talking about? I don't know anything."

"Okay, so then I need you to help me find out the truth."

Leo didn't think he could be more surprised, but he was. "Are you insane?"

"You could find out."

"I am not going to do your investigating for you. Besides, this is all ridiculous. You're acting like it's some stupid murder mystery. The guy was an asshole. He could have wound up in that lake because of a dozen different reasons."

"So you agree then that he was murdered?" Harrigan asked.

"No! It was probably an accident. Maybe he was drunk and drowned."

"Perhaps," Harrigan said, "but I don't think so." He reached into his inside jacket pocket. He pulled out a black object, and held it in the air. It was a videotape. "Catch," he ordered, then threw it across the living room to Leo. He jumped up and caught it. "Put it on."

Leo stared at it, and then at Harrigan. This all seemed so stupid. A stranger shows up to reveal some deep dark secret about his boyfriend's past, with a videotape to prove it? "What is this?" he asked.

"Just put it on," he repeated. Leo hesitated. "What are you afraid of? If you don't believe me, it won't hurt you to watch. What more could you possibly discover?"

Leo hated Harrigan's cocky attitude. He hated his being there in that moment. He hated everything about him. But Leo realized that he had to find out what was on the videotape, especially if it had anything to do with Matt.

He walked over to the television, extracted a porn video from the VCR, and placed it to the side. He glanced back at Harrigan, who gestured with his head to proceed. Leo inserted the tape, sat down, picked up the remote control, and turned on the television. He hit play. A few seconds of fuzz were followed by a glitching picture, then clarity.

A dark black woman with shoulder-length hair parted to the side appeared in the screen. Her name, Giselle Mahoney, was on the bottom of the screen reporting for Channel 7 News. Also at the bottom was the date of the report: April 29, 1996. Just over three years ago. She spoke into the camera with an investigative reporter's voice. "I'm here at Cranberry Lake in New Jersey, where less than two weeks ago a mystery unfolded when a father and his two children fishing found the remains of a body in the lake." The camera panned back and to the side to reveal a shot of the lake, with hills and houses dotting it in the distance. "The body was unrecognizable, but an analysis of dental records and research into missing persons reports has helped police identify the man as one John Pierce of Brooklyn. But what is most shocking is that Jack, as he was known to family and friends, has been missing since 1975."

A picture flashed on the screen of a man dressed in 1970s clothing with black, plastic-frame glasses and salted brown hair. Leo jumped back in his seat. There was a slight resemblance to Matt, though older and with different colored hair. The picture stayed on the screen as the reporter continued to talk about who he was, that Jack Pierce had been the only son of a successful commercial realtor. Both of his parents had died in the early 1960s, and despite inheriting some property from his parents, he was unsuccessful as a realtor himself and continued to lose money and property that his father had built up through the years.

The camera showed a new image, a cabin, red with white trim, an open-air front porch with wooden rocking chairs, and a detached garage off to the side. The house was weather-beaten and old, almost nostalgically so. "This cabin," the reporter continued, "was the summer vacation home of Jack Pierce and his family. It was sold to a neighboring family shortly after his disappearance. According to longtime resident and widow Mrs. Whitman, the Pierces were a loving family who got along with their neighbors." An elderly woman suddenly filled the screen, who answered unheard questions. "They were a nice family," she croaned. "I remember Jack being very outgoing and friendly with everyone. He and my husband used to fish together. They had been coming here for years when my husband and I built our home here. We only saw them during the summers, and then one day, they left. His wife sold us the house sometime later. I remember that she was quiet. They had two lovely children."

Another picture flashed onto the screen, and it too startled Leo. It was a family photo of Jack with his "nice family." Leo had never seen this photo, or any for that matter, of Matt or Millie from their past. The photo dated from around 1970. A much younger and softer Millie with long blonde hair and a dark dress was holding in her arms a quiet baby. She was identifiable with her high cheekbones and hazel eyes. She wore a limp smile on her face. Standing to her left before her was a thin Theresa as a child with long hair brighter than her current mousy brown. She stared into the camera, almost in fright. Jack stood behind and to the right of Millie in a polyester suit, his face aglow. The reporter's voice continued.

"Jack Pierce is shown here from an old family photo with his wife Millicent and their children Theresa and Matthew. Their current whereabouts are unknown, although one relative of the deceased who lives in New York believes the family relocated to California many years ago."

The camera returned to the reporter, the lake and hills behind her visible. "At this time, the family has not been located, although the police say that an investigation is pending. One officer I spoke with told me that there may be some evidence of trauma to the victim, so this may not have been an accidental drowning. The family member, who declined to be identified, has adamantly denied rumors that Jack's business dealings weren't always aboveboard. For now, one can only speculate on how Jack Pierce disappeared all those years ago and wound up in Cranberry Lake. I'm Giselle Mahoney for Channel Seven News . . ."

The videotape went fuzzy. It ran as Leo stared at the black and white lines and the scratchy noise echoed in his head. He didn't move.

Leo hit the mute button. Silent fuzz played. "I told you she lied," Harrigan said.

Leo turned his head toward him. "You don't know that," he said, although he could sense less confidence in his own voice. "That news report said nothing about Millie knowing anything."

"Do you know when a missing person's report was filed on him? Six months after he disappeared. Do you know who filed it? Mrs. Hunter, Millie's mother. She claimed that her daughter had left her husband because he used to abuse them. She moved to get away from him. He never showed up to claim responsibility for his children. That was why they were filing the claim, because no one knew where he was."

"All of that is possible, you know," Leo replied. "Jack Pierce was an asshole to his family. He used to beat them. Did you know that?"

"So I've heard."

"You've heard?" he repeated. "That man was a fucking nightmare! He made their lives hell. No one is sorry he's dead, and none of them ever missed him."

"Your boyfriend didn't care about what happened to his father?" Harrigan asked.

Leo hesitated before replying, "No." He knew he was lying, but he felt compelled to do so. He suddenly realized with each passing second that he couldn't say another word to Harrigan. He had to get him out of the house. "You need to go," he said. Harrigan didn't move. "I said get out of my house!"

He stood tall and walked toward the front door. "You can keep the video," he said, his attitude returning. He opened the door and stepped onto the front porch. He turned and lit a cigarette. As he exhaled, he said, "I'm going to find out the truth about what happened to Jack Pierce, with or without your help." He paused a moment. "Don't be a fool, Leo. You wouldn't want to become an accomplice after the fact."

Leo looked up at him quickly. "An accomplice to what?"

Harrigan didn't answer. He simply exhaled, the smoke encircling his head in an creepy glow from the porch light. "I'll be in touch," he said. He turned and stepped away from Leo's vision. He heard the porch door squeak open and slam shut behind him. Leo was alone again, the house silent, the remote control in his hand.

He stared at the fuzzy lines in the television. Then, he rewound the tape and released the mute on the remote. He watched the program again. He heard the telephone ring, but he didn't get up to answer it. He heard Armando's voice leaving a message, but he didn't respond. He watched the news program a third time. A couple of minutes later the phone rang again, and Armando left him another message. His initial thought had been that Harrigan had doctored the tape somehow, but he knew now that wasn't the case. When they showed the picture of the family, he paused it and tried to use the slow advance button to clear the tracking. After his fifth try, he got a picture that was more clear. He stared at the picture for a long time, examining their faces, their demeanors, staring at the baby that had been his lover and the woman holding him that was his friend. He rewound the program again and watched it for the fourth time. The visual images of the lake, the cabin, Matt's family, and Matt's father penetrated his mind, and the words describing Jack and his family from the videotape and from Harrigan repeated in his head. He finally shut off the television and dropped the remote control onto the table, but it replayed in his mind.

He was in shock, but not like when Matt had died; it was more confused silence. It didn't make sense. Matt's father had been dead since 1975. There was a missing person's report filed at that time by Millie's mother. Millie had sold the cabin a year later. They were a nice family. They were an abusive family. Too many ideas. Too many mixed messages. One thought, however, stayed clear in his head, and it disturbed him: Matt had never known his father was dead. No one had told him. Not even Leo, although he had thought Jack's death was recent.

What if Harrigan was telling the truth, and Millie had known all along that Jack was dead? What did that mean? Did Millie know more than she was telling? And why would she not tell anyone? Was this her great secret? Or was it even worse?

Leo shook his head violently. This was ridiculous. Harrigan was spooking him. He was acting like their lives were some dark Gothic closet, the body of Jack Pierce waiting to spring from its depths. He was overreacting to Harrigan's insinuations. There was a perfectly logical explanation for the whole situation. Harrigan was making him paranoid and getting him to jump to conclusions. This wasn't an Agatha Christie book or a Jessica Fletcher episode; this was real life.

He needed a joint. He moved on the couch and reached over to the ebony box. He opened the lid and saw the last remaining joint. He lit it with a lighter. He closed his eyes, sucked in, and tasted the burning sensation in his nostrils and throat. He choked slightly, then inhaled more. He opened his eyes slowly and leaned back into the couch. He felt his body and mind relax. Thoughts of disappearance and death filtered away.

He heard the squeak of the screen door. He turned his head and looked at the open front door and for a moment thought it might be Harrigan again. Then, as the footsteps got closer and the figure appeared in the porch light, he remembered it was Armando. He quickly bolted up and extinguished the joint on the hardwood floor by his feet.

Armando knocked on the door pane. "Can I come in?" he asked.

Leo tried to control his breathing. He felt oddly guilty. "Sure," he said.

Armando entered, taking slow steps into the room. "Are you all right?" he asked. Leo looked back at the television. He didn't respond. He heard him sniffing and he asked, "Is that. . .?" Leo glared up at him quickly, and Armando's voice trailed off.

"Look, Armando," he said, "I'm sorry, but I'm not into this right now."

He shrugged, his hands in his pockets. "Okay. I'm just checking to see how you are. You didn't answer when I called."

Leo stood and faced him, his arms crossed. "Sorry. I've got stuff on my mind." He could sense a harshness in his own voice. It bothered him that he was speaking to Armando this way, but he couldn't stop himself.

"So, uh, how did it go with the PI?"

"Fine." Leo shook his head. "I don't want to talk about this."

"You sure? The guy seemed pretty intense about what he needed to talk to you about. Something about Matt's father being missing?"

Leo exploded. "I said I don't want to talk about this!"

Armando took a step backward and raised his arms. "Shit, calm down, Leo! All right, I get the message. Sorry for prying." He turned and started walking.

Leo felt terrible. He rubbed his face with both of his hands and groaned furiously at himself. He took a few large steps forward. "Wait, Armando, I'm sorry." He turned around. "I need sleep or something. Can we do this another night."

"Hey, it's okay. No problem." He turned and walked toward the door, his hands in his pockets again. When he reached it, he turned back one last time. "I'll call you?"

Leo hesitated a moment, then nodded. "Yes, of course. Sorry about tonight."

Armando said good night, then left. Leo waited until the screen door slammed, a car door opened and shut, and the vehicle drove off before he walked to the front door, shut it, and locked it. He turned his back to the door and banged his head against the wood.

He looked down at the floor where he had been sitting on the couch. The joint was still laying there. He went back to the couch, tore off his shirt and shoes along the way, and plopped himself back on the couch. He reached down quickly, scooped up the joint, and lit it again. Marijuana infused the air.

He smoked the joint for another minute, taking deep breaths and allowing the smoke to infiltrate his nostrils and burn his throat. With each puff, he fought desperately to forget the night. The disappointment of the situation with Armando was starting to go to the side. It was the words of the detective, the images from the video, thoughts of Millie, all of these things echoed in his mind.

None of it made sense. Millie didn't know anything. There was no way that she could know anything about Jack's disappearance or his death. She could never have kept silent about this all these years. Matt must have asked her through the years, and she probably told him the same thing: to get over it and move on, his father was a bastard for abandoning them, and he was better off without him. But what if she had lied to him? What if, for some reason only she understood, Millie had known that Jack was gone for good? Could she have kept it a secret for all these years from Matt and Theresa? And if so, why?

He remembered a few sessions with Matt and Dr. Tate, and mention of Matt's missing father had come up during those sessions. He remembered their discussions about Matt's anger toward his mother. And then he remembered one time when he had come home from teaching and he saw Matt hunched over the dining room table writing furiously. He asked him who he was writing to. He was reluctant to tell him, but then he mentioned the advice Dr. Tate had given him, to write his feelings down, to write letters to people. He could write to get all of his anger out. No one ever had to read the letters. They were his own private thoughts. He could say whatever he felt in them and use the letters to tell people exactly how he felt. And he could destroy them afterward and let the anger or sadness burn away.

It was then that Leo remembered a particular letter, addressed to MOTHER, one he had removed from his lover's body. No one knew he had it. He had not read it because he never wanted to betray Matt's private thoughts. Now, however, he needed to know.

High, the joint finished, his mind restless, his breathing heavy, he jumped up and stumbled into the office. He went right to the desk. He opened the small drawer, knowing exactly where he had placed it that night after the funeral. He looked down at it in his hands and saw the folded envelope with MOTHER written in Matt's handwriting.

He hurried back to the living room and sat on the couch in its glowing lamp-lit atmosphere. He swallowed and could feel his heart beating harder. He licked his lips to quench them. He hesitated no more, then used his index finger and inserted it into the open space in the flap. He tore through the second seal affixed with tape that someone, maybe Millie, had used to close it before placing it in the casket with Matt. He removed the few sheets of loose-leaf paper and unfolded them. His hands were shaking, and his brain was panicking, telling him not to do it. He took a quick breath and read.

He could sense his betrayal of his lover's mind with each word and phrase, but this was quickly overshadowed by what he read. He was startled by what a son could say to his mother, the level of anger beyond what he imagined him capable of revealing. But deeper, into the recesses of the letter and Matt's mind, Leo learned Matt's secret that he had kept from them all.

When he had finished reading the letter, his hands were shaking and his eyes were misty. He fought to control his emotions and breathed deeply. He needed to see the news report once again, so he played the tape, and glanced every now and then at the images on the screen and the letter before him. They were connected, linked by a single family, now infamous on television and wracked on paper. The news report changed to black and white fuzz again, but he didn't turn it off. He leaned back in the sofa and closed his eyes to think. He rested the letter in his lap, and breathed deeply to concentrate. Without warning, he drifted off to sleep.

– ELEVEN –

"You have no idea what it's like," Matt once said to him with an edge to his voice.

Leo had made the mistake of asking Matt about his cutting. By this point he was fully aware of the problem, having sat in one or two sessions with Matt and his doctor. They were able to discuss it openly in that setting, but Matt would never talk about his problems when they were home. It was as if he were living two separate lives.

"I'm only asking you because Dr. Tate thought it would help you to talk more."

"I don't want to talk about it." He took a hit on a joint, then passed it to Leo. He looked down at it. There was only a knuckle length left. He had to hold it near the edge where it was burning in order to inhale. He did so sharply, and the burning sensation scorched his throat like always. He felt more lightheaded though, so it was adding to the two other hits Matt had let him smoke. He went to extinguish the remaining bit, when Matt stopped him with his hand on Leo's arm. "What are you doing?"

"There's nothing left. I was going to put it out."

Matt took it from him and managed to hold the very last bit of the joint and inhale it. He made a wheezing sound, taking in more air than pot. Only then did he squash it out against the wooden frame of their screened porch.

It was twilight late in September 1997. The crescent moon was visible in the humid western evening sky. They were sitting on their porch swing. Leo stared toward the screen door, regretting that he had said anything about the cutting.

"It's a release," Matt said. Leo looked up at him. "The cutting," Matt continued, as if Leo hadn't understood him.

Pierce
© 2007 by The Haworth Press, Inc. All rights reserved.
doi:10.1300/5849_11

"What are you releasing?"

He shrugged. "Pain. Anxiety. Grief." He scoffed, then took a swig of his Corona. "You know what, that's all bullshit. That's the psycho-doctor's analysis." He shifted in the bench and looked into Leo's eyes. "Do you want to know what it's really like?"

Leo nodded, afraid to break contact with Matt's hazel eyes, flaring in an odd way.

"It's like fucking," he said. "It's like an orgasm. You know when the orgasm hits and you're about to shoot, how it happens in that one instantaneous moment? Your nerves are on edge and your entire body is on fire?" His eyes were excited, his pupils dilated. In the darkness lit only by the porch light Leo could see he was flushing. "It's an unbelievable sensation! Cutting is like an orgasm to me. When I bleed, it's like I'm coming, and then I feel this sense of total exhaustion." He moved closer to Leo, so that he could smell his breath. "Even the preparation, getting a knife, choosing my spot, it's like foreplay. I go into this trance. It's like I'm fucking myself and nothing else in the world is going on."

Leo was frightened. His heart was pounding and his mouth was dry. He broke Matt's gaze and drank the last drop of his beer.

"Aren't you glad you asked?" Matt said, then laughed.

Leo looked back at him. He was leaning against the swing, trying to make it move with his one foot against the floor. Leo's own feet planted firmly stopped the swing from rocking. Matt drank the end of his beer, then dropped the empty bottle on the floor with a clatter. He looked back at Leo with a wicked grin. Leo watched him suddenly reach down and grab at his shorts.

"Check this out, Leo. I'm fucking horny."

Leo looked away. "You're weird sometimes," he said.

"Why?"

"Because of what you said. How could cutting yourself be like an orgasm?"

"I was speaking metaphorically. You're the grad student. You couldn't figure that out?"

Leo looked back at him and found himself relaxing a little. "It didn't sound like you were trying to be poetic."

"I wasn't trying to be anything. You asked me a question, and I answered it. All right, so maybe I exaggerated, but it's better than the fucking garbage Tate feeds me. It's like he's trying to program me into some little psycho robot."

"Dr. Tate is trying to help you recover from your cutting. Did you forget you were in the psychiatric ward not too long ago?"

"No, I didn't forget!" he said loudly. A mourning dove in the bushes outside flew away. "And I don't need you to keep reminding me."

Silence. "I'm sorry," Leo said.

"It's all right," Matt replied. He was calm now himself.

"I was trying to help."

"You know what would help?" Matt grabbed Leo's arm and led his hand to Matt's shorts to feel his hard-on.

"No, Matt, not now."

"Come on, Leo, I'm fucking horny. You know pot does that to me." Leo heard a snapping noise and looked down to see that Matt had pulled the front of his shorts down. His erect cock was upright in the air. He was moving Leo's hand over it. "Oh, yeah, that feels good."

Leo continued to stroke Matt, the beer bottle in his other hand. He moved forward to put the bottle down, and tried to use the maneuver to take his hand away, but instead Matt took advantage of it and grabbed at the back of Leo's shorts. His hand was down them in a flash. Leo could feel Matt's fingers running up and down his ass crack. "Matt, stop, I don't want to—"

"Leo, loosen up!"

He didn't have a moment to react. Matt yanked Leo's shorts down. His buttocks were resting on his hand and the cold seat. He hardly knew what was happening, Matt moved so fast, but his own cock was rising now from Matt's fingers playing with his ass. Matt was kissing him now, then sucking on his naked cock. He was suddenly lying on the bench with his legs up and Matt was on top of him. Matt wet his palm with spit and coated his hard cock. "Matt, stop, I don't want to do this. Not out here." He was feeling vulnerable on the swing, outdoors, with the neighbors nearby.

"I told you to relax, Leo."

He could feel the head of his cock push in. It was sharply painful. He wanted him to use lube, a condom even. He felt Matt push his way in and Leo gritted his teeth in agony, afraid to scream aloud in pain or pleasure, in case the neighbors heard. Matt was on top of him, kissing him on the lips. Leo tasted pot and Corona mixing with the same flavors in his own mouth, but for some reason they turned him off. He felt the friction in his ass as Matt fucked him and the swing creaked with their motion. He stroked Leo off at the same time. At the last moment, Matt pulled out, and he shot his come on Leo's shirt, and jerked Leo off onto his shirt as well.

Matt was shivering. "Damn, that was hot," he said. Leo didn't respond. Matt stood and pulled his shorts back up. "I need another beer. You?" Leo nodded quietly. Matt went to the door, then turned back toward him. "You better get dressed and get rid of that shirt before the neighbors see you." He laughed at his own joke and went inside, leaving Leo to pull his shorts back on and take off his shirt. His ass was burning and his cock stressed. It was suddenly very damp outside, and he went indoors. He swore to himself that he'd never ask Matt about his cutting problem again.

Leo had woken up, startled to find himself asleep on the couch. His head pounded and his neck ached. The television was on, the videotape long over and rewound, and a new channel shouted the morning news. He saw the scattered pages of the letter on the floor, and he reached down and put them together, then placed them neatly on the coffee table before him. He rubbed his head. He took Tylenol for his headache, turned off the television, then went to lie down for a while. He slept a few more hours, but he tossed and turned. He skipped breakfast, choosing to stay in bed. He only got up for lunch because hunger won out.

As he ate, he wondered why he was involved. He was only the Pierce-in-law, wasn't he? Why had he found himself privy to information he never wanted to know? Why did he know more about Matt's mind-set and feelings now, when he could do nothing about them? He could have done more to help him had he known about it when he was alive. But now? He could do nothing, and it frustrated him.

All of his time with Matt, his attempts to do things for him, to re-unite him with Millie, to save him from his own demons, he had done it all without ever knowing the whole story. None of it had any meaning compared to the latest information that had come to him. And he was furious because he couldn't imagine doing anything that could help matters.

He sat back in the chair and closed his eyes. He replayed in his mind the videotaped news program, Giselle Mahoney regurgitating information and flashing photos on the screen. It was all still vague, though. The videotape didn't reveal any great truths, except that Jack Pierce had disappeared almost twenty-five years before. There was no other truth than that. The letter came back to him. It haunted him more. He had read it and could hear Matt's voice as he read the words. It was as if Matt were speaking his true feelings for the first time. And yet, there were missing pieces to the story, pieces he didn't want to know about.

He tried to block the whole thing out of his head again. He finished eating his lunch and threw out the remnants. He cleaned out the re-frigerator of leftovers. He rearranged kitchen knickknacks. He looked for anything to do to distract him. He thought of his students' assign-ments, and remembered he needed to refresh himself on *Oedipus the King*. He pulled out the textbook and breezed through the play that he had read half a dozen times already. It was a play of revelations and family drama, a Greek tragedy. His academic mind reflected on the parallels to his own life, the constructed drama of Matt and Millie, the revelation of information with each arriving messenger. He saw the triangulations once again. It wasn't a completely accurate portrayal. Incest between mother and son certainly wasn't the issue here, but the unfolding of the truth was similar.

He glanced at the microwave clock. It was after two-thirty already. He was supposed to be at Millie's therapy session at three. He would be late. He didn't want to go, but he got in his car anyway.

He drove slowly. The afternoon sun was hot and blinding. He squinted behind his sunglasses. He was on Roosevelt Boulevard, ap-proaching the entrance for the Bayside Bridge to head north to Clearwater. He was in the right lane. And then, without any warning, he panicked. With no reason, he changed lanes and cut off a car whose driver blared his horn. Sweat spread over his body. His armpits and face were wet. His heart was pounding.

It was an odd moment then, a moment when Leo suddenly understood how Matt might have felt seconds before his crash. He could sense Matt driving across the Howard Frankland bridge at a high speed to think and clear his head. He could envision him with tears in his eyes, confused and frustrated. He could sense how in a single second, he had taken his hands off the wheel, perhaps to wipe his eyes, to stop the tears, or just to let go, to pray for a moment that someone else would guide his life and stop the torment. That single moment in time could have been suicidal. Or, it could have been an attempt to ease the pressure off of himself, to turn it over to some other power. But it failed. The car lost control, and he had flown headfirst into the median, his body thrown from the seat, windshield glass slicing and penetrating his beautiful body. All from that single moment when he might have wanted not to kill himself but to have someone else take over.

Leo forced himself to focus on the road before him. He controlled his breathing to calm down. He would have to go a different way to the hospital. He reached US 19 and should have gone north. Instead, he moved into the left lane and headed back to St. Petersburg. He knew where his mind was taking him. He hadn't been there since Christmas. Prior to that, it had been for what would have been Matt's thirtieth birthday in late October. He stayed on US 19 until he turned onto 54th Avenue. Ten minutes later, he stopped at a traffic light and turned right down 20th Street. He was at Sunnyside Cemetery, an oddly appropriate name for a final resting place in Florida.

He turned off the car, stepped outside, and shut the door. He hesitated a moment to get his bearings in the hot sun. The cemetery was larger than it looked. It was oddly laid out with three rectangular plots of land separated by local streets, the last plot turning south to create an L-shape. It was separated from the main streets by ranch-style posts. Leo looked out across the cemetery and located the oak tree and the cement bench. Matt was three plots in.

Sunnyside was a traditional cemetery with headstones marking the graves of individuals, unlike most other Florida cemeteries that had flat stones in the ground. Leo walked slowly on the gravel path. He made his way to the oak tree and cement bench commemorated for someone he didn't know, then turned down the row until he came to the third headstone. He should have brought flowers or some other token. Not that Matt would know, of course. Flowers served the purpose of letting other people know that someone was mourned. They were for the living, not the dead.

Matt's marker was a simple, square, gray, granite block. He looked down at the headstone. Engraved in a tall font, it read:

MATTHEW PIERCE
SON, BROTHER, LOVER
OCTOBER 28, 1969—APRIL 28, 1998

And below that, at Millie's insistence, were two lines of poetry by Christina Rossetti:

WHEN I AM DEAD, MY DEAREST,
SING NO SAD SONGS FOR ME.

Leo squatted. He kissed his fingers, and touched the stone heated from the afternoon sun at Matt's name. He sighed to himself. "Hey, Matt," he spoke aloud, slightly conscious of anyone around at the time. "Sorry I haven't been by more often. Busy with school and everything." He swallowed. "So things fucking suck lately," he confessed. "But I guess you know that." He hesitated a moment, glancing around. He saw a woman with flowers entering the cemetery. "I miss you, you know. A lot. Too much, I think. It's been over a year now, and for some odd reason, I cannot get over you. It's not like you were a saint or anything," he chuckled. "God knows, you were a pain in my ass a lot." He smiled more now. "I meant that in an emotional sense, but it applies physically too."

He was silent. Leo wondered why people asked the dead questions. They didn't answer. They never did. He had come in the past and sat by Matt's grave and asked him why he had died, if he had killed himself, why he had been so angry that night. Never was there an answer.

"Hey, I met someone," he said, changing the subject. "His name is Armando Sedilla. I know how much you loved the Latinos, so maybe if I'm lucky I'll get to have my first, huh?" He wondered if Matt would be shocked or upset. He grew serious. "We haven't had sex though," he explained. "I thought we would, but I fucked that up."

He changed positions so that his weight was leaning on his left leg during the squat. He breathed deeply, and glanced around again. He saw the woman go to the row of graves one over from him and walk down toward the end. He turned his head back to Matt's stone and looked more intently at the speckles of black, white, and gray in the granite, and the engraved words that stated Matt's private information publicly. He looked down toward the ground then and was surprised to see something he hadn't noticed before. It was a bouquet of flowers wrapped in clear cellophane. They had been lying on the ground facing away from the stone and hidden by the overgrown grass. Leo picked them up.

The price sticker from Publix for $3.99 was still on the plastic wrap. The flowers were shriveled up. He had no way of knowing how long they had been there, although he could guess it was at least a few days. He had never known anyone else to have brought Matt flowers before. Yet, knowing last week was the anniversary of Matt's death, Leo realized anyone who had known Matt could have been by to leave them. It was what he should have been doing. Not getting high and drunk on his front porch swing commemorating the horrific night.

He couldn't get out of his head that maybe if he had changed something or did something differently, Matt wouldn't have argued with him. He could have stopped pressuring him about Millie. He could have told Matt that whatever he wanted was fine with him, and they wouldn't have fought, and he never would have died.

"I guess it is my fault," he said. He dropped the flowers. He shifted his weight onto his other leg. "What was I supposed to do though?" he continued. "You never helped me to understand. You never told me anything that made sense. I wanted to help you. I wanted to do whatever I could. I wanted to know why you hated her so much, why you couldn't let me be friends with her. Why, Matt? Why?!"

He looked up and saw the woman glance in his direction, then quickly focus on her own grief. He felt foolish for the moment, but his emotional outburst continued. He stood up. "Matt, I'm serious," he said. "Why couldn't you have told me?" He stared at the stone and the grass before it. "I read your letter. I know I shouldn't have. I had to though. You never shared with me your true feelings. And now I have more questions and I'm more confused than ever before, thanks to that fucking Harrigan asshole!" He knew that Matt didn't know who he was, though, so the exclamation was worthless.

"What am I supposed to do? How am I supposed to let go of all this? How do I move on with my life when I don't even understand what happened? I want to know why you were so pissed off that night. I feel like I pushed you to the edge of a cliff, and I don't know why you were even on the cliff. God damn it, Matt, why couldn't you just tell me what happened?"

He wasn't crying. He was angry. And he felt hopeless and more disgusted and with less direction than he had before. He walked to the cement bench and sat down forcefully. He doubled over with his hands rubbing his face. He sat up again, running his hands through his hair, shutting his eyes to concentrate, breathing deeply. He tried to focus on the serenity and the nature of the peaceful cemetery. Instead, all he could hear was the traffic roaring by on 54th Avenue. He realized he hated this place.

He opened his eyes and gazed back at Matt's grave. A mourning dove had landed on the headstone. It walked from one end to the other, then back again. It stared at Leo, or so it seemed. Then, it cooed, ruffled its gray-brown feathers, and flew away.

A thought occurred to him. It was so obvious, silly even, though it was missed by so many people. The dead had no answers. Only the living did.

He got up and walked to his car. He glanced over his shoulder and watched the back of Matt's headstone grow smaller with each step. He felt more relieved and calmer. He was glad he had come, if even briefly. He felt more in control now, and was resolved as to what he had to do.

Thunder echoed as he drove home. A minute or so after leaving the cemetery, another afternoon rainstorm poured down on his car and slowed his progress. He pulled into his driveway twenty minutes later. He went right into the kitchen, dried his face and hands on a dish towel, then checked his messages.

The two from Armando from the previous night were still there, and he deleted them. There was a call from his mother, wanting to know if she was going to see him for Mother's Day on Sunday. She also then commented angrily about Leo having revealed Theresa's secret. Leo shook his head in amazement. He had wondered how long it would take for Theresa to report back to his mother about what Leo had done. He hit delete.

He was surprised when he heard Armando's voice again, and listened to the new message. "I'm checking to see how you're doing. I hope you're all right after last night. I do want to see you again, so I hope you'll call me." He rattled off his phone number and hung up. Leo saved the message, although he couldn't deal with him right now.

He looked at the clock on the microwave. It was 4:04. Their session might still be going on. He got undressed and dried off. He went out to his front porch and watched the storm rage outside. Rain was flooding his overgrown lawn. He sat on his porch swing to relax with the soothing water. He had decided he would wait a little while longer, then call Dr. Bauer.

Just as the rain was letting up, the phone rang. He went inside and answered it. He was greeted by a British-accented voice. "Oh, hello, Leo. It's Dr. Bauer."

"Hi, doctor. I was going to call you."

"We were surprised you weren't at the session today. Are you ill?"

"I had things to take care of and I couldn't make it."

"Well, I'm releasing Millie tomorrow. We had another good session today and I no longer believe she's a danger to herself. She's agreed to see me on an outpatient basis at my office once a week."

Leo swallowed, realizing if he were going to do this, he had to do it now. He couldn't wait until after she was released. "Dr. Bauer," he said, "is there any possible way we could have a session tomorrow before she goes?"

He heard her hesitate. "I was expecting to release her in the morning. I don't know if I can schedule—"

"I'm sorry, Dr. Bauer, but it's important, for Millie's sake. There are a few things that we need to discuss. I'd rather we did it while she was still there."

The urgency in his voice must have carried through the phone. "All right," she replied. "Can you come tomorrow afternoon? Say at one p.m.?"

"Yes, that's fine." He would head over right from school.

"I'll notify Millie and her daughter for the meeting."

Leo thought of the message his mother had left him, and he knew having Theresa there would make things worse. "I don't think you need to call Theresa," he said. "This has more to do with Millie and me. And Matt," he added.

"I see." She was hesitant.

"It's nothing serious," he said, closing his eyes as if to hide from the lie. "I need to clear the air about a couple of things. You know how the two of them didn't get along. I want to talk to her about that." He continued before she could interrupt him. "I'll see you tomorrow at one." He quickly hung up.

– TWELVE –

Leo sat nervously in the doctor's office the next afternoon after his class, waiting for Dr. Bauer and Millie to arrive. He looked at the Impressionisti prints to soothe him, but it didn't work. His stomach was tense. The folded letter was searing a hole in the back pocket of his jeans. He had been questioning to himself since that morning whether this was the right thing to do. He knew that when he produced the letter, Millie would know he had betrayed a confidence shared between mother and son, a confidence Leo never was supposed to know about. He had decided that he would bring up the letter only if he had to. He would speak to her only about Harrigan and see what she had to say.

The door to the room opened and they came in. Millie seemed refreshed and was wearing a little makeup, something Leo swore he had never seen her do. It was applied with exuberance, as if to prove that she was ready to go home. He could see in her hands a pack of cigarettes and a lighter. Leo stood when they entered, and she gave him a hug and kiss.

"Please, let's sit," Dr. Bauer said. Millie sat on the sofa to Leo's left as she had these past few sessions. She watched him. "Leo asked for us to meet. Since he missed the session yesterday, I thought this would be a good idea."

Before Bauer could continue, Millie grinned and said, "I'm going home today, Leo. I'd really hate to have to stay here any longer." She paused a moment, then plunged. "So let's have it. What did you want to talk about?" She was leaning forward, her arms crossed over her chest. She stared at Leo with a challenging, if not fierce, stare.

Pierce
© 2007 by The Haworth Press, Inc. All rights reserved.
doi:10.1300/5849_12

He had no choice but to confront her in the same way. He leaned forward, his hands clasped together on his legs. "Harrigan came to see me the other night." Millie didn't respond.

"Is he the private investigator Millie hired to find her husband?" Dr. Bauer guessed.

Leo waited to see if Millie would respond, but she didn't. She stared at him. Leo met her gaze, but answered the doctor's question. "So she claims."

"I did hire him," Millie said quickly.

Dr. Bauer said, "You said you were avoiding him because you hadn't paid him."

"That's right."

"No, it's not," Leo replied. "He was hired by relatives of Jack Pierce's, to find you."

He could see her eyes darken. "That's not what happened at all. I'm amazed how willing you are to believe a complete stranger over me."

"I didn't believe him at first. But he showed me an interesting videotaped news program from when they identified the body and—"

"Wait!" Dr. Bauer interjected. They both turned toward her. "Your husband's body?"

"Ex-husband," she replied matter-of-factly.

"Millie," she continued, "you didn't answer my question." The doctor was disturbed.

"Maybe Leo should answer it. He seems to have all the answers."

"I'm not asking Leo. I'm asking you."

"I am telling you the truth. I don't know what he's talking about."

"Leo," Bauer said, and he turned toward her, "tell me what happened."

Leo found himself glad to have turned from Millie. She was frightening him. "Harrigan came to see me the other night. He told me Millie hadn't hired him, that he was sent to find her. He also told me they found the remains of Jack Pierce's body three years ago in Cranberry Lake in New Jersey. He's been dead for over twenty years now." He explained briefly about the videotape as well. "Harrigan thinks Millie knows more about this than she's letting on."

Bauer turned toward Millie. "Is all this true?"

"Lies, I tell you," she said, with too much comical flair.

"Millie, don't mock this situation!" Dr. Bauer was angry. "This is serious."

"Don't talk to me about serious," she replied viciously. Millie was facing Bauer now, her hands fumbling with her cigarettes on the table, her eyes set on the doctor. "In case you hadn't noticed, I'm the one suffering here. I'm the one who took those pills."

"And why did you take those pills, Millie?"

"Because of my son."

"Because he was killed."

"Yes, of course, because he was killed!"

"And how did it make you feel?"

"I'm furious! I'm angry! And I'm disgusted with myself and what I did to him!"

Leo watched her reaction, while his own chest and face flushed with growing anger.

Bauer spoke. "Millie, did you hire that detective?"

"I already answered that."

"Millie, I'm asking you a question. You have to be honest with me. It is important to your recovery that you tell me these things. There's no reason for you to lie. We're here to help you." Millie was looking off to her left, her arms crossed tightly over her chest. "Millie," the doctor encouraged, "what happened with Harrigan?" She didn't respond.

Her silence confirmed at least one thing for Leo. She had lied about hiring the man, as Harrigan had said. Which meant Harrigan had looked for her. Which meant only one thing. . .

"Harrigan did find you, didn't he?" Leo asked. Bauer looked toward him, but Millie stayed turned away. "Not here though. In Hollywood. Am I right?" She didn't respond, but she embraced herself tightly and rocked forward slightly. A sense of realization was occurring to Leo. He glanced at Bauer, then back at her. "That's why you moved here, isn't it? You didn't move to reunite with your family. You moved to get away from him." Millie didn't respond. "Millie, why did you lie to me? You told me you moved here to reunite with your son."

"No!" she snapped her head toward him, her finger pointing sharply and shaking at him. "I never said that. That's what you wanted to believe! I let you try to reunite us. I wasn't going to work against you, but I wasn't going to be an active participant either."

Leo's stomach was churning. Matt's assumptions about his mother were right. She really didn't want anything to do with him. She didn't care about him at all. Which meant her reasons for attempting suicide were lies too. Bauer couldn't see that, though. She couldn't see beyond her need to heal.

As if on cue, Bauer continued to work with Millie as her doctor. "Tell me how you feel, Millie. Right now, confronted by this."

"I'm pissed! Where does he get off asking me questions like this? He has no right."

Bauer continued to ask her about her feelings, and Millie turned her focus back to Bauer. Leo watched, and with every word coming out of her mouth, all he could think was that each was a lie. He was amazed at how angry he was becoming. Never in the past few years had he ever imagined he would be this incensed with her. They had discovered such strong amicability between them, and their friendship had been one of companionship, in spite of Matt. Now, with each passing second, Leo could sense how Matt had hated her. He could feel the letter burning in his back pocket, a son's words dying to come out. He could hear nothing of Millie's spoken words, but sense only that they were garbled sounds. None of the actual words meant anything. It was staged for Bauer's sake. He suddenly yelled angrily, "This is fucking bullshit!" He stood and began pacing behind his chair.

They turned toward him. Dr. Bauer said "Leo, please, it's—"

"Don't you get it? You're making this all about Millie. I'm not here for Millie, I'm here for Matt. None of this is about her. It's about her son!"

"Leo, we know that."

"No, you don't! You don't get it at all! Matt is the one who died in the car crash last year. Not us! He's the reason we're here."

"Leo, I know you're upset, but this is not helping."

"Oh, no," Millie said vindictively, "let him rant. He's been needing to do this for a long time. He has to accept the truth about what happened to Matt in that car crash."

Leo turned on her. "Don't even suggest that to me."

"Why not?" she replied. "You know damn well that he was suicidal. Why are you so shocked by the thought that he crashed his car purposely? It's obvious."

"No, it's not! He was doing much better with everything. He stayed away from you and suddenly he was starting to do better. They even gave him a promotion at work."

She scoffed. "Promotion? They shoved him in an office to shuffle papers because they couldn't afford him as a liability!"

Leo was in utter shock that Millie was being this harsh and cruel. None of it was true. "I can't believe you. He was your son."

"Yes, I know that. And I loved him as best as I could. He'd never let me get near him. I couldn't help him. I know I failed him." She paused. "That's why you're angry, isn't it? You think you failed him too. You think it's your fault he killed himself."

"No!" he screamed. He stopped pacing. The room blurred. He wiped at his eyes.

"It's true, Leo. He killed himself."

"No, God damn it! I am not going to be responsible for his death!"

Silence. Leo slammed his fists into the top of the chair. His fury was burning. He couldn't be responsible for Matt's death. His last words and actions weren't responsible for killing his lover. He suddenly reached into his back pocket and yanked out the letter furiously. He unfolded it and flashed it in the air. "Recognize this?" he asked Millie. He wiped at his eyes. He saw her confused look, then watched as she focused on the letters on the front of the envelope. "Do you recognize it?!" he yelled.

He could see then in her hazel eyes illumination. Her cheeks paled. Then, her expression quickly flashed into fury, disappointment, and despair. "Oh, Leo," she said, "you didn't."

"I did," he replied. He sounded proud of his accomplishment, but inside he was sickened by his actions. He didn't want to do this, but she was forcing him. He felt as if someone else was controlling his words. "Care to hear what it says? Or do you remember most of it?"

Dr. Bauer quickly stood and positioned herself between them. "Leo, give that to me." He hesitated. "Leo, I have to see what it is. This is getting out of control. I need to know what is happening." She was asserting her dominance in the situation. She looked at him with determination, her hand forward. Leo turned it over to her. She opened the envelope and scanned the letter. She turned toward Millie. "Do you know what this is?"

Leo could see her hesitate, then nod slowly. "It's a letter from my son."

Bauer turned back to Leo. "Was this among Matt's things?"

Millie interrupted him before he could respond. "No, he got it from Matt's dead body. I put it in his casket before they sealed it."

Bauer glanced back at Millie, then returned her gaze to Leo. He could see that she was disturbed by this, but she said nothing. Leo breathed heavily. He suddenly realized how horrible he seemed. He had stolen something from his dead lover's body placed there by his mother. He had always known this was a bad thing, but now confronted by his own actions, he realized how detestable it actually was. He returned Bauer's gaze and responded quietly. "I didn't do it purposely," he said slowly. "I was the last one with him before they closed the casket." He swallowed back his tears, the vision of his lover lying motionless in the box flashing in his mind. "I didn't know what it was, but it wasn't there beforehand. I took it out, and I saw what it said on it. I was confused. Then they took him away before I could put it back." He looked beyond Bauer to see Millie. "I didn't mean to take it. It happened so fast." Millie stared off before her. He looked back at Bauer. "I only read it the other night for the first time, after Harrigan visited me."

Realization seemed to penetrate Bauer's mind. She glanced back at Millie and then looked at Leo again. She returned the letter to him. "Why don't you sit down," she suggested. "I'm stepping out on a limb here, but I want you to read the letter aloud."

"What?" Millie shrieked and jumped from her seat. Even Leo was surprised.

Bauer sat in her chair and faced Millie. "I think he should read it. I believe it might do both of you some good."

"You're not serious."

"Absolutely. It's apparent that you haven't been honest with me, and I refuse to discharge you not knowing the whole truth." Leo was impressed with Bauer's resolve.

Millie was furious. She looked at Leo with disgust, then grabbed her cigarettes and lighter and walked toward the door. "I'm not staying for this bullshit."

Bauer issued an air of command accentuated by her English accent. "Millie, if you walk out that door, you will not leave here, today or any other day, until I say so. Do you understand me?" Millie had stopped right at the door. "I suggest you return to your seat. Both of you," she continued, looking at Leo this time. He didn't hesitate. He sat with the letter in his hands. He was amazed by Bauer's authority. Even Millie slowly stepped away from the door and returned to her place on the couch. She looked away from both of them, though, and crushed her cigarettes and lighter in her right hand. She crossed her arms sharply over her breasts.

"Thank you," Bauer continued. She turned her attention to Leo. "Please read the letter."

Leo glanced at Millie, but she had not changed position. She stared away from both of them. He glanced at Dr. Bauer, who encouraged him with a nod. He removed the letter. He lay the envelope in his lap. He unfolded the pages of loose-leaf paper slowly and stretched them slightly so that he could better read the words. He cleared his throat, breathed deeply, and read Matt's words aloud for the first time.

Mother,

I decided I should write you a letter because it's the only way I can talk to you about all the shit I've always felt was so bad about me and you and our relationship. I'm writing this letter to say good-bye to all the pain you've caused me.

How stupid is that? I'm laughing to myself because I realize I had written something like that to you at least a dozen times in my head or on paper, but I never told you or sent you the letter. I don't know why. It's weird. I guess I was afraid to get you upset, even though I'm so fucking pissed off at you.

I know you think I'm overreacting to everything, making a big deal out of stupid stuff. I've heard you say it before: "What's done is done." But I can't let it go. I hate you, and I cannot bring myself to get through this hatred. My shrink says I'm only hurting myself, and Leo too. I've hurt myself all along with the cutting and attitude, so I'm used to that. But I don't want to hurt him. He doesn't deserve that.

I hate you because you were drunk so much. I hate you for ignoring me. I hate you for the way you treated Theresa. I hate you for abandoning me.

I hate you for letting my father hit me and doing nothing about it. I blame you for every time he hit me. You could have stopped him, and you didn't.

I hate that you took me away from my home after Grandmother died and dragged me off to Florida without even asking me.

And I hate you for never once taking a minute to even think about or tell me that maybe you felt bad for all of these things that you did to me.

It all seems so weird, because now that I've written it I'm wondering if what you always say is true. Maybe none of it does matter now. And I guess I could probably get over all of these things, if I wanted to. But you know that isn't it. You know that there is one more thing that I hate you for, that I can't get out of my head. It has been the one thing that has always frightened me about you. I've never been able to speak about it. I still haven't even told my shrink. I don't know if I ever will.

I hate you because of what happened to my father.

There. I said it.

Mother, I was there. I heard what happened that night in the house at Cranberry Lake. The screams woke me up. I was shivering in my footed pajamas with my teddy bear. I heard what happened. I heard the noises and the screams, and I couldn't move. I think I peed in my pajamas I was so scared. And then I ran back upstairs to bed and hid under the covers and cried until I fell asleep.

I don't understand for sure what happened, but I know it was bad. I think I blocked some of it out. But I know it was bad, because you woke me up in the middle of the night and said that he had left us. Then you took us back to Brooklyn to Grandmother's. And Theresa never said a word. I kept asking you what happened, but you wouldn't tell me. You just yelled at me to shut up. And you left Theresa and me at Grandmother's. You left us! You never came back! The police even came to Grandmother's once, but none of us could tell them where my father or you were. The only thing I remember hearing Grandmother tell the police was that you had had a fight with my father, that he had hit you, and had taken off.

My father was gone. My mother was gone. You both had abandoned me. I was so confused and upset, and I had no one to explain it. Grandmother repeated the same story over and over until it was what I believed.

And Theresa didn't speak. Did you know that she didn't speak for almost two weeks after you left us at Grandmother's? Did you even care?! How could you? We didn't even see you again until she died.

I was six years old, Mother. How could you fuck with the mind of a six-year-old like that? And then come back years later like nothing had happened, and drag me off to Florida without even talking to me?

God, I hate you. I've always hated you. I once asked Theresa about every-thing that night, but she said she doesn't remember. I think I hate her too.

Why are you all so fucking silent?

What happened to my father?

And why can't I ask you this to your face?

I don't know if this is helping me or not. I don't even know if writing this makes any difference at all. It isn't easy to talk about these things. But I have to do this for Leo's sake, because I don't want to hurt him. I don't ever want to hurt anyone the way you hurt me.

I want to kill myself. I will never be able to get over this. And I know that I will never be able to confront you and know the truth. I'm too afraid of you. My nightmares tell me things, but I get confused and I can't remember the images. And then I start to cut myself again.

My God, what the fuck did you do to me?!

Matthew

Leo lowered the letter into his lap and sat back in the chair, glanc-ing at Millie, then Dr. Bauer. Neither spoke. He breathed deeply to calm himself, and fought off the chill of Matt's voice echoing in his mind. He had betrayed his lover's feelings by reading aloud what had been just for Millie's eyes. And now not only had he stolen the letter and read it, but he had used it to confront Millie with its contents.

"Millie?" Dr. Bauer said, breaking the silence. She leaned forward and gazed intently at her. "How do you feel?" Her arms were still wrapped tightly around her. She gazed to her left still, ignoring both of them. "Are you angry?" Bauer asked. "Are you sad? Do you feel betrayed?" Millie said nothing. Bauer came forward and leaned across the glass-top table. She reached out with her hand as an offering. "Millie, it's all right. You can be sad or angry or whatever you want to feel. It's all right." She held her hand out longer. "Come," she invited with a quick gesture of her slender fingers, "take my hand." She didn't move. No sound emanated from her. Not a yell, nor a cry, nor a simple sigh. She was silent. Bauer lowered her hand, returning it to her own lap. "Please, Millie. Tell me something. What do you feel? You must feel something," she encouraged.

Leo looked down, hating himself in that moment. The betrayal was unbearable. It was a pressure on his head and chest.

"I feel. . ."

Leo jerked his head up. Millie had spoken. She turned her head slowly to look at Bauer and Bauer gazed back at her with hope in her eyes. "Yes?" she encouraged. Her eyes were wide as she encouraged her patient to acknowledge her sense of self.

"I feel . . ." she repeated. Then with a silent sigh, she finished her sentence, speaking as if to Bauer, but really speaking to no one at all. "I feel nothing."

It was a letdown even Leo hadn't expected. And yet, oddly, it made sense. It was the only appropriate thing she could have said. He scoffed to himself. She practically glowed or swooned when she spoke about Swinburne and Rossetti. But her family brought out no emotions other than bitter acceptance.

"Millie," Bauer said, "I know it probably seems as if you feel nothing, but look within. You know there is pain and hurt. You can let it out. You can tell us how you feel."

"I feel. . ." she said again, somewhat more animated this time. Her eyes were focused on Bauer this time. Leo could see her blink as he looked at her profile. He thought he could see tears in her eyes, but realized it was the reflection from the light in the room.

"I don't care how you feel," Leo suddenly interrupted.

"Leo!" Dr. Bauer replied with suppressed anger.

He didn't know why he had spoken or why he had said those words. They had come out of him without thinking, but he realized then that despite his guilt for having betrayed Matt, he was angry because she was claiming she felt nothing. Her dead son's words had echoed in the room, confessing secrets he never had understood, and she felt nothing. He was enraged.

"How could you feel nothing?" he asked. Bauer tried to interrupt him, to tell him this was inappropriate and to get him to back off, but he ignored her. "You read this letter. You heard his words spoken again. How could you feel nothing?"

Millie looked downward. She squared her jaw and breathed deeply. He couldn't imagine what she was thinking in that moment, but she made no reply.

"Did you hear what Matt said to you?" he continued. "He blames you for everything, including things that happened with his father. What happened to the man?"

"He was a nightmare," she said softly, not looking at him.

"I don't give a shit what type of person he was!" Leo yelled. "Don't you see that Matt used to cut himself because of something that happened with his father?"

Millie moved slowly, gently putting her squashed box of cigarettes and lighter on the table. She leaned back. She looked off to the left again, then stood. She crossed her arms as she started to pace. She even started to bite on a fingernail. He had never seen her do that before. She shook her head slowly. "I can't," she said softly.

"You can't what?" Bauer asked.

"I can't tell you." She paced slowly, her face revealing troubled thoughts.

"You can't explain what happened to Matt?" Leo asked. "It's obvious that whatever happened to Jack, you're the reason Matt freaked out the way he did. You're the reason he wound up cutting himself! You're the reason he's de—"

She stopped in her tracks and looked at him. He had almost said it, blaming her for his accident. Almost. But he had held back. She stared at him, her eyes angry, but shaken. There was a hesitancy, as if she wasn't sure what to say or how to feel. Confusion. Leo felt the same way, he realized. Too many emotions colliding at once. He calmed himself, focusing on Jack. That was what he needed to know.

"Millie, you have to tell me," Leo said more calmly now. He looked back up at her, the letter in his hand again. "Millie, you owe it to Matt to tell us what happened to his father. He died never knowing the truth."

She was looking at him, her eyes full of confused emotions. "I'm afraid," she said then. He could hear her voice trembling. She looked away and paced.

Was she truly frightened? Her words surprised Leo. In his mind, Millie was afraid of nothing. Yet, he could see her biting her fingernails and how she seemed so lost in her own thoughts. He had never seen her act this way before.

"What are you afraid of?" Bauer asked for him.

She stopped and bit her thumbnail. She glanced up at Leo again. "I never knew he had witnessed anything," she said clearly, in a voice he recognized as her usual calm voice. She stopped biting her nail and crossed her arms. "I had always thought, and prayed, that he was asleep, that he never heard anything that night. You have to believe me when I tell you that. I was terrified my children would be hurt. I didn't care about myself." She looked downward. "I didn't want them near my children."

"Someone was going to hurt them?" Bauer asked.

She nodded slowly. "I was afraid that they would." She looked up at them quickly. "I really believed they were going to come after us next."

"Who?" Leo asked this time, uncertain what she was going to say, and feeling himself grow nervous as he prepared to hear the truth for the first time, a truth even Matt had never known.

She spoke firmly, looking at Leo with a determined gaze. "The men who killed Jack."

Bauer realized the gravity of the situation and quickly went to her side. "Millie, it's all right. You're safe. Leo and I are the only ones here." She took Millie's hands in her own, then stroked Millie's hair to soothe her. "Nothing you say will leave this room. I promise."

Millie gazed at Leo. "There was this man. His name was Salvatore. I never knew his last name. He was Jack's business partner." She hesitated again before continuing. "He was in the Mafia, I think."

Leo blinked. "The Mafia?" he asked, almost mockingly.

"Yes," she replied, nodding toward Bauer, who still worked to comfort her.

"You expect us to believe that your husband was killed by the Mafia?" he asked.

"I knew you wouldn't believe me. But you know what? I don't give a shit!"

"But the Mafia?" he scoffed.

Millie's anger flared. "I said I thought he was in the Mafia!"

Bauer put up her hands between them. "That's enough," she commanded, her accent taking control of the room again.

Leo was in shock. She was lying again. He couldn't believe she was doing this.

"Look," she said to Leo, "I know it seems ridiculous. But this guy Salvatore did exist, and he was a shady businessman."

"Why do you think he was in the Mafia?" Leo asked more calmly now.

"Oh, please, I grew up in Brooklyn, for Christ's sake! We were surrounded by Sicilians! Half the neighborhood fraternized with Mafia cousins in Hoboken or God knows where else!"

Bauer intervened once again. "Why don't we sit down," she suggested. "We should discuss this more calmly now. I don't think it's important whether or not this Salvatore person was involved in organized crime or not," she said, looking at Leo, as if to tell him to drop the interrogation. "We're talking about what happened to Jack," she added. She guided Millie back to the couch, and this time sat beside her and held her hands in her own. "Millie, tell us about the night Matthew was referring to in his letter."

Millie glanced at Leo for encouragement. He leaned back in the wing chair and listened to what she had to say. He tried to imagine it as she described it, as Matt might have seen it as a child, or even as an adult in his hazy memories.

"Jack was involved with commercial real estate," Millie began. "He had inherited the business from his father, but he was a complete failure with it. I didn't know how badly things were with him when we first got married. I found out afterward.

"You have to understand, Jack was a terror at times. When we first got married he was a total gentleman to Theresa and me. Afterward, everything changed. The first time he hit me was because I had redecorated the living room.

"Oh, he was all apologetic and made up to me, but it went downhill from there. I won't insult your intelligence with the whole cycle. You know the story of abused women. They stay in the relationship because they feel trapped or frightened. I felt both. And then I was pregnant and we had another mouth to feed." She scoffed. "I could tell you stories. . ."

Dr. Bauer interrupted her. "Millie, focus on that night."

She took a breath and folded her arms again. She glanced at Leo sharply. "Theresa was sleeping next door at the Whitman's house. She was friends with their daughter Mary." She paused. "They just showed up one night. We used to go to the lake every summer to the house Jack's family owned. It was the one time of the year I had any reprieve from him. Theresa, Matthew, and I would have over two months of sheer bliss. But then he'd always join us toward the end of the summer and the nightmare would begin again.

"It was 1975, toward the end of summer. One night this guy Salvatore and some of his 'associates' showed up unexpectedly. I had never met them, but I could tell Jack was frightened. I'd never seen him scared before. Jack sent me upstairs. From my bedroom I heard them talking downstairs, and then I heard yelling. There was a loud noise, and I swear I heard Jack cry out. I rushed downstairs to check on him, but the front door slammed shut and it was quiet. I ran to my bedroom window overlooking the front of the house. I saw them roughing him up and leading him away."

Millie looked up at her audience. "I was very frightened. He never came back. I had no idea what happened, but I knew it wasn't good. I didn't know what to do, but I thought the best thing would be to get away, as quickly as possible. I woke up Matthew. We packed up everything, his clothes and toys, Theresa's things, my things. I got Theresa then. We got in the car and drove right to my mother's house. I dropped the children off, making her promise to keep them hidden away for a while."

She sighed and looked off into the distance. "And then I took off. I was so frightened by what had happened, I thought for sure they might come look for me or my children. I didn't know what happened to Jack, but I knew it wasn't good. I admit that running away did have one advantage. I wouldn't have to put up with Jack's beatings anymore. I took advantage of that moment to get away from him."

Millie looked at Leo and Dr. Bauer. "No one ever heard from him. I called my mother almost daily to check on Matthew and Theresa. I made her keep them home for a while until I was convinced no one was looking for any of us. Eventually she told me we had to file a missing person's report. I sold the cabin and our home in Brooklyn to use the money to support my children. I filed for divorce on grounds of abandonment. And I made a life for myself in California, where I tried to forget everything about Jack, and knew that my children were living a life better with my mother than I ever could have given them."

Leo and Dr. Bauer listened without interrupting her. Leo had attempted to avoid meeting Millie's occasional glances at him, but when he did look up at them, he noticed more than once that Bauer was listening to her intently, stroking her hands as she sat beside her on the couch. At times he also noticed that she would turn her head slightly, as if trying to hear what Millie wasn't saying. Millie's story focused on the facts of that night. He imagined Bauer was trying to determine how that night had made her feel.

Millie seemed completely genuine in the telling of her story. But there was something that wasn't working for Leo. Why the secrecy all of these years? Had she been that afraid?

That was it. Millie was afraid. It didn't make sense to Leo. The whole time he had known her, she had been like a tigress. How could she have been afraid all of these years? How could she have given off this bullish, aggressive attitude since the day he had spoken to her on the telephone, and been so afraid the entire time?

Bauer spoke. "Millie, who else knows about all of this?"

She breathed deeply for a moment. "I told the police."

"The police questioned you?" Leo said with surprise.

She met his gaze and nodded. "Yes. About a month or two after they found the body. They sent an officer from New Jersey to Hollywood to question me."

"How did they find you?"

"I was using Pierce as my last name then." She hesitated, trying to find the right words to explain her actions from years ago. "When I moved to California, I switched my name back to Hunter to be safe. Only when I moved to Hollywood did I start using Pierce as my last name again. It made things less confusing with Matthew going to school."

"When did you start using Hunter again?"

This time she hesitated before responding, as if anticipating Leo's accusation. "When I moved over here."

"So you did run away from Harrigan after he found you."

"He wouldn't leave me alone! He kept insisting that I had lied to the police. They believed me. I didn't understand why he wouldn't." She looked over at Bauer. "I moved over here to get away from him, and I thought changing my name back to Hunter would get him away from me."

Leo scoffed, shaking his head. "Obviously that didn't work."

"It did for a while," she retorted. "But then he found me. He showed up at my door about a month or so before Matthew died. And it's because of him that we're sitting here and I've told you all of this."

"And, what? You're not afraid of this guy Salvatore and his people now?"

"Of course I am, Leo. If I wasn't, I would have told the story to everyone, including Matthew, a long time ago."

Bauer said, "I think we've had quite a difficult meeting, and it's time we stopped."

"Wait," Leo said. "One more thing." He had looked at the words Matt had written, and something occurred to him. He looked at Millie and met her gaze. "We did all this because of the letter that Matt wrote." He held it aloft in his right hand. "Matt is the reason that the truth has even come out." He paused a moment, thinking how to word his question. "You realize that he saw something that night, don't you? He witnessed what they did to his father."

"Leo, I swear to you, I never knew that." She spoke with a clarity to her voice. "I am not lying when I tell you that I never knew that, not until I had read that letter. I never knew."

"You didn't know that Matt had probably seen his father killed?"

She looked at him with a fierceness in her eyes. "Leo, I swear, I never knew it. I thought he was asleep the whole time."

"You realize this was what did it to him." He could feel a wave of emotional understanding in the pit of his stomach. "This is why he started cutting himself. His psychiatrist had told us that sometimes cutting victims base their illness on a tragic event in their lives."

"And he died," Bauer added, "never understanding the truth about what happened to his father. How tragic."

Leo looked up at Millie, and she averted his gaze. Too quickly.

And there it was again. He watched her for the next few seconds. She was not responding, emotionally or otherwise. He knew then in that moment that she still hadn't told them everything, and that she wasn't going to.

He stood abruptly. He looked at Bauer, who seemed complacent, then at Millie, who avoided him. He glanced at the letter in his hand, then placed it and the envelope on the glass table beside her cigarettes. "I think this belongs to you," he said to Millie, his voice somber. "Excuse me," he said, then exited Bauer's office. He could hear Millie calling after him, but he kept moving, struggling with the cries bursting within him. He left the hospital, more confused and angry than before. All of it was lies, or all of it was true. Whichever, he knew she hadn't told them everything.

– THIRTEEN –

He could feel a familiar prodding from behind, between his legs. He knew he was in bed, pretty sure he was asleep. But the prodding was waking him. He recognized the earthy smell that was his lover. He didn't open his eyes, but inched himself closer to feel the prodding start to penetrate him. The body of his lover pressed naked hip against hip, chest against back. Small puckered lips brushed against the soft sensual nape of his neck, just behind the ear, sending chills down his body. An arm came around to embrace him tightly, then reached down and touched him. It felt good, but for the damp sensation. There was a warm wetness like some special lubricant he didn't recognize, first running along his torso, then dripping from the lifted arm. He rotated his head back without opening his eyes to kiss the lips on his neck. He tasted the liquid on his tongue, and he choked. He opened his eyes and sat up choking more. He reached with his hand to his mouth and pulled it away. Blood stained his fingers. He looked down and saw blood on his torso, hips, and cock. He turned quickly to tell his lover, and then he screamed. Matt looked up at him, naked, erect, bleeding. The blood seeped Christ-like out of knife wounds on his body. The wounds flashed close-up in his eyes, the slice of a sharp knife or serrated glass stretched across his muscles and tissue. The blood seeped from the cuts in beautifully horrific displays of gravity and tension. "Matt, you're bleeding!" he shouted. But his lover was unphased. He tilted his head back toward the pillow. "You wanted to know the truth," he said. "This is it." Leo jumped out of bed, his instinct to call for help, when he bumped into Millie, puffing on a cigarette in his bedroom, looking down at him over silver half-eyeglasses. "You wanted to know the truth," she said. "Now you know." He screamed again, then turned and saw Matt kneeling on the bed now,

Pierce
© 2007 by The Haworth Press, Inc. All rights reserved.
doi:10.1300/5849_13

his erection surrounded by bleeding wounds drenching the sheets, his voice echoing his mother's words, "Now you know." Leo looked back from one to the other, uncertain which way to turn, screaming.

The telephone rang, and he was sucked into sitting up, gasping for breath. His heart pounded and his body was drenched in a cold sweat. He flailed in the bed, panicking for a few moments, looking for Matt, but seeing no one. No Matt. No Millie. Just himself, lying in his bed alone, the morning sunlight peeking in from the vertical blinds on the window. The phone rang again. He realized it had been a nightmare, but it was taking him a moment to calm down. The phone rang a third time. He reached across the bed and grabbed it off the other nightstand. He wiped his brow with his hand and breathed heavily into the phone, managing to say hello.

"Leonardo? What's wrong?" It was his mother.

"I'm okay. Nightmare, that's all."

"Ah, *sì*. Nightmares, your fears." How wise she was at times. "Sunday is Mother's Day!" she exclaimed suddenly. "You come for dinner? I make veal parmigiana!"

Leo fanned himself with the sheet. "Mamma, I haven't thought about it. Can I—"

"Ah! What's to think about? I'm your mamma! You come for Mother's Day!"

"We'll do something—"

"You can't make plans now? It's a couple of days before, and you can't come to see your mamma on Mother's Day? Giorgio would never do that to me!"

Leo breathed deeply. He wanted to hang up on her. Instead, he changed his tone and was exceedingly sweet. "Mamma, how about we do something different for a change? I'll take you out for dinner. We'll go anywhere you want."

She paused before responding. "There is this new Italian restaurant near Tyrone mall." She mentioned someone from the Italian-American Club who had gone. "She enjoyed it very much. It's called Carrabba's."

"Mamma, it's not new. It's been there for a while."

"Well, it's new for me. But if you don't want to go there—"

"No," he said, desperate to get off the phone. "That's fine. We'll go to Carrabba's."

"It may be expensive. I look for coupons."

"You do that."

"Do we need reservation?"

"Yes, probably. Why don't you make one?"

"A che ora?"

"I don't know. Whatever time is good for you, Mamma. I have to go. Call me when you have the reservation, and I'll pick you up a half hour before." He hung up before she could reply, and he flopped back into the pillows with a sigh of relief and exhaustion.

After a few moments, he turned on his side. He looked over at the nightstand and gazed at the photograph of the two of them, their happy moment caught forever on film. He reached out with a finger and touched Matt's face, right at the spot where Leo could see the sharp upturned grin on his face as he kissed Leo's cheek. They were beautiful together. So different from the flash of nightmare, his lover sliced and bleeding. And the words.

He hadn't pursued the truth for himself. He had done it for Matt. It had been his intention to know only for Matt's sake. Matt had died not knowing the truth, and Leo owed it to him to help understand that great mystery of his life. The problem, Leo realized, was that Matt was no better off knowing. He was dead. He heard in his mind Millie's words from the day before. He felt guilty that he had let Matt down, that he could have done something to stop him from driving off that night and dying in the car crash.

What if Matt had killed himself? What if it was intentional? It would have had serious repercussions on Leo's life. He never would have received the insurance money, and he never would have been able to stay in the house. His entire life would have been transformed. But it went beyond the mundane, and he couldn't believe it. It would have meant Matt had given up, on himself, and on them.

Why was Millie so focused on believing her son had killed himself? He thought about the letter Matt had written to his mother, and the brief mention at the end of him wanting to kill himself. Could it be that that convinced her? A few simple words? Millie was so different from him in her reading of the same events, and almost needed Leo to validate her belief. Perhaps for her it was about justification, that after everything she had been through with Matt, she needed to believe he had chosen to end his own life as poetic justice. Maybe that really was her guilt, that she had failed him as a mother. Perhaps she needed to believe it to justify her own role in his life, almost a martyr complex in some ways. And what struck Leo is that for as much as he didn't believe Matt had killed himself, she did believe it. They had different versions of the same story. It was almost, he realized, like her explanation for Jack's death.

Millie had been precise about what had happened to Jack. She had described the events very well, as if they had never left her mind, even though they had happened over twenty years ago. And she had said and acted like she was frightened. But Leo didn't get it. There was something to the story she told and the fear she exhibited. It seemed almost theatrical. What if she had made it up?

Then again, what if it were true? Her story was plausible. Peculiar maybe, but plausible. There really was no reason to doubt her story. And even if she had stretched the truth a little, or been a bit dramatic, it didn't change the fact that Jack was still dead.

He looked at the framed photograph. "You'd doubt her, wouldn't you?" He knew the answer to his own question. "You would want proof."

How could he get proof, though? He wasn't about to ask Harrigan. He thought about Theresa. She might know something. But supposedly she didn't remember anything. Besides, Millie had said that she wasn't even there the night that Jack had disappeared. She probably wouldn't have missed him either. But he wondered if he could be discreet somehow, and find out from Theresa how he might research this information on his own. She was a librarian. He had figured out that librarians knew everything, or at least how to find out about everything. It was a stupid thought though. He couldn't ask her. He would have to think of something else.

Leo forced himself out of bed. He opened the vertical blinds and the light stunned him for a moment. He realized he had no idea what time it was, and glanced at the clock on the other nightstand. It was after nine-thirty already. He was going in the shower, but stopped to look out the window again. He heard the roaring of a motor and saw his next-door neighbor mowing her lawn. He looked down at the shrubs and grass outside of his own house and knew he was overdue to do the same before the neighbors complained. The lawn was almost a foot high after not having mowed it in two months or so. He grimaced to himself, not really wanting to do this. His neighbor was dripping in sweat already. He could just imagine the humidity.

He dressed in a pair of shorts and tank top, then made coffee and toast for breakfast. He flipped on the television to check the local weather on the eights of the hour. He was hoping for news of a morning shower, to excuse him from cutting the lawn. No such luck. The Weather Channel showed him the map of the Tampa Bay area. Words came up about early morning sun, then information about another tropical storm. More storms were on the way, continuing through Mother's Day. He read the special warning of heavy rains to start late tonight, with local flooding and severe lightning.

Leo turned off the television with a sigh. He'd mow the lawn now before the rains came. He shook his head in disgust, then got off the couch. He put on his sneakers, unlocked the door, and grimaced as he stepped into the humid morning on his front porch. He stretched and stifled a yawn. He finally opened his screen door and stepped outside, walking through the yard into the back where he had the shed with the bicycles, lawn mower, and remnant picket fence. He waved to his neighbor as he passed. The straw smell of dried grass was thick in the air. As he walked, it scratched at his calves. Florida crabgrass was coarse and weedlike, not to mention filled with fleas and other vermin. You didn't run barefoot through Florida lawns. It was nothing like the soft lawns he remembered from New Jersey. He reached the shed and pulled out the mower, edger, trimmer, and container of gas.

He added gas to the mower, remembering Matt showing him how to attach the dispenser on the plastic container of gas in order to pour it into the mower. The heady smell rushed up his nose, and he looked away. His eyes watered. When he was finished, he sealed the container and put it off to the side. He bent over the mower and pulled the cord with force. Nothing happened. He tried it two more times, then the mower roared. He remembered that he was supposed to get control of it right away. It had sprung to life and was starting to inch away on its own.

Cutting the grass with this old machine was extremely difficult, especially with the lawn at this height. He considered starting in the backyard, but then realized he should do the front yard first, in case he decided to stop and finish the job another day. He pushed the mower along the side of the house, mowing a semistraight line through the grass. It was then that he realized that he had forgot to put the bag on it and that grass was shooting against the house. He would have to rake it all up afterward. He sighed in exasperation. He was awful at this outdoor landscape stuff.

He pushed the mower all the way to the front of his property. His neighbor had already done her front lawn, and had been kind enough to do the small portion of his lawn on the one side of the driveway. Leo was able to start on the main property. He went all the way down toward the sidewalk area and started moving in a horizontal direction, the motor resounding in his ears and vibrating in his hands.

He was about halfway through the front yard, lost in thought about ripping out the overgrown shrubs around the front porch. As he turned around with the mower, he was only half conscious of the large truck newly parked across the street. Then, he jumped back. Standing in his driveway was Armando.

He was wearing a brown cap and his brown shorts. His brown shirt had the top few buttons open, a light patch of dark hair visible right away. He wore dark aviator sunglasses. His smile was framed by his neatly trimmed goatee, and he shook his head with laughter. He had his hands in his front pockets. Leo quickly turned off the lawn mower and used the bottom of his tank top to wipe the sweat from his brow.

"Working hard?" Armando asked.

Leo nodded with a grin. "I hate doing this."

"Yeah, I kind of figured that. This place looks like a jungle."

"Thanks," Leo muttered, only mildly insulted.

"You know, I could help you."

Leo glanced at the truck. "Aren't you working?"

"Not now! Some other time."

"Well, thanks, but I need to do it this morning though. Storm tonight."

"Yeah, I heard. Sorry I can't help you now."

"No problem." Although, admittedly, Leo was disappointed. He could have used the help. And he wouldn't have minded hanging out with Armando. He caught a glimpse of his chest in his open shirt again, and he felt himself responding. Almost instinctively, he asked, "Did you want a drink or anything? Iced tea?"

"Lemonade?" Armando said suggestively.

Leo closed his eyes and shook his head. "Do you need to keep reminding me?"

Armando laughed. "I would have a drink, but I have deliveries to make."

They were silent for a moment. "So . . . why are you here?" Leo asked.

"Delivery in your neighborhood." He pointed across the street to the house where the little girl with pigtails lived. "I saw you outside, thought I'd stop by." Leo nodded in response. Armando looked downward. "You haven't called me," he said.

He looked away sheepishly, then back at him. "Yes, I'm sorry about that." He wiped his sweating brow again. "It's not you, Armando. I've been busy with stuff."

He nodded slowly. "Well, I'd still like to see you again."

Leo was glad to hear this. At least he hadn't botched up everything. "So would I." He thought he'd plunge. "What are you doing this weekend?"

Armando made a face, his hands moving from his pockets to one another over his stomach. "I'm going to Orlando this weekend, for Mother's Day. But, I'm free tonight."

"That's good. We can do something tonight."

"I can't go partying or anything though. I have to work on an article tomorrow morning before I leave. I have a deadline on Monday."

"That's fine with me."

"Great! I'll call you after work to figure out a time."

"Sounds good. I'm looking forward to it."

"Me too!" he said. Armando smiled, then turned and walked to the truck. Leo watched the sexy Latino ass and muscular calves with the brown boots. He was surprising himself how much he liked this boy. Not only was he hot, but he was interesting, and interested in Leo.

Armando was getting into the truck, when suddenly Leo realized something. Armando worked for a newspaper. Which meant he probably knew something about how to get news information. Maybe he could help him. Without hesitating, he called to him. A car passed, so he had to wait a moment. The truck started in the meantime. He called more loudly and came to the truck. Armando stepped down from the seat and stood on the bottom step above him. Leo looked up at him. "What's up?" Armando asked over the rumbling of the engine.

He wasn't sure how much he should go into right now. This certainly wasn't the most appropriate time or place. He decided to keep the information to a minimum for the moment. "This newspaper you work for. Do you have the ability to do research, or do they have researchers or something?"

He nodded. "They have one news librarian on staff. I don't usually go to him for help though. Why, what's up?"

Leo considered his request then. "Is there some way, maybe, that you could help me do some research?"

He couldn't see Armando's eyes, but he saw his head jerk back. "You want me to help you do research on your dissertation? I don't know anything about—"

"No," he interrupted him, feeling foolish for the moment, "this has nothing to do with my dissertation." He really wasn't sure how much he should say at that moment. Another car drove past and he moved in toward the truck to avoid the car. He looked back up at Armando and said, "It has to do with the other night, when that PI was here."

"Oh," he replied, his surprise evident. He was serious now, and was thinking about that night. "About your lover's father being missing?"

Leo hesitated, then nodded. "Yes, but it's more complicated than that. If you're too busy, I can find—"

"No, it's okay. I can help you. Or at least try. I should be done working by around three o'clock or so. Let me go home first to get showered and ready, and then I'll come over."

Leo nodded in acknowledgment. "That sounds good. Thanks. I'll take you to dinner afterward as a treat."

Armando smiled. "Yeah, okay. I'd like that."

Leo was smiling now too. "All right. So I'll see you a little later." Armando chuckled. "What's so funny?" Leo asked.

"You have me intrigued, Dr. Vasari."

Leo found himself amused by the comment. Instead of responding verbally, he did so physically, reaching up with his hands to touch Armando's calves.

"Stop it," Armando said jokingly, his legs twitching. Leo ignored him and traced his fingers lightly and slowly toward the back of his knees, caressing the dark hairs with a magnetic sensation. His hands moved further upward and entered the bottoms of his shorts. He grabbed the bottoms of his thighs and squeezed a bit, then tried to go higher, but his hands could only reach to the middle of his thighs. He saw movement above him then, Armando responding inside his shorts.

"That's it, stop it!" Armando said more forcefully now with a laugh and shiver. "I have to go!" He quickly stepped up and away from Leo, who now dropped his hands with disappointment. Armando sat in the seat of the truck. "You are bad, Dr. Vasari!" he said. Leo grinned back, then winked. "I'll see you later," Armando said, looking toward the road. He glanced back at Leo one last time and adjusted himself.

Leo laughed, stepped away from the truck, and went back to his side of the street. The truck rumbled down the brick-paved road, leaving Leo feeling oddly giddy and happy. He liked this guy. As he watched the back of the truck disappear, though, he wondered how much he could trust him with Millie's story. He would have to think about how much he could say about the research that needed to be done. The last thing he wanted was a news story coming out afterward about what he had told him. He didn't think Armando would necessarily do that. But then he realized that he really didn't know him very well at all. He had to be careful and keep most of the information to himself for Millie's sake.

– FOURTEEN –

After finishing the lawn, Leo took a long, cool shower and ate a quick lunch. He paid bills, then decided to clean up before Armando arrived. He moved a few pieces of furniture back to their proper locations and fluffed pillows on the couch and chairs. He rearranged knickknacks scattered throughout the house. He straightened his mother's painting of his great-grandmother over the couch, then stepped back to look at it. It had been up there for a while. He decided to exchange this one and a few others with the ones stored in the office closet to give the place a different feel. He sat on the floor in front of the closet and flipped through the framed paintings. He found a Byzantine-looking Madonna whose face resembled his mother's. It was creepy how she had venerated herself, but aesthetically it was beautiful with rich gold and ruby hues. He pulled out another one of Saints Catherine and Dominic, and the angel that his mother had given him for his birthday. He finished going through all of them and carried the three into the living room where he exchanged them for others hanging about the place. He carried the removed pictures and put them in the closet in front of the others. He turned to leave the office, then hesitated. He crouched and pulled out the painting he avoided most.

When he thought about the photograph of his lover and he in his bedroom as compared to this painting, he found an interesting contrast in the presentation, even though they were both portraits. The photograph was humanistic, romantic even, a snapshot, a moment frozen in time when the person who took the picture saw Leo snuggle up to Matt and Matt turn and reach upward to kiss Leo.

The oil painting, on the other hand, was austere. The association with them as saints was a little frightening. In contrast to the photograph, it idealized them. He still found the portrayal of himself to be inaccurate. But the figure of Matt was oddly uncanny to him. Perhaps it was the way she had depicted his spiked blond hair or cheek bones. The portrayal was anachronistic to the trecento style of the painting, but somehow it made Matt's face more lifelike. They didn't touch each other, which added to the austerity, but the keys to their house lay on the ground between them. They were joined by property and destiny, the painting said. But there was no passion in this painting. Respect. Decency. But no passion.

The most creative aspect of the painting was the name association. It was also the part that bothered Leo the most. The arrows. Blood dripped from these wounds. The shocking symbolism bothered Leo tremendously. His mother wasn't psychic of Matt's future or even conscious of his cutting problem, but her forethought of his skin being cut and blood pouring forth was frightening. And beside him stood Leo's persona, unable to do anything to help him. His mother's creativity had added something surreal, almost psychological, that perhaps said more about Matt and Leo's relationship than the photograph of them as intimate lovers.

He quickly put the picture back in the closet with the rest of the paintings. They had never hung this picture before, and he certainly wasn't going to now. It would serve only to haunt him. The photograph on the nightstand did that enough.

Armando was coming over soon. Leo quickly ran into the master bathroom and washed up again. He looked around in his closet and drawers for something decent to wear and found a nice pair of Geoffrey Beene jeans he hadn't worn in a while and a new dark blue Polo shirt he had picked up when he had been shopping on his birthday. He gelled his hair again so that the waves of dark hair almost parted to the side and pushed upward. It wasn't a new look, but one that he hadn't tried in a while. The more he got ready for what he imagined was his date, the more he realized he was giddy and nervous about seeing Armando again. He took a deep breath looking at his reflection and forced himself to remember that there was serious business to take care of first. He needed to get Armando's help on the research first.

He heard a knock in the distance. He took one last look at his appearance, turned off the bathroom light, and headed toward the living room. He opened the front door and smiled when he saw Armando standing there. He was wearing jeans and a beige, checkered, short-sleeve shirt with the top few buttons open. On another person, the habit of revealing chest hair might have seemed obnoxious, but Leo found it irresistible.

Armando's hand suddenly came from around his back. In it he held a wrapped bouquet of mixed flowers: yellow asters, white daisies, baby's breath, a green fern, and a single red rose. Leo's mouth dropped. "You did not buy me flowers."

Armando made a face. "No, I bought them for the lady next door, but she wasn't home, so you can have them."

Leo mimicked a laugh. "I've never had anyone give me flowers before." He was twenty-nine, and he had been with Matt for four years, and he had never once received flowers. In contrast, Leo had given Matt flowers three times: once for their first anniversary, second for his promotion, and third for his funeral. "Thank you," he added, taking them, smelling them, luxuriating in their beautifully mixed sweet scents, quickly hiding his lament with joy.

He leaned forward and they kissed and hugged on the threshold. Leo stepped aside and told Armando to come in. They entered the house and Leo shut the door behind him. He told Armando to get comfortable and went to find a vase. He had to look through a few cabinets and found an old wine carafe that he could use.

As he put the flowers in water, he heard Armando's shoes walking on the hardwood floor in the dining room. "Did you just get this painting?"

Leo carried the flowers into the dining room and set them on the table not far from where he had last set the Swinburne and Rossetti books. He stood beside him, looking at the painting. "No, I've had it for a while. I changed them around though." Armando pointed to the signature in the lower right corner. Leo's mother always signed her work with her full Italianate name, Rosa Vasari, with a flourish. He answered his unspoken question. "They're my mother's paintings. Ever since my father died, that's been her grief therapy."

"Is she totally religious?"

Leo thought about the interesting question a moment. "No, I wouldn't say that. I think she's more into the ritual of Catholicism, but not so much all of the doctrines." Leo wondered about his reaction to the painting. "Do you like it?"

Armando hesitated, nodding slowly. He glanced at Leo quickly, then back at the painting. "It's. . .interesting."

"You hate it."

"No!" he said defensively, his face a look of fear. "It's not my taste. It's beautiful, if you like that style."

Leo laughed. "It's all right. I'm not crazy about them either."

Armando relaxed. "Okay, I feel better now. Why do you have them hung up then?"

"Do you really have to ask? My mother painted them. I have no choice." As an afterthought, he added, "Matt actually used to like them." He regretted saying it as soon as he did. They looked at each other and there was a moment of awkward silence. Leo changed the subject as quickly as he could with the first thing that came to his mind. "Do you want a drink?"

"Boy, you keep pushing that lemonade on me," he said jokingly.

Leo chuckled. "Sorry, no lemonade. Iced tea if you want it."

"Sounds good, thanks." Leo went into the kitchen and poured out glasses of iced tea for both of them. He was walking back into the dining room with the glasses and coasters when he heard Armando ask, "Are these yours?"

Leo entered to see him holding the Swinburne book. He was carelessly flipping through the pages. In an odd moment, Leo felt fearful and upset that he was touching the books. But he restrained himself from jolting forward and taking the book away. "Um, kind of," he replied. "They're very rare, so be careful with them."

He didn't seem to get the hint. He stopped flipping and opened up the book at an area where the spine was breaking. He looked at one of the poem. "I don't understand poetry at all," he said. "It never makes sense to me. I prefer straight prose."

"Well, you're a journalist."

"Yeah, I guess," he said. He put the book down, and Leo felt a sense of relief. Armando took one of the glasses from Leo.

"Actually, those books are probably a good segue into what I need your help with."

Armando drank some of the iced tea. "What do you mean?"

Leo pulled out the chair at the one end of the table and motioned for Armando to do the same with the chair on the side. They both sat and Leo gave each of them a coaster. Leo drank some of the tea also, then set it down.

"It's kind of a complicated story," he said to Armando. "Are you sure you want to hear this?"

"If you want me to help you, you need to tell me."

Leo nodded in acknowledgment. He was still hesitant. He didn't want to betray Millie. That much he knew for sure. He wondered what Armando might know already. "What did you pick up on from the other night with the PI?"

Armando arched his eyebrows for the moment. "You mean, other than the guy being an asshole?" Leo grinned in agreement. "He showed up wanting to talk to you about your boyfriend's father being missing." Leo nodded. "How long was his father missing?"

"Over twenty years." He wondered how he should begin, then decided to blurt out the most obvious fact. "They found his body three years ago in a lake in New Jersey."

Armando jerked backward in his chair, his eyes opening wide. "No way! That's messed up. What happened? Did he drown?"

Leo realized that he didn't exactly know the details of Jack Pierce's death. "The only thing I know for sure is that his skeletal remains were found in the lake. They identified him from dental records and a missing person's report filed over twenty years ago." Leo considered again telling him everything that Millie had said, but he was still hesitant. He thought about the story he had known all along up until just the other night, and it occurred to him that might suffice for now. "From what I understand, he was pretty abusive to Matt and his family. He apparently took off during the night and they never heard from him again."

"He left, just like that? That sounds odd."

Leo realized now how odd it did sound, and it made him realize how Matt must have questioned it all his life, how or why his father could disappear like that without any warning and never try to see his son again. "Harrigan, the PI asshole," Leo continued, "was the one who told me his body had been found. He's trying to find out what happened to him." He mentioned also that someone in Jack's family had hired him.

"So he tracked down Matt as his son down here in Florida? How weird," Armando said.

"Actually," Leo replied, realizing he could say this, "Harrigan tracked down Matt's mother first. He never spoke to Matt."

"I didn't know his mother was in the picture."

Leo scoffed. "Yes, well, that's a whole other story," he said. Leo pointed to books on the table. "That's the connection to those. They belong to Millie, Matt's mother. She gave them to me." Leo chuckled suddenly. "You know, this is kind of strange. It just occurred to me that those books were the two packages you delivered to me."

"For real?" He suddenly reached over and picked up the Rossetti, flipping through it. This time, though, Leo didn't feel the same sense of panic he had a few moments beforehand when he had handled the Swinburne. Apparently Armando was supposed to touch those books.

"So what do you think?" Leo asked.

He put the book back down. "I think you've got quite a story there! It's like some sort of scandalous family drama. It would make a great article."

Leo paled. "You're not thinking about writing about this for a story, are you?"

"Please. No. I do pieces on being a Latino and entertainment bits. I don't do society columns or crime pieces." Leo wasn't convinced, though, and it apparently showed in his face. Armando grew serious. "Leo, it's all right. I swear. I'm not going to write about this. You asked me to help you with research, that's all. I promise."

Leo felt a little relieved. "Can you think of how I can find out more information?"

"Sure, you should talk to Matt's mother. What was her name? Millie?"

"I already spoke to her. She doesn't know anything more than what I told you," he lied, looking down, then drinking the last of his iced tea.

Armando sat back in his chair. "All right, so we're thinking about news stories? Is that what you meant earlier?" Leo nodded. "You want to know if there are any news articles that you can read up on the case?"

"Yes."

"Leo, actually, you don't really need me to do this. You're at USF. They have newspaper databases like LexisNexis and NewsBank. And if they found the body three years ago, then there's going to be information in the database, probably in full text."

Leo felt sheepish. "I had no idea." He silently scolded himself for being such a poor researcher. "So I have to go over to Tampa?"

"No, you could do it right here at their St. Petersburg campus library." Leo's feeling of stupidity must have shown. "Haven't you ever been there?"

"Uh, no, actually. I've been going to Tampa all these years."

"Oh, my God. Leo, the campus is like five minutes from your house. They have a beautiful new library they built a few years ago. I used to use it when I was at the Poynter Institute." He drank the last of his iced tea, then checked his sports watch. "It's after four-thirty," he said. "We can head over there now and look up some of the information if you want. I think they're open for a few more hours."

Leo nodded in agreement and put the glasses in the sink. He was embarrassed by how silly he felt, but at the same time he was grateful that Armando was willing to help. They met in the living room and Leo put on his sneakers. As they were walking out, Armando mentioned about a notepad and pen or pencil. Leo was going to go back inside for them, but Armando told him he had some in his own car. Leo thought about the cliché of a reporter having a notebook ready for a story, then reminded himself that Armando was doing this to help him, not for a story.

Armando volunteered to drive. Since they were going to the USF campus, Leo realized he could bring his parking tag to make it easier for them, so he retrieved it from his own rear view mirror. Leo hopped into the passenger seat of the white Hyundai, and Armando handed him a small notepad and pencil from somewhere in the rear seat of the car. He encouraged Leo to write down some of the facts that he knew. It would help make the research easier. Leo tried to pay attention to where Armando was driving so that he could come here in the future, but at the same time wrote down the facts as he knew them.

Jack Pierce had disappeared when Matt was almost six. That was in August 1975. It had taken place at the summer house at Cranberry Lake in New Jersey. Jack's body had turned up in the lake in mid-April 1996, just over three years before. Leo considered other bits of information from what Millie had told him and what he knew about Matt's cutting problem, but he didn't want to write them on the paper. The only thing he did add was a line beneath this information, and the name *Salvatore* under it.

– FIFTEEN –

Armando wasn't joking when he said the campus was five minutes away. It was located on the South side near the Salvador Dalí Museum. As Armando parked, Leo felt foolish that he had forgotten the campus even existed. It was a small, beautiful campus on the western side of Tampa Bay. From the seawall, Leo could see yachts docked at the marina. Each of the few buildings on campus faced the water. They walked toward the ascetic white library. Once inside, the windows brought in natural light, which gave it a warmth, unlike the Tampa library with its yellowing cinder-block walls and fluorescent bulbs. Large, contemporary sculptures hung from the third-story ceiling. Shelving was relatively sparse, allowing for growth. There was still a smell of new construction, sawdust, and paint, even though it was a couple of years old. Only about a dozen students were visible on the main floor, and a reference librarian sat reading.

Armando and he walked toward one of the research computers and sat before it. Armando opened up Netscape and easily manipulated the database list looking for what he wanted. Leo watched him skim through a Web page or two as he quickly found what he was looking for. Leo was amazed. He pulled open a database and asked Leo what he wanted to look up first. Leo considered the idea, then consulted his notepad. "I guess Jack Pierce, Matt's father."

Armando typed in the name and clicked a few more boxes related to types of news products and dates. He clicked on search. After a few seconds, a message came back saying there were too many hits. They had to narrow down the search. Leo told him to add Cranberry Lake. They were pleasantly surprised when it brought up about a dozen news articles.

doi:10.1300/5849_15

Scanning through the titles, Leo was immediately surprised to discover how some of the top hits were directly related to what he wanted to know. He caught phrases like "body found" and "identified" and "police investigation." A few hits didn't seem relevant, but Armando suggested they go through them one at a time. The relevant news stories all came from the local *New Jersey Herald* newspaper, with the exception of two from the *New York Daily News*. They started at the earliest relevant story near the bottom of the list. The story dated from April 30, 1996, the same date as the video news broadcast. Like the video, this article revealed that the body found two weeks earlier had been identified as Jack Pierce, missing since 1975. There was nothing new in this article. Armando e-mailed it to Leo, just in case he needed it later.

The next article went into more depth. It described who Jack Pierce was, his connection to Brooklyn, and his life as a commercial realtor. There was even a similar quote Mrs. Whitman who had lived on the neighboring property and eventually bought the Pierce's house. Leo scanned for any references he recognized. He saw Millicent Pierce's name and mention of two unnamed children, believed to be in California. The police were quoted as saying that they were working to identify the whereabouts of Mrs. Pierce and her children. She was not a suspect, but wanted for questioning. They e-mailed that article. Armando suggested printing them out as well. "You never know with e-mail if it's going to get there." Leo agreed, so they sent it to the networked laser printer and would retrieve it afterward.

Another relevant *Herald* article was dated about three weeks after the last one. It was an update to the story with a headline that caught Leo's eye: "Pierce victim of organized crime." Armando eyed him curiously, but Leo didn't say anything. The police were quoted in the article as saying they had ruled out that the Pierces were in California, but were still looking for them. The article went into more details about Jack Pierce's business dealings, mentioning a few building projects that had failed in the 1970s under questionable circumstances due to Pierce's ineptitude. Then, appearing for the first time, was the name Leo had been searching for: Salvatore Portavia. He was Jack's business partner starting around 1972.

Portavia was long rumored to be an associate of the New York-based Gelotti family. It was unclear whether he was a blood relative, but evidence suggested that he had worked with members of this suspected organized crime family. Portavia was charged and convicted of racketeering in 1985. He died a year later in prison from an apparent heart attack after turning state's evidence and agreeing to cooperate with investigators in the prosecution of Vincent Gelotti for murder.

"Shit," Leo said with surprise, sitting back in his chair. "Salvatore did exist."

"Yeah, I caught that, about the organized crime association. Were you going to mention that part?" Armando's voice sounded both excited and cautious.

"I didn't really know." He glanced at Armando, who looked at him with disbelief. "All right, so maybe I heard something about the guy and organized crime. I wouldn't worry about it."

"Worried? Who said I'm worried?" Armando said jokingly. "The guy's dead."

Leo sighed. "I didn't know he was dead. I was hoping there was something else about him."

"Like that he confessed to killing Jack Pierce?"

Leo nodded, then exhaled heavily. "I guess that was a long shot, wasn't it?"

"Not necessarily. There are a few more articles left."

Leo agreed. He moved closer to the monitor. Unconsciously, he moved forward to manipulate the mouse when he felt Armando's hand do the same. They looked at each other and laughed. "Sorry," Leo said, pulling back.

"I'm not," Armando said. He glanced around quickly and without a moment's hesitation kissed Leo on the lips.

Leo flushed, then saw that Armando was even more red. He laughed. "You're nuts. You'll get us thrown out."

Armando shifted in the seat and cleared his throat. "Not until we finish our work."

They glanced back at each other and smiled. Leo hated to admit it, but he found their joint effort oddly romantic. If he had seen another couple doing something like this, he would have found it sickening.

He clicked on the word "next" and pulled up an irrelevant article. He clicked again, and a good article came up, this time from the *New York Daily News*. The article was a lengthy recap of much that had been published in the local New Jersey paper, but there was additional information related to Brooklyn. It went into more detail about Jack's business dealings and described additional information about Salvatore Portavia's suspected crimes and how the two caused the eviction of numerous tenants in the early 1970s in a scam to demolish buildings for new development. The article gave an address in Bay Ridge where Jack Pierce's family had lived until 1975. Property tax records showed that the Brooklyn house had been sold five months after he was reported missing. The article went on to report that he had been declared officially missing with the Brooklyn police department in the spring of 1976 by his mother-in-law. At the time of Jack's disappearance, the Pierce children were living with their grandmother and his wife was in California. She had filed for divorce on grounds of abandonment. There was a quote at the very end by a woman who was Jack Pierce's cousin.

"It's disgusting what happened. My aunt and uncle were the sweetest people, and my cousin an upstanding citizen. I don't believe any of these rumors about his business dealings. I blame that woman he married. She takes off with all of his money, and he's declared missing? They should arrest her."

There was no justification for the woman's remarks other than her own opinion. It was then that Leo jolted and reread the last part of the article. "That son of a bitch," he muttered. Leo pointed to the woman's name on the screen: Mrs. Agnes Harrigan.

"Isn't that the PI's last name?"

"Yes. Unbelievable."

"It could be a coincidence," Armando suggested.

"I seriously doubt it. He has to be related to Jack. No wonder he's been hounding Millie all this time. He has some personal vendetta."

"What do you mean he's been hounding her?"

Leo remembered that he hadn't told Armando everything. He felt more trustful of him, but he waved off his question for the moment. "I'll tell you later. Let's finish up here."

They e-mailed and printed that article and continued to the last few dated about two weeks later. Both claimed that Mrs. Pierce had been discovered living in Hollywood, Florida. Investigators were in the process of questioning her although she was not considered a suspect. They also made mention that the Sussex County Coroner's Office had issued a statement that due to the nature of the body's remains and where it was found, it was impossible to rule Jack Pierce's death as being anything more than an accident. They could not explain how his remains could have stayed underwater all these years, nor could they explain the marks on two ribs and clavicle bones, suggesting that he may have suffered from some trauma. The *Herald* also quoted an anonymous source in the police department who said that it was possible Portavia was partly responsible for Pierce's death. He commented about how the body might have been dumped in the lake weighed down with blocks, "classic Mafia style." It ended with him saying that there was no way to prove anything one way or the other. The *Daily News* article quoted Mrs. Harrigan again that she suspected, without evidence of course, that her cousin's wife had something to do with Jack's disappearance. She pointed out she had run off with all the money. The reporter countered her claim by noting that Pierce and Portavia's business was broke. In January 1976, before Jack was officially declared missing, Portavia filed for bankruptcy. One year later, he reopened a brand new commercial real estate company with two partners related to the Gelotti family.

Leo and Armando found one last article from the New Jersey paper. It was dated from early July 1996 and was a single paragraph. The reporter highlighted the current status of the investigation, claiming that Millicent Pierce had been interviewed by police and she had told them about the visit of Salvatore and two other men in August 1975. She had gone upstairs, heard arguing downstairs, then the front door slam. She never saw her husband again. Her family was scheduled to return to Brooklyn the next morning, and they did so without Jack. Rather than return home, however, she brought them to her mother's house because she had decided to take this opportunity to leave her husband because he used to physically abuse his wife and children. The reporter praised her resolve and encapsulated the remainder of her story that Leo already knew. After filing for divorce she put both houses up for sale. When asked about money that he had left behind, she noted that there was none. His disappearance had left the family penniless, which is why she had sold both houses.

This last article noted that the police had declared the case closed. With lack of evidence to suggest otherwise, Pierce's death was declared accidental. There were no other articles on the case. They e-mailed and printed out these last remaining articles. Armando went to retrieve them from the printer.

Leo sat back and stretched. He found himself relieved more than anything else. He was very glad he had done this research, and that Armando had agreed to help him. Leo was at peace now, he realized. Millie had been telling the truth. And while there was little evidence to suggest that Portavia had killed Jack Pierce, if Jack had been killed, then Portavia and his cronies had to have been the ones to do it. Leo breathed deeply, glad that he had proved to himself that everything was all right.

He regretted, though, that Matt had never known any of this. He might have found peace years ago if he had been able to connect his hazy memories of hearing the fighting downstairs, and seeing something, whatever it was, that made him realize his father had been killed. It had scarred him and made him block out the scene his whole life. It all made sense now. And Millie wasn't to blame. She had chosen never to say anything because she believed it would devastate her children. She was protecting them. And she had never known what Matt had witnessed, until she had read that letter.

"You okay?" Armando asked, interrupting Leo's thoughts.

He got up. "Yes. Thank you, for all of this," he said, taking the twenty-odd pages of printed text from Armando.

"No problem. I'm glad I could help. But you know I have a bunch of questions now."

Leo nodded slowly. "I figured as much. I'll tell you what I can."

"Good." He glanced at his watch. "It's about six o'clock. How about some dinner?"

"Let's go downtown. I'll treat you to a nice restaurant."

As they left the library, they could hear thunder rumbling in the distance. Dark clouds were gathering over the bay. They drove to the Ovo Café on Central Avenue between 4th and 5th Streets, someplace Armando had never been before. They arrived in a matter of minutes. Armando parked in the street, then put money in the meter. As they were walking inside, the first drops of rain started to come down.

The Ovo Café was sleek in its design. Tan and black colors were accented by brightly polished silver chrome. The smartly dressed young hostess took them down the short black-and-white tile walkway surrounded by half walls, a martini bar behind one side, smoking diners behind the other. They were brought to a table in the larger dining area. Reproductions of works of art by Toulouse-Lautrec and Picasso adorned the walls with thick black glossy frames. The hostess showed them to a table that normally sat four. She handed them menus and removed two of the place settings.

Armando nodded in approval, looking around. "This place is beautiful."

Leo opened his menu and saw that the selection hadn't changed. "The food is great. They specialize in pierogies, of all things. The gourmet pizzas are delicious too."

A young man came to the table and greeted them warmly, telling them his name was Josh. He was probably no more than twenty years old, waiflike, with pale skin and blond hair. He told them the specials for the night and took their drink order for the house chardonnay. When Josh brought them their glasses of wine, he took their dinner orders. Leo ordered one of the pierogie dishes with ham and asparagus, and Armando went with a barbecue chicken pizza. They also ordered salads. When Josh left, Leo raised his glass to make a toast. "I want to thank you for helping me."

"You're welcome, but I'd rather we toast to our second date."

"Second?"

He nodded. "Karaoke with Whitney and fine dining with Suzie."

"I don't know if I like that being our first date. That night ended disastrously."

"Not all of it. We entertained those kids in the parking lot."

Leo laughed. "All right, to our second date."

"And may it end more pleasantly this time," Armando said, raising his eyebrows suggestively. The clinked glasses and drank. The wine was bitter and chilly for Leo's taste, but he drank it anyway. He was setting his glass down when Armando spoke again. "So how do you think he died? Accident or murder?"

Leo was taken aback by the direct question. "Does it matter?" he asked.

Armando shrugged. "I guess not. Just curious to know what you think."

Leo sat back in his chair and considered the two possibilities. He hadn't had a chance to think this through based on just the articles, although he had the advantage of knowing more than Armando at this point. "Murder," he replied.

"You think this mob guy really did him in?"

Leo considered how to respond. Armando had been good enough to help him, so he knew he could reveal more facts at least.

"What Millie said to the police in that article, I already knew about. Portavia was there the last night Jack was seen alive." Armando raised his eyebrows inquisitively. Leo went on, telling him about Portavia and other guys showing up, and how afterward they never saw Jack again.

Josh interrupted them with their salads. As they ate, Armando asked, "So all of this research you wanted to do was to confirm her story? Or was it to challenge something Harrigan told you?"

Leo considered the options. "Both."

"Did Harrigan accuse Millie of knowing more than she was telling."

Leo nodded. "But he's an asshole. She told him the whole story she told the police and he doesn't believe her."

"Do you believe her?"

Leo hesitated, his fork in midbite. Revealing this truth made him seem a little harsh. Why wouldn't he believe Millie? Shouldn't he have instinctively? "I guess this is where the story gets complicated. You have to understand that Millie and I are very close. Much closer than she was with her own son." He explained the significance of the books she had sent him.

Armando finished chewing salad. "Why did she send them to you?"

Leo drank more of the bitter chardonnay, then spoke frankly.

"Millie tried to kill herself on the anniversary of Matt's death. She sent those books to me as parting gifts."

"Oh, my God," Armando muttered. He had finished most of his salad, so he put his fork down and pushed the plate away. "Leo, that's awful. So this just happened?"

Leo nodded, then sighed. He was finding this difficult to talk about. "That first morning we met when you delivered the first package. It was one year ago that the police came and told me Matt had died in a car accident."

Armando shook his head in dismay. "Leo, I am so sorry."

Leo drank more wine and looked at Armando over the rim of the glass. He could see genuine concern on his face, and it comforted him. But he could sense pain inside himself from talking about all of this. He realized that he could probably tell Armando about the months after Matt's death, how he would sit on the front porch swing and re-live the horror of that night. He sensed that he could tell Armando all of this, and he would understand. But he didn't, in case he was wrong and it sent Armando running away.

"How is she now?" Armando asked.

"She survived. She was Baker Acted. I went to visit her a few times. After Harrigan showed up at my door that night, I decided I needed to find out more information from her, so I asked her. She told me the story." He realized he was making it sound like nothing, but there was no point in bringing up all the sordid emotional details.

"Matt never knew anything about his father?"

Leo shook his head, then pushed his finished salad away. "She was protecting him from the truth. Unfortunately, he didn't know that, so he resented her his whole life. He didn't talk to her for years at one point. And, unfortunately, he died not knowing the truth about his father, because she believed it was better for him not to know all these years." He purposely left out the story of Matt's cutting problem.

"But she told you," Armando remarked.

"I guess she felt like she had to. I was confronting her with information. Harrigan had been hounding her already, and she told him the same thing. And to answer your question from before, I did believe her more, but I needed to clarify a few facts for my own curiosity."

Armando shook his head in sympathy. "This whole situation is sad. It's a shame you're being dragged through the whole thing." He was silent for a moment, then continued, speaking almost analytically. "You know, if Harrigan is related to Jack, then he does have some sort of personal interest in finding out what happened to him. I mean, if she told him the same story as she told you, why is he still harassing her?" Armando hesitated, as if to consider his own question, then added, "And what about this money that the cousin kept talking about? Do you think he's pushing Millie because of the money they feel like they have a right to have?"

Leo shrugged. "I guess it's possible." He thought about how Millie had said in the beginning that Harrigan was harassing her for money. Perhaps that part was true too.

Josh returned with their dinners. He cleared away the salads and served their food. He also lit the oil lamp on the table, and they noticed the rest of the servers were doing the same at all of the tables. They continued eating and the conversation consciously drifted into other areas such as their families and work. At one point there was momentary silence, not of awkwardness, but of comfort for a change. As they ate, the lightning and thunder were their only interruption.

Suddenly, the lights went out and the restaurant was illuminated solely by oil lamps. There was a momentary stir from the diners, but it returned back to the same quiet background din as before. Armando and Leo looked at each other over the last of their food. The oil lamp made Armando's skin glow an amber color. He lifted his glass of wine and it too shimmered in a beautiful white gold sheen. The effect was sensual. Leo drank from his own wine the effects of the atmosphere. It was euphoric, a different kind of high. He found himself smiling almost for no reason, and Armando did the same. Leo realized then how much he was enjoying Armando's company, and lamented for a moment that he had allowed this part of himself to die for so long. A touch of sentimentality over Matt almost crept to the surface, but the lights came back on unexpectedly, and it fortunately distracted him from continuing with this thought.

Oddly enough, the diners at the various tables cried for the lights to go out again. Armando echoed their sentiments, and the hostess was kind enough to oblige. She dimmed the lights to an atmosphere similar to what they had had a few moments before. There were cheers throughout the restaurant. Armando simply looked over at Leo and said, "Much better." Leo felt a foot rubbing against his leg, and he looked over at Armando's sheepish grin. Leo shook his head, laughing. Josh suddenly returned and asked if they wanted more wine. Without hesitation, Leo raised his glass.

They finished their dinners and drank more wine. They continued talking about some of the things Armando had written in his "Latino Living" columns, and Leo went into more details about his dissertation, something he rarely felt comfortable doing. Leo was shocked when Armando told him he would like to read some of it. Only Millie had ever expressed such a sentiment. It occurred to him that he hadn't told Armando the same thing about his columns. Now he made it a point to himself to remember to pick up a copy of the paper and read them.

They ordered a chocolate cheesecake dessert to share and drank a third round of chardonnay. Both were feeling the effects. Armando started fanning himself with his cloth napkin and mimicked a Southern belle with the vapors. Leo flushed and laughed loudly from the silly joke. They realized people at the other tables were looking at them, so they tried to control their laughter.

As Leo paid the bill, Armando asked him what his plans were for the weekend. Leo told him about taking his mother to Carrabba's for Mother's Day. Leo added, "I'm going to call Millie also. Now that she's home, I want to take her out and go book shopping. We haven't done that in a very long time."

"You know, it's a little strange, being it's around Mother's Day."

"What do you mean?"

"Well, the whole situation with Matt dying and his mother trying to kill herself. You mentioned that they never had a close relationship."

Leo sighed loudly. "Matt hated his mother." There was certainly no point denying it.

"I guess if you were abandoned by your mother as a child you might resent her."

Leo was a little surprised to hear him say that, but in actuality it was nothing he hadn't thought of himself through the years.

Armando sat back and drank the last of his wine. "Don't you find that whole thing strange though, that she abandoned her children? I mean, if she was so afraid of that mob guy, why would she leave them with her mother in Brooklyn? Why didn't she take them with her to California?"

Leo went to answer, then realized that he couldn't. He had never thought of this before. It did seem odd when he thought of it. Taking them with her to California would have seemed the most obvious thing to do in order to protect them. But Millie was also determined to move on with her life. She did file for divorce. She felt like she had an opportunity to be free for the first time in her life. Free in the full, literal sense, without children or a husband or any responsibilities. In a way, he couldn't blame her, although it did seem strange.

They left the Ovo Café feeling extremely light-headed from the wine. They said good night to the hostess and stepped outside. The wind had picked up, but the worst of the rain had subsided temporarily. They stood in front of the restaurant, uncertain what to do next. Armando checked his watch and showed it to Leo with a surprised look. "It's after eight-thirty!"

Leo was equally surprised that they had been in there all that time. They looked at each other for a moment, then instinctively this time, Leo took the initiative and kissed Armando on the lips. He didn't care who was watching. It seemed the appropriate thing to do, and he was thrilled to have done it. When they parted a moment later, Armando looked pleasantly surprised, and he took Leo's hand. "I think we need to go back to my place," Leo suggested. Armando squeezed his hand, and they walked to the car.

The ride back was quiet. Armando had to turn on the windshield wipers as the wind blew a light mist. It took them a little longer to return to Leo's house because Armando drove carefully from having been drinking. They reached Leo's house in about ten minutes and he parked in the driveway behind Leo's Tercel. Leo was about to get out when Armando reminded him about the papers they had printed out at the library. He grabbed them off the floor. Armando then put his hand on Leo's forearm as if to caution him. Leo looked up quizzically at him. Armando had an annoyed look on his face. He pointed toward the front porch with his chin.

"You've got company," he said.

Leo looked toward the porch through the misty rain, and saw a tall shadow standing near the front porch door. He could see the light of a cigarette in the shadows of the porch light. It was Harrigan.

"No fucking way," Leo said.

"What do you want to do?"

Leo jumped out of the car and Armando quickly followed. He stormed up the front steps of his porch and yanked open the screen door. Armando was right behind him as they entered. "Get out," Leo ordered.

Harrigan puffed on his cigarette, then dropped it onto the wooden floor of the porch and extinguished it with his shoe. He exhaled in their faces. "I see your friend Millie is out of the hospital. Did you get her to tell you the truth?"

"Yes, she told me the truth. The same truth she's told you and the police, but apparently you're too damn stupid to realize this. You've obviously got some vendetta against her that you won't leave her alone."

He grinned. "I don't know what you're talking about."

"What is it? Money?"

"Money again? Is that what she told you?"

"No, but apparently it's something your mother is hung up on!" He saw Harrigan's eyes flinch. Leo flailed the printed pages into his suited chest. "It's all right here, asshole. I know you're related to Jack Pierce."

Harrigan took the pages from him and thumbed through them in the dim porch light. He started chuckling. "Did your homework, I see." He glanced up at Leo mockingly. "What happened, you afraid someone like your dear friend Millie wasn't telling the truth?"

Leo scoffed. "No, asshole, I didn't believe you were telling the truth! And why should I? You show up out of nowhere and start harassing all of us."

"So you decided to play boy detectives then?" He quickly glanced away, then back. "Oh, I'm sorry. Gay boy detectives?"

Armando pushed his way forward. "Hey, watch it!"

"Get off my porch, and don't come back," Leo said with force. The wine and his anger were making him flush and dizzy. There was a bright flash of lightning that illuminated the neighborhood, then a loud crack of thunder that roared for a few seconds. The rain started to pour down harder.

Harrigan glanced out the screen at the weather, then turned back to look at Leo. His face had a determined, serious look. "You're satisfied then?" he asked.

"Of course I'm satisfied. I know all that I need to know. Now get out of here."

"You think it was Portavia, don't you?"

Leo rolled his eyes and glanced at Armando. He looked back at Harrigan, determined not to continue this conversation. "It doesn't matter what I think. I don't care whether it was him or not. It was ruled an accident."

"But it wasn't an accident, according to Millie."

"And? What's your point?"

"I interviewed Portavia's wife after I heard about the police interview with Millie. The widow claimed her husband was in the Hamptons when Jack was killed."

Leo scoffed and was about to respond, but Armando spoke for him. "You're joking, right? You went to this woman and asked her what she remembered about her dead mob husband on a particular night twenty years ago? How the hell would she remember that?"

"Portavia's wife shouldn't be able to remember, but Millie should after these years?"

Leo yelled in response. "Millie was the one who was victimized! Of course she's going to remember what happened!" Leo suddenly grabbed Harrigan's arm fiercely.

"Don't touch me!" Harrigan demanded, pulling himself free. Lightning flashed.

"Then get the fuck off my porch," Leo ordered over the thunder.

Harrigan pushed past them and flung open the screen door. He walked down the steps, then suddenly turned fast and waved the papers in the air. "You don't mind if I keep these, do you?" he asked as they started getting wet, then turned and hurried to his car parked across the street, shoving the papers in his suit jacket pocket.

Leo wanted to go after him to get the papers, but Armando stopped him, his hand on his shoulder. "Let him go. You've got all the articles in your e-mail, so don't worry about it." They watched Harrigan drive off in the pouring rain. Then, Leo turned and moved to the front door. He fumbled with his keys and unlocked the door, flinging it back against the wall with a loud bang. He flipped on the lights as he entered. He heard Armando close the door behind him. Leo kicked off his shoes and they slammed into the wall by the dining room. "Calm down, Leo," Armando said. "He's gone now."

Leo turned quickly to Armando. "God, he enrages me! He's such a fucking pompous asshole, thinking he knows everything."

He closed his eyes and put his hand on his forehead to rub his temples. The effects of the wine and the adrenaline rush were giving him a massive headache. He heard footsteps before him, but kept his eyes closed. He felt Armando's arms around him and he was pulled tighter to Armando. When he opened his eyes and put his arms around him in return, Armando was looking into his face with a smile, and came in for a kiss. Leo responded, although the pounding in his head was intense.

Armando's arms moved up and down Leo's back. He kneaded Leo's muscles strongly, while his lips pressed against Leo's. The combination of the hands and the lips and the goatee brushing against his face were stimulating him, and he could sense not only himself but Armando responding between their legs.

Armando broke apart for the moment, and kissed him quickly once, then twice. He reached down and tugged at the bottom of Leo's shirt. He lifted it out of his pants and pulled it over his head to reveal his bare chest. The chill in temperature made Leo's nipples harden fast, and his cock grew. Armando dropped Leo's shirt on the floor, then hugged him close again. He moved down with his face and started to rub his goatee over Leo's chest. Leo shivered. He looked down at Armando's head as he saw him lightly rub himself against Leo, then come up and with his tongue dart around Leo's left nipple, then the right one. The pain in his head was still intense, but the chills down his body were counteracting it. He reached out and started unbuttoning Armando's shirt.

Armando stood upright, and let Leo remove his shirt. It slid to the floor, and Leo stared down at the light patch of hair on his chest, the same patch he had seen sneak peaks of a few times already and had wanted to touch. He reached with his hands and started to intertwine his fingers through the hair, then squeezed his nipples slightly. Armando's eyes closed and he put his head back, hissing in response. Leo came down and kissed Armando's chest, licking areas of the hair he loved, and used his tongue to circle Armando's left nipple. He was moving to the right nipple when Armando suddenly lifted his head up again and turned it slightly. He reached up with his arms and brought Leo's face to his. They started kissing harder, and Armando's tongue flitted into Leo's mouth. Armando moved their bodies closer to each other so that their hard cocks were pressing against each other through their pants. He pulled apart, and breathed deeply. Leo did the same, trying to calm the pain in his head. Armando pushed him backward slightly, guiding him toward the living room couch.

Leo sat down and Armando reclined on top of him. Armando ran his fingers through Leo's gelled hair and down his body as he kissed him, rubbing his goatee against Leo's face and licking his lips and tongue with his own. Leo's hands moved downward and explored his bare back, feeling smoothness until he came to a small tuft of hair at his lower back. He ran his fingers through the hair, then continued downward, grabbing Armando's ass with his hands, squeezing the muscles. Armando groaned and shivered.

Armando moved downward. He used his goatee and lips to rub and kiss Leo's chest and nipples. He didn't feel the same chills he had before, but a more warm wave cascade through his body. Armando moved further, and kissed at the trail of hair around his navel. Then, as he kissed Leo's happy trail, he moved to Leo's jeans. He opened the button and unzipped them, revealing the top of Leo's underwear. He licked at the trail and started to lift the band of the underwear, his tongue flickering at the trail as it moved downward.

The pounding in Leo's head grew stronger and he could feel himself getting dizzy and flushed. Without warning, he suddenly lifted his head and felt a rush as he pushed Armando back and told him to stop. He breathed more heavily, and pulled himself out from underneath Armando. Unconsciously, he buttoned his jeans and zipped up. He leaned forward, his elbows resting on his knees, his hands on his head, as he caught his breath and the dizziness started to subside. Armando quickly sat beside him and put an arm around his shoulders, comforting him. "What's the matter?" he asked.

Leo could only shake his head. "I'm sorry, I can't."

Armando pulled back and sat against the couch. "What happened?"

Leo turned toward him and saw the look of disappointment and confusion on Armando's face. "I don't know. I just can't do this." He was confused himself. The dizziness was still there, but going away. "Maybe it's the wine," he said, knowing that wasn't completely the truth. Armando wasn't as easily convinced either, and he looked away. "Look, Armando, I'm sorry, it's not you. I think it's all of this stuff that's happening. I'm under a lot of pressure and stressing out."

"Maybe I should go," Armando said and started to get up.

Leo quickly grabbed his arm and pulled him back. "No, don't go! I want you to stay." He felt like such a fool, and he knew he was acting like one, sending mixed signals. Armando gazed at him, and Leo tried to appeal to him using his eyes and his words. "I'm serious. I don't want you to go. I can't do this, though. I'm sorry." He took a deep breath, then looked away at nothing. He could sense the real truth behind what was happening, and it both aggravated and disappointed him. "I guess I'm not ready."

Armando looked down for a moment, then back up at Leo. "Haven't you been with anyone since. . ."

Leo was grateful he didn't finish the rest of the sentence. "No, not really." He looked back at him and forced a smile. "I'm sorry," he apologized again.

Armando put his arm on Leo's shoulders again. "Are you sure you want me to stay?" His disappointment was evident, but more masked this time.

"Yes!" Leo replied, perhaps a little too quickly. He loved his arm on his shoulders. It comforted him greatly.

Armando picked up the remote control with his other hand. "Some TV then?" Leo nodded. Armando flipped on the television and handed Leo the remote. "Do you want your shirt?"

Leo looked at him. "No, forget that. Can we just lay here for a while?"

Armando paused, glancing at the television for a second, then back at Leo. He had a small grin. "Sure. Come here." He leaned back against the couch and pulled Leo toward him so that he was leaning against his chest slightly. Armando leaned further into the corner of the couch, and wrapped his one arm around Leo's shoulders and neck. Leo reclined into him, and they watched television. Leo flipped through a few channels until they came to some action movie neither of them had seen before. He left that on and put the remote down. They stayed like this. When that movie ended, they left the channel on to see what was coming on next. Both of them had seen the movie before, but neither of them had the energy to change the channel. The wine took its effect, and they fell asleep lying against each other.

– SIXTEEN –

They slept soundly until lightning illuminated the house and an explosive crack of thunder jolted Armando and Leo awake. Shortly afterward, Armando got ready to leave, much to Leo's and his disappointment, but they agreed to speak over the weekend. Before Armando left Leo apologized again for things.

"It's not necessary," Armando replied. "I understand. I mean, I'm not happy, but I understand. We'll take it slow, that's all." They kissed, and Leo leaned against the door frame as he watched Armando rush to his car in the pouring rain.

Leo slept for a few more hours. He spent most of that Saturday working on his dissertation. He found himself excited to be working hard on his research, and felt alive again reading through his old notes, finding sections from the works around him to quote, demonstrating how characters conveyed his thesis. He realized he was going to have to work on the Swinburne and Rossetti poems too.

He was interrupted by three phone calls that afternoon. The first was his mother confirming their plans for Mother's Day. The second was his friend Doug checking up on him. The last call was from Armando. Leo quickly stopped what he was doing to talk to him for half an hour.

The next morning he continued working on his dissertation, citing poems by Swinburne and Rossetti and discussing their relationship to the change in the perception of the woman during the 1860s. He found it difficult at times to see how he could make the poetry fit with the fiction of Mary Braddon and Wilkie Collins, but he figured he would continue in this vein and let Palmer help him sort it out afterward. By lunchtime, he was ready to give her drafts of two chapters.

Pierce
© 2007 by The Haworth Press, Inc. All rights reserved.
doi:10.1300/5849_16

Afterward, Leo drove to an art supply warehouse in Clearwater to buy two prepared canvases and a few tubes of paint as Mother's Day gifts. As he left, he wondered what he should get Millie. He was relatively close to where she lived and he could stop by and visit her. She was home now, presumably discharged by Bauer a few days ago. She would be waking up in her own bed, not some strange bed in the psychiatric ward at the hospital. She would be able to sit at her own kitchen table, smoke a cigarette, and make her own coffee her way. She would not have to worry about rules or regulations with everything she did.

He decided not to visit her unannounced. She might be angry at him after their confrontation, and he didn't want to make things worse by dropping in without calling first. He considered calling from his car, then realized that he had left his cell phone at home. He would have to wait to call her when he got home, which he did about an hour later. Leo picked up the cordless phone in the kitchen. He had not called her house in a while, but he remembered the number instinctively as he dialed. He was jittery. The phone rang twice, and she answered the phone in the nasal Brooklyn accent he had come to adore.

"Hello?" she asked.

"Happy Mother's Day, Millie."

"Leo," she replied, after a pause. "Thank you."

Leo paced in his kitchen. "So, how are you?"

"Fine, I guess. I'm home." Her responses were stilted.

"When did Dr. Bauer discharge you?"

"That same day," she said.

There was an edge to her voice, but Leo ignored it, sounding forcefully gleeful. "You must be glad to be home!"

"Yes." Then, her tone seemed to change slightly and her voice elevated. "I think if I had to stay there another night with those freakin' loons, I would have killed myself!" Leo wasn't sure what to say. "That was a joke," she said matter-of-factly.

Leo forced a laugh. "Yes, I figured that." He hated that this conversation was so surface-level. There was too much tension, too much left unspoken. He heard the clicking of her cigarette lighter as she fired up a cigarette. He heard her inhale, then exhale. He swore he could sense the smoke coming through the phone.

"I had a visitor yesterday," she said.

"Anyone I know?"

"Harrigan."

Leo's eyes widened with surprise. "He really is a pain."

She puffed on her cigarette. "He had some interesting papers with him. Some news articles from the Internet."

Leo shut his eyes. It never occurred to him that he would bring those papers to Millie and tell her where they had come from. He sighed in frustration. "Millie, I'm sorry about that. I swear to you that I was trying to get the facts straight. I was trying to do it to get rid of him."

"Well, unfortunately, it isn't working." As an afterthought, she muttered to herself, "Apparently, nothing is."

"Millie, I really do apologize. I didn't expect you to find out about the articles. He got me so angry the other night—"

"Forget it. It's all right." He heard her inhale the cigarette again. He could almost see her in his own mind. She would be sitting at her retro black and white kitchen table with ash burning at the edge of her cigarette, unconscious of the fact that she should have flicked it off by now. "I was surprised to see how much had been reported when they found the body."

"I'm sure it was big news at the time," Leo suggested.

She took a long drag on her cigarette. "I guess."

A thought occurred to Leo. "Hey, you know I figured out that Harrigan was related to Jack. His mother—at least, I guess it's his mother—was quoted in one of the articles. Agnes Harrigan? She blamed you for everything."

"Oh, God, that was her name!" She sounded excited. "You know, when he first approached me in Hollywood and told me his name, I asked him if he was related to Jack. He told me no. I thought the name Harrigan sounded familiar, and he looked like someone I used to know, but I couldn't think of his mother's name to prove it." She paused to smoke. "That woman was nuts. She hated me. I think she always had a crush on Jack. He used to dote on her when they were young. She probably thought he was going to leave her money."

"Well, it explains why he has a personal interest in this whole thing. I don't understand what he's trying to find out though. He needs to let the whole thing go."

She didn't respond right away. She smoked. "He's never going to let this go," she muttered, sighed, then added to herself, "There's little choice left."

"Choice for what?"

"Nothing." She spurted back to life. "What's going on with you to-day? Taking your mother out?"

"Yes. She wants to go to Carrabba's for dinner."

"Tell her I send my best when you see her."

"I will."

"Take care, Leo."

"Wait!" he said, catching her before she hung up. "I want to do something with you too, for Mother's Day."

"Oh, okay," she replied. He heard her exhale again.

"How about book shopping and lunch? Like we used to do?"

"Sounds good," she said, at a distance. "We haven't done that in a long time." She sounded nostalgic.

"How about Thursday after my morning class?"

She hesitated. "I have a few things to do on Thursday."

"Friday then?"

She considered. "Friday will be good. Actually, Friday should work out perfectly."

"I'm looking forward to doing this with you."

"So am I, Leo. I'll see you then."

They hung up, and Leo felt himself beaming. She wasn't upset with him as he thought she might be. He would look forward to Friday all week.

Just after 5:00 p.m., Leo parked his Tercel in front of his mother's house. Another car was in the driveway. As he approached the front door with his wrapped gift in hand, it occurred to him that it was Theresa's car. He hesitated to open the front door, but did so. When he entered he called to Rosa. His mother responded loudly, "Leo-nardo! *Vieni qui!* In the living room!"

He went inside and saw his mother and Theresa sitting across from each other on the floral wicker furniture. On the coffee table was a mixed arrangement of flowers in a basket. Rosa Vasari rushed forward and embraced her son tightly. She had had her hair dyed and was wearing a yellow floral-print frock that unsettled him. They kissed and he gave her his present, wishing her a happy Mother's Day. She squealed in delight, then hurried to show him the flowers. "Look! From Theresa. *Che bellissimi!*"

"They are beautiful," he agreed. He looked at his ex–sister-in-law. "Hi, Theresa."

"Leo," she replied, then drank from the glass of water on the coffee table.

There was a stiff silence in the room. Leo felt as if he had intruded on a conversation. He glanced at Theresa, but she was looking away, fondling the ferns in the floral basket. She was definitely angry with him.

Rosa broke the silence. "Leonardo, you want a drink? *Acqua? Vino?*"

He saw his mother was drinking a glass of red wine. "I'll have what you're having." She beamed, reached up, and kissed him on the cheek. She put his gift on the floor beside the coffee table, then hurried into the kitchen. Leo sat in his mother's place. Theresa still wouldn't look at him. She drank from her water glass again.

"So," Leo said, forcing conversation. "I spoke to your mother before. She sounds well."

Theresa glared at him. "No thanks to you," she muttered.

"What is that supposed to mean?"

She looked toward the kitchen, then back at Leo. She spoke in a low voice. "I told you from the very beginning to stay out of this. You should have listened."

"What was I supposed to do? Harrigan was starting to harass me too, you know," Leo said. Theresa turned her attention to the ferns. In the silence that followed, a thought occurred to Leo. "Look, this may seem like a bad time to discuss this, but can I ask you something?"

"What?"

"When did you find out about what happened that night?"

She hesitated. "She told me after Harrigan first came to see me. But I believed my mother when she told me the story."

"I believed Millie." He was uncertain if he sounded convincing. "Look, you know that I went to Millie for Matt's sake."

"Oh, please, Leo, leave my brother out of this. He's dead. You went for your own selfish reasons."

Leo was angry at her remark, but he restrained himself. He knew she was right. He was saved from further conversation by his mother, who entered carrying a tray with Leo's glass of wine and a platter of crackers, two cheeses, and red grapes. Rosa set it down on the coffee table. *"Mangiamo!"* she said proudly, handing the glass of wine to Leo and cutting a slice of cheese and putting it on a cracker for her son. When she offered the same to Theresa, she shook her head and grabbed her purse.

"I'm sorry, Rosa. I have to go."

"But you just got here!"

"I'm having dinner with my mother also. I have a bit of a drive from here." She stood and put her purse strap on her shoulder.

Rosa was sad, but hugged Theresa. *"Mille grazie* for the beautiful flowers."

"You're welcome. Happy Mother's Day." Rosa walked her to the door.

Leo sat quietly waiting until his mother returned. He ate another cracker with cheese and a grape and drank some of the merlot. He wondered whether or not his mother had realized Theresa and he had not said good-bye to each other. He was about to eat another cracker when his mother walked up to him again and slapped it out of his hand. *"Che hai fatto?"*

Leo stared in shock at her. "Mamma, what the heck is your problem? And stop with the Italian, will you? Jesus, you're not even Italian!" She glared at him, her eyes betraying hurt. He calmed down. "What did you just ask me?"

"Why did you tell Theresa and Millicent about what happened to her?" Her accent was gone, he noticed. But he was more concerned at the moment about what she was asking him. Leo had forgotten his mother knew about this. He looked away sheepishly. "It was a secret," she continued, "You weren't supposed to say anything!"

"It came up during the session. I was angry and I—"

"You shouldn't have said anything. Now Theresa doesn't trust me anymore."

"Oh, I don't believe that for a second. Did you forget the flowers she gave you?"

His mother scowled, but didn't respond. She grabbed his unfinished glass of wine and the other glasses on the table and put everything on the tray. She lifted it and headed toward the kitchen. "We have to go." Her accent was back.

When she returned, Leo rose from the sofa. She got her purse from her bedroom and declared herself ready. "Don't you want to open your gift first?" he asked.

"No, we're late. I will open it when we come back."

Leo rolled his eyes in frustration, but forced himself to ignore her attitude. They left the house and drove the fifteen minute ride in Leo's car to the restaurant. It was raining lightly at this point, and his mother lamented that she didn't have her umbrella with her. She then complained that she was uncomfortable in his car and wished he had driven hers. They didn't speak the rest of the ride.

When they got to Carrabba's the parking lot was packed. He dropped his mother off at the entrance and found a spot toward the end of the lot. The rain came down harder. He ran fast in the rain and dealt with being wet and cold in the air-conditioned restaurant. He asked his mother if she had checked in with the hostess. "No, it's Mother's Day," she retorted.

Leo grumbled to himself, and went to the hostess. He gave their last name, and they were told to wait for a few minutes. She handed him a pager. The time passed slowly as they waited in silence amid the clamor around them. Leo looked up toward the open kitchen area and saw chefs preparing dinners and servers bustling about with dishes toward the tables. The sharp smells of garlic and rosemary filled the air. Families came in and out in large groups hugging and kissing one another.

He looked at his mother seated beside him. She was gazing blindly before her, ignoring the people and chaos. She seemed consciously ignorant of everything. He wondered what she was thinking about in that moment. Then, he noticed that her right eye was watering, and a single tear fell from her eye. He looked away, a slight pang of sorrow and guilt aching in his heart.

It was just the two of them celebrating this special holiday. His brother was away. His father was long dead. He looked back at her, and saw she had attempted to disguise the tear by touching her eyes with a tissue.

She was insane. She was dramatic. She drove him crazy. But she was his mother, and she had given him life. She didn't always do or say things the way he would have liked, but at the age of twenty-nine, his mother was alive and well and omnipresent in his life. For that he should be grateful, not angry. He leaned in suddenly and rested his head on her shoulder. "I love you, Mamma," he said. He gave her a quick kiss on the cheek.

She turned toward him and kissed him back. "Thank you, *mio figlio*." She wrapped her other arm around his neck and hugged him. She then wiped at the tears forming in her eyes again. He told her to stop or her mascara would run, and she laughed.

The pager went off, and Leo helped her stand. They were shown to their table. It wasn't the best location, and he thought she seemed upset, but this time held her tongue. He asked the hostess for a different table, and his mother looked relieved and pleased that he had done this for her. The hostess found another table just getting cleared off. It was a booth along one of the windows. He looked at his mother and she nodded with a smile. They sat there instead.

Their server was a pretty girl with blonde hair. They ordered glasses of merlot, which she brought them. Rosa was hesitant about what to order. When the young server told her about the specials, Leo's mother was intrigued by the veal saltimbocca and ordered that. Leo went with one of the restaurant's chicken dinners, Pollo Rosa Maria. They both ordered house salads.

Leo raised his glass of wine. "To my mamma, on Mamma's Day!"

She smiled and clinked glasses. They sipped, and his mother made a face. "Too dry."

He didn't respond. He thought the wine tasted velvety smooth. His mother sighed. He knew the drill and played along without fighting. "What's wrong?"

"I wish Theresa and you would get along."

Leo was genuinely confused by this. "Why? She and George are divorced now. Technically, she's not even part of the family anymore." In the back of his mind, he recalled Theresa having said something similar to him after Millie's suicide attempt.

"I think of her as family!" Rosa objected. Leo had to agree that she was more like family to his mother than George was. "I'm going to miss her," she continued.

"What do you mean?" He drank more of his wine.

She looked up at him with sad eyes. "She's thinking about moving away! She applied for jobs in Jacksonville and Orlando."

Leo was actually impressed by this news. He had always wondered if Theresa had the guts to get on with her life. She hadn't seemed to do much since George had left her. "That's not too far away." Orlando made him think of Armando suddenly, and he wondered if his family were having dinner at this hour, or if he were on his way back home yet.

His mother didn't agree or disagree with his statement. "She's had such a difficult life," she lamented, heaving another sigh. "Her mother, her marriage. . ." She shook her head. "She always wanted children."

"She could always adopt."

"She wanted to have her own children." Rosa drank from the glass of wine, but didn't make a face this time. "I think she regrets never keeping her baby."

Someone different brought them their salads and served them. Leo dug his fork into the salad and was about to eat when he paused and looked back at his mother. "Wait. What baby?" His mother looked up at him quizzically as she chewed on her lettuce. "You said she regrets never keeping her baby. What baby?"

Rosa held a tomato aloft on her fork. "The baby she couldn't keep," she said.

"Mamma, I'm confused. You told me she had a miscarriage, and that she couldn't have any other children."

"She had the miscarriage because of the abor—" Rosa suddenly dropped her fork in horror. *"Dio mio!"* she exclaimed, making the sign of the cross and looking heavenward.

Leo put his fork down also. "Mamma, what are you talking about?"

"Niente."

Leo scoffed. "Oh, no. You've got to tell me now. You started to say something." He thought about what she had started to say, and even though it seemed so obvious, it didn't seem possible. "Theresa had an abortion?"

Rosa shut her eyes and shook her head.

"Come on. You have to tell me. You already let it out. Just finish the story."

"No!" she said.

She drank more of her wine and Leo saw it was making her face and neck flush beneath her makeup. It occurred to him that she was concerned Theresa would know she had said something and would be angry with her again. He said to his mother, "Look, I promise I'm not going to say anything to anyone. I won't let Theresa know that you told me." That seemed to ease her mind. She relaxed some. "Did she have an abortion?" he asked again.

She glanced around the restaurant, as if Theresa were lurking in the shadows spying on them behind an artificial ficus tree. She leaned in closer to Leo and nodded slowly. Then, she said softly, *"Era terribile!"*

"When did this happen?"

"When she was a teenager."

Now Leo was stunned. Theresa, his ex–sister-in-law librarian, had not only tried to commit suicide at some point in her life, but now also had had an abortion as a teenager. It certainly changed everything he ever thought of her as a meek, conservative woman.

"Does George know about this?" he asked.

Rosa shook her head. "I don't think she ever told him. She told me when she was in the hospital. That's why she couldn't have children. They ruined her when they did that terrible thing, and she couldn't have children after that."

Leo had to admit that it was very sad. This news certainly made him wonder a lot though. How could she have allowed herself to get pregnant? Who could have been the father? Presumably some boyfriend she had at the time. Her grandmother must have gone crazy. "How old was she anyway? Eighteen?"

Rosa gazed at her untouched salad, her fingers interlocked in prayer. "Fourteen."

"Fourteen?!" he replied loudly. His mother looked up in shock. She shushed him and appeared ashamed for having said anything. She made the sign of the cross again and said a quick silent prayer, glancing around the restaurant. Leo wasn't sure how to react to such news. Without any warning he chuckled. His mother glared at him. "I'm sorry," he said. "I don't know why I find this amusing."

"It's not funny!" she said angrily. "Theresa was my only hope for grandchildren!"

Leo grew serious, trying not to take the comment personally. "Not necessarily," he retorted. "If you're lucky, George's bimbo will get pregnant."

His mother rolled her eyes in frustration and sat back in the bench. She stared out the window in silence and watched the rain.

The news was shocking and sad. He was seeing Theresa in a whole new light now. Another thought then occurred to him. If Theresa had been fourteen when she had the abortion, someone would have had to take her to have it done. "Did Millie know about this?"

His mother glanced back at him with a look of self-satisfaction. "Millicent made her have the abortion. Otherwise, she would have kept the baby."

"You can't blame Millie for making her have the abortion."

"No?" she challenged. "Her mother forced her to kill that little innocent baby."

"How was she supposed to raise a child at fourteen years old?"

Rosa waved a finger at him. "Your *nonna*, your father's mother, God rest her soul, she was fifteen when she was married and sixteen when she had her first son."

"Mamma, that was in. . .what. . .1920? Things were different then. Besides, *Nonna* was married. Theresa wasn't. She shouldn't have been sleeping around at fourteen."

His mother didn't respond. She looked back toward the window. She reacted slightly to the lightning flash that illuminated the parking lot on this side.

A man arrived with their meals. He took away their salads and served their entrees. The young girl who was their initial server stood just behind and asked how everything was. She offered fresh parmesan cheese and sprinkled some on both their meals. Leo's mother asked for water with lemon, and she quickly returned with it for both of them.

They ate quietly. Halfway through their dinner, Leo finally broke the silence by asking nonchalantly, "Did Theresa tell you who the father was?"

"No, she did not," Rosa responded firmly. "I didn't think that was appropriate to ask."

Leo shrugged. "It might seem important to me to—"

"I don't want to talk about this anymore!" she exclaimed.

Leo was taken aback, but said nothing. Apparently he had gone too far. He changed the subject. "Food is delicious. How do you like yours?"

She shrugged her shoulders. "The veal is tough. Look how hard I have to cut it."

"Let's send it back."

"No!" she replied, horrified. "It's all right. I'll eat it."

"Mamma, really, if it's not good, we'll send it back."

She shook her head. "It's delicious. You eat." She put her fork and knife down. "Thank you, though, for offering to please me."

"It's okay."

She seemed to lighten up. "I'm very proud of you, you know."

"What do you mean?"

"You're going to be a doctor!"

He chuckled. "Not a medical doctor, a professor."

She shrugged. "So? You'll still be Dr. Vasari. College professor. I am very proud."

"Except for the gay thing." It had come out without thinking and he regretted it.

She stared back at him, and he glanced away. When he looked back, she averted his gaze this time. Then, she shrugged. "Ah, so nothing is perfect!" She dove into her veal and ate. "I would rather you had a nice boy with a good family and career, than do like your brother and run away with a stupid blond waitress half your age!"

"Is everything all right here?" the blond server asked, suddenly standing at their table.

Rosa turned to her with a horrified look. "We weren't talking about you, *mia cara!*" She reached out with her hand and caressed her forearm. "You are a beautiful girl. But my son," she pointed toward Leo, "he is gay, so you are not his type."

Leo and the server looked at each other in shock, and both started laughing because they didn't know what else to do. "That's okay," the girl said to Rosa. "I was just checking on how your meal was."

"*Delizioso!*" Rosa said. She kissed her fingertips and demonstratively threw them upward. The girl laughed and said she was pleased, then left the table. "So what else is new?" his mother asked, not missing a beat. He watched her take a gulp of her merlot, and he realized that she was getting drunk.

Since she had opened the door and homosexuality seemed to be an open topic at the moment, he said rather proudly, "I've started seeing someone."

"*Magnifico!*" She took another gulp of her wine.

Leo expected her to start asking about him, what he did, his name, his family, and so on. He started to tell her they were taking things slowly, when she cut him off by putting the glass down sharply and speaking aloud. "I am seeing someone too."

Leo stared back in amazement. He sat back to process this information. "What do you mean you're seeing someone? You've never dated anyone before."

"Then it is time for me to date a man too." She proceeded to go on for ten minutes about her gentleman friend, Giacomo from Sicily. He had only recently joined the Italian-American Club. He had been in the United States since the 1950s, but had retired and moved to

Florida a few years ago. She went on and on. The only time she changed the subject was when she commented about how good the wine was and drank more.

Leo didn't interrupt her. He sat back and listened to her in silence. He couldn't comprehend his mother with another man other than his father. She idolized him. It was incomprehensible. He listened, half amused, half amazed. His only remark to her finally was, "Well, Dad is probably turning in his grave." It slipped out, more as a joke than anything else, but he could tell immediately afterward from her silence that he had upset her again.

When another server came by and asked if he was done eating, he realized he hadn't taken another bite of his food in a while. He had lost his appetite. The server took it and Rosa's empty plate away. They decided to have dessert and coffee at home.

The rain let up as he drove back to her house. The entire ride she sat with her arms folded and stared out the window. They were approaching the house when Leo finally felt compelled to say something. "Did you enjoy your dinner?" It was a lame question, but it was the only comment he could think of.

She focused back on him, putting her hands in her lap. *"Sì, grazie."* She paused a moment, then said, "You are a good son." She leaned over and took his hand in hers and squeezed it. He returned the gesture and smiled at her. She scolded him then for looking away from the road, so he turned back quickly and concentrated on his driving.

When they arrived at the house, the rain had stopped, so they didn't have to hurry inside. He was getting ready to go, when she suddenly remembered that she had a gift to unwrap. He felt a little foolish that he had forgotten this as well. They went into the living room and sat on the matching couches. His mother opened her gift and was very pleased with his choice of paint colors and canvases. "I wasn't sure if you'd like it," he told her.

"They are perfect. Beautiful colors." She pointed to one of the paintings surrounding them on the walls, a medium-sized canvas she had depicted her sisters in, dressing them in ancient togas of bright colors. The background was an intense gold. "That is like this color you bought me." Leo thought it was garish, now that he saw it on a painting. But she was satisfied.

"You know who that is, don't you?" she continued, referring to this same work. He told her he knew, that she had told him the story of her sisters. She started to point out one or two other paintings from her seat on the couch. She told him anecdotes about who they were and why she had depicted them in certain ways, stories she had told him before. He knew the basics, but never remembered the specifics.

"And you know that one?" She pointed to the large one on the wall, her centerpiece, her masterwork. The portrait of his father. "He was a good man, your father," she said, sighing sadly. She looked into her lap.

"So you've said," Leo replied. "I have a difficult time remembering things about him." He wasn't sure why he said that. It was somewhat true. He actually believed he wanted to forget him. Oddly though, the one thing he most wanted to forget was the one thing he remembered most vividly. He had never told his mother about how his father had walked in on him having sex with another boy. Not that he ever would tell her. Leo's father had never spoken about the incident to Leo or to anyone else, as far as he knew or hoped.

"It's a long time now since he passed away," Rosa said.

Leo nodded slowly. "Fifteen years."

She looked back up at the painting. "He was very proud of you," she said.

Leo scoffed without warning or hesitation. "Proud? Uh, I don't think so."

His mother seemed taken aback. "He was proud of you."

Leo shook his head. "Mamma, he was proud of George because he was into sports and other macho things."

She shrugged. "Okay, so he was proud of your brother because of the sports. But he was proud of you in a very different way. He knew that you were smart and that you would make something of yourself."

Leo wasn't convinced.

"I'll never forget what he said to me, two nights before he died. He said, 'Rosa, you keep an eye on our boys. Giorgio will need your guidance. But Leonardo . . . he will need your love, your support, and your acceptance.'"

Leo felt a cold chill through his body. Two days before he had died. It was the closest Leo had ever thought of his father acknowledging what had happened, or even admitting that he had loved his son, despite what he had seen that day in Leo's bedroom.

"He really said that?" he asked, his voice trembling.

She looked at Leo. When she spoke, her voice was normal. She had no accent. "I never knew why he said it, but I tried to give you what he said I should. I hope I did."

He couldn't respond. He felt cold. Oddly cold. The dead had no answers. Only the living did. He would never understand his father's words, what they really meant, not for certain. He had never heard them spoken. He could only listen to what his mother told him now, and accept her words as truth.

"Earlier," she said, "after Theresa left, you mentioned about me not being Italian."

Leo looked away sheepishly. "I'm sorry about that. I didn't mean—"

"No, it's all right, Leonardo. It's true." She paused. "Do you know why I speak Italian, or have an accent sometimes, or even changed my name to Rosa?"

Leo looked at her. He shook his head, because he really didn't know for sure.

"It was because of your father." She shifted positions slightly and looked up at the portrait again. "When we were young and in love, before we had you and your brother, your father would hold me in his arms and teach me little Italian words and phrases. I thought it was so romantic. What did I know about Italy? I was a girl with a German father who had been taught how to make bratwurst, not veal parmigiana."

She closed her eyes, lost in her own memories. "Your father would hold me close to him and whisper to me, 'You are *mia Rosa, bella donna.*'" She opened her eyes and Leo could see tears. "And I remember the first time he said that to me. We were in the back seat of his '57 Chevy, of all places!" She chuckled, then wiped at her eyes. "I asked him what it meant, what he had said to me. And he told me, 'It means you are mine, and that you are my beautiful lady.'

"It sounded so wonderful, so true and romantic and heartfelt. It had such intense meaning when he said it in Italian. In English, it sounded so silly. But in Italian, it was like music, and it seemed so real. Your father started to call me Rosa, and I never objected." She looked at her son. "I speak Italian and pretend to be Italian, because it's the only way I know how to keep your father alive in my heart."

Leo didn't know what to say. She wiped away the tears streaming down her face. He watched her, absorbing himself in her feelings and beginning to understand his mother, and his father, for perhaps the first time in his life. They were like Matt and he and so many others. They weren't just his parents. They were people, and they had all the sensations and fears that everyone had.

Rosa suddenly chuckled and commented that she must look like a mess. She was about to say something else when the telephone rang. Instinctively, she got up and hurried to answer it. Leo heard her from the kitchen exclaim with her accented English, "Giorgio! Why you wait so long to call your mamma?"

Leo stood and looked at the portrait of his father. The old man looking down at no one, as she had once told him, seemed different somehow. Leo could swear he saw a small grin on the man's face. It was not no one that he was looking down upon, but rather all of them, his mother most importantly, with a subtle hint of joy in his heart.

He decided to leave. He passed his mother in the kitchen and saw her back to him as she preyed on his brother's guilt. He grinned, perhaps in satisfaction, perhaps in love. He said, *"Arrivederci,* Mamma," but she didn't hear him. He left his mother's house with a sense of ease for the first time in his life.

– SEVENTEEN –

Leo was glad to see that finally the sun was shining and the wave of tropical storms had stopped. The days following Mother's Day were miserable from the unending deluge, but Leo took advantage of the bad weather to focus on his teaching and his dissertation. Armando and he went out for dinner and a movie one night. Their date ended with a kiss good night and a recommitment to take things slowly.

It was now Friday, and Leo was standing on his front porch drinking a cup of coffee. A mourning dove landed outside his screen and he bid it good morning. He was going to spend the afternoon with Millie, and had arranged to see Armando again that night. He got ready. On his way out the door he saw the Swinburne and Rossetti books on the dining room table. It had occurred to him that Millie might want her books back, so he took them with him.

Traffic made the trip to Millie's nearly forty-five minutes long. Leo always found the name of the community—Queen's Manor—to be funny. According to Millie, there was no royalty, but quite a few queens. Her own next-door neighbor was an aging Liberace. As he approached her mobile home, he saw Millie sitting on the mortar-colored concrete steps smoking a cigarette, her cream-colored bag clutched in her lap. Leo drove to the end of the street, made a U-turn in the cul-de-sac, then pulled up in front of her home. Millie got up and threw her cigarette to the ground. She was wearing a peach T-shirt, off-white clamdiggers, and sandals. As she came closer to the car, he saw that her gray-blonde hair was brushed into place and she wore a little bit of makeup. Leo had to admit that she looked pretty good for someone who had been discharged from a mental hospital a week ago. She opened his car door and stepped in. They greeted each other with an embrace and Leo could sense no hesitation from her.

Pierce
© 2007 by The Haworth Press, Inc. All rights reserved.
doi:10.1300/5849_17

That could only mean that she was comfortable with things and all would go well today.

"You've gained weight!" she said, settling into her seat and putting on her seat belt.

Leo wasn't surprised she had noticed. She had been the first one to point out how much weight he had lost after Matt had died. "Probably too much," he replied.

"Bullshit. You needed to gain some weight. You were looking anorexic." She paused a moment, then, turning back toward him, said as if in a revelation, "You're seeing that UPS guy, aren't you?"

Leo grinned sheepishly and could feel his cheeks flushing. "Yes."

"Oh, that's wonderful, Leo! You'll have to tell me more about him, like how big he is."

As always, her question took him off-guard. "I'm not discussing that with you!"

She blew it off with a wave of her hand. "Please, Leo. You have to let this old broad live vicariously through you. When you haven't had sex in as long as I have, stories are all I have to go on." Leo laughed as he shifted the car into drive. When they reached the first stop sign, she said anxiously, "So tell me about him!"

He smiled as he turned left. "We're taking it slowly."

She nodded her head in assent. "That's smart. Get to know him better first. Very mature of you." She turned toward her window. "Boring, but mature," she added sarcastically.

A minute later, they had passed through the iron gates of Queen's Manor, turned onto Belcher Road, and headed south. They agreed to shop first, then have lunch afterward. Rather than follow the same route he had taken to get here, Leo turned onto East Bay Drive and followed this as it turned into Roosevelt Boulevard. He drove past the St. Petersburg-Clearwater airport and realized he was heading in the direction of Feather Sound, where Armando lived with his aunt. He was excited to see him that night. With that thought in mind, he turned to Millie.

"You are happy for me about this guy?"

"Of course I am. Why wouldn't I be?"

"Oh, I don't know. Because you're my mother-in-law."

She looked squarely at him. "First off, I was your mother-in-law. I'm not anymore." Leo couldn't help but look away. "And secondly," she continued, "I'm your friend." He glanced back at her, and she reached out with a hand and rubbed his shoulder. "I think it's wonderful that you've finally met someone. You've needed this for a long time now."

"It's been very difficult year," he commented.

She nodded in agreement. "For both of us." They were quiet for a moment. Then, she shook her head and shifted positions to face him more. "Okay, this is depressing. I want to hear more about him. What was his name? Armando?" she said with an exaggerated accent.

As Leo turned onto I-275 and headed south, he told her more about Armando's job and schooling, and gave in to tell her what he looked like when she pressured him to share some details. They laughed and chatted as he continued driving, as if nothing had ever happened or changed between them. It made Leo feel inordinately comfortable.

About fifteen minutes later he exited onto 5th Avenue, then turned down a side street, taking the shortcut to the parking lot behind the cream-colored concrete building that was Haslam's on Central Avenue, one of the largest new and used bookstores in the country. By the time they had arrived, his stomach was grumbling and he wondered if perhaps they should have eaten first. With the size of this store, he knew they were going to be a while.

Neither of them had been here in a long time, so it took them a moment to adjust to their surroundings. Continuing to their left was every nonfiction topic from art to zoology, but before them, beyond the new fiction, were the used book and antiquarian sections. They headed in that direction. They entered, and could smell almost instantly the delicious aroma of old books, like a musty research library.

"Did you ever finish reading *Lady Audley's Secret?*" he asked her while they browsed. He remembered she had been reading it when she was in the hospital. He was holding in his own hands an Oxford edition of *Aurora Floyd* by the same author.

Millie was farther down the aisle browsing, running her fingers across the spines of numerous books. She glanced at him over her half-rim glasses. "Yes, I finished it."

"What did you think?"

"I think she got a bad rap in the end."

"You don't think she got what she deserved?"

"Exiled to an asylum in Belgium for something she never did? No, I don't think so."

"What do you think she deserved as punishment?"

"Why should she have been punished?" They were now standing before each other, their attention on the conversation and not the books. "She didn't do anything."

"Are you kidding? She was an egomaniac."

"I don't think so. She wanted to better herself and get out of that hellish life she had been living. She didn't mean to hurt anyone."

"What about the fire? She didn't mean to set that?"

"All right, so there was that. But she was desperate by that point. I still don't think she should have been sent off into exile like that. Her husband wound up getting rid of her in the end, remember, not the other way around?"

"Which husband?"

Millie scoffed. "Yeah, come to think of it, both of them!" Millie turned toward the books again. Leo did the same, but then he heard her ask him a question. "What do you think should have happened to her?"

He turned back to her. She was still casually browsing the shelves. He thought for a moment about her question. "I don't know, to be honest with you. I mean, hubris did her in. It really was like Greek tragedy in some ways."

"Is that why you're using it in your dissertation? Does she epitomize your 'Clytemnestra Complex'?"

"Well, I wouldn't say Lady Audley epitomized her. I mean, Clytemnestra killed Agamemnon because she had a lover and wanted the throne for herself. Lady Audley took on a whole new identity to better herself and tried to bump off her husband after he came back from the dead and threatened to expose her."

"So why are you using the book in your dissertation?"

"Because it was about hubris. Clytemnestra had hubris, obviously, and was struck down by her own son in the end as punishment. Lady Audley had hubris because she had a goal, something she wanted to accomplish, and nothing was going to stop her. Including her own son, come to think of it."

"Then you think she was punished for trying to better herself?"

"No, she was punished because of what she did in order to better herself."

"But did she deserve it?"

Leo actually hadn't considered this before. "Well, I'd say she deserved some sort of punishment. Although, I don't think at the end of the twentieth century we have the right to impose our values and mores in determining her judgment."

Millie nodded slowly, as if in assent, then went back to the shelves. "I'm going to look down here," she said, moving away.

Leo smiled. He loved Millie. She was so easily able to get him thinking about things in a way no other person had been able, except for maybe Palmer. But his dissertation professor didn't count; that was her job. Millie did it out of friendship and genuine interest. She didn't ask questions about literary interpretation or plot explanations. She asked about ethics or morality. She challenged him to come up with reasonable explanations for why things were important. Sometimes they were in agreement on things, other times not. But she always managed to trigger something in his brain that made him think about something he hadn't before. It occurred to him now that he might need to rewrite some of that information on hubris and punishment in his dissertation.

Holding the Braddon book, Leo turned to look behind him and discovered the poetry section. He was standing in the S section, with used paperbacks and a few torn hardcovers of works by Shakespeare and Shelley before him. He continued downward and found a single volume of poetry by Swinburne with a light brown binding. He pulled it out and walked it over to Millie. "Look," he said. "Swinburne. *Poems and Ballads* and *Atalanta in Calydon* in one volume."

She took the book from him and glanced through it. "This came out in the 1970s. I still can't believe that no other edition of his poetry has been published since then."

"Do you have this one?"

"No."

"Then I'll buy it for you," Leo said.

"Oh, no, don't bother."

"But you don't have it."

"That's all right."

"Millie, this is your Mother's Day book-buying trip. I'm supposed to buy you a gift."

She smiled. "Lunch is fine."

"Well, are you going to get anything?"

"Probably not."

"But you always buy something. You always find something unique in this store."

She shrugged. "I can be different today."

Never had they left a bookstore without at least one book in Millie's hand. They had only just arrived, though. He would give her time. She was bound to find something. He took the Swinburne back from her. "Never mind. I'm buying this for you whether you like it or not."

She chuckled. "All right, twist my arm."

Leo left her to continue browsing in the fiction aisle while he walked toward the literary criticism section. He laughed to himself when he discovered a misshelved copy of one of Palmer's books on women writers of the 1890s. He had read through some of it once before. He decided to buy it. It was probably a good idea to have a copy of his dissertation professor's works on his bookshelf.

He continued shopping and checked on Millie a few times. She had moved to the poetry section and spent more time here. After about an hour and a half, his stomach was grumbling more fiercely, and he suggested they eat. Millie agreed, and they made their way to the cashier. Leo held five books in his hands, having picked up two additional criticism books. Leo was startled, however, that Millie had nothing. "You really didn't find anything?"

She shook her head, putting her eyeglasses away into her bag.
"No."

"You know that's very strange."

"Leo, I have plenty of books, some of which I've never had a chance
to go through. I don't need anymore."

"Except for one more Swinburne, right?"

She smiled. "Yes, except for one more Swinburne."

The cashier called to him, and he moved forward with his purchase.
Millie had pulled out her green and white pack of menthol cigarettes
and motioned to him that she was going outside to smoke. Leo joined
her a few minutes later. She was leaning against the window of the
store, her head raised upward toward the sun, her eyes closed. She inhaled and exhaled without moving, and Leo asked her if she was okay.
She opened her eyes and looked at him. "Just enjoying the warmth of
the day." He nodded in acknowledgment. She took another drag on
her cigarette, then dropped it and extinguished it with her sandaled
foot. "Come on. Let's eat."

Leo had suggested that they go to The Garden, a restaurant on
Central Avenue, about fifteen blocks east. It was near the Ovo Café,
which Leo pointed out to Millie as the place of Armando and his second date. The Garden had been around for a few years now and spe-
cialized in Greek and Middle-Eastern food. Lamb and couscous were
often on the menu, but it was accentuated by other forms of Mediterranean cuisine, including pastas and fish. The inside of the restaurant
was rustic with wood-beamed ceilings and darker furnishings, but the
walls were painted a bright rust-orange color and were decorated with
large paintings and sculptures by local artists. The art changed every
couple of months, so the restaurant doubled as an art gallery. The
hostess sat them outside in the patio area at Millie's request. She was
interested in absorbing as much sun as possible today. She also lit up
another cigarette.

There were only two other tables outside with people seated at
them. The atmosphere here was relaxing, with large oak trees dropping occasional leaves on the broken stone ground. The tables and
chairs were white wrought-iron, not completely comfortable but appropriate for the environment. Their server was a gangly young girl

with frizzy black hair and a pierced nose. She asked them what drinks they wanted, and Millie suggested determinedly, "Let's have white wine."

Leo looked at her in surprise. "You don't drink. At least, I didn't think you did."

She ignored him. "Two glasses of chardonnay." The girl left.

"Since when do you drink wine?"

"I'm keeping you on your toes, Leo. A lot has happened recently . . . over the past year. I'm going to enjoy the rest of my life." She took a sharp drag on the cigarette and exhaled toward the sky. The sharp minty tobacco smell filled the air around them.

Leo watched her and shook his head. This was Millie. Unpredictable. Uncanny. One never knew what would come from her next. The server returned with their drinks. Leo immediately raised his glass. "To life."

Millie clinked glasses with him. "To life, however short and sweet it may be." She gulped down her wine while Leo sniffed and tasted his. She puffed on her cigarette again. The server told them about the specials of the day and asked if they wanted a few minutes to go over the menus. Millie replied by saying, "No, I'll have that special, with the grilled tuna and that couscous stuff." Leo quickly scrambled through the menu and ordered a gyro sandwich with a Greek salad.

The server left, and Leo watched Millie take another drink from her wine. He had to laugh. "You're really enjoying yourself, aren't you?"

"Why shouldn't I? I'm having lunch with my good friend Leo."

And she was alive, he realized. She was celebrating her release from the hospital and the fact that she had managed to survive her suicide attempt. He sat back in his chair. "I guess Dr. Bauer is a miracle worker."

Millie nodded slightly. "You could say that."

"Your sessions are going well?"

She smoked. "As well as can be expected."

Leo looked away, and flicked a few small leaves off the table. He took another drink from his wine. He considered Millie's celebration of life, and realized there was much to be learned from this. She was enjoying that which she had almost lost—her own life. He had spent a year mourning his lover's death, but he realized that he too was beginning to enjoy his own life, thanks to Armando. He questioned to himself if it was good to depend on another person to revitalize yourself. Millie seemed to be doing it on her own. She didn't have anyone in her life to snap her out of her depression. He would have to live by her example. He took another swallow of his wine.

The server brought their lunches a few minutes later. Millie raved about her tuna, spiced and grilled then laid on a platter of greens with couscous on the side. Leo's gyro sandwich was nothing special, and he regretted that he hadn't ordered something exciting to match Millie's exotic dish. They talked about different things while they ate. Millie was giddy to hear that Rosa was dating someone. He told her about his classes that week, and she shared some gossip about her neighbors.

When they were finished eating, Leo paid the bill, thanking their nose-pierced server as they departed. They walked out to the car and Millie smoked a cigarette on the way. Leo asked her if she wanted to stop anywhere else. The digital clock on a downtown bank tower told them it was 2:47. She walked to the passenger side of his car and looked up at him, squinting her eyes slightly in the bright sun. "There is one place I would like to go."

"Where?" Leo asked.

She threw the cigarette away. "The cemetery."

It wasn't so much that Leo was bothered that she wanted to go to the cemetery. They had spoken about Matt a bit. He was his lover and her son. It seemed natural that she would want to go. The problem was that Leo and Millie had not been to the cemetery together since his funeral. It had been the beginning of the worst year of Leo's life and what would amount to be not only neglect for his lover by hardly visiting his grave, but neglect for his friend by hardly visiting her either. He agreed to take Millie to the cemetery, trying to comply without hesitation.

They didn't speak for a while. Once they were on 4th Street, Millie asked him, "Is there a Publix around here?" He told her there was, in the Northeast Park Shopping Center at the next light. "Could we stop there for a minute?" He turned into the parking lot and dropped her off at the front door.

As he drove up and down the aisles of the parking lot, unconsciously avoiding cars that pulled out of spots and surprising others by not taking them, he fought against the twisting in his stomach. He finally sighed in frustration and shook his head. He knew it was guilt. He was subjecting himself to his own feelings of pity for having given up on his lover in his grave and for abandoning Millie in the process.

"Why do you feel so guilty?" he asked aloud, turning a corner and moving up another lane. "You haven't done anything wrong," he told himself. "Millie totally understands. And Matt is gone. You have to move on with your life." He took a deep breath, but the pain didn't subside. As he reached the end of the lane, he saw Millie standing outside the store holding in her fist something wrapped in a brown plastic bag and putting what looked like her wallet or eyeglasses into the pocketbook hanging from her elbow.

He stopped in the fire lane in front of the store and she got in. She thanked him for stopping, and then removed the plastic bag. He caught the fresh sweet scent before he realized that she was holding a bouquet of flowers wrapped in clear cellophane. The flowers were a multitude of beautiful spring blooms. He noticed the little price tag sticker at the edge of the cellophane that had the store's name and $3.99 imprinted on it. He looked at her, but she was gazing into the flowers and smelling them. He glanced back at the road before him, turning onto 4th Street again. As he merged into the traffic and continued on his way, he could feel the anguish in his stomach churning even more. He glanced back at her and asked, "You've been visiting him, haven't you?"

"Every month," she replied, glancing away from the flowers out the windshield.

"But . . . how?" He knew it was a stupid question, but she didn't drive anymore, and the cemetery was far from her house.

"Taxi," she said. She looked over at him. "How else am I going to get there?"

He looked away. "Every month?"

"Yes. I go on the anniversary of the morning when you called me and told me he was dead." She paused. "Didn't you ever wonder who left the flowers?"

Leo didn't respond. How could he tell her that in the past year, he had only visited Matt's grave a couple of times, and he had never once until a week ago even noticed flowers had been left there by anyone? It made him feel even worse. They drove in silence the next ten minutes it took to get to the cemetery.

By the time they turned onto 54th Avenue, the local elementary school was letting out, so traffic was heavy with yellow school buses and parents' cars. They slowed down to fifteen miles per hour as they passed through the school zone and the crossing guard let them pass. As he came to 20th Street, he made a left and parked the car at the main entrance. He hesitated a moment before turning off the car, staring out the windshield, feeling worse by the minute. Millie was quiet too. Suddenly, she stepped out of the car with the flowers and closed the door. She probably believed he wasn't going to go with her, which is why she had hesitated as well. He realized that she would have been right. He didn't want to join her. He felt foolish and guilty and stupid about the whole thing. He watched her walk toward the grave, knowing its location as easily as he did, down from the large oak tree hovering over the concrete bench. He shook his head in disgust and self-pity, then realized he was being an asshole. He turned off the ignition and got out of the car.

He squinted in the bright afternoon sunlight and heard children squealing amid the honking horns and accelerating buses, noises that seemed so incongruous near a cemetery. He took a deep breath, then followed Millie's footsteps on the dirt pathway along the concrete wall. He reached the oak tree, and stood beside it, watching as she sat in the dirt with her back almost toward him, the flowers in their cellophane wrapping laying against the granite headstone. He could hear her murmuring, and he looked down at the soil, his sandals, the concrete bench, anywhere but at Millie. A mourning dove landed on the concrete bench, cooed, then fluttered away.

He heard her groan and looked up again. She was getting up, stretching her muscles, brushing off her pants and shaking out her sandals. She picked up her bag and walked over to him. She sat on the bench, then reached into her bag for her cigarettes and lighter. He looked away, toward the school buses and traffic, then at the dove that had landed on another headstone. He heard the clicking of Millie's lighter once, twice, then could smell the crisp burning of the cigarette, and hear her exhale. He watched the bird waddle along the stone. He finally asked her, "What do you say to him when you visit?"

She inhaled and exhaled, menthol wafting in the air. "It depends. Sometimes I talk about what's going on in the world. Sometimes I apologize for how I fucked up his life. Other times, I tell him I forgive him for fucking up mine. And then sometimes I just tell him how much I love him and wish he were alive so that we could be like a real mother and son should have been."

The bird flew into the oak tree and disappeared from his view. Leo looked down at Millie, and she met his gaze. "You really loved him, didn't you?" She nodded slowly. "Even though he apparently hated you."

She shrugged. "He never understood me or what happened to us. I blame myself for that. I was trying to protect him and Theresa, that's all." She took a drag on her cigarette, half of it now ash dangling from its end. "Everything I did was for their benefit or protection. I've been accused of abandoning my children, but I left them with my mother because I was in no condition to raise them. I had to get away. I would have destroyed all our lives if I had let them stay with me at that time."

Leo moved toward Matt's grave. He stood before it, hands in his pockets. He saw on the gray granite his name, his dates, his condition in life as son, brother, and lover. And then he saw the fresh flowers, and felt a wave of despair over how she had been visiting him every month since he had died, while Leo had languished in his own self-pity. He turned to Millie.

"Do you know what I do every month while you're visiting him? I sit on my porch swing getting drunk and smoking pot, praying for the ceiling to come crashing down on me or for me not to wake up again. I pray for anything to make all the pain go away. I pray for the past year to have been a fucking nightmare from hell, and that the police never came to my house that night, that it was all a mistake, or that he had played a trick or something, and he's alive, and he comes home, and we kiss and hug and wind up in bed making love to each other and then curling up in one another's arms and sleeping until the birds wake us up and we start all over like we did every other fucking day."

She finally flicked the ash from her cigarette. She took another puff, then extinguished it on the bench. She exhaled a cloud of smoke into the air and gazed at him through it. "You loved him very much, Leo. You've been grieving."

"No, you've been grieving. You come and visit him every month. Do you know how many times I've visited him? I think like three times since the funeral! I'm wallowing in self-pity because I can't deal with the fact that he's dead. He kept talking about how he hated you. My God, he should have hated me!"

"Leo, he was crazy about you. He could never hate you. Everyone grieves differently. You can't blame yourself for how you're handling it."

"But I'm not, don't you see? I'm not handling it at all! It's my fault that he's dead!" He paused. He had admitted it out loud for the first time. "You were right, what you said during the session with Dr. Bauer. I blame myself because of how he died. Do you know what happened that night? Do you know that we fought? About you, of all things! I came home from food shopping and I was so pissed at him because he was keeping you apart from me. I tried to be understanding over and over, but meanwhile I was hurting you and me because we couldn't be friends. I was resenting him for all of this. I believed he should have gotten over all of his anger issues with you years ago, or at least learned to reconcile that you were a presence in our lives. But instead he kept pushing you away, and I was hurting because of it."

He paced. "I saw he was upset and distraught that night, but I didn't care. I was a total bitch to him. We got into a fight. I told him I was inviting you to my birthday dinner, and he threw a fit." He scoffed. "He threw a jar of sauce at me, for Christ's sake! And then he stormed out of the house." He met Millie's gaze. "I never spoke to him again. I drove him to his death that night. And you're right. I don't know if he committed suicide or not, and that's what has haunted me all year, that instead of helping him I may have driven him to kill himself!"

Leo turned and stared at the headstone in front of him. "Did you?!" he screamed. "Did you kill yourself because of me?!" He fell to his knees, anger and fury and despair bursting within him. Tears suddenly were burning his eyes and he fought through hazy vision to stare at Matt's name on the stone. He pounded the ground with his fist. "I killed you, didn't I?" he yelled. He rocked in a fetal position, hitting the ground. He rolled forward so that his head touched the soil and he cried into the ground, wetting the dirt that covered his lover. He pounded the ground, crying, "I killed you."

Millie was at his side on her knees then, her arm around Leo's back, the other on his arm, stopping him from pounding the soil. She comforted him, rocking him slightly. She positioned him more so that he wailed in her lap, wetting her pants and shirt with his tears. His body shook, and he could feel the sensations of grief shudder out of him. She rocked him like a mother would her son, helping him get over his pain.

"You didn't do anything but love him," she said. "You loved him with all your heart, and he loved you back the best he could." He could hear her as if in the distance, his own grief shuddering through him still. His tears flowed, but his cries were stifled more as she rocked him and he tried listening to her words.

"He loved you more than ever I knew he could love someone. He had so many problems, and you were the best thing that ever happened to him. He was fortunate to have you." He could hear her words, but they seemed at a distance. He tried to focus on what she had to say, because he knew she was comforting him, even though the pain racked his body and the tears poured from him. "You didn't kill him, Leo. It wasn't your fault. Don't blame yourself." She reached down with her hands and took his face in them. She turned his face upward toward hers, and through his tears he could make out her own sad, drawn face. "Listen to me," she commanded, bringing his attention to her and silencing his tears. "You're not the reason why he died, Leo. I am."

Leo wiped at his eyes and shook his head. "No, don't say that. It's not your fault."

She scoffed. "Oh, Leo, but it is. More than you know."

He sat up. "Millie, it's not your fault. I was the one who fought with him that night before he left. He was angry at me."

"No, Leo, he was angry at me." She shook her head and sighed. "I saw him that night too. When he left you, he came to see me."

Leo sniffled and sat up straighter. Millie positioned herself so that she sat in the soil again, and looked at him, nodding her head. "I don't understand," he said.

"He came to see me that night. When he left you, it was around dinnertime, right?" He nodded. "He must have gone to a bar or something, because he showed up at my house after ten or so." He eyed her curiously, wiping his eyes dry. "He pounded at the door, screaming for me to let him in. I was already in bed. I knew who it was right away, and I was totally shocked to see him. I let him in, even though I could tell he had been drinking. I was furious with him. We argued in my kitchen for a few minutes. And then I told him to leave. I didn't want to speak to him like that."

Millie looked at Leo. "I walked into my living room, but he didn't say anything, and he didn't leave. I turned around and looked at him, and for a moment I was frightened because he had a look in his eyes that reminded me so much of what his father looked like when he was drinking and was ready to hit me. I told him to get out, but he stood his ground. Then he reached into his pocket and threw something on the floor.

"I asked him what it was, and he told me to pick it up. I was so angry with him. I reached down and saw it was a folded envelope. I opened it and saw the word 'Mother.' He told me it was a letter, and he wanted me to read it, right then and there. It was the same letter that you brought to the session that day, the letter I wanted to bury.

"I didn't know what to do," she continued. "I was so pissed and scared at the same time. But he didn't move. I was going to tell him to leave again, but I saw how angry and upset he was, and he screamed at me to read the letter. So I opened it, and I could tell from the first opening words that it was some psychotherapy bullshit. I yelled that I didn't want to know about his inner feelings, but then he stared at me, and I swear I could see tears in his eyes, something else that I hadn't seen since he was a little boy. He pleaded with me. 'Read it,' he said. 'Please, Mother.'

"I got through the first few sentences, but then I had to sit down on the couch because I couldn't keep myself steady the more I read. I was horrified and shocked and terrified. When I finished reading the letter, I didn't know what to say. I asked him what he wanted. 'To know the truth, once and for all!' he screamed. 'I've suffered my whole life because of something I don't know about, and I can't take it anymore.'

"'What do you want to know?' I asked him.

"'I want to know what happened to my father! The truth!' he yelled.

"So I decided then and there that I had to tell him. All of it, because for the first time in both of our lives, I realized that everything that had happened to him in his whole life, his anger toward me, this cutting thing when he was a teenager and now, all of it was because of that night. He had been suffering all of these years because he couldn't remember what he had seen happen to his father. He had seen his father die and he had no conscious memory of the whole thing. All I had done was try to help him forget because I thought it was better that way."

Leo was confused. "But you didn't know what happened to Jack. You said so yourself. We're only guessing that Matt witnessed something, but we don't know that for sure."

Millie closed her eyes and shook her head. "No, Leo, you don't understand. I knew all along that he had seen something. I didn't just discover it a year ago."

When she opened her eyes, she explained. "Do you remember once, when we first met, I asked you what Matthew remembered from his past?" Leo nodded. "Do you remember you mentioned something about a stuffed animal? You said he had mentioned to you once about always wondering what had happened to that teddy bear, that he remembered it as being one of his most favorite toys as a child?"

"Yes," he said, his voice shaking.

"Leo, I've had Teddy Pierce all of these years, and I never told him."

"Why not?"

"Because I found it that night, when we left. Afterward, I went back to check on things, and I found the bear in the living room. I don't know how I didn't see it before. I picked it up, thinking it was odd that it was there, thinking Matthew must have dropped it on the way to the car. But then I saw that there was something wet on it. It was blood. I freaked. I didn't know what to do with it, so I put it in a plastic bag and hid it in the back of the station wagon. I never said a word to Matthew. I couldn't give it to him, not like that. I figured I'd wash it, or maybe throw it out. But something stopped me, and I realized then that none of it made sense, how the bear had gotten in the living room, because I remembered that Matthew had gone to bed holding it, like he always did. Which meant he had to have come down at some point afterward. I was too petrified to think what might have happened, so I shoved it in the plastic bag and left that night with it." She swallowed and met Leo's gaze. "I've had that stupid teddy bear all this time, Leo."

"But, Millie, how do you know that he saw something that night? You said yourself that Jack disappeared with the men and that you had not seen them go. Why do you think it was blood?"

She ignored his question, looking away. She continued with her story. "I told Matthew the truth. I told him what happened to his father. I told him everything, from the beatings to what had happened to his sister. And I told him what I had told the police afterward about Salvatore Portavia. He was confused and upset. And then he said he didn't believe me. So I showed him the bear.

"I had kept it all these years wrapped in a plastic bag. I unwrapped it, and gave it to him. He took it from me. 'It's Teddy Pierce,' he muttered. I nodded, then came to him. 'Do you remember now?' I asked him. He shook his head, but I could see from the look on his face that he was frightened. There was a softness in his eyes and face that I remembered from his childhood, from when he would run to me with dandelions from the garden and come to me to heal his cuts and lay down with me when we would cry ourselves to sleep because of what his father had done to us. He looked like the child I remembered, the little boy who used to sleep with Teddy Pierce. But he shook his head, as if fighting not to remember. He looked at the bear, and I saw him

touch the stain, where the fur had turned dark brown after all of these
years, and I saw in his face that he knew, that he finally remembered
what had happened that night.

"'I was there,' he said. 'I saw what happened.' His face had a
twisted, horrific look. His eyes were bloodshot, and he started to cry.
He suddenly screamed aloud and slammed his fist against the kitchen
table. He was moaning in agony, remembering the night and what he
saw. I tried to hold him, but he wouldn't let me. He pushed me away.
I begged for him to let me help him, like I used to when he was a
child. I apologized for what I had covered up for all these years, that I
had lied to him all these years. I told him that I had only done it for his
own good. He didn't listen to me, though. I could see how much he
was hurting, and I wanted so much to help him and make him understand, but he pushed me away. 'I have to go,' he said. I begged him to
stay, but he ignored me. I knew he was in no condition to drive. He
reached the door, and turned back. He put the teddy bear back on the
kitchen table, then looked at me, tears streaming down his face, his
eyes bloodshot and his face stained with tears and puffed red. And
then he said to me, 'You should have kept lying, Mother. I wish you
never told me the truth.'"

Millie's eyes were wet with tears. "He left. I tried to chase him, but
he drove away. I was so upset, and I cried for hours and hours, holding
that fucking stuffed animal and his letter in my lap until I fell asleep
on the couch. And then when I woke up, it was from the phone ringing. It was you, Leo, telling me my son had died in a car crash, and I
knew that it had been my fault all along. He had killed himself because I had helped him remember the truth."

Leo was stunned silent. He had listened to her story, and he realized
that his own anger at himself over the past year couldn't even begin to
compare to the anger and pain Millie had been suffering from. He felt
utterly stupid.

"It wasn't your fault, Leo," she muttered. "It was mine."

He looked at her, and shook his head. "Millie, don't believe that.
You did what he asked you to do. He wanted to know the truth, and
you told him. I still don't believe he killed himself. It was an accident,
because of the wet roads. The police said so. He was stupid, not wear-

ing a seat belt or drinking and driving. He left us no signs that it was a suicide." He could see that she didn't believe him. "Millie, I blame myself for Matt's death because I felt like he was angry at me. You were right when you said that he loved me, because no matter what had happened between the two of us, we always made up and worked to make things better. That was how we did things." Leo realized as he was saying these words that he was comforting himself, and he was startled to discover an odd sense of peace settling in his mind and heart.

"He didn't kill himself over me," he continued. "And he didn't kill himself over what you told him." Leo considered the story of Jack Pierce's death and realized that the story was tragic, even knowing that Jack might have been attacked or killed in his own house then taken into the lake, and that his son had witnessed it. It was a nightmare to think Matt had endured such tragedy as a child and had suffered his whole life from it, but it still wasn't Millie's fault.

"Millie, you had nothing to do with it. You weren't even there when Jack was killed. You were upstairs. You had no idea all of this would have happened to him. You said it yourself. You were trying to protect him from the truth. He demanded to know the truth, and you were forced to tell him what happened. It's horrible, but it's not your fault."

Millie shook her head. "Oh, Leo, you don't understand. It is my fault."

Leo took her hands in his. "Millie, it's not. You have to forgive yourself too. We both do. Neither one of us is to blame." He looked at the headstone, then moved one of her hands to touch the ground where Matt was buried. He covered her hand with his own. He looked at Millie, realizing he was coming to terms with forgiving himself, and wanting only to have her do the same. "It's not your fault that Matt couldn't handle the truth when he was finally confronted with it. And he didn't kill himself over it."

"Oh, Leo, stop, you don't understand. He couldn't handle knowing the real truth."

"Having seen Portavia kill his father? I know, I understand that."

"No, Leo," she said forcefully, pulling her hands away from his. "That's not what Matthew saw that night."

Leo looked at her in confusion. "I don't understand."

Millie moaned in frustration and ran both of her hands through her hair. "Oh, for Christ's sake!" she yelled. Specks of dirt flaked off of her head, but she didn't care. "Leo, Portavia was never at the summer house that night. He didn't kill Jack. I made that whole story up when the police questioned me after they found his body."

She sighed deeply. She met Leo's gaze. She spoke frankly and peacefully, and confessed to him for the first time the real truth. "Leo, I killed Jack. I killed my husband, and my son saw me do it."

– EIGHTEEN –

Leo was unable to speak. He watched her get up, he heard her joints creaking. She brushed off her pants and walked back to the cement bench. She sat down and pulled out another cigarette from her bag. She lit it and exhaled slowly to calm herself. She then met Leo's gaze again as he sat in the grass and soil by Matt's grave. He listened in silence as Millie spoke.

"When I first met Jack," she began, "I wasn't crazy about him. My mother thought there was something wrong with me. Here was a man with money who was expressing an interest in me, a divorced schoolteacher and mother living at home with her own mother. I was a total failure in my mother's mind, so any man who would be interested in me was reason enough for me to take him. Frankly, she was driving me crazy, and even though I want to say that she was wrong, I did feel like a failure.

"We met at the New York Public Library. The principal had asked me to look up statistics on segregation in the schools. That was big then. Jack was going through zoning regulations or something like that. He didn't look like most men I might have wanted to date. He was older, more professional. I was about your age when we actually met, maybe a little younger. I had blonde hair that I used to wear long then, and a pillbox hat style that I couldn't let go from my infatuation with Jackie Kennedy. Leo, I looked good.

"We literally bumped into each other and knocked everything in our arms all over the place. He was all apologetic and offered to buy me a cup of coffee. I turned him down, but he insisted, so I gave in. Like I said, I wasn't crazy about him. There was something about his attitude. He was a little pompous. But I was polite, and even gave him my phone number when he asked.

Pierce
© 2007 by The Haworth Press, Inc. All rights reserved.
doi:10.1300/5849_18

"He called, and my mother pressured me to go out with him. I agreed, and it went from there. He was surprisingly understanding about my being divorced with a child. He seemed even overly excited by the idea. He was an only child and his parents were dead. I think I felt sorry for him, especially when he told me how much he always wanted to have a family. Theresa was five when all of this was going on. She was adorable then, with straw blonde hair." She smiled from the memory.

"Leo," she continued, "you need to understand that Theresa was my entire sense of being at that time. My whole purpose was that I was working to support my daughter. She had no one to turn to but me. Her father was out of the picture. My mother was there, but I was Theresa's mother, and it was my responsibility to raise her. But when the facts were laid before me, and Jack proposed, I realized that my own hesitations about him and our incompatibility needed to take a backseat to what my daughter needed, a stable family with two parents and an income that would give her everything she would want. My mother was ecstatic, Jack was thrilled, even Theresa was excited. Jack had made an impression on her with gifts from the beginning. Only I was uncertain about my decision, but I put my hesitations aside for everyone else's sake. I didn't realize how stupid that was until afterward.

"We got married at city hall in 1967. An aunt and that cousin of his were the only people on his side to attend. Theresa and I moved into his family's home in Bay Ridge, which was kind of upper crust at that time. Everything was going okay. I quit teaching because I didn't need to work anymore, which I only sort of regretted. I spent more time with Theresa. She had started at a new school and liked it, which was good. We settled into a normal routine. He'd come home around five-thirty every night. I'd have a cocktail waiting for him. Dinner would be in the oven, ready to be served twenty minutes later. It was like *Father Knows Best*."

Leo watched her from his place beside Matt's grave, listening intently, almost numb with anticipation. Her cigarette had been burning in her fingers. She had only paused to inhale a few times. The ash was nearly the length of the cigarette itself, and suddenly it fell in a giant lump. Without hesitation, almost instinctively, she brushed it off her pants, stamped out the burning end, tossed it aside, and lit another cigarette.

"I can pinpoint exactly when everything changed," she said, exhaling as she spoke. "It was in 1968, the Friday of Memorial Day weekend. We were supposed to visit that cousin of his in Queens for a barbecue on Memorial Day. I had been redecorating the living room. I was excited for Jack to come home and see what I had done. There were new drapes and carpeting. I did everything in gold ball fringe and red velvet. It was all the rage then.

"He walked in and I could tell he had a lot on his mind from work, but I couldn't restrain myself. I ignored his pleas to be left alone with a drink. He grumbled and allowed me to lead him by the hand. 'What do you think?' I asked, like a pathetic wife.

"He walked around the room in silence, then turned toward me with this look I'd never seen before. 'What did you do?' he asked.

"'You don't like it?' I remember I was devastated.

"'What in God's name did you do?!' he yelled.

"'Jack, please, it's not a big deal.'

"'You destroyed what my mother spent her life putting together, just to make this place look like a whorehouse!' He ran over and ripped the drapes off the windows. I had spent all day sewing those fucking drapes, and he tore them down like they were rags. He went crazy, knocking things over and breaking new ceramics.

"I begged him to stop. I was crying. He rushed at me then and without a single moment's hesitation lifted his hand and wailed me across the face. I fell back into a chair, clutching my stinging cheek, and stared up through my tears in utter horror.

"He came at me and slapped me across the face again. He lifted me by the shoulders and shook me in the chair. 'How could you destroy what my mother did? I want this place to look the way it did before!' He slapped me even harder this time. My face was burning, and I was sobbing. I begged him to stop. He finally got off of me. 'Now fix my fucking drink!' he said, and stormed off.

"Leo, I don't think I was ever more frightened in my life up until that point. He was like some other man. I forced myself to get up and make his drink. I didn't know what else to do. I did spit in it, now that I think about it. But it didn't change anything. This was only the beginning. It started from there and just kept going, not too often at first, but whenever it happened, it was totally unexpected. One time it was because dinner was cold. Another time the television was broken. I never had any warning, and there was never anything in particular that seemed to set him off. I wound up drinking vodka martinis to keep myself calm whenever he was coming home, just in case. From there I went to straight vodka. But that happened over the next few years.

"The morning after that first time he hit me he shocked me by apologizing and telling me about the cabin he had in New Jersey. I never knew anything about it. It was the first time he had ever mentioned it. We cancelled our plans to go to his cousin's barbecue and drove out to the cabin, all three of us. And we had the most incredible weekend.

"Leo, I loved that cabin. It was cozy and quaint, not like some log cabin. I didn't have to do any redecorating here. It had old world charm and antiques, but up-to-date appliances. It was so peaceful out there. The air was fresh and clean. You could smell the pines and hear the wind blowing through the trees. The house was right on the lake, just up from the water. At the bottom was a wooden pier. And the lake itself was beautiful. Cranberry Lake. It seemed to stretch on for miles, but it was probably my imagination at the time. Jack taught Theresa how to fish, and she was thrilled. We only stayed that first weekend, but Jack promised we could come back for the summer.

"It became our annual ritual. We'd go there for the summer months. Jack usually didn't join us because of work. He'd show up every once and a while, stay for a few days, then disappear again. Things between us got worse, and as his temper and drinking flared, so did my drinking and my desire not to be around him.

"I had Matthew just before Halloween in 1969. I was so lonely, Leo. That's why I got pregnant. I never should have otherwise, the same way I never should have with Theresa. I got pregnant with Theresa because I missed my father and I was trying to make Larry love me more. I had Matthew because I wanted someone to love me that wasn't Jack. We named him after my mother's father. I thought for sure Jack would put up a fight, since this was his first-born son. He didn't even care. He left to take Theresa to the Bronx Zoo while I was nursing Matthew in the hospital.

"My life went on like this. I was drinking more whenever he was coming home. I stopped caring about the house, the laundry, the cooking. Jack and I would fight all the time. He'd wind up hitting me. He used to smack Matthew in the head if he was screaming in his high chair. At first I went ballistic and tried to protect him. He beat the crap out of me that night, so badly that I had to go to the hospital. I didn't give a shit anymore after that.

"The only good periods were when we'd escape to Cranberry Lake. It got to the point that I desperately looked forward to the summer months. Jack would be gone for long periods of time, and I could focus my energy on Theresa and Matthew. My drinking would slow down. I'd actually be able to talk to my kids too. We'd play games in the forest, go fishing on the lake. I became a pretty good fisher. I learned to drive so I could take us around the whole area and visit the local farms to buy produce and go to craft fairs. A cabin was built next door to us one summer, and that's when Theresa became friends with the girl next door. She was a year or two younger than her, but they got along great.

"It was just beautiful, Leo. All of it. I used to pray years later for the ability to return to those peaceful days and nights when I enjoyed my life with my children and was able to make apple pies and play hide-and-seek. Those were the best days of our lives.

"And then he would show up and make our beautiful, peaceful lives hell all over again. He was like a tornado that sucked all the happiness out of our lives when he blew in and out. The worst was when he'd stay a week or longer. I wanted to die.

"Just to show you how awful he was, how mean-spirited . . . one time I was reading them Christina Rossetti's 'Goblin Market' from a book of poetry my father had given me years before. We were sitting in the living room trying to be as we always were when he wasn't around. He suddenly grabbed the book from my hand. He was swaying with a cocktail in his other hand. 'What the fuck is this shit anyway?' he asked. 'What're you reading this bullshit to them? It's all garbage. They need to learn about real life. Put on the TV.'

"'I'm not doing that, Jack. Besides, they like it.'

"He rolled his eyes, then scowled down at Matthew and Theresa. 'Do you like this bullshit your mother's reading you? Wouldn't you rather watch TV?'

"They both looked at me, and I could tell they were frightened. They didn't know what to say, and I was afraid to speak for them. Suddenly, Theresa shocked me, and she said, 'I'd rather watch television, Daddy.'

"'Good!' Jack said triumphantly. He switched on the TV. Theresa was immediately fixated, while Matthew stared at me with frightened eyes. He looked at his sister, and then at the TV as well. He was only about three years old at the time, so I can't imagine what else he would do.

"Then I heard a ripping noise, and the next thing I know, Jack was tearing the book to shreds. He ripped out pages, broke the binding, threw the whole thing into the garbage. I was furious with him! I was about to say something, but I hesitated. I looked back at my children, and their eyes were glued to the TV. I did nothing. I let him destroy the book my father had given me, and I let my children watch TV. I fixed myself a drink and went to bed."

Millie puffed on her cigarette. "I think probably the strangest part of that story I just told you has to do with Theresa. It was the first time I ever heard her speak in agreement with Jack against me. She started to do it all the time after that. She was about ten then. Jack gave in to her every whim. He took her to places like the zoo, the park, the gardens, to Coney Island even. He'd never take his son. I didn't understand it. He'd buy her gifts for no apparent reason, and he treated her like she was some God-damned princess. Needless to say, she got nasty with me a lot and ignored everything I told her to do. It drove me crazy, when I cared to think about it. The problem was, I was so fucking stupid and drunk I never knew what was really going on."

Millie looked directly into Leo's eyes. "He was sexually molesting her, Leo. He was molesting her, right under my nose, and I was clueless."

"Oh, my God," Leo muttered in shock, glancing away.

"I don't know what Theresa remembers from her past. She'll probably hate me for telling you things about her, but I have to because it has to do with what happened to Jack. Theresa developed early. She got her period when she was eleven. Fortunately she was visiting my mother when it happened, so I was able to come over and help take care of it. I figured I should explain to her about why it happened and everything, and she responded with a wise-ass remark, something like, 'I'm not stupid, mother, I already know about sex.' I passed it off as nothing and ignored her. Her attitude got worse, though, and then her grades started to fail. I tried talking to her, but she ignored me. I probably should have tried harder.

"And then, the most incredible thing happened. She got pregnant. This was in June 1975. School had gotten out, so I took them right from school to the cabin for the summer. Theresa didn't want to go. She kept insisting that she wanted to stay in New York with Jack. I couldn't imagine why. She always wanted to go to the cabin. She loved it there as much as Matthew and I did. She was friends with the girl next door there. I couldn't figure it out.

"We were there a few days when one morning I heard her throwing up. I didn't think anything of it, figuring she had a stomach bug. She didn't want to come fish with us or do anything. She was very tired and wanted to lie down all the time. I wanted her to go to a doctor, but she resisted. And then, one afternoon about a week later, I sneaked into her room to check on her. I remember the light coming into the room lit up her body on the bed. She was laying on top of the comforters on her back. Her shirt was pulled up from her belly.

"I almost had a heart attack. She was pregnant and starting to show. I wanted to kick myself for not realizing the signs earlier. I couldn't believe it. I panicked. I woke her up, demanding to know what happened. She denied everything, telling me I was crazy." Millie shook her head. "Leo, when I think back to some of the things I said to her. I called her a cheap whore and a slut. I thought she got pregnant from somebody at school. I kept asking her who the father was, but she refused to tell me.

"I knew what I had to do. There was no way she was going to keep this baby. I looked in a phone book. I found there was a women's clinic about thirty miles away in Hackensack. I brought her there immediately, despite her tantrum. I made her abort the baby. I know that makes me a terrible person, but you know, I was horrified to think that she could have slept around and gotten herself pregnant. I couldn't even begin to imagine what she thought she'd do with a baby at fourteen years old. She was going to throw away her entire life. And I was terrified to think what Jack would do or say. I thought he'd kill her and me.

"She hardly spoke to me afterward. She was furious with me. I was saving her life and her future, but she wouldn't listen to me. I figured I'd let her stew and things would get better. But her attitude that summer was awful. I guess I don't blame her, thinking about the situation now. It was horrible what I did, but I know I did the right thing.

"What I never imagined, though, was what would happen next. Never did I think that my entire life and the lives of my children could so drastically change because of her pregnancy and the abortion."

Leo swallowed and ventured to speak. "Did Jack know she was pregnant?"

Millie shook her head. "He had no idea. I wasn't going to tell him at all, but he found out. He showed up for one of his whirlwind visits. It was August, two months after the abortion. I never even thought about it at the time, but the medical bills went to our home address in Brooklyn. So Jack showed up all of a sudden, and for the first day we're all on edge like always. He kept trying to get Theresa to do things with him, but she resisted."

Millie peered at Leo with a determined look. "Theresa was sleeping next door at the neighbor's house. I remember that for a fact." She paused, smoking. "Matthew had gone to bed upstairs. He was sleeping already, I thought."

Millie sighed, then gazed into the distance. "I was sitting outside on the front porch with a fruit bowl and a kitchen knife. I remember it was so peaceful outside. There was this incredible summer breeze.

The sky was lit up with the thousands of stars in the sky. It had to be around midnight by this point. And then Jack called me inside.

"I shook my head in frustration and fought the urge to scream. I figured it was easier to go along with what he wanted, otherwise he'd start a fight. I brought the tray inside and went into the living room, setting it down in front of the chair I usually sat in to read. 'Can I fix you a drink?' I asked him.

"'Are you blind?' he said. He held his cocktail in the air like some fucking king. He was sitting at the side table going through papers and smoking his Camel cigarettes. I poured myself a vodka. 'What is this shit?' he asked. He turned in his seat and held papers in the air. He said they were medical bills from a doctor in Hackensack. I realized obviously what they were.

"'I'm sorry, I forgot to tell you about that. I was sick and—'

"'You had to go to Hackensack to get better?' he said.

"'Female problems,' I said to him, hoping that would satisfy him.

"'What was wrong with you that no one here could take care of you?'

"'Jack, there aren't that many doctors here. We're in the middle of nowhere.'

"'Well, what's this shit?' he asked, trying to pronounce the names of the medical tests, hitting the papers. 'Do you know how expensive this stuff was? You've got your fucking nerve going and spending money without discussing it with me first!'

"I was furious. I downed the last of my drink. I don't know what made me say it, but I knew he'd change his whole tune when he knew the truth.

"'For Christ's sake, Jack,' I yelled, 'it wasn't for me. It was for Theresa.'

"'Theresa? What's wrong with her?'

"'She was pregnant.'

"He said, 'Was?' and I remember thinking to myself that it was so strange that he didn't say 'Pregnant?'" She scoffed and shook her head.

"I told him I made her abort the baby. He didn't say anything. I explained what had happened, and how she refused to talk about it.

And then I told him that I had no idea who the father was, and I saw his face go white. He wasn't saying anything to me. Nothing. I'd never seen him look like that before, because I thought he'd flip out. And then I swear something in my head said, 'Well, of course he's quiet. He's the father.'

"I had no way of knowing. At least, at the time I didn't think so, but of course afterward I could see the signs. But it was so strange. It was like I knew without any doubt." Millie inhaled sharply on her cigarette.

"What did you do?" Leo asked.

"I asked him. He didn't say anything. I asked him again. Then he tried to reason with me. And the more I asked him, the less he denied it, until finally he said that yes, he was probably the father."

She scoffed again. "I went out of my mind. I started screaming. I couldn't believe it. He had admitted he had gotten my daughter pregnant! Not only was he beating me and his son, but he was having sex with my teenaged daughter!"

She seemed to stare off, beyond Leo, to some different memory. "I went crazy. He came toward me and tried to calm me down. He even slapped me to shut me up. I pushed him away, and he came toward me again with his hand in the air. That's when it happened.

"I grabbed the knife on the tray and I just started stabbing. I was like an animal. He tried to fight back. I must have punctured a major artery somewhere, though, because he went down clutching at his body. I kept stabbing him. I was enraged at what he had done to my children, to me, how he had ruined our lives. There was blood everywhere. I'd never seen so much blood in all my life. And then I stopped, gasping for air, holding the knife. He collapsed to the floor.

"He lay there staring up at me. I couldn't speak. I saw his eyes roll up into his head and his body convulse. There was blood coming from all the cuts in his chest. It was pouring out all over the Oriental rug. It just kept coming out of him. He was making these gurgling noises, and I saw blood seeping from his mouth."

Her eyes moved from the distance beyond Leo and focused on him again. She smoked more of her cigarette. She chuckled then. It was eerie, emanating from her, and it gave Leo chills.

"Do you know what I did next? I started kicking him. Don't ask me why. I kicked him, wailed him with my foot. I think I was screaming too. I don't know if I was trying to hurt him even more, or if I was trying to revive him. I didn't know what I was doing.

"Finally, I stopped. I was gasping for breath. My heart was pumping like crazy. He wasn't moving. I guessed he was dead, but then I was afraid to touch him and find out. How stupid is that? I had stabbed him to death, but I was afraid to see if he was dead.

"I looked around. The blood was a lake around his upper body and head. I looked down at myself, and I had blood all over me. I freaked. I threw the knife down onto the tray and I started ripping my clothes off. The next thing I knew I was in the kitchen and my clothes were in the garbage. I washed myself, scrubbing my hands and arms and face with a scouring brush to get all of it off my body. I went into the unwashed laundry basket where I had some clothes, and I put on something dirty.

"I was dying for a drink, but I didn't want to go back into the living room. There was a fresh bottle of vodka in the freezer, so I poured myself a few drinks. I sat at the kitchen table, drank that vodka, and lit a cigarette to calm myself.

"Only when I was more relaxed did it occur to me that I had to do something to get rid of the body. I couldn't let Matthew or Theresa ever find out what I had done. They needed to forget everything about him, especially what he had done to them. He was a horrible man, and now he was dead. I was relieved to know that he wasn't going to hurt my children again. But I also knew for a fact that I had to protect them from the truth, from ever knowing what had happened." She extinguished her cigarette, then closed her eyes and breathed deeply.

Leo could sense that he was probably pale from shock. His numbness had spread throughout his body. Gradually, he could feel the cool grass and cold dirt beneath his hands, and realized he had been gripping the grass and tearing at the soil during her story. He glanced over at the gravestone and the gray granite of Matt's name stared back at him. He cleared his throat, and tried to speak. He had to repeat the first few words to make them come out clearly. He looked back at Millie. "I guess that's about when Matt went downstairs."

She fired her eyes open. "It had to be, sometime in that time period, because I never saw him." She fumbled in her bag and lit another cigarette. He watched as she seemed to remain calm with each inhale and exhale. It relaxed her, as it had that night, along with the vodka.

"What did you do?"

She pursed her lips. "I got rid of the body." She smoked, then continued. "Leo, there was so much blood, I was in shock. I forced myself to go back toward the living room. I was standing at the entrance to the living room. The bottom of his feet were facing me. I stared at him lying there with the blood all near his chest and head. I think I started to panic when I realized the blood was seeping into the hardwood floor and I'd never get it clean. I had to get him out of there as quickly as possible. I forced myself into the room. I tried not to look at him.

"I started to move in a frenzy. I cleared all the furniture out of the way, then picked up the end of the Oriental carpet by his feet. I don't know how I managed to do it, with his lifeless body lying on top and blood seeping out of it. But I did it. I dragged him into the foyer and watched this stream of blood follow us.

"I started to go crazy thinking of ways to get rid of the body. I thought about burying him, but I knew someone would find the body eventually. I had to come up with something better. I opened the front door and looked out toward the lake, and that's when it hit me. I would dump his body into the lake. They did it in the movies, didn't they? Organized crime and stuff.

"I rolled the carpet around his body. I tied him up with rope. Of course when I did it, blood started to run out of the one end and I was filthy again. I knew I had to move fast. Somehow, I lifted the one end of the carpet with his body in it. Good God, Leo, it was so fucking heavy!

"I dragged him down the steps and through the trees. I had to stop and rest a couple of times, but I reached the sloping hill toward the wooden pier. I rolled him down to the pier, holding on to him as much as possible. I tripped at one point, and he got stuck on roots or something. I finally managed to get him down to the pier, and then I dragged him over toward the boats.

"We had two fishing boats tied to the pier. One of them wasn't in such great shape, but Jack never wanted to throw it out because it had belonged to his family. I figured I'd better use that one. I somehow managed to roll him into the boat without it capsizing or me falling into the water. I looked down at the end of the pier and found some square cinder blocks, the ones with holes in the middle. I ran back inside at that point, because I realized I needed more rope. Then I tied the rope through the cinder blocks and attached them in different ways to the ropes around the carpet. I tied the second boat to the first with a simple knot. I got into the first boat with the carpet, put on my life jacket, and rowed out into the lake.

"There was no moon that night. It was very dark outside, but when you're in the middle of the lake, exposed like that, the stars provide enough light for you. The problem was, I was concerned they might show too much. I really was terrified someone was going to see what I was doing. I was also afraid there might be people fishing, because you know fishermen go out in the middle of the night. I had to move fast, so I paddled even harder.

"I listened as I rowed. The only sound I heard was that of my oars hitting the water. I finally decided that I was close enough to the middle of the lake. I decided to sink the boat. It was the easiest thing I could think of. I tried banging away to make a hole, but it echoed. I stopped and waited for a few moments. No lights came on. I heard no other sounds. I tried using one of the cinder blocks instead. I scraped it along the bottom of the boat where it was eroding. I was surprised that it didn't take very long. The water started seeping in fast. I grabbed the oars and put them into the other boat. Then I climbed into it myself, and quickly untied the string that connected the two boats. I paddled a foot or so away, and then watched.

"The water was gurgling into the boat. I could see that it had risen near the top, and then the boat started to go under. It moved at an angle, and the carpet stood upright, which scared the shit out of me. The boat went under, the carpet with it. The water bubbled for a few more seconds, and then everything was quiet.

"I sat there for a few minutes, just watching the spot like I was waiting for something. I had some fearful moment when I thought Jack would pull a Houdini and rise from the water laughing like a maniac and come after me. But nothing happened. I looked around. I was surrounded by water and the stars. I remembered then that I was not finished with what I had to do, and I paddled back to shore."

Millie extinguished her cigarette on the bench. She didn't light another. She clasped her hands together, and looked at Leo. "I went back into the house, and cleaned the most obvious bad areas in the living room and foyer. I couldn't worry about doing a perfect job, not yet, because at that point I needed to get Theresa and Matthew away. I had already decided I was going to take them to my mother's. I turned off the lights in the living room so they wouldn't see anything. I showered, got dressed, and then got all their stuff together. I woke Matthew up and got him into the car, then woke up the neighbors and took Theresa. I packed up the car with their suitcases and told them we were going to Grandmother's."

Millie sat up and crossed her arms. "When we were on our way, Leo, I have to tell you I felt so unbelievably relieved and grateful that I had gotten them away from the house and they hadn't suspected anything. I couldn't believe how easy it was. Then, out of nowhere, Matthew asked me, 'Where's Daddy?'"

She sniffed. "I hadn't planned for that question. I had moved so fast to take care of everything and had gotten rid of his body and had gotten them away from the house without any suspicion. But it never occurred to me that he would ask me that. I realized other people were going to ask me the same question. I said quickly, 'He's gone.'

"That wasn't good enough for my inquisitive little boy, though. 'But where did he go?' he asked again. I looked in the rearview mirror and he seemed very confused. He was rubbing his sleepy eyes and yawning. I snapped. I guess it was the pressure of everything, I don't know. I screamed that he had left us. Then, the more I thought about it, it seemed to make sense to me. I would pretend he had left us like my first husband had. I know it seems ridiculous now, but at the time it was logical. I figured I could pretend I was a terrible wife and couldn't keep a man around. It seemed to satisfy him. He didn't ask me again."

Leo swallowed his nervousness. "What about Theresa?"

"She was very quiet. Never spoke a word. I don't think she said anything the entire drive. She looked out the windshield and said nothing to me."

Millie paused, then continued her story. "The whole drive I repeated that their father had left us, and how it was for the best, and how we'd be fine. Stuff like that. I did this all the way into Brooklyn. It took an hour and a half to get there. I think when we arrived it was almost four in the morning. My mother was shocked to see us. I told her the same thing I had said to Theresa and Matthew, that Jack had left us. I asked her to watch them for a while, that I had more to do. She agreed. And then I said good-bye to them. Only Matthew seemed upset. He cried, but I told him I'd be back."

"You lied to them," Leo muttered.

"No, not at all. I had every intention of going back."

"But you left them."

"At that point with my mother, but I was going back to join them."

"So what happened?"

She sighed. "I drove all the way back to the cabin and got there after five-thirty. I was completely exhausted, but I had to force myself to stay awake. I think I chain-smoked the whole ride. I stopped for coffee at an all-night diner. I finally got there. And then I had to get the place cleaned up, perfectly, so that it looked like nothing had happened.

"I was mopping the hardwood floor in the living room, when I suddenly hit something. I saw it slide across the floor, but I had no idea what it was. I bent down, and I was surprised to see that it was Teddy Pierce. He loved that thing. I had bought it for him when he was born, and he always slept with it. I couldn't figure out why it was here and why he hadn't noticed he didn't have it with him.

"I picked it up, and then I dropped it. It was wet, in the lower half of the bear. It was stained a different color. I knew it was blood. My instinct was to throw it out, but it was Matthew's favorite toy. Something held me back. I was totally confused as to how it had blood on it, because I knew he had gone to bed with it."

Leo glanced at the tombstone. "That's when you realized he had seen the body."

She nodded, almost to herself. "He had to have seen something. He must have come downstairs when I attacked Jack. Or he must have gone into the room before I got rid of the body. Maybe he only came downstairs after I had gotten rid of the body. I didn't know. I had no idea what he saw, but I knew that he had seen something.

"But when he had spoken to me, asking where Jack was, he gave me no reason to think he knew what had happened. Nothing. So I started to wonder if maybe I was making the whole thing up. Maybe I was panicking for nothing. Maybe I was wrong, and he hadn't gone to sleep with the bear, and I had dropped it. I didn't know anymore."

"But you kept the bear?"

She nodded. "Yes. I don't know why. I couldn't get rid of it. It was Matthew's favorite stuffed animal. I didn't want to lose it.

"I finished cleaning up. I got all my stuff together. I went through the whole place and took whatever I wanted, anything that I liked in particular. I had already decided I wasn't coming back here. There was no way. I figured if I sold the cabin, maybe I could buy something else and we could go have a different summer home where we could make new memories.

"The sun was rising by the time I was ready to go. I was so exhausted, Leo. I had been awake all night, and I had done everything I told you. I stood on the pier smoking, looking out toward the lake, watching the sun rise over the fir trees. He was gone. It was all over. We could move on with our lives, and my children wouldn't have to suffer because of him anymore. I knew it had all worked out for the best, and even though I was shocked by what I had done, I had no regrets. That man was a bastard, and now he was rotting at the bottom of the lake.

"I left. I drove off, waving good-bye to the Whitmans next door, assuring them the family emergency was going to be fine. They waved me off as if everything was normal. They suspected nothing. As long as his body didn't turn up anytime soon, everything would work out fine." She eyed him. "You want to talk about pressure? Think how I felt for years afterward, waiting for that body to turn up." She glanced off again. "And then I heard nothing about it or about his body ever showing up. It was weird in a way. When we finally filed a missing person's report, I thought someone would find his body. When I sold the cabin to the Whitmans the following summer, I thought for sure someone would discover something. But nothing ever happened. I couldn't believe that no one suspected anything, and that no one had found him."

There was silence. Leo's thoughts were on Matt as a child. "You never did go back to them, though."

She shook her head. "No, I didn't. I stood on that pier and looked out at that lake. After what I had done during the night, despite the fact that I had no regrets, I realized that it was already too late. I had completely let them down. I had allowed my daughter to be molested and my son to be beaten, and I had done nothing about it."

"You were being abused yourself," he said.

"I realize that now, but I didn't then. At that time, I blamed only myself. I had let everyone down, my mother and me too."

Leo hesitated, then said, "But you did do something about it, like you said."

"I told you, though, it was already too late," she said quickly. "The damage had been done. I needed to let them heal. The only way they could do it would be for me to go away, far, far away from them. My mother could give them a normal life, maybe the kind of normal life she always wanted me to have. With me around there'd always be suspicions and doubts and questions and they would never trust me.

"I didn't make a conscious decision not to go back. I was so tired that morning when I left, Leo, I wound up going the wrong way on Route 80. I was supposed to be going east, but I was suddenly heading west, and I didn't realize it until I was near the Delaware Water Gap. That's when I realized I had to keep going, and let my children heal with my mother's guidance, and without me as a reminder of all that was bad."

She looked at him with hopeful eyes. "You know, I kept in touch, at first. I don't know if Matthew ever told you that. I did stay in touch. My mother was furious with me and would scream and yell whenever the children weren't around. I kept telling her that I couldn't come back, not right away, that I was a terrible mother and they deserved better and that I needed time to figure things out. She agreed that I was a terrible mother, but for leaving them like their father had." She paused. "She believed the story that Jack had left us. It was almost too easy, in a way. You would think that people would have found it odd that I had two husbands who had abandoned me, but people didn't question it. My mother didn't either. She chalked it up to my being a failure."

She sighed. "And then as the years passed, I just lived my life. I worked. I dated. I discovered drugs and Swinburne, thanks to a couple of boyfriends I had out there," she joked, but Leo did not laugh. "And, yes," she continued, "I kept less in touch with my children. I thought it was better that way. They had gone on with their lives, and so had I. I even forgot about Jack and what I had done, and when I remembered, it used to make me feel better to think that maybe Theresa and Matthew had forgotten all about him as well."

Millie sat up and looked around her. She fumbled in her bag, perhaps to get another cigarette. Leo interrupted her by asking, "So is that everything?"

She had a cigarette in her mouth and was about to light it. She took it out. "Yes, that's everything," she said with a serious tone. "Is there anything you want to say to me?" she asked, almost challenging him.

Leo could feel the cool grass and soil in his hands still. It was a sharp contrast to the sun beating on his hair, and the sweat on his forehead and chest. He realized how hot it was when he felt the coolness from the ground. He gradually released his hold on the grass and soil. He turned to look at Matt's gray granite stone, but found he could not look at it right now. It was bothering him too much. It was all too much. "We should probably go," was all he could say. His voice was frigid. He couldn't even look at her. She picked up her bag, and led the way to the car. He followed. They both got inside and Leo drove toward her home.

The traffic was heavy at this hour. The silence in the car was so obviously purposeful it was unnerving. They reached her house a very slow forty-five minutes later. As she opened the car door, she hesitated and turned to him, but he didn't look back at her.

"Leo, I know this was quite a lot to hear and it's probably difficult for you, but I want you to remember something very important. I love my children. I always have. And everything I did was for their sake. All of it was for them. I'm not your Lady Audley or an example of your 'Clytemnestra Complex.' I didn't do any of it for myself, although I admit I did wind up gaining a life in the process. I did it for my children, not for me."

Leo looked down at the steering wheel. She continued to get out of the car. "Wait!" he said. She turned back as she was about to alight from the car. "Your books," he said, oddly remembering them in that moment. He reached into the backseat and grabbed the two old books and the one new one. He handed them to her. She looked back at him, but didn't thank him. She got out of the car and slammed the door.

"Shit!" he muttered under his breath. He got out of the car, but stayed on his side. "Wait, Millie," he said, knowing that he had to say something to her, because he didn't know what else to do. He watched as she walked up the front steps of her mobile home. She turned back to face him, her bag in one bent elbow and her books in the other.

"I'm sorry, Millie," he said hesitatingly, "I don't know what to say." Only one thought entered his mind: try to justify her actions and make it easier for her to deal with the truth. "It was self-defense," he explained. "You didn't mean to do it. He was terrible to all of you. You were defending them from him." As he spoke he realized he was trying to help himself deal with the truth.

She paused a moment before speaking, then smiled in an odd, sardonic way that was true to Millie's form. "It's okay, Leo," she said in her Brooklyn accent. "You'll be all right. It's not like you'll be driving into a cement median and killing yourself."

He leaned his head down against the car, realizing how much she had suffered. Not only was she guilty of killing her husband, but she inadvertently had killed her son as well. All of the guilt that Leo himself had felt for the past year couldn't begin to compare to how Millie had felt for almost twenty-five years.

The slamming of the screen door made him look up again. She had gone inside and closed her door. He had no other choice but to go himself. He drove away.

– NINETEEN –

When Leo approached his house, he saw the white Hyundai parked in the driveway. He swore aloud. He had completely forgotten he was going out with Armando that night. He sighed as he sat with the engine running. He was going to be bad company tonight. He should cancel the date. Then, he looked out the window of his car and saw Armando smiling and waving at him from the screen porch. Leo found himself smiling back. He was glad to see him.

He turned off the ignition and stepped out of the car, grabbing his books. He headed up the steps of the porch and Armando held the screen door open for him. Leo gave him a kiss, and Armando embraced him tightly. Leo started to pull away after a moment, but Armando's arms were still around him. He relaxed and continued to hold him, waiting for Armando to let go first. He did finally, then kissed Leo again. "I missed you," he said with a sheepish grin, running his hands up and down Leo's arms.

Leo smiled, his arms tingling. "Me too." Neither of them spoke for a minute, and Armando started to hug and kiss Leo again. This time Leo pulled away. "I have to shower and stuff. I wasn't expecting to find you here." He regretted that his tone sounded harsh.

Armando pulled back. "I figured I would just come over. I hope that was all right."

"Yes, that's fine," he said with more exuberance.

"You sure?"

He nodded. "Absolutely. Sorry, I'm a little out of it right now. Long day. Let me shower and get ready. I'll be fine afterward." He turned and unlocked his front door.

He moved inside and headed into the office to put his books on his rolltop desk. He heard Armando call to him from the living room.

"I forgot to give you something." Leo wondered if he had brought him flowers or some other gift. He stepped out from the office and saw him holding a box. "It was on my delivery route today, but since I knew I was going to see you tonight, I broke a few rules and decided to bring it with me."

"Who's it from?"

Armando glanced at the label. "Millie. Hey, didn't you see her today?" he added.

He nodded slowly. "Yes."

"How did it go? Did you have a good day?"

What a question. *Good* day? Shocking perhaps. Interesting. Emotionally gut-wrenching. But *good*? Hardly.

"It was fine," he lied to Armando. "Put it on the dining room table." What could she have possibly sent him? She hadn't said a word to him about it all day. Probably another book. He had no desire to deal with it.

Twenty minutes later, he was dressed and ready to go. He was hungry. He hadn't eaten since his lunch with Millie. He found it surprising that after everything that had happened today he was actually going on this date. If he were lucky, being with Armando would help him forget about things for a while.

He marched into the living room and saw Armando watching television. He got up and shut it off when Leo came in, confirming he was ready. "I saw a commercial for the new movie *The Mummy*," Armando said. "It's supposed to be pretty good. Brendan Fraser is in it, which is good enough reason for me to see it." Leo didn't even know who the actor was. He agreed though, trusting Armando's judgment.

They left the house, taking Leo's car for a change. They went to Steak and Ale and would go afterward to the movie theater across the street from Tyrone mall. The restaurant was dark inside because of the dark wood, Tudor-like paneling, and leaded windows with colored glass. Their waiter was a husky man in his midtwenties with a military-style haircut. He took their orders quickly, Armando having prime rib, medium rare, and Leo the New York strip, medium.

They were sitting eating salads for some time when Armando commented, "You've hardly spoken all night."

"That's not true."

"Yes, it is." There was an edge to his voice.

"I guess I have a lot on my mind. Why, what's up?"

Armando shrugged. "I don't know, you tell me."

Leo put his fork down. "Nothing's up. I'm trying to enjoy my dinner with you." He glanced at the table across from them where an elderly couple sat with their granddaughter who cut their meat for them into bite-size pieces. He saw their waiter handling orders at another table.

"Sometimes you seem very distant," Armando said. "You go from one extreme to the other."

"I have no idea what you're talking about."

"Well, take for instance that whole situation with Millie. I know you only gave me enough information to help you."

Leo tensed. "What do you mean?"

"What happened after that PI showed up that night? I asked you on the phone the next day and the day after that, and you kept telling me you didn't want to talk about it."

"Because I didn't."

"And now?"

"There's nothing to talk about!" He could feel perspiration on his brow and upper lip.

Armando shook his head in frustration. "What about today? I know you saw Millie today. Did that guy see her again? Did she talk to you more about this?"

"Why do you want to know all this?" Leo couldn't help feeling suspicious.

"Because I'm interested to know. And I'm involved." Armando was sitting forward, his forearms on the table.

"You're not involved. It has nothing to do with you."

"I am involved! I'm involved because you asked me to help you, and I'm involved because we're seeing each other."

Leo noticed out the corner of his eye that the elderly woman had pointed to her granddaughter and husband. All three were looking at them now. The waiter came over, asking if everything was all right.

They both said yes, and the waiter told them their food would be coming out shortly.

Leo lowered his voice when he replied. He wiped at the perspiration on his forehead and lip with his linen napkin. "Look, Armando, it's not a big deal." He found himself trying to think of something to avoid talking about the whole situation. "I don't like talking about things that make me uncomfortable like this. It's just the way I am. Besides, there's nothing else to tell you about the whole situation." He hoped his lie was convincing.

Armando didn't respond. Then, he sat up in his seat and shrugged, throwing his hands up. "Okay, whatever."

A different server interrupted them with their dinners, inquiring who got which steak. She left, and they stared at their meals in silence.

"Looks good," Leo said.

Armando grabbed the salt and pepper and doused his prime rib.

Leo couldn't touch his food. He glanced away again. He met the gaze of the elderly woman, and she looked away. They were annoying him now. But he realized Armando and he were probably making a spectacle of themselves. It was his own fault. He was being a jerk and pulling away. Armando was right though. He did owe him some explanation. "Armando, I'm sorry. Today was. . ." He thought about what to say. "It was difficult today."

Armando sat back in his seat and stopped cutting his steak. He seemed to relax more. "Why? What happened?" He drank from his glass of soda.

Leo hesitated before responding. How was he supposed to tell the new guy he was seeing that his former lover's mother had confessed to killing his lover's father and dumping his body in a lake? He couldn't tell him any of it. It wasn't exactly everyday conversation. "It was rough emotionally," he said. "We reminisced a lot about the past. And I didn't want to tell you because I didn't want it to interfere with our plans." He hoped that was convincing.

Armando nodded slowly. "I see."

"Look, Armando, you knew from the beginning that I had a lot going on. I hate that it affects you too, because I really like you a lot, and if you don't want to see me anymore—"

"Hey, calm down, Leo. Of course I want to keep seeing you. I like you a lot too." He reached out and grabbed Leo's hand. He pulled it toward him and kissed Leo's curled fist, his goatee rubbing slightly against Leo's fingers, his damp lips wetting his knuckles. "I just want you to know that you can talk to me about anything. If you want to talk about Matt or how you feel or about Millie or whatever. You can talk to me, okay?"

Leo didn't have a chance to respond. "How is . . . ?" they both heard and looked up at the waiter, whose face revealed a shocked look from their intimacy. Armando let go of Leo's hand. The waiter's face was red, uncertain what to do.

Armando recovered first. "Everything's fine."

"Right," he replied and hurried away.

Armando shook his head in disgust. "I hate homophobes. Gay people are everywhere. He needs to get over it." He pointed with his fork across the room. "And so do those old people at the next table."

Leo chuckled. "You noticed them too?"

Armando rolled his eyes. "How could you miss them? They keep staring at us."

Leo cut into his steak and was about to eat a piece, when a silly thought occurred to him. "He's probably still in the closet."

"Who, the old man?"

"No, the waiter."

He hadn't thought his comment was that funny, but Armando laughed aloud. "Good point," he said. "I bet he's going to be a drag queen when he grows up."

They enjoyed the moment. They both then looked at the table across from them. The elderly woman was still staring at them. Armando stuck his tongue out at her, and she quickly turned away. They both laughed harder.

Leo was relaxing, and his face was taut from smiling and laughing. It was a good feeling, one that he didn't have very often. It only seemed to happen lately when he was with Armando. He did like him a lot, probably more than he had realized before, and he didn't want to screw this up. "Armando," he said, growing serious. Armando looked back at him, chewing food in his closed mouth. "Thank you. I appreciate knowing I can talk to you. I may take you up on that offer one day."

Armando swallowed his food, then smiled and winked.

Leo remembered then that he did want to talk to him about something. "Oh, and by the way, I happened to catch this week's 'Latino Living' by A. J. Sedilla." He took a bite of his buttered baked potato. "'Latino Lovers'? Rather catchy title."

Armando put his fork laden with meat down. "Did you like the column?"

Leo nodded slowly, enjoying both his dinner and seeing his nervous reaction. "I found it rather . . . intriguing. I'm somewhat curious to find out if everything you suggest is true." He couldn't help but be pleased when he saw Armando turn red.

After dinner they walked to the movie theater. They waited on line for a few minutes, they got tickets and went inside. Armando bought a soda for them to share as they watched the movie. They were enthralled by *The Mummy,* grimacing along with the rest of the audience when the scarabs poured out of the mummy's face and cheering when the damsel Evie was rescued by the hunky O'Connell. Leo was intrigued that the heroine had been a librarian, and thought of Theresa. "Somehow though," he said, "I can't see her chasing mummies in Egypt."

As they walked back to his car, Leo risked public spectacle and persecution from the cars passing them on 22nd Avenue. He quietly slipped his arm around Armando's waist and lay his head on his shoulder. He could feel Armando's warming response, and he put his arm around Leo's waist as well. They walked in silence for a few moments, when Leo asked, "Do you want to spend the night?" It had come out without hesitation or forethought.

Armando stopped. They broke apart and Armando turned to look at Leo. "Are you serious?" His face was like a child's anticipating a potential surprise party.

"I'm not promising anything—"

Armando put his one hand up. "Don't. It's okay. I'm just glad you asked." With that, he came forward and kissed Leo. They heard a horn blare, but no comments were shouted. Neither of them were sure how to take it, but they didn't really care. They got into Leo's car.

Once they were home, Leo played his answering machine and Armando listened with him as he heard his two messages. The first surprised him, as it was from his brother calling to let him know he was returning to Florida, that the fucking cunt he had been with had left him. George then asked Leo to help him look for a place when he came home. "You know I love Ma," he said with his heavy Jersey accent, "but I ain't livin' with her."

Leo shook his head in disbelief. "My brother has never asked me to do anything with him," he told Armando.

"He's a bit homophobic too?"

Leo scoffed. "To put it mildly. Hey, I'll tell him my new friend Armando is going to come with us and we know of a great place right near the Suncoast Resort, so he can have drinks with us at Sunday T-dance." Armando laughed.

The second message was from Palmer, letting Leo know that she had read the latest work that week on his dissertation and she was very pleased with his progress. She wanted to meet with him to discuss the Swinburne and Rossetti.

"Weren't those the two poets that you got those books from Millie?"

Leo nodded. "I added poetry to my dissertation after she had sent me those books. I thought they might add a new angle." He deleted his messages.

"What is the title of your dissertation? You never told me."

Leo rolled his eyes. "'The Clytemnestra Complex: Literary Murderesses in. . .'"

His voice trailed off. Something had occurred to him for the first time. Clytemnestra. Agamemnon. Electra. Orestes. The entire myth started to unfold around him. The coincidence. The murder. Millie. Jack. Theresa. Matt. It wasn't unlike Greek tragedy. There was no direct similarity, although at first it was tempting to see parallels because of the drama and the interpersonal relationships. But Millie was no Clytemnestra. Even she had said that herself.

Leo shook off the whole thought. It was too disturbing. He walked past Armando and entered the living room. Armando called to him and followed him. Leo turned quickly to face him. "You must think I'm nuts."

"I am confused. It's like you went into some other dimension. You were telling me the title of your dissertation—"

"Let's forget all about that. No work talk now. My dissertation is the bane of my existence sometimes, and I'd like to forget it for a while." Leo glanced at the VCR and saw that it was 11:21. "Do you want to watch TV or something?" he asked, heading for the remote control.

Armando grabbed his arm and stopped him. He turned him around. "No, I want to go to bed," he said, then kissed Leo hard, his tongue pushing into Leo's mouth as his goatee rubbed against his face. Their arms intertwined around one another, and then Armando pulled away. He unbuttoned his shirt slowly, flashing the small patch of dark hair on his chest, then one of his nipples, which he rubbed to make it hard. He took a few steps backward toward the hallway, then removed his shirt and tossed it onto the floor. He turned and rubbed his ass with both hands, moaning, then turned his head back toward Leo and winked. He walked down the hallway. Leo grinned, then scurried after him, squeezing his ass as he moved past him, hurrying to the bedroom first.

They cuddled in bed. Leo had changed into boxers, making Armando turn around while he changed, despite his protestations. Armando wore his white Calvin Klein briefs to bed, and Leo couldn't help but notice they fit him quite well, forming a beautiful package in the front and contrasting nicely with his light caramel skin.

Leo lay on his back. His right hand lay beneath Armando, running his fingers along his shoulders and back. Armando lay on his side facing Leo and had his arm stretched across Leo's torso. He ran his fingers delicately over Leo's chest hairs, tracing his nipples. Leo shivered from his touch. Armando gently caressed his sternum, using a single finger to move down his happy trail toward his boxers, where Leo could feel himself stirring. Armando moved his single finger under the waistband of his boxers, gently playing back and forth across his abdomen. He moved a little closer with his whole body, kissing his chest and licking his right nipple. Leo could feel Armando's cock swollen against Leo's hip and thigh, and he was pleasantly startled to realize how big Armando was. He felt skin then, and realized the head of his cock was rising out of his underwear. He glanced down and he could see the tip of the swollen head in its hood.

He lay his head back, trying to enjoy the moment. He wanted to do this. Armando was watching Leo's cock grow in his shorts. He moaned as he nibbled on his nipple and moved his hand from the waistband of Leo's boxers to the gaping slit in his shorts where his cock was starting to peek through. He reached inside and grabbed Leo, squeezing enough to make it harder. He sucked at his nipple at the same time, and Leo inhaled sharply from the intensity of the moment. His shut his eyelids and could feel his eyes rolling back from the pleasure of the moment. He could feel his body tingling from the caresses, the sucking, the licking, the squeezing, as well as Armando's uncut cock rubbing against his thigh. Armando got up from his reclining position. By the time Leo opened his eyes, he could feel the air hitting his cock as Armando pulled it through the slit in his boxers and wrapped his lips around to swallow him. Leo exhaled sharply and moaned. It had been so long since anyone had sucked him like this. It was too much.

"Stop," he said. Armando ignored him. He continued to go up and down on his cock, licking it with his tongue inside his mouth. "Armando, stop," he said again.

Armando pulled away. He was reclining over Leo's leg, his torso resting on his right elbow and he gazed up at Leo over his erection. "You don't want me to stop," he said, then engulfed his cock again, sucking hard.

Leo's body convulsed slightly, and he forced himself up onto his elbows. "Armando, no, really, you have to stop." He ignored him, sucking even harder. Leo was torn, the pleasurable sensations of his tongue and lips around him, overwhelming him as he fought not to do this. His head rolled back, and he breathed deeply. He tried to deaden the tingling through his body, but it was so difficult. Then, without thinking, he turned his head to his left, and saw the photograph.

"Armando, that's enough. Stop!" He spoke forcefully enough that Armando did stop.

"What?" He stroked him slowly, but Leo started to pull his body away.

"I can't do this," Leo said. Armando stopped stroking. He scoffed. "I'm not into this right now."

"You're joking, right?"

His cock softened.

Armando looked away, shaking his head. "Unfuckingbelievable," he mumbled.

"I told you I couldn't promise that anything was going to happen."

"I know, but for Christ's sake, you could at least try to enjoy it a little!" He paused a moment, then added, "Is it me? Are you not attracted to me?"

Leo rolled his eyes. "Oh, my God, are you kidding? I think you're hot!"

"Then what the hell's the problem?"

Leo threw his head back onto the pillow in exasperation. "It's me, all right?"

"No, Leo, it's not all right. We've been seeing each other for a couple of weeks now, right? And we still haven't had sex. If you don't want to fuck yet, that's fine, but could we at least have some physical intimacy?"

Leo raised himself with one hand beneath his head. He looked back at him. Armando was beautiful. Here was this gorgeous Latino who wanted to have sex with him. Even better, wanted to be with him, like a couple maybe, and he couldn't even relax enough for a blow job. "Armando, I know what you're saying. But I haven't been with anyone like this in so long. I'm not used to the intimacy."

Armando shook his head in disgust. Leo saw him glance at the photo, but Leo didn't acknowledge what he had done. Armando hesitated a moment, then looked at Leo and said, "I know you're going to get pissed when I say this, but it's been over a year since Matt died. You have to move on with your life. You're only twenty-nine, not eighty-nine."

Leo sighed and looked up in frustration. "Armando, I know that, but there's so much going on with the whole thing, it's overwhelming sometimes."

"Like what? Tell me something so that I can understand what's going on with you."

Leo looked at him. He could see he was willing to listen, was open to helping him cope. He wanted to open up to him, tell him things, make love to him, but it was so fucking difficult. He didn't know where to begin. He thought he had to say something, anything to make the situation better. He said quickly, "Do you want to know where Millie and I went today? To the cemetery. We reminisced about Matt and the past, while we sat there at his gravestone."

Armando was receptive to whatever Leo had to say. "That must have been special."

Leo eyed him sharply. "Special? It was a fucking nightmare!"

He met his gaze. "Why?"

Leo was startled that he didn't get it. "I just told you we visited Matt's grave site, and you think that was special?"

"Well, I assumed so, considering all that Millie has been through lately, that the two of you were able to spend quality time, talking about the person who meant so much to you both."

"Matt hated his mother," he said matter-of-factly.

"Why did Matt hate his mother?"

Leo thought about how to answer the question, then shook his head, exasperated. "It's such a long story, I can't even get into it."

Armando glanced away briefly. "Okay, so why don't you tell me why the visit was so bad."

Leo wanted to shout it out loud, to scream to him, "Because Millie told me that twenty-five years ago she killed her husband, then dumped his body in the lake!" But he didn't of course. He couldn't acknowledge publicly to anyone what she had done. It would give too much credence and validity to the whole thing, and it would cause him to question his friendship with her and his relationship with Matt, the years they had all known each other. Acknowledgment would mean that everything he had known was a lie and that nothing had been the way he had assumed all these years. So he said nothing to Armando.

"Leo?" he encouraged.

He looked away. "I don't want to talk about it."

He could hear Armando's frustrated sigh. He saw him out of the corner of his eye as he got up from the position he had been in and moved to the other side of the bed. He yanked up the sheet and got under it. He lay with his back turned to Leo and grumbled, "Good night."

Leo turned onto his side away from Armando. He looked at the photograph. All he wanted to do in that moment was smash the glass and tear up the photo. He turned out the light instead.

– TWENTY –

Three hours later, Armando was snoring lightly beside him, but Leo lay on his back, unable to sleep. He was disgusted with himself. He couldn't imagine why he was treating Armando so badly. He wanted to be with him, and he knew he would be good for him. But he couldn't do it. He couldn't open himself up to him. He didn't need a therapist to tell him that part of it was his fear of being hurt again, or of being abandoned physically and emotionally, things related to past relationship issues with Matt. All of that was obvious. And all of that would have been normal. But now Leo had been given extra baggage he could have very nicely done without.

He lay there wondering why Millie had told him. Why, after all of these years, had she waited until that afternoon to say something to him? It was like she had been waiting for a specific moment to expiate her sins. He was no priest though, and he could offer no penance. Why did she choose to tell him the truth?

He couldn't take the insomnia anymore. He was getting angry. Her actions had made Matt who he was, and Leo had been the one who had had to deal with his issues, consistently offering to help him but blinded by the truth as to what was actually wrong. He sat up in bed. He moved slowly so as not to wake Armando, but he could hear motion. Armando rolled onto his back, his snores becoming a little louder as his mouth opened. Leo couldn't help but smirk. He could see Armando's beautiful form in the darkness, his face at rest, eyes closed, goatee surrounding an open mouth with choking snores coming from it. His hair was skewed. His right hand covered the patch of hair on his chest, and his left hand touched his stomach, half hidden by the sheet. Leo shook his head, angry again at himself for how he was letting Armando down. He got out of bed and left the room.

Pierce
© 2007 by The Haworth Press, Inc. All rights reserved.
doi:10.1300/5849_20

He thought maybe he would watch TV, but quickly changed his mind. Infomercials and biblical talk shows were the only shows on at this hour. He walked across the hardwood floors trying to dampen the squeaks in the boards echoing in the quiet house. He grabbed a Corona from the refrigerator to help him sleep. As he drank it, he leaned against the kitchen counter. In the dim light he could see into the dining room where the flowers Armando had given him, now wilting, were dropping petals onto the table. There was a nasty decaying smell exuding from them even from this distance. He had to throw them out. He finished his beer quickly, then went into the dining room and picked up the vase. As he did so it banged into the unopened package that was from Millie. He set the vase back down and ignored the falling petals and rancid water. The box stared up at him.

The only reason why he was hesitating opening it was because of his last conversation with her. He couldn't deal with anything she might have given him now. He knew he was being ridiculous. It was probably just another book. But she hadn't mentioned or she had forgotten that she was sending him something, which he found strange. All she would have had to say was, "Oh, yeah, and I sent you my book of poetry by Browning," or Tennyson, or any other Victorian she had in her collection.

He reached in the kitchen utensil drawer for a serrated knife. He carried it to the dining room and picked up the package. He moved into the living room and sat on the couch. He set everything onto the coffee table, then turned on the lamp on the end table beside him, near the ebony box where he kept his joints. He picked up the package. It wasn't flat like the others he had received from her, but wider and longer. It was very light too. He realized it couldn't be another book, unless it was some odd-shaped paperback curled inside. He shook it and heard something scratch against the sides.

There was no point in continuing to guess what it could be, so he took the knife and cut through the tape and label. He opened the flaps of the box easily enough, and saw something wrapped in white tissue paper. He set the knife down, then removed the item from the box. It was soft, in some areas cushy, in others mushy and dead. He put the box onto the table, and unwrapped the tissue paper.

For the most part it had brown fur, but the tummy, inner ears, and pads at the ends of the feet and hands were dirty white. Plastic brown eyes stared back at him with a vacant stare, and a tiny, worn, black pom-pom was its pathetic nose. The stuffing in the arms and legs were full, but the body and head were practically deflated. Leo held the teddy bear aloft in the light, and stared at the dark brown stain on the lower left side of the stomach area, continuing all over the legs, and onto the back, including the little brown tail.

He threw the bear onto the coffee table. Why would she send this to him? What was going on with her? She had made her confession to him and sent him Matt's old teddy bear, the same teddy bear that she had found almost twenty-five years ago soaked in her husband's blood, the same stuffed animal she had kept all of these years, for no reason, until she had produced it to show Matt, to remind him of what had happened that night. The bear had helped drive him into the median.

Leo embraced himself. He was freezing suddenly. He wrung his hands over his face, wiping desperately all of the thoughts penetrating his brain. He was breaking out in a clammy perspiration. It was like everyone was screaming at him. He could hear her confession all over, her words in the cemetery, his mind's eye showing him the night Matt's father had been killed, Millie stabbing him over and over in anguish for what he had done to her daughter, Matt watching from the doorway in horror as his father was killed by his mother, hiding until she stepped away, then going to see his father and watch him die, dropping his teddy bear near a pool of blood as he hid from his mother again, desperate not to let her find him.

"What the fuck are you doing to me?!" Leo screamed, rubbing his face and temples fiercely. He could feel his eyes burning. He shivered. He was aflame with angst, his head ready to burst. Why was she sending him this too? The confession wasn't enough? Why did she feel like she could burden him with all of her guilt? It was too much. He couldn't take this. He had had to bear with Matt and his pains for so long, he couldn't take on Millie's as well.

"What's going on?" he heard from the entrance to the living room.

Leo looked up sharply and saw through his teary eyes Armando standing there. He looked tired, but was alert. Leo quickly wiped at his eyes. He tried to tell him it was nothing, that he could go back to bed. He came to Leo and with a quick shove pushed the coffee table away. He fell to his knees in front of Leo and reached up with his hands. "Leo, what's the matter?" He took Leo's hands, but Leo struggled to use them to hide his tears. Armando overpowered him, though, and moved Leo's hands away. He used his own hands to stroke Leo's face. He cupped Leo's face with them, and used his thumbs to wipe at the tears in his eyes. He saw Leo shivering and quickly reached up to hold him tightly, to warm and comfort him. He rubbed his hands up and down Leo's back, but he shivered still. Armando got up quickly and raced back into the bedroom. He came back with a T-shirt and the bedsheet. He made Leo put on the shirt and wrapped the sheet over his shoulders. He sat down again on the floor in front of him and held his one hand and wiped at the tears with the other. Leo started to shiver less. After a few minutes, he had calmed down enough that he took a deep breath and saw Armando again with clear eyes.

"Thanks," was all he could muster.

Armando smiled, continuing to wipe at Leo's face with his free hand. "No problem."

Leo chuckled. "I'm not a wacko, you know."

Armando smiled. "I know that. And I also know that you're keeping way too much inside and it's destroying you."

He was so right. Leo knew it. And all of these hang-ups were in Leo's mind, and all they were doing were hurting him, and Armando now.

"Look," Armando continued, "I don't want to pressure you, but I told you I'm here for you if you need to talk. I am a pretty good listener."

Leo glanced toward the box on the coffee table. "I opened the package."

Armando followed his gaze. "Was it another book?" Leo hesitated a moment, then shook his head. Armando reached toward the tissue and picked up the bear. He showed it to Leo. "This is what she sent?"

Leo nodded. He could feel himself tense, but he breathed slowly to calm himself.

"Cute bear," he said, bringing it closer to the light with his one free hand. He started brushing at it. "Kind of pathetic looking," he added with a chuckle. "It's stained though."

Without forethought, Leo said, "It's blood."

Armando stopped brushing the bear. He met Leo's eyes. "Blood? Are you sure?" Leo nodded. "Whose bear is this?"

"Matt's."

"Why is there blood on it?"

"It's his father's blood." He let that sink in, and continued before Armando could ask another question. "Matt dropped the bear in the blood after he saw his father killed."

Armando's eyes widened and his mouth fell open. "What? Matt saw. . .? But I thought that business partner . . . Sal whatever . . . took Matt's father away from the house that night he disappeared? How could. . .?"

Leo shook his head. "None of that happened."

"Leo, it said in the news reports that Millie told the police. . ." His voice trailed off again, almost suspecting what Leo was about to say.

"It turns out none of that ever happened," he said hesitatingly.

"Then what did happen?"

"She killed him."

Armando swallowed, his Adam's apple moving nervously. "Millie killed her husband, and Matt saw it happen?"

Leo nodded slowly, clutching the sheet around his shoulders as another chill ran through his body. "She stabbed him, more than once." He could hear his voice was a monotone. "Then she wrapped his body in a carpet, dragged it out of the house and into a boat, tied weights to it, and dumped his body into the lake."

Armando stood suddenly. He was holding the bear still. He looked like he didn't know whether to drop it with disgust or examine it more closely. He paced. "This is fucked up," he said. He stopped and looked at Leo. His face was blank with shock.

Leo regretted opening his mouth. Not only had he betrayed Millie, but he was scaring Armando. He got up to take the bear from him. "I never should have said anything."

Armando pulled the bear away from him and held it aloft. "No. What are you talking about?"

"I never should have told you. All I've done now is add you to my fucked up situation."

"Leo, I wanted you to tell me."

"I don't think you had this in mind when you said it."

Armando glanced away for a moment, his eyes revealing this was true, but he surprised Leo then by gently pushing him backward. "Sit down," he said.

"Just give me the bear and forget about it," he said.

"Leo, sit down," he ordered, pushing him more. Leo did as he was told and sat on the couch again, the sheet clutched tightly around him. Armando put the bear on the table, and lowered himself before Leo and sat on the floor. "Look, I'm not going to deny that you shocked me with what you just said, but that doesn't change anything. I want you to feel comfortable enough to talk to me. I'm not going to judge you or anyone you know or love. Trust me. Let me be there for you. I want to do what I can to help you." He reached with the other hand and squeezed Leo's two hands in his.

Leo looked into his eyes and he could sense that same trust he had seen before. He had to open up to him, if for no other reason than to let him know that he appreciated his concern and did trust him. He glanced at Armando's hand covering both of his. He met his gaze, his beautiful dark brown eyes. "Where do you want me to start?" he asked.

Armando shrugged. "It's totally up to you."

"This could take a while."

Armando smiled and squeezed his hands again. "I'm not going anywhere."

Leo took a deep breath, sat back in the couch, looked into Armando's eyes, and opened up for the first time, telling him the detailed story of his life with Matt and Millie.

He began with how Matt and he had met, and the early years of their relationship. He told him about how angry Matt was when Millie moved to town and his reactions whenever Leo tried to reunite them. He explained to Armando about how Millie had abandoned her children and left them with her mother while she moved to California, how this had happened the morning after Matt's father had been killed, and how she returned, swept him off to Florida without any warning, exposing him to a brand new life full of alcoholism and unhealthy relationships.

"Matt hated her," Leo said, "and I could never understand why. It never made sense to me. I asked him over and over, but he wouldn't discuss it. I used to think he was jealous because I had a better relationship with her than he did. I mean, I can understand him being resentful and hurt that she had abandoned him, and the alcoholism and stuff, but his hatred was so deep-rooted and violent."

Armando looked away for a moment. "If he witnessed . . . it . . . maybe he blocked out the whole thing. Children have a way of coping by blocking things out of their mind."

"You're probably right. Millie told me that when her children asked what had happened to their father, she repeated that he had left them. She told her mother the same story, so that was all Matt ever heard. He was only six at the time. He probably did convince himself that it never happened." Then, something occurred to Leo. "Although, I wonder if maybe he did remember, in a different way." Leo then told Armando that Matt had been a cutter.

Armando looked confused. "I don't understand. You mean he actually used to cut himself?"

"I know it seems strange. It's a weird phenomenon for people who aren't aware of it. Basically, it's an attempt to get rid of pain. It's kind of confusing."

Armando seemed more conscious now. "Well, actually, now that you mention it, I think I know what you're talking about. There was a girl in my freshmen class in high school who I swear was anorexic. I heard one day that some girls found her cutting herself in the stall in the bathroom. It was a big deal at the time, and no one understood it. The girl wound up transferring to another high school."

"It's more common with teenaged girls, but boys are known to do it also." He told him about the night he discovered Matt cutting himself in the bathroom, the blood, his zombielike state. "He was admitted to the psychiatric ward for attempted suicide, but a doctor who was trained in self-mutilation was able to help him." He paused. "I blame myself, you know. It was only because I forced Matt to interact with his mother that he started cutting himself again."

"Whoa, Leo, it's not your fault. He had a serious problem. And like you said, it probably was connected to witnessing what he saw as a child."

The interesting thing was that Leo realized now, perhaps for the first time, that Armando was right. The self-mutilation predated Leo. It was based on the early childhood trauma of what he had seen. Matt's psychiatrist had said that most of the time self-mutilation was a by-product of other emotional problems, but that occasionally it stemmed from early childhood trauma. Dr. Tate had seemed very interested in supporting Matt's questions about what had happened to his father, now that Leo thought about it. Not that it helped him when he had discovered the truth.

"Leo," Armando encouraged, "what did Millie tell you about . . . Matt's father's death."

Leo told him about his phone conversation with Millie on Mother's Day, how Harrigan had visited her again. He continued by telling him about their book shopping trip and lunch that day, and how they had gone to the cemetery afterward. "We were there at Matt's grave, and we started talking. I broke down." He paused. "I told her that ever since he'd died I blamed myself for what happened to him, how I angered him and how he stormed out of the house and wound up dead afterward."

"I didn't know that happened. You had a fight?"

Leo nodded. "I blamed myself for sending him into that accident because I got home that night, saw he was upset, but ignored it and argued with him about wanting Millie to come to my birthday dinner. He was furious." The night flashed in his mind.

Armando shook his head. "Leo, you know it's—"

"I know, it's not my fault that he was killed." He scoffed. "I didn't realize that until today. Millie told me that he showed up at her house that night." He recounted what she had told him about Matt's visit and the letter, and how she had told him the truth about what had really happened to his father, that she had killed him. He told Armando about the beatings, the drinking, and Theresa's molestation, pregnancy, and abortion. He told him what had happened that night, how she attacked Jack when she discovered what he had done. She had killed him, and then she had gotten rid of the body.

Leo sat back, weary from the storytelling. Armando still held onto his hands, but he was silent. Leo came forward again and removed one of his hands. He brushed Armando's hair, running his fingers through his thick locks. He reached down and kissed him on the lips. Armando smiled. "Thank you," Leo said.

"For what?"

"For listening. For making me feel comfortable and safe enough to talk."

"How do you feel?"

"A lot better. I'm exhausted."

Armando chuckled. "I can imagine."

"But I also feel like some huge boulder is off my shoulders. I am so glad that you were willing to have me talk to you."

"I'm glad I could be here for you."

Leo heard Armando's stomach grumble. He glanced up at the VCR clock and saw it was 5:29. He was surprised that their conversation had gone on for such a long time. "Do you want breakfast?" Leo asked.

Armando eyed him suspiciously. "How could you want breakfast all of a sudden?"

Leo shrugged. "I don't know. I'm Italian," he joked. Armando smiled. Growing serious, Leo added, "I want to do something to thank you."

Armando shook his head. "Don't bother."

"All right, how about just cereal, then we go back to bed?" Armando nodded in agreement. Leo threw off the sheet and got up. They headed into the kitchen. Leo brought out the milk, two bowls and spoons, and the Cheerios. Armando sat down to eat while Leo leaned against the counter. He watched Armando. He seemed pensive. "What's going on?" he asked.

Armando glanced at him. "I'm sorry. I'm thinking about everything Millie told you."

"What about it?"

"I don't know. I guess I'm a little confused by a couple of things you told me. Maybe it's because you were retelling the story and it wasn't coming right from her."

"I don't understand." Leo wondered if it was just this, or was he saying this to cover up his true feelings, his disbelief and horror at what Leo had told him.

Armando looked away, as if pondering something. "Well, I don't know Millie, so I have no idea how big or how strong she is, but don't you find it odd that she was able to get rid of the body by herself?" He paused as if to let the words settle in Leo's mind. "Dead bodies are pretty heavy," he added, "from what I've heard, obviously."

Leo was surprised by Armando's words, but he calmed down. At least it didn't seem as if Armando was traumatized. Leo thought about Millie's body size. She hadn't changed much in all her years, although presumably she would have been stronger when she was younger, not to mention healthier, prior to her worst years of heavy drinking. He doubted she could do it by herself today, but about twenty-five years ago, she probably could have. He thought so. He told Armando that.

He eyed him. "You really think she could have wrapped up her husband's body in a carpet, weighed it down, dragged it outside, put it in a boat, and drowned the body, all by herself?"

"Well, why couldn't she? The adrenaline from the whole situation would have kicked in and enabled her to do all that. I mean, come on, she actually killed someone. Obviously she panicked afterward."

Armando nodded. "Okay," he said, but he didn't seem convinced.

Leo crossed his arms. "What are you thinking? That someone helped her?"

He shrugged. "I don't know."

"Like who?"

He shrugged again. "I really don't know. Look, ignore me. I have no idea what I'm talking about." Armando was eating a spoonful of cereal. "I think my journalist-type brain works overtime and I get these weird ideas in my head."

They continued to eat quietly. Leo finished his cereal. He put his bowl and spoon into the sink, then turned back and took Armando's from him when he was finished. He was returning the milk to the refrigerator when Armando asked him, "It's kind of strange that you got the teddy bear today . . . or yesterday, whatever . . . don't you think?"

"Why?"

Armando rose and came toward him as Leo turned. He hugged Leo, and whispered into his ear, "Ready to go back to bed?"

Leo nodded. "Why did you ask me that, about the bear?"

Armando had walked into the living room and picked up the sheet from the couch. "Considering everything she told you yesterday, it's a little strange that the bear showed up yesterday too."

"Why do you think that's strange?"

They had reached the bedroom. They both climbed back into bed. Armando unfurled the sheet and it billowed like a parachute over them. Once they were settled, they turned toward each other. Armando answered his question. "She would have had to have shipped the bear to you at least a day beforehand. She sent it UPS, remember? I told you it was on my delivery route."

"And. . .?"

"And then she wound up telling you everything the same day it arrives? I just think it's weird, that's all."

It was weird, now that Leo thought about it. Coincidental. Oddly coincidental. And for some reason, he was beginning to feel strange himself.

"There was no note in the box?" Armando asked.

"No," Leo replied.

Neither of them spoke for a moment. Then Armando asked him, "Why do you think she sent it to you?"

"I guess as a memento or something."

They were looking into each other's eyes. "It still seems strange to me. Especially that you got the bear on the same day."

Leo nodded, his head rustling in the pillow. "It's not like she planned on telling me the whole thing."

Armando pursed his lips. "Unless. . ."

He didn't finish his sentence. Leo didn't need him too. Unless Millie had every intention of confessing to him yesterday. That would explain why she wanted to go to the cemetery. She had the whole thing planned. But the idea seemed absurd. His stomach was tightening.

"Are you sure there wasn't a note?" Armando asked again.

Leo blinked, thinking for a moment. "I didn't see one, but I'm going to look again."

Leo threw the sheet off him and got out of bed. He ran into the living room to the coffee table with its strewn tissue paper and empty box. As he moved closer to it, he kept thinking about the last time she had sent him packages with no notes.

He reached down and grabbed the open box. There was nothing inside. He picked up the rest of the tissue paper on the table, and suddenly something dropped near his feet. It was folded. His stomach churned. He dropped the tissue paper on the coffee table, and slowly squatted to the floor. He was afraid to pick up the folded envelope, uncertain what it could be, but somehow suspecting what it might be.

He took a sharp breath, and quickly reached for the envelope. He unfolded it with two hands. The back flap had once been sealed and taped, and as he turned it over nervously, he realized it was worse than he imagined. The front of the envelope read MOTHER in Matt's handwriting.

Anguish washed through him. It wasn't a sense of sadness or even despair, but rather fear and panic, knowing that the teddy bear and the letter could mean only one thing. He felt dizzy suddenly.

"Leo, did you find something?" he heard from behind.

Leo stood slowly. He was shaking. He turned to face Armando, the letter folded in his hand still. All he could say was, "We have to go."

"Where?" he asked, sensing Leo's panic.

"To Millie's. Right now."

– TWENTY-ONE –

They arrived at Queen's Manor in less than half an hour. They passed through the entrance gate, and drove through the streets faster than they should have. They parked in front of Millie's house, jumped out of the car, and ran up the stairs. Armando was as concerned as he was, and Leo couldn't help but appreciate that he was sharing this with him. It made the situation easier to handle.

Leo rang the doorbell and banged on the screen door. There was no answer. He called Millie's name aloud a few times, opened the screen door, and banged harder on the inner wooden door. It was quiet. He turned and said to Armando, "What do you think we should do?" He noticed a neighbor jogging by and another walking her dog. They both stared at them in the dawn light, but neither said a word.

"Look," Armando replied. He was pointing toward the door.

Leo glanced back and saw that the wooden door had sprung open a few inches. It had popped from his knocking. Without hesitating, Leo pushed the door in and they entered. For a moment he felt like they were breaking and entering. He forced himself to stay calm by focusing on Millie. He called her name aloud. They were standing in her black-and-white kitchen with its red appliances. It had been quite some time since he had been in her place, and thoughts of coffee and book discussions flooded him. He pushed them aside. "Millie!" he called.

What if she were asleep? He was probably scaring the living hell out of her, but he didn't care. He called her name again. It was quiet, as if she wasn't home. Then, after the eerie stillness of a few seconds, Armando said to him, "Wait." He turned his ear toward the interior of Millie's home. "Do you hear that?"

Pierce
© 2007 by The Haworth Press, Inc. All rights reserved.
doi:10.1300/5849_21

Leo realized that his heart was pounding in his ears and that was the only thing he could hear at the moment. He breathed deeply and focused on what surrounded them. The refrigerator grunted and the air conditioner blew. Then, he heard something new. "What is that?"

"It sounds like water running." Armando hesitated a moment, then looked at Leo. "Do you think she's in the bathroom?" His voice sounded cautious.

Leo considered his question, and then a strange sensation overcame him. He burst out laughing.

"What?" Armando asked.

Leo replied over his laugh. "I can't believe this. Of course she's in the bathroom! She's probably in the shower!"

"Oh!" he said in agreement, exhaling a sense of relief. "Whew! I was getting nervous there."

Leo breathed deeply too. "Tell me about it." The front door was obviously left open because she had already been awake and probably outside smoking a cigarette and drinking coffee. She was taking a shower to get ready for her day. It was Saturday. Theresa was probably taking her to the Oldsmar Flea Market earlier than usual for the best buys. That had to be it. Leo couldn't help but feel a little stupid in that moment, but was grateful for feeling that way and not something worse.

He shook his head in disbelief. He turned back toward the kitchen while Armando entered the living room. Leo pulled out a chair from the kitchen table, his usual side chair when he would sit and have coffee with her. He sat down now and said, "We'll have to listen for when the water shuts off so we can let her know——"

He cut himself off by what he saw on the table.

At the same time, Armando said from the living room, "Um, Leo, come here."

On the kitchen table before him were two envelopes. One had Theresa's name on it. The other Leo's. Beneath his envelope were the new Swinburne book of poetry he had bought her, and the Rossetti and Swinburne books he had returned to her.

"Leo," he heard again from the living room. He could hear concern in Armando's voice.

Leo stared at the envelopes as he stood. He walked slowly into the living room, but could not stop staring at the envelopes. He was shaking.

"Look," he heard Armando say.

It broke Leo's gaze from the kitchen table to where Armando was pointing, downward, toward the olive green shag carpeting. At first Leo didn't see anything. As he looked further, though, he could see discoloration. He stepped forward, and he heard a soft squishing noise. The carpet was wet. Worse, it was still getting wet.

"I don't understand," Leo muttered.

"It has to be coming from the bathroom."

Leo looked back at Armando. He grabbed his hand. They walked together slowly, their feet squishing in the water. Leo's dizziness was returning.

As they moved closer to the bathroom, their feet were immersed in a quarter-inch of water and the carpet was drenched. It was like walking through a muddy lawn. Their feet were getting soaked. They could hear the water running inside. Leo glanced down. Water was seeping out from underneath the bathroom door. He looked at Armando, afraid to do anything.

Armando took charge. He held Leo's one hand and used his other to pound on the thin wooden door. It echoed throughout the hallway. "Millie!" Armando yelled. Only running water replied. He met Leo's gaze. "We have to go in," he said nervously. Leo breathed deeply, then nodded in agreement.

Expecting to have to break the lock on the door, Leo was surprised when he was able to turn the handle without any problem. He threw the door open, saying Millie's name. More water poured out soaking their feet, and they stepped back involuntarily. They both looked into the avocado-green-tiled bathroom with its vanity mirror lights on. They could see water flowing over the lip of the bath tub, the curtain pushed off to the right hiding the taps.

Leo moved inside first. He had let go of Armando's hand to enter. He was shivering. Each step through the water was more and more difficult. He hardly took steps, just sloshed bit by bit until he was closer to the tub. He could see a dark form in the water, and he knew what he would find, but he had to keep moving forward, to see for sure, in case he was wrong. He stopped when his feet hit the rim of the tub, and he forced himself to lower his head. His breathing was shallow and his heart was pounding in his throat. He felt weak. He looked.

Millie was underwater, her eyes closed as if in sleep, her hair floating about her like strands of dancing fine silk. Her face was still, her mouth agape. The water made her appear fishlike, her skin bluish and scaly. Her limbs were rising, but had not broken the surface, the force of the water apparently keeping her body submerged. She was fully dressed with a cardigan sweater over a T-shirt, as if she were cold. He noticed a rock on the bottom of the tub near her pockets, and he knew she had done that to weigh herself down.

The dizziness became too much and his legs gave out from beneath him. Armando caught him as he fell. He heard Armando call his name aloud, but he couldn't respond. Armando's voice was like a distant echo. He started to retch, and Armando guided him to the toilet. Leo could feel his knees and legs in the water on the floor, but the sensation was surpassed by his being sick. Leo vomited everything he had eaten, puking until he could feel his esophagus burning and corpuscles bursting in his face.

He retched, his stomach convulsing, nothing but air escaping his body. Armando held him, rubbing his hands up and down his back, telling him it was okay. His voice came closer. He could feel his lips against his head as he murmured soft words to him. Finally Leo caught his breath and stopped retching. Armando tore off strands of toilet paper and wiped Leo's mouth and the surrounding area. He flushed the toilet and guided Leo away from it. Leo leaned against the cheap wooden vanity cabinet and caught his breath while Armando cleaned the area. When he was finished, he sat on the floor by Leo and held him.

Leo tried to pull back. "I'm a mess," he muttered, his voice croaking.

Armando eyed him with a bit of fury. "Leo, stop. It's okay."

Armando came forward and held him. Exhaustion and grief overcame Leo, and he cried. The tears came slowly at first. The harder Armando held him, the more the tears came. Leo was sobbing, his stomach aching, his body shaking as he mourned once again, this time for the loss of his closest friend. Armando rocked him and held him close, and Leo could feel him crying as well. It made him hold onto Armando even harder.

The minutes passed slowly. Eventually they separated and Armando kissed Leo's lips and cheeks, licking his salty tears, then letting him dry his face on his shirt. When he was calm again, Leo forced himself to crawl from the vanity toward the tub. He had to see her again. Armando tried to stop him, but Leo insisted. He propped himself against the tub and looked at her still, blue face floating freely with her gray-blonde hairs whisping about. She looked as if she were asleep in the wind, Ophelia resting in a porcelain-based river.

He heard Armando behind him, and then he saw him move behind the curtain and turn off the water valves. The sound of the rushing water slowed until it was a trickle, and the surface of the water continued to seep over the lip, until finally it stopped and the water was still.

"She must have accidentally drowned," Armando said.

Leo knew otherwise, but couldn't say it. He said nothing in response. He suspected that Armando knew that what he had said wasn't true either, but that he was saying it just to say something or to provide hope or belief that maybe there was some other unintentional explanation for what had happened. But it was senseless to think such a thing. This time Millie had succeeded.

They stayed in the bathroom for what seemed like a very long time. Armando finally told Leo that they had to call the police. Leo nodded, but he had a difficult time leaving her. He stared at her for what he knew would be the last moments he ever would, then managed to break away and allowed Armando to help him stand and lead him out of the bathroom.

Armando grabbed a towel from the linen closet and they dried off as best they could. Armando followed him into the kitchen. Leo sat at the table and stared at the envelopes. He heard Armando pick up the phone and call 911, reporting that they had found Millie Hunter drowned in her tub. When he hung up, he turned to Leo. "What about her daughter?" he asked. "How do we get in touch with her?"

For some odd reason, Leo felt as if he knew the answer to the question. He didn't know Theresa's number by heart. But he knew from the envelopes staring at him that Millie had this all planned out. He picked up the envelope with his name on it and turned it over. His phone number was written on the back. He picked up the envelope with Theresa's name and turned it over. Her number was there as well. On the table behind the envelope was an empty pharmaceutical bottle for Valium. Leo handed the envelope to Armando.

Millie had planned all of this out so resourcefully, so succinctly. She had planned everything from sending him the teddy bear and Matt's letter, to confessing the truth to him, to writing out letters with phone numbers on the envelopes in case someone else found her. She had taken her pills, dressed, put rocks in her pockets, ran the bathwater, and immersed herself. The Valium would have taken effect quickly enough if she had taken the whole bottle, and if the overdose didn't kill her, she would have fallen asleep in the bathwater and drowned.

He turned back to the table and stared at the envelope with his name. He wanted to throw out the letter and forget it ever existed. He couldn't handle more news, more truths, more confessions. He couldn't take anymore. But he also felt that he had come this far with her, that she had been able to bare her soul to him in a way she never had been able to with anyone else. She knew he would be able to take the news and handle all of it. She had her reasons, although he didn't necessarily understand them. Perhaps that was what was in the envelope.

"Hello, Theresa?" he heard Armando say behind him, his voice shaking slightly. "My name is Armando, I'm a friend of Leo's." He heard him pause. "We're at your mother's house." He hesitated. "You need to come over right away." Another pause. "I'm sorry, Theresa, I don't know how to tell you this. Your mother's passed away."

Leo breathed hard as he heard Armando put the phone down. He stared at the envelope, his name emblazoned in blue ink on the front in her cursive handwriting. He had come this far. He had to keep going. He tore open the envelope, pulled out the letter, and started to read.

> *Dear Leo,*
> *I suspect since I saw you things have been tough. I'm to blame for all of it, and I apologize. I never wanted you to suffer. I care about you as if you were my own son, the one special child I never had, that understood me*

*and allowed me to be my own person without judging me or questioning
me. I would never want you to suffer because of what I did with my life.*

*You're probably wondering why I told you my story about what hap-
pened to Jack. I'd like to tell you that I didn't intend to bring it up to you,
that I never intended to burden you or Matthew with this information.
But then I would be lying. The truth is that I planned to tell you everything. If not today, then sometime in the future, maybe when I was on my
deathbed, who knows. But circumstances changed all of that.*

*You have the right to know that your guesses were right on for a few
things. I did run away from my children, now that I think about it, because I couldn't face them. And I did run away from Harrigan when he
found me in Hollywood and wouldn't stop harassing me. It was the only
thing I could think of. I'd like to think I get credit for at least running to
my children this time, rather than away from them like I did almost
twenty-five years ago. I didn't choose to move to Clearwater to be reunited
with my children, but being possibly reunited with them was a potential
perk. Unfortunately, that didn't work out exactly as I would have liked,
but as I've always said, what's done is done.*

*It's all too much for you, I'm sure. I don't regret telling you everything,
but I do regret that it might put you in a bad position, unable to know
what to do with this information. I would like to hope you'll do nothing
with it. Keep it between you and me. I'd prefer that Harrigan never find
out. And Theresa too. Although, to be honest with you, Theresa understands more about the truth than even she realizes.*

*Like I said, you don't have to do anything. I've decided to make the
choice and end my own life so that there is no going forward with what
might happen next. I would like to think that I'm taking control of my
own destiny and not leaving it up to people like Harrigan or—don't be
upset when I say this—you.*

*Since I'm in such a confessional mood lately, I guess it's only fair that I
tell you that I tried to kill myself a few weeks ago because I couldn't take
Harrigan's harassment anymore. I tried to end my life to stop everything
from ever coming out. The fact that I did it on the anniversary of Matthew's death. . .well, I could say it was just coincidence, but maybe deep
inside I did miss him so much and regret how much of our lives were spent*

in anger or disregard for each other that I couldn't take the guilt anymore. Maybe.

I also want you to know that I'm not angry with you for bringing Matthew's letter to me. I admit I was furious at first and shocked that you would have done that. When I tried to kill myself a few weeks ago, I was angry because it didn't work and I couldn't figure out why I was still alive. But when you brought me the letter and told me Harrigan had seen you, I realized my suicide didn't work because I had unfinished business. That business is done now.

I'm giving you back the Rossetti and Swinburne poetry books I had sent you originally. I really want you to have these. The Rossetti book was a special gift from you, and it meant a lot to me. I grew up reading Rossetti and often found her words comforting when times were tough, like after my father died. The Swinburne book has followed me since my days in California and I have always cherished it for its lush language and imagery and its hope of enduring love. Please keep these and treasure them always. And please keep the new one you just bought me. Mark that one up for your research.

I wish you the best of luck on your dissertation. You are going to make one fabulous professor. Just be sure to teach them poetry along with fiction.

Good luck also with your new relationship. Armando must be a special person to make you smile again and to bring you back to life. You deserve all of that happiness you seek, Leo, and I want you to be happy.

I love you, Leo. I love you for the joy you brought to my son's life. You made his days the best ever, knowing how sad he was for so long. And I love you for the friendship you brought to this old broad's life. Your unconditional friendship has meant the world to me.

I hope you will understand and forgive my burdening you with the truth. I think that you will, and when you do, you will understand why I told you my story. That stupid cliché that the truth will set you free does have some merit, in a strange sort of way. But I think something else about truth is more powerful.

The truth is what you make it out to be. Truth is not fact, it's what you believe.

All my love,
Millie

– TWENTY-TWO –

"The Lord is My Shepherd; I shall not want. . ."

The people in attendance mumbled along with the minister. His voice was accented with exaggerated flair. He was a tall, spindly man with thick glasses. Leo tried to focus on the minister's words. He looked at those around him, and wondered if Millie would have been as equally distracted. It was scorching hot outside. He wondered why they weren't standing under a funeral tent to protect them from the sun. Millie had made her own funeral arrangements, though, so he imagined her saying to the funeral home director, "Five hundred dollars for the tent? Screw that. Let them sweat."

It was about 10:20 on Tuesday morning. He'd be teaching right now, he realized, had Millie not killed herself. He had been having nightmares from finding her in the tub. The image of her submerged and blue burned in his mind. He fought to push the thought away and breathed deeply. He looked at the dark brown casket and floral arrangements, and then glanced at those around him for a distraction.

There were about fifteen people at the funeral. Everyone was dressed in some form of black, gray, or navy. They all wore sunglasses, except for the minister. Leo recognized Charlie the librarian. He and a few others who worked with Theresa had come. Dr. Bauer was there; Leo wondered how she was handling Millie's death. Millie's Liberace neighbor and another couple from Queen's Manor were also there. Funeral home and cemetery workers hovered along the perimeter, waiting to finish their job.

Armando was standing to his left. He had taken the day off to be with him during the funeral. He had even gone with him to the wake the night before. Leo moved his hand closer to Armando's and squeezed it. Armando glanced back at him and smiled.

Pierce
© 2007 by The Haworth Press, Inc. All rights reserved.
doi:10.1300/5849_22

His mother stood to his right. George was on the other side of her. He had flown in on Sunday morning. Leo was pretty sure he had been scheduled to come then anyway, and that he hadn't rushed because of Millie's death. Oddly, though, George was standing beside Theresa. It was very strange seeing the two of them together. George had gone to the wake with their mother. Toward the end, after their mother had encouraged him numerous times, he had made a point of speaking to Theresa. Leo didn't hear what they had to say, but he watched them leave the room together at one point. He realized that his mother was pushing George to make amends with Theresa. He only hoped Theresa wasn't stupid enough to take him back.

Everyone was standing. There were no chairs. No one seemed to be crying. Even his mother had dry eyes. He almost wondered to himself if it was because no one was all that upset, or was it because they were thinking about grocery lists and laundry? Or maybe it was because they had all done their mourning in private. He wanted to believe this was the case. He knew that was what he had done, to a large extent. He was resolved to her passing now. She had killed herself in order to maintain silence. It all seemed to make sense. She had planned out everything so beautifully, it was frightening.

Leo blamed Harrigan. Millie had been content to keep her secret and never bring it to the surface. Even after Matt had died, she would have been able to keep silent and never worry about the truth coming out. But that asshole had been pressuring her for so long that she had cracked, and she had killed herself to keep the truth away from everyone, especially Harrigan. The only thing he still didn't comprehend was why she had told him. She claimed she knew he could handle knowing the truth. But what was he to do with it? He wanted to ask her. If he were given one final wish regarding Millie, it would be to know why she had told him, maybe ask her over one last cup of coffee and a poem or two. It was hopeless though. He would never understand, and he had to accept that. The dead had no answers.

He was going to miss her terribly. When he had lost his father, it had been like something was missing from the normal routine of their existence. When Matt had died, it was like a vacuum had sucked all the energy and air from his existence, and he was left to waste away in self-pity and despair. The difference this time was that he wasn't responsible, and there was nothing he could have done to prevent it. Her absence was going to be one of those things he would realize more intensely in weeks to come when he would come across a new tidbit of Victorian criticism on Swinburne and go to call her, or he would want to go book shopping and take her along. Those were the moments when he would realize how much he missed her, and he would mourn again.

The blaring of a horn from a truck passing on 54th Avenue interrupted the minister and jolted all of them from their thoughts. The minister lost his place. The sun was burning down on all of them, and Leo couldn't help but wish the minister would shut up and the funeral would be over. He didn't feel sacrilegious or heretical for thinking such a thing. Millie would have been the first to yell, "Jesus Christ, get on with it, will you? It's friggin' hot out here!"

Leo scanned the surrounding area, looking for Matt's tombstone. Millie had chosen to be buried in the same cemetery as her son, but had selected a plot far enough away so as not to bother him. Sunnyside Cemetery was divided by 20th Street. Millie's grave site was on one side of the street, Matt's the other. Since their arrival, though, he hadn't yet figured out where they were in position to one another.

He looked across the street and saw a man in the distance. To his right was a large oak tree. Leo recognized the tree. He realized there was the cement bench beneath it, and that the row of tombstones alongside it was the one that included Matt's. The man was standing in front of Matt's grave, in fact. Leo looked more closely at the man and recognized him. He was dressed more casually and wore sunglasses. It was Harrigan.

He felt Armando squeeze his hand, and he looked at him quickly. Armando gestured toward everyone else with his head. Leo realized he had missed something. Everyone was looking at him. He saw Theresa coming toward him with her hand outstretched. She held a piece of paper in it. "My mother wanted you to read it," she said.

He took the paper from her. He glanced down and saw it was a photocopy from a book. The heading at the top told him it was an excerpt from poetry by Swinburne. He looked over her shoulder toward Matt's grave site. Harrigan was still standing there, watching them.

He focused back on Theresa and nodded slowly in acknowledgment. Millie had left instructions for this too. He released Armando's hand and gently wiped his wet palm on his suit pants leg. He moved forward to where the minister was, looking in the distance. He saw that Harrigan realized Leo had seen him. He shifted uncomfortably and turned away.

Leo now stood facing the casket, holding the piece of paper in his hand. It was strange to be standing where the minister had stood moments before. The minister had stepped to the side, and he smiled broadly at Leo as he took the lead. Leo looked at those present, and he was nervous, almost like the first day of every semester when he walked in to teach a new class. He looked at the paper. The beginning of it was bracketed in black marker, identifying what he was to read. "This is the beginning of the poem 'The Triumph of Time,'" he said. "Algernon Charles Swinburne was one of Millie's favorite poets." He shuffled his feet. He had read poetry aloud for his students, but never for family and friends. He stared at the flower-draped casket, wondering if she could hear him. He read.

> Before our lives divide for ever,
>   While time is with us and hands are free,
> (Time, swift to fasten and swift to sever
>   Hand from hand, as we stand by the sea)
> I will say no word that a man might say
> Whose whole life's love goes down in a day;
> For this could never have been; and never,
>   Though the gods and the years relent, shall be.
> Is it worth a tear, is it worth an hour,
>   To think of things that are well outworn?
> Of fruitless husk and fugitive flower,
>   The dream foregone and the deed forborne?
> Though joy be done with and grief be vain,
> Time shall not sever us wholly in twain;
> Earth is not spoilt for a single shower;
>   But the rain has ruined the ungrown corn.

He looked up at his family and friends. His mother was dabbing at her eyes with a white handkerchief that contrasted sharply with her black dress and veiled hat. Armando smiled at him in support, and discreetly gave him the A-OK with his left hand. Leo smiled.

"Thank you, Leo," the minister said. "And now Millie's daughter Theresa is going to read."

Leo stepped away and Theresa exchanged places with him. As he returned to his spot, he pocketed the paper. He looked back toward Matt's grave. Harrigan was gone. He scanned the surrounding area to see where he might be, but he couldn't find him anywhere. He felt Armando's hand rubbing up and down on Leo's back, and it comforted him. He returned his attention to Theresa.

"My mother's other favorite poet was Christina Rossetti. Mother wanted me to read the poem 'song,' which she read at my brother's funeral." Leo looked away, uncertain he wanted to hear the poem engraved on his headstone. He knew he might break down. But this was what Millie wanted. He heard her sniffle, then clear her throat.

> When I am dead, my dearest,
>   Sing no sad songs for me;
> Plant thou no roses at my head,
>   Nor shady cypress tree:
> Be the green grass above me
>   With showers and dewdrops wet:
> And if thou wilt, remember,
>   And if thou wilt, forget.
>
> I shall not see the shadows,
>   I shall not feel the rain;
> I shall not hear the nightingale
>   Sing on, as if in pain:
> And dreaming through the twilight
>   That doth not rise nor set,
> Haply I may remember,
>   And haply may forget.

There was a catch in her throat as Theresa finished reading the poem. She wiped at her eyes behind her sunglasses. Charlie moved

forward to comfort her and took her back to her place. She leaned on
him, her head resting against his shoulder. They were more close than
Leo had realized. Her emotional response also told him how close she
had been to Millie. The minister quickly ended the ceremony, giving
his final benediction. The group dispersed.

During the wake the night before, Leo's mother had graciously volunteered to host a luncheon at her house after the funeral. Theresa
had protested at first, but Rosa insisted, wanting to do something
to help Theresa in this difficult time. The funeral now over, the guests
headed toward their cars to follow Rosa's lead.

Leo turned to Armando. "Could you give me a minute?" Armando
nodded, and Leo walked toward a headstone nearby. He picked up a
plastic bag that he had placed there earlier. He walked along the
gravel pathway and came to the street. He crossed quickly and continued through the cemetery. He reached the oak tree and the cement
bench. He walked around it and stepped over a branch that had fallen
from the tree. He passed the few tombstones until he came to Matt's.
It was undisturbed. The flowers Millie had left for him on Friday were
wilted, but still wrapped tightly in plastic. He squatted and picked up
the flowers. They were Millie's last gift to her son. He replaced them
along the front of the headstone. He reached into the plastic bag and
removed two items: the teddy bear and the letter. He had decided
that morning to leave these two items at Matt's grave. It seemed only
appropriate, as they were so much a part of Matt's life, and death. He
lay the letter down beside the flowers and put Teddy Pierce on top of
it. The stuffed animal shifted slightly and rested its head against the
flowers.

Leo ran his fingers over the front of the stone, feeling the polished
granite. He wondered when he would return again to the cemetery.
Instinct told him that of course he would return, especially now that
two loved ones were buried here, mother and son. But he considered
too that there really was nothing here that was Matt, nor would there
be anything that was Millie. Just decaying physical manifestations.
Still, he imagined he would come back again someday, perhaps once a
month, visit each of them, pay his respects, bring them flowers. But
he knew also that over time he would not visit as much. His visits

would decrease, like everyone's visits to cemeteries diminished. Cemeteries existed to remember those who had passed on, but unless you visited your loved ones or took care of their markers, this physical manifestation of their existence disintegrated as quickly as memory of them did. Leo wondered though if that was a good thing or a bad thing. Remembering stopped you from living your own life.

"I figured you might come over here," he heard a voice say.

Leo jumped and turned around quickly. He was face-to-face with Harrigan. "What are you doing here?"

"I'm not allowed to come to the funeral of a family member?"

"Family member?" Leo shook his head in disgust. "You have no right to disturb us."

"I can come here if I want. Free country."

Harrigan had no heart, no care for anything he had done. He was responsible for everything that had happened to Millie, and he didn't give a shit. Leo wanted to hit him, use the branch near the cement bench. "It's your fault she's dead," he blurted out angrily.

He nonchalantly took a cigarette out of a pack in his pocket and lit it. "I figured you'd say that." He exhaled into the air.

"It's true," Leo continued. "If you had left her alone, she never would have killed herself."

"I was after the truth."

"You knew the truth, and you still wouldn't leave her alone!"

He took a long drag on his cigarette. "You and I both know that story about the mob guy was total bullshit." Leo didn't respond. He certainly didn't intend it to support Harrigan's statement, but his silence apparently told Harrigan something. He nodded. "Yeah, I figured as much. I guess there's no chance of me finding out from you what the truth really was?"

"I don't know what you're talking about," Leo said. He looked away. He saw Armando on the edge of this section of the cemetery, his hands on the fence, staring at Leo and Harrigan, waiting for Leo to call him over.

Harrigan continued. "You know, if she told you the truth, maybe she told it to Theresa, or one of her other friends, or maybe you told it to your friend."

Leo turned back to Harrigan. The man had a grin on his face. Leo tried to remain calm, but he was starting to shake inside. "Why don't you leave us alone?"

He took one last sharp drag on the cigarette, then tossed it to the side. It landed on the ground before a headstone nearby. Lee could see it smoldering. "What's the matter?" Harrigan asked. "Afraid I'm going to push you to kill yourself too, like Millie, or your boyfriend here?"

Leo was enraged. He stepped forward with his hand outstretched. He had never hit anyone before in his life, but he wanted to smash Harrigan's head in. "You're a fucking asshole!" he screamed. He made to wail him with a fist, but Harrigan put out a hand and stopped him. He was bigger and stronger than Leo, and easily pushed him back.

"Leo!" They both turned and saw Armando running toward them.

Leo took a deep breath. His wrist and arm hurt where Harrigan had shoved him. "It's all right," he said as Armando came forward. He was more in control now, but his anger hadn't dissipated. He had to rub his wrist and arm, but did it so that hopefully no one noticed.

"Get lost," Armando said to Harrigan.

Harrigan chuckled. "Yeah, I'm out of here. Have fun, boys."

Armando came to Leo. He hadn't missed Leo's attempt to nurse his injuries. "Did he hurt you?" he asked.

Leo shook his head. He looked up and watched Harrigan's back as he walked away. He was furious, but there was nothing he could do. There was no point in continuing this. He was better off letting him go and hope for the best. Just like Millie had done, even though it had gotten her nowhere.

He was unprepared then when Harrigan turned to the left and walked along the pathway. The side profile of Harrigan with his mustache and sunglasses rushed to Leo in a flash. He had seen that profile before. He realized that on more than one occasion he had thought he knew Harrigan, that he had seen him before, but could never remember when or where. Suddenly, the memory jumped into his mind like a replayed video recording.

Leo was driving. He was upset. He wanted Millie to come to his birthday dinner. He was going to invite her regardless of what Matt said. He knew it would piss him off, but he didn't care anymore. He had groceries in the trunk. He was going to try to make his mother's lasagna, but use jarred sauce instead of making his own. He pulled up to his house, and had to wait a moment as a car pulled away. He was unconscious of the action, but he turned his head as the driver passed him. He wore sunglasses and had a mustache.

It had been Harrigan. Harrigan had been at his house that day. He had spoken to Matt.

Without hesitation, Leo ran. His shoes slipped on the grass, but he ran after Harrigan anyway. The image of Harrigan driving away from his house on that day, that last day that he had ever seen Matt alive, echoed in his head as he charged toward Harrigan. At the last possible moment, as he was upon him, his rage flying in his mind at the realization of what Harrigan had truly done, not so much to Millie, but to Matt, he screamed aloud, jumped upward, and threw himself on top of Harrigan.

The attack took Harrigan by surprise, and he lost his balance as Leo clung to him, kicking at his legs to knock him to the ground. He pulled on his shirt and heard it ripping from his tugging. Harrigan was yelling too, and his sunglasses flew off his face. He reached behind him, somehow managing to maintain his balance despite Leo pulling him down and kicking at his legs. He grabbed at Leo's face. Their bodies twisted. Harrigan knocked Leo's sunglasses askew. Then he snapped his neck back and smashed the back of his head into Leo's forehead and left eye. The lens of his sunglasses pierced into his skin. Leo could feel sharp pain in his face and a wetness that he knew was blood. Harrigan wasn't finished though, and he yelled and pummeled himself backward, falling with Leo. Leo maintained his hold, but it wasn't enough. Not realizing where they were, Leo fell back against a grave monument with Harrigan's full weight crushing him. The pain shot into his back as Harrigan smashed fully into him, pushing harder and harder to get Leo to release him. Leo yelled out in pain.

Harrigan spun around and grabbed Leo's collar and the neck of his tie, preventing him from falling to the ground. He lifted a fist with his other hand and was about to pummel it into Leo's bleeding face. "Fucking punk!" he screamed.

In a daze, Leo saw the motion just to the right of Harrigan's head. The oak branch wailed Harrigan. The force of the impact sent Harrigan to the ground. He had released Leo from his fist, and Leo sank to the ground. He watched Armando hover around Harrigan, waving the tree branch, screaming at him to take another shot. Harrigan was on his feet again quickly, but this time he held a hand to the side of his head. His balance was off.

"Get the fuck out of here!" Armando shouted.

"You're fucking nuts, you know that?!" Harrigan shouted, glancing at Leo. They all were catching their breath. No one moved or spoke for a moment. Pain was shooting through Leo's back and chest. His forehead and eye were stinging. Blood was starting to blind his one eye. He wiped at it with his suit jacket. He saw Harrigan spit, then turn and walk away.

"Wait," Leo muttered through his breaths. "Wait!" he commanded. Harrigan stopped and turned to face him. He glanced at Armando, who still held the branch aloft, prepared to strike again. "You were there," Leo said. He struggled to get up, refusing Armando's help. He forced himself up, despite the pain in his body. "That night. When Matt died."

Harrigan turned to look at him. "What are you talking about?"

"You were there!" Leo yelled. He stepped forward, hobbling slightly. "At my house. The night Matt died."

Harrigan held his head. His facial expression changed. "How did you know?"

"Because I saw you! I came home just as you were driving away." Harrigan didn't respond. "Why were you there?" He still didn't say anything. "Answer me, damn it!" Leo ordered.

His eyes shifted, then returned to Leo. "All right, yeah, I was there."

"You told him, didn't you? About his father."

Harrigan nodded. "He deserved to know the truth. He'd been wanting to know for years what happened to his father, and his mother wouldn't tell him."

"You had no right to tell him anything!"

"I didn't?" He scoffed. "He wanted to know. He paid me, for Christ's sake!"

Now it was Leo who was startled. He couldn't speak. Armando asked the question he could not. "Matt hired you to find his father?"

Harrigan shuffled his feet, then shook his head in frustration. "Not exactly. Matt did hire someone to find out about his father."

"Who?" Leo managed to ask. "Who did he hire?"

"Buddy of mine, another PI in Miami. The guy wound up calling me, though, because he knew I was in the New York area. Imagine my surprise when it turned out that he was looking for the same information I already knew. I had been trying to track down Millie after she had left Hollywood, and here comes her son contacting my buddy to help him find out information I already knew. So, yeah, I paid him a visit, told him who I was, his long-lost cousin, and I shared with him everything I knew."

"What did you tell him?" Leo asked.

"The same stuff I told you. I showed him the videotape, and the files I had been keeping, news clippings, things like that. I told him his father's body had turned up in the lake after being missing for over twenty years. I told him his mother had lied to him."

"You had no right to do that," Leo said.

"I had every right! The kid wanted to know, so I told him. And then he paid me, told me he wanted me to find out the complete truth. Then he told me to go, said you were coming home, and he didn't want you to know anything about this." They were all quiet. "Look," Harrigan continued, "I was just as surprised to hear that he had died in that car crash that night, but it wasn't my fault, so don't try to blame me for it. I decided to keep investigating, for his sake, I guess. He was my cousin, I figured I owed him."

"I thought you did it for your mother's sake."

He shrugged. "Yeah, her too."

Leo shook his head in disgust. "You are so full of shit. You did this for your own fucking selfish reasons."

"You know what? Screw you! I don't owe you any explanation. I didn't do anything wrong."

Leo moved toward Harrigan. He held one hand to his forehead and eye, the other to his chest. He was still angry, but not in the enraged way he was before. Hearing about that night with Matt had somehow calmed Leo. It didn't change how he felt, but he was less out of control.

"Let me tell you something," Leo said, continuing toward him slowly. "You did do something wrong. You told him information he wasn't ready to handle. You didn't know anything about his mental state or his emotional problems. It wasn't your right to bring him this information, and to harass his mother, his sister, and me afterward. I blamed myself for Matt's death because I thought I had pissed him off that night. Then I found out that Millie had seen him that night, and he had brought the information to her, and she was forced to tell him everything."

"She should have told him a long time ago," Harrigan muttered.

"That was not your decision to make!" Leo yelled back. "Millie had her reasons. She was protecting her children. She was always protecting her children."

"Protecting them from what?" Harrigan asked. "Let me guess . . . the truth?" Leo could see that even now he was fishing. "I'm right. She told him what really happened, didn't she?"

Leo wondered if he should acknowledge this, if he should shout it all out and tell Harrigan. It would get him off of their backs once and for all. They would never see him again, and everything would be over. But he couldn't do that. He needed to protect Millie and Matt. That was why Millie had told him, he realized. She knew Harrigan wouldn't leave this alone. She told Leo the truth because she knew he would do the right thing, and that was to protect his loved ones. And then Leo smirked, because he also knew that there was no way in hell he could ever consider giving Harrigan the satisfaction of knowing the truth.

"Leave us alone," he told him, feeling an inner strength rising. "All of us. Theresa, me, Armando. Even Millie and Matt. Go home. Get out of here. And if you don't, I will go to the police and tell them how you have been harassing every one of us, and that you drove Millie to her death. I bet you I could help them come up with something like manslaughter or some other crime to make you suffer the way you made her suffer."

"Bullshit," was his reply.

Now it was Leo's turn to scoff. He could sense Millie within him, almost cheering him on in his mind. "Don't fuck with me, Harrigan. Millie taught me a thing or two that you wouldn't want to know about." He watched Harrigan's face as the implication registered.

Leo turned toward Armando. "Let's go," he said. Armando nodded slowly, dropped the branch, and helped Leo. They walked away from Harrigan. They heard nothing from him, but after a few seconds, they heard him walking away on the path in the opposite direction. The pain was fierce in Leo's chest and back and on his face, but the inner strength he felt made the outside pain easier to handle.

When they reached the cement bench, Armando made Leo sit down. He took off his own sunglasses, then took Leo's hand away from his forehead and looked at the cut. "Jesus," he said, "you're going to have a nasty black eye."

Leo stretched, and the pain shot through his torso. Armando helped him take off his jacket and tie. "My chest and back are killing me too," he admitted. Armando tried to rub both, but Leo pulled away from the pain. He apologized, but Leo waved it off. He started chuckling then, and Armando asked what was so funny.

"You were pretty amazing with the tree branch," he said.

"Me?" Armando replied shocked. "What about you with that attack? I better not piss you off." They both laughed, then Armando said, "Don't take this the wrong way, but you look awful. You better clean up before we go to your mother's."

"I have a better idea. Let's skip my mother's, and just go home."

Armando nodded in agreement. They both got up. Armando took his arm and helped him. They were stepping away, when Leo hesitated and looked back at Matt's headstone. "Wait a second," he said. He walked toward the grave site. He noticed Armando wasn't following him, though, so he motioned for him to join him. He could see he was reluctant, but he followed. Leo took Armando's hand and they stood before Matt's grave site.

"Matt, this is Armando. Armando," he said, looking at him, then pointing downward with his free hand, "this is Matt."

Armando looked awkwardly toward the headstone. "Um, hi, Matt. Nice to meet you," he said hesitatingly. He looked back at Leo, obviously feeling strange.

"I told you he was a hottie," Leo said to Matt, then looked at Armando, who blushed.

There was silence. Leo looked down at the flowers, the teddy bear, and the letter, then looked up at the stone, staring at Matt's name, dates, and the quote by Rossetti. He read the lines again to himself: "When I am dead my dearest, Sing no sad songs for me." He had done just the opposite. But he had had no idea how to do anything but grieve for him as he had. He was about to step away, when suddenly a mourning dove landed on the top of the stone and cooed a soft warbling noise. The bird stared up at Leo, and he thought it odd that the bird had been so brave to approach them. It made him smile. Then, after a few moments, the bird cooed one last time, flew away, and Leo and Armando left the cemetery.

– TWENTY-THREE –

When they reached the house, Leo went into the kitchen and took two Tylenol. He phoned his mother and told her they wouldn't be coming over. She reacted by squealing about how much food she had. She insisted he speak to Theresa, who she assumed would convince him to come over. "Theresa," he said, "sorry, we're not coming over."

"No problem. Don't worry about it." He could sense his mother's disappointment in the background. He was about to hang up, when Theresa said, "Wait, Leo, can you come to my mother's later? I'm packing up her things. I was hoping we could talk."

Leo hesitated before responding. He wasn't sure he wanted to go back there. But he realized that she needed him to go, maybe to help pack, otherwise she never would have asked. He owed it to Millie. And he was curious to know what she wanted to talk about. He agreed, hoping his hesitancy wasn't obvious.

Armando called him from the bathroom, where he was waiting to clean Leo's wounds. He lay the cordless phone on the counter and followed Armando's voice. He realized he was in the main hall bathroom. Leo never used this bathroom anymore. Armando had the bright white lights on. Arranged on the counter were a bottle of peroxide, cotton balls, and Band-Aids. He entered the bathroom slowly. "Sit down," Armando commanded, pointing to the toilet seat.

As he sat, Armando wet cotton balls with peroxide. He commented, like a good nurse would, that it was going to hurt, but when Armando applied the disinfectant to Leo's facial cuts, it stung more than Leo had expected. He jolted backward involuntarily. Armando reassured him, commenting, "Look, after dealing with Harrigan, I think you can handle a little peroxide." Leo smiled and nodded, and Armando continued to wash the wound.

Pierce
© 2007 by The Haworth Press, Inc. All rights reserved.
doi:10.1300/5849_23

Leo watched Armando nurse him in the mirror. The glass of his broken sunglasses had sliced through his right eyebrow and created a diagonal cut almost an inch long that moved from his forehead to the bridge of his nose. The bleeding had stopped, but the peroxide was making it bubble and ooze. Armando blew on the cut to cool it. A few seconds later, the cleaning and the burning had stopped. He put small Band-Aids on the area. "You need to put ice on that eye now, and ice on your chest and back."

As he had watched Armando in the mirror, he felt one of the most amazing sensations. He was being taken care of for the first time in a very long time. He stood and waited until Armando had turned back to him after sealing the peroxide and putting things away. Leo reached out his arms and took hold of Armando's sides. "Thank you," he said, and then, "I lo—"

Leo stopped midword. He knew shock was apparent on his face, reflected as it was in Armando's own stare back at him. Leo faltered and looked away, feeling his face flush. "I appreciate your help," he muttered finally. He was afraid to look back at him.

"You're welcome," was the reply. Armando stepped away. "I'll make the ice packs."

He felt like a fucking idiot. Armando thought he was crazy. How could he love Armando after only a couple of weeks? Leo couldn't be falling for him that quickly. They hadn't even had sex yet.

He looked at his reflection in the mirror. His hair was messed from the scuffle earlier. His eye was turning black and blue already, but the cut was bandaged. He was still wearing his shirt, tie, and suit pants, disarrayed and dirty as they were. His neck and face were tinted pink from his idiotic moment. He wasn't sure which was worse, the realization of what he had almost told Armando, whether it was actually true, or if he had just made an ass out of himself. For all he knew, Armando was doing all of this out of pity for Leo.

Armando called him from the kitchen. Leo turned, shut off the lights, and left the bathroom. He hurried into his room to change clothes. Removing his clothes was more difficult than he imagined, the pain in his chest and back intensifying as he stretched to undress and dress himself. He came out a few minutes later in a tank top and shorts. Armando was sitting on the living room couch still wearing his dress clothes, the sleeves of his white shirt rolled up as he waited to administer the ice packs he had made with dish towels. He had Leo sit beside him, and positioned ice packs to his back and chest. He made Leo hold the one on his chest, then held a third ice pack to his eye. Leo was shivering from the freezing packs applied to his body.

They were silent for what seemed a long stretch that was probably no more than two minutes in reality. Leo looked at Armando with his one visible eye, and saw he was looking away. He was distracted, upset. Leo felt so stupid. "You can go if you want," he muttered.

Armando looked back at him. "What?" His eyes were open wide.

"You don't have to stay," Leo said, "if you want to go."

"Why, do you want me to leave?"

"No," Leo replied, gazing at him, almost begging him for forgiveness with his one good eye. "I want you to stay. I just thought maybe . . ."

"What?" he encouraged.

"I thought maybe you'd had enough of taking care of me and wanted to go home."

Armando scoffed. "I'm helping you because I want to."

Leo looked away. "Well, I wasn't sure."

Armando pulled his hand away from Leo's back and pushed him against the couch to put pressure on the ice pack. The motion caused him some pain. He put the other ice pack from his eye onto the table. He got up and paced.

"I'm sorry," Leo said, wiping his wet eye. "I didn't mean to get you upset." The ice packs were melting. Water dripped down Leo's back and chest.

Armando stopped. "You really don't know how I feel about you?"

"I'm not sure."

"And you were in a relationship for four years? How is that possible?"

Leo looked away in pain. The question had hurt him as much as the aches in his body did. No matter how Leo felt about him, Armando had no right to question his relationship with Matt. His feelings apparently showed on his face.

"Okay, now I'm sorry," Armando said. He sat down beside Leo again, and they looked at one another. "I didn't mean that," he continued. "I'm just surprised by you sometimes. I have been with you through all of this because I want to be here for you. And I've been pretty damn understanding about not having sex. But it's all because I care about you very much." He put his hand on Leo's hand that held the ice pack to his chest. "Leo, I've never felt this way about anyone before."

He was sincere. Leo could sense it without question. He leaned forward. The ice pack fell from his back, but he ignored it. Armando moved in as well. They kissed. Then, Armando leaned his forehead again Leo's, and Leo yelped in pain. The special moment suddenly gone awry, they both laughed.

Armando took the ice packs away from him, cupping them as much as possible to prevent them from dripping everywhere. "I'll go change these," he said. He got up and headed toward the kitchen. He stopped and turned. "Oh, by the way, I 'lo—' you too," he said and winked.

– TWENTY-FOUR –

As Leo entered Queen's Manor he found himself grateful that he would not have to pass through Millie's demesne again after today. He approached her mobile home and saw three cars parked in front of it. One was Theresa's, another he didn't recognize, but the third was his mother's. He didn't expect to see even this many people here. He parked and walked across the street. On the way the front screen door opened, and Leo saw Charlie exit, talking to someone as they both carried boxes outside. Leo blinked in disbelief as the second person came into view. It was his brother.

"Hi, Leo," Charlie said when he saw him.

"Hey, bro," was George's response.

Charlie giggled. "Oh, my God, I just remembered you two were brothers. How weird is that? You two are so different!"

"Not so different," George said.

He opened Charlie's car door and tossed in the box he held. He took Charlie's box and put it in as well. As he bent over, Charlie glanced at George's ass in jeans. He gazed at Leo and said, "One can only hope," shifting his eyebrows suggestively.

Leo was stunned into silence by his brother's presence and his friendly cooperation with Charlie. As for Charlie's taste . . . Leo shook it off. "Where's Theresa?"

"Inside," Charlie pointed. "We should take a break, don't you think, George?"

"Hey, fine with me," he said. George noticed Leo's face then. "What happened to you? Your boyfriend didn't do that, did he?"

"Of course not. I . . . walked into a wall," he said, knowing it was a ridiculous explanation.

Pierce

© 2007 by The Haworth Press, Inc. All rights reserved.

doi:10.1300/5849_24

"That was stupid." George continued, "It better not be your boyfriend, cause I'll beat the crap out of him."

Leo didn't know how to respond. It was unlike his brother to even suggest defending Leo. Fortunately, Charlie spoke for him. "Yes, I bet you could beat him up with those arm muscles." Charlie smiled brightly at him, then turned back to Leo. "I'll go get us drinks, George." Charlie pushed Leo up the stairs, following close behind. As they entered, he whispered to him, "Your brother is so hot!"

Leo stopped and turned to him. "Charlie, you know my brother is straight, right?"

Charlie squinched his face. "Straight? What is that all about? No man is really straight." Inside, he opened the cooler on the floor near the door and took out two beers. He lifted them high to Leo. "Especially when there's alcohol around."

"Are you taking another break?" Theresa had come from the living room.

"This is hard work!" Charlie moved forward and planted a kiss on Theresa's cheek. "How're you holding up?"

She nodded. "I'm okay." Charlie exited quickly, closing the door behind him.

Leo pointed after him. "You know he's plying your ex-husband, my brother, with alcohol to make a play for him."

She rolled her eyes. "Show Charlie any man who can walk and Charlie's after him. He won't get far. George is as straight as they come."

He was surprised by Theresa's casual attitude, then saw it was complimented by her own attire. Her light brown hair was tied in a ponytail. She wasn't wearing glasses. He caught the latent scent of cigarettes, but he was sure the smell was from Millie's house. Theresa was wearing an old Disney T-shirt with Goofy on it and denim shorts that made her hips and thighs look larger than usual. He realized he hardly ever saw her this casual, which was probably why it stood out so noticeably. It was a sharp contrast to the conservative black dress she had worn at the funeral.

"I was surprised to see George here," Leo said.

"He followed me, at your mother's insistence. I think she's pushing us back together."

"You're not though, right?" Leo realized his opinion was too obvious.

She shook her head. "I would never get back together with him, not after what he pulled. Besides, I'm moving to Jacksonville next month."

"Well, don't be surprised if my mother encourages him to follow you." Leo shuffled his feet, continuing to make small talk. "So you got a new job?"

"Yes, I'm the new Head of Public Services in the library at Florida Community College at Jacksonville," she said proudly. "It's a good salary, and a whole new beginning for me."

"That's great," Leo said. He couldn't help but wonder to himself how Millie's death played into Theresa's new beginning. Her passing was coincidental, but like so many other things, perfectly planned and timed. Leo looked into the black-and-white kitchen with red appliances that had been one of the surprises of Millie's mobile home. It looked sparse now. Only the red oven stood out. Every other splash of color was packed in boxes, and they were surrounded by black and white.

Theresa suddenly came forward and looked closely at his face. "What happened to you? Your eye is swollen."

Leo wouldn't have told his mother or George. But he realized that after everything he had been through with Theresa and Millie, he had to tell her. "I kind of bumped into Harrigan."

He could see the name register with her and she grew serious. "Where?"

"At the cemetery. I saw him during the funeral, hanging around Matt's grave." She looked away uncomfortably. "Don't worry, he's not going to bother us anymore," he reassured her.

She met his gaze. "After the way he hounded my mother? I'm not so sure."

"I think I got my point across for him to leave us alone," he said, feeling proud of himself.

She shrugged. "I guess it doesn't matter now anyway. I doubt he'll follow me to Jacksonville. It's a shame that you had to get hurt to deal with him, but if it helped, then I'm glad." As an afterthought, she said, "Actually, I don't even know what I'm worried about. It's not like we know anything different from what my mother already told him."

His first thought was that she too was obviously covering up the truth. But then he looked at her face, and he could tell that Theresa still didn't know the truth that Millie had told him. Even though Theresa did not know that her mother had killed Jack Pierce, Leo couldn't help but wonder if Theresa at least suspected the truth. Of course, it was also possible that Theresa was unaware that Millie had told Leo anything.

The clicking of a lighter caught his attention. Theresa had lit a cigarette. She replaced the lighter on the kitchen table near where she had a white and green pack of cigarettes. He hadn't seen them before now. Next to them was an ashtray half-filled with butts. Menthol filled the air. "You're smoking?" he asked incredulously.

She shrugged. "I know, it's bad. I haven't smoked since I was in college. After your friend called me that morning and I was on my way here, I got an overwhelming desire for a cigarette. I stopped at a Citgo and bought a pack. Needless to say, I can't stop now." Unconsciously, he inhaled the singeing smoke of sweet menthol tobacco. It was like Millie was in the room again.

"So," Leo said, forcing conversation again, "did you need my help with anything?"

She shook her head. "Not really. I've packed up the stuff that I want to keep. Mother's books are going to the library, like she wanted. I'm going to have a garage sale over the weekend and try to get rid of the furniture. I put the unit up for sale." She puffed on her cigarette.

Leo nodded, glancing around some more. He peered over her shoulders into the living room. He could see the paneled walls were now stripped bare of their pictures. The beaten couch was still there, as were the end tables and 1950s-style lamps on them, but the ruined shag carpeting was gone.

"You know," she added, "if you want to take anything, you can. I'm sorry, I guess should have mentioned that."

"No, that's all right," Leo said. He hated to admit it, but he actually wouldn't have minded peering at her book collection one last time. It was packed at this point, ready for donation though. He was almost disappointed. Then he was disappointed with himself for desiring something that belonged to his dead friend. Wasn't it enough that she had already given him books from her collection? "Did you want to talk to me about something?" he asked, more to change the subject in his own mind.

"Oh, yes." She pulled out a chair from the kitchen table, and pointed to another one. He took hold of it and realized it was the same chair he had sat in on Saturday morning. He forced himself to sit.

Theresa took a drag on the cigarette and flicked ashes into the ashtray. She hadn't developed the habit of letting the ash linger. "I have to ask you something," she continued. "Mother wrote in the note she left me that she wanted me to check with you about a stuffed animal that she sent you. And that if you didn't get it I needed to follow up with UPS about it. Do you know what she was talking about?"

Leo was taken off guard. "I got it the other day."

"What was it, a birthday gift or something?"

He wasn't sure how to reply. "I don't know if I'd call it a gift." He gazed at her through the cigarette smoke. "It was Matt's teddy bear."

"Oh," she replied, her eyebrows arching quickly in surprise. She inhaled the cigarette so that the end burned orange. She flicked the ash. "I had no idea she had any of Matt's toys left. She certainly never kept any of mine."

"This one was. . ." He thought of the right word. ". . . special, I think." He thought about telling her that he had left it at Matt's grave that morning, but he held back. He could see that she was distracted.

"I don't remember anything Matt had that was special," she continued. She sounded perturbed. "Everything we had at my grandmother's got tossed in the trash after she died, courtesy of my mother. I don't think she saved anything that was my grandmother's either."

"This was from before you lived with your grandmother. She found it the night. . ."

She encouraged him to continue when his voice trailed off. "What night?"

He met her gaze. "The night your stepfather was killed."

She went to speak, but didn't say anything because the door opened. She extinguished the cigarette, squashing it firmly in the ashtray. George and Charlie came inside. "We're getting the last of the books," Charlie said. He continued into the living room with George behind him.

Leo looked back at Theresa, but she was gazing into the kitchen. Charlie groaned from the weight of the boxes, and George helped him get them out the house. As they walked past them again, George said to Theresa, "This is the last of it. We're taking them over to the library, then I'm heading back to Ma's. Unless you need me for anything else."

Theresa looked up at him. "No, that's fine. Thank you."

"Well, I'll call you later."

"What for?"

He shrugged. "I don't know . . . just talk, I guess."

"George, there's nothing for us to talk about."

Charlie and Leo looked at one another for a moment. Leo sensed that Charlie was uncomfortable in the midst of their domestic squabble. It ended quickly, though, when George grumbled something unintelligible, then opened the door to follow Charlie outside. On the way, they heard him ask Charlie about getting a beer after they were done. They didn't hear Charlie's response. The wooden door closed, followed by the screen door slamming outside.

They were alone again, and it was quiet. Theresa broke the silence by getting up and opening the cooler. "Do you want a beer or something?"

He was startled to think she might be drinking too. He was relieved when she pulled out a bottle of Zephyrhills springwater for herself. "No, I'm fine," he said to her. She shut the cooler and sat down again. As she opened the bottle, Leo said to her, "I'm surprised Millie was so interested in knowing if I had received the bear."

She didn't respond to his statement, but instead asked, "What do you know about that night anyway? What did Matt ever tell you?"

Leo leaned back in his chair. His fingers grabbed at the end of the table, picking at it. "Nothing."

"Look, if you don't want to tell me—"

He looked up at Theresa quickly. "I'm serious. Matt never told me anything. He mentioned about going to the cabin during the summers when he was very young, but he hardly remembered anything from then. He hardly ever spoke about his father either. All I knew for the longest time was that Jack had taken off one night. Matt never knew anything about what had happened to him." As an aside, he added, "You know, not knowing the truth drove him crazy." He had meant it figuratively, but in some ways he realized there was an added dimension.

She shook her head. "What that poor kid went through," she said.

"With the cutting?" Leo asked, realizing it probably wasn't necessary.

She looked down at her bottle, then drank some of the water. "I guess my mother told you he did it when they moved to Florida?" Leo nodded. "I guess he was trying to kill himself."

Leo considered it somewhat ironic that she was able to speak of Matt's cutting problem as attempted suicide but was not seeing a connection to her own attempt years ago. He didn't bring it up, but responded to her last remark.

"He wasn't trying to kill himself. He never was. He was crying out in pain, trying to get someone to listen to him." He looked down at the table and picked harder at the table. "I don't think anyone heard him. I don't think even his doctor was able to penetrate what was happening to him. I think the most he ever got was that it had to do with Jack's disappearance."

"So what do you know about the night Jack died?" she asked.

Leo sat up in the chair. "Just what Millie told me." His response was neutral, revealing nothing, he hoped. Again, he wondered what she knew. Her response surprised him.

"Which story?"

Now he was confused. "What do you mean?"

"You know what I mean. My mother liked to make up stories. Sometimes she would change things, events, cause confusion. She lied to us a lot."

He grew defensive. "I think any lies she told you were to protect you."

She nodded. "Yes, I've heard that one. She liked to protect herself too, though."

"I don't think you're being fair," he replied.

"Look, I'm not saying that my mother deliberately tried to hurt Matt and me. You're probably right, she did try to protect us. But I also think she was interested in protecting herself. Why else did she abandon us?"

"She told me you were better off living with your grandmother, that she was a terrible mother."

She drank her water and scoffed. "Well, at least that's true." Leo was getting angry with her attitude, and it was evident on his face. "Leo," she continued, "there's no point in you getting upset. You knew my mother for only a short time. She's been very good these past few years. But do you know what it's like not to speak to your mother for years at a time? I was a teenager living with my grand-mother, helping take care of my little brother, while my mother lived in San Francisco, or wherever the hell she went, writing us whenever she felt like. She never left a phone number. She would call once every six months, maybe. It was very difficult for us."

Leo looked away and nodded slowly. "You're right. I can see what you're saying." He remembered their book talks over coffee, right here, at this very table. Those were vivid, living memories for him. But then he considered that this was also the same woman who had killed her husband and dumped his body in the lake. Millie had been many different people. "What do you remember from that night?" he asked Theresa, more out of curiosity.

She looked away for a moment. "Actually, I have no idea what hap-pened that night. All I knew was that Jack had taken off. I heard the story from my mother about Jack's business partner and Jack disap-pearing only after Harrigan first came to me. But for some reason I've never felt right about that story."

Leo shifted in his seat. So she did have her own suspicions. "What do you mean?"

"I don't know. There are things about the night he disappeared that don't make sense to me."

"Well, I guess you wouldn't have known anything firsthand from that night anyway. Millie told me you weren't there."

She drank from her water bottle. "I know. I was sleeping over at the house next door. Mary . . . something-or-other. I can't remember her name."

"Whitman," he replied.

"Yes, that's it. How did you know that?"

"Harrigan's videotape," he replied, remembering the old woman on the videotape, the woman who would have been Mary's mother.

Theresa looked away again. "You know what's strange, though? I don't remember sleeping over there. Apparently I did though, and Mother picked me up the next morning and we went straight to Brooklyn. But I don't remember any of it."

Leo eyed her curiously. "That seems strange."

"I used to think so. There's a lot from my childhood I don't remember. I can't seem to recall any solid memories of anything before living at my grandmother's."

Leo found himself interested in this. He shifted in his chair to face her. He had memories of being seven or eight, going to the Catholic elementary school in New Jersey, having snowball fights with the twins next door, watching educational filmstrips at the library, and earning his first dollar allowance for washing dishes. He could also remember things like his brother constantly teasing him about the boogie man in the window at night, his mother cooking the most amazing dinners, his father teaching him how to ride his bicycle without training wheels, and his father suddenly missing from his life. He could remember these things very clearly.

"I don't know how to explain it," she continued. "They're like flashes and sensations. But once I lived with my grandmother, I can recall full memories like everyone else. It's almost as if I woke up one day and everything was clear from the time I was at Grandmother's."

"How old were you then?"

"I don't know. Fourteen or so."

"Did you ever tell Millie?"

She nodded, drinking again. "I did. Years ago. She told me not to worry about it, that she couldn't remember things from her early years either."

Leo wondered why so much would have been lost for her, although he recalled his own conversations with Millie, about how Jack had been abusive and Millie had been drinking. Matt had apparently purposely forgotten things. "They say that children with traumatic childhoods often block them out as a coping mechanism. Do you think that's what happened to you?"

"Probably."

"Maybe you should go talk to someone about it," he said.

"I've thought about it. I haven't had time though. There's been too much going on with Matt, George, and now my mother."

"I heard that you didn't speak for a few weeks after you got to your grandmother's. Do you remember that?"

She looked at him oddly. "No. Did Matt tell you that?"

He nodded, lying, not wanting to discuss the letter, now with the teddy bear at Matt's grave. "Well," he continued, "considering the traumatic childhood, especially how abusive Jack was, I'm not surprised most of your memories are gone."

"Jack?" she said, looking surprised. "The good memories I do have are with him." Leo's confusion was evident. "Let me guess. You heard from my mother how horrible Jack was."

"Millie spoke venomously about him."

She nodded. She drank the last of the water from the bottle. "I've heard those stories too. But they don't make sense to me. Before Jack came along, I had no father. My own had taken off when I was born. I knew nothing about what a father was. And then I remember this sensation of unbelievable joy, that a father was taking an interest in me. He came out of nowhere. It was like magic. I have these mental flashes of us doing things. I see us sharing a milk shake. I feel him pushing me on the swing at the playground, and I'm laughing out loud swinging up into the sun. I can feel him holding my hand while I'm feeding a goat, probably at the Bronx Zoo. They're not complete memories. I can't tell you anything specific about what we did, but I see flashes of us doing wonderful things. I can feel him holding my hand, and squeezing it to tell me he much he loved me." Her eyes seemed vacant and lost in thought. "And when I think about him, I have the most amazing warm feeling inside me. He made me feel loved, unlike anyone else." She had a dreamy look about her. "I wonder about my mother's stories."

Leo tried to hide his shock. "You think your mother made up the stories about Jack drinking and beating all of you?"

"Jack never hit me. Jack loved me."

"Okay, so he didn't hit you, but he did abuse you." She gazed at him blankly. "Sexually," he continued, meeting her gaze, and feeling very uncomfortable all of a sudden. He shifted in his seat and looked away.

"Jack never abused me. He loved me." She spoke like an automaton. Her voice was mechanical, as if she were reciting a sentence she had said over and over, as if to convince someone of its truth. "He loved me," she repeated.

He moved forward in his seat. His mouth was dry. "Theresa," he said, "he got you pregnant, didn't he?"

"Who told you—?"

She stopped herself. She was furious, but she no longer spoke so oddly. She shook her head angrily. She smashed the plastic bottle in her hands so that it collapsed with a loud bang, causing Leo to jump back in his seat. She put the bottle back on the table, and took a cigarette from the pack. She flicked the lighter twice before the flame rose and the smell of menthol filled the air again. She looked upward, exhaling a cloud of smoke around them. Leo couldn't help but cough slightly, more out of nervousness.

"She really told you everything, didn't she!?" She stood and paced in the kitchen. Leo turned in his chair and watched her. He had never seen her this agitated. As she smoked and paced, her face was flushing with anger. "Look, don't get me wrong, I guess it was my mother's decision to tell people what she wanted, but she had no right to tell you about that."

Theresa flailed her arm out with the cigarette, pointing toward Leo. "She made me have an abortion! Do you realize that? She made me kill my baby! I wanted to keep that child. I was so happy when I found out I was going to have his baby. I would have my own little baby, like Mother had Matt, but Jack would love us even more than them!"

Leo listened to her tirade, uncertain what to say or how to respond. She was unhinged. She kept pacing. Her face was red, her eyes wide.

"He told me he would. He told me he'd love me forever! And then she had to ruin it all! She dragged me to that fucking clinic and forced me to have an abortion! I wanted that baby!"

There was a pause, but she kept pacing. Leo swallowed and ventured to reason with her. "Theresa, you were only fourteen at the time. There's no way you could have raised it."

"Yes, I could have! Jack would have helped me!"

"And, what? You'd all wind up living together like a happy family?"

"Yes!" she screamed.

Then, she looked away, and started to calm down. Leo could see her slowly return to the woman he knew before. She stopped pacing. She breathed deeply. "Oh, my God," she muttered. "I sound like an idiot."

Leo watched her, waiting cautiously to see what she would do or say next. She returned to the table and extinguished the cigarette in the ashtray among the numerous butts already there. She sat down, then rubbed her face and shook her head. She looked up at Leo.

"I'm not psychotic." He turned back in his chair completely to look at her. She continued to explain. "Obviously, the fourteen-year-old in me thought it was the perfect resolution. Of course there was no way it could have worked out. But I do still have a difficult time with this, because my mother did make me have an abortion, and the doctor apparently didn't know what he was doing. I could never carry a child after that." She met Leo's gaze. "That baby was my one opportunity to have children, and my mother took that away from me."

He breathed deeply. "Don't you think it was Jack's fault for getting you pregnant in the first place? He had no right to touch you. If he had never touched you, you wouldn't have had an abortion and things would have been very different for you."

She nodded slowly, gazing off into her unrealized future. "My mother never would have left us. I would have had two kids by now probably. George and I would have lived very different lives. He might have even loved me more and we wouldn't have divorced." She wiped at her eyes with her fists. When she looked up at Leo again, her eyes were bloodshot and wet, but she wasn't crying. "I guess you're right. I've been blaming my mother this whole time for something that was Jack's fault." She shook her head. "Now that I think about it, I wish I had been able to tell her I didn't blame her anymore."

"I don't think she ever realized that you did blame her. She never told me that."

"Oh, she knew."

"I really don't think so."

Theresa grew serious. "No, Leo, I know for a fact that she knew. I told her right to her face that I blamed her. In front of Jack, no less."

"What do you mean?"

"It's another hazy flash memory. I hear myself screaming at her, telling her Jack loved me and that she had killed our baby."

"When was this?"

She shrugged. "I have no idea. But I see Jack in the flash, so it must have been that summer after the abortion, right before he was gone."

"What else do you remember?"

She closed her eyes, pausing a moment. "I hear all of us yelling. I can still smell Jack's Old Spice cologne. He's angry and shocked. He doesn't know what to do or say. And my mother. She's right in front of me. She looks horrified, almost as if she'd been drinking."

Leo thought about what Millie had told him from the night Jack had died, how he had been angry because he had discovered the medical bills for Theresa. That was how Jack had found out about the abortion. Theresa hadn't even been there. So what was Theresa remembering? Was it even a memory, or the wishful thinking of an inner adolescent?

Leo asked, "You told Jack you were pregnant with his child?"

She opened her eyes. "Well, of course I. . ." Her voice trailed off. "What?"

"I was going to say that yes, of course I had told him. But, I don't actually remember telling him. I remember that flash I just described to you." She pondered the situation. "Do you think that's how I told him? In some sort of teenaged emotional outburst, in a fight with my mother?"

"I have no idea." Leo was confused by all of this. It contradicted Millie's story. He thought about what Theresa had said a little while ago, about Millie making up stories. "Can you remember anything else?" he encouraged, though with hesitation.

She sat back and closed her eyes again, as if to replay the memory. "I hear me yelling. Everything is blurry. I think Jack reached out to me, or my mother. I can't tell."

As she continued talking, something occurred to Leo. Millie had told him that Jack had found out about the pregnancy and abortion only moments before she had killed him. But now Theresa was saying she had told him. The timing was off. It was all wrong. Theresa wasn't even there that night.

"Okay, that was strange," Theresa said, interrupting his thoughts, looking at him. "Mother was sitting with a tray in front of her. She had been peeling an apple. There's a knife on the tray." She met his gaze. "How weird is that? I mean, I don't think I ever saw my mother eat an apple. Did you?"

"No, now that you mention it." Leo did find the detail odd as well, but his mind was on what she had said before. He realized he was feeling very uncomfortable.

"Why would I see her peeling an apple?" she persisted, closing her eyes again.

Leo didn't respond. Millie had told him that Theresa was sleeping at the neighbor's house. Theresa knew this too, but she had no memory of it. Millie had made a point of emphasizing this fact first during her confession at the psychiatrist's office, then afterward in the cemetery. She had been insistent. Theresa had been next door. Was it a lie? Or was it possible that she had been mistaken about how Jack had discovered the news about the pregnancy and the abortion? Maybe Theresa had told him sometime sooner in such an emotional outburst.

But then why wouldn't Millie have told him that when she had told him everything else? Why not that detail? It didn't make sense.

"The apple is green," Theresa continued, "but when I look back at it, it's got red on it." She seemed frustrated. "Why is everything so blurry? Wait, the knife's gone." She paused. "Leo, I see red . . . every-where."

Leo turned his attention back to Theresa. "What do you mean?" His heart was pounding harder. He could feel perspiration on his fore-head. He wasn't liking this, not at all. Something was very wrong.

She opened her eyes again. "There's suddenly red . . . everywhere." He could hear the concern rising in her own throat.

Had she been there that night? Had she actually witnessed her mother killing Jack? Was Millie trying to hide this fact from Leo? If so, why? She had told him so much already.

"Leo, I don't understand all of this. What am I remembering?"

"I don't know," Leo muttered in response.

All Theresa knew was that Jack had been taken away by his busi-ness partner that night and had apparently been killed by him and his associates. Theresa knew the story that Millie had told the police and Harrigan. She had no idea that Millie had killed Jack. He could feel his concern rising, yet he needed to understand more. There was something missing in this story, something he had to understand. But something was warning him not to push things too far. He thought about what she had said . . . there was red everywhere, just like how Millie had described it . . . all of the blood . . . everywhere. He could see that Theresa was agitated. She had opened her eyes again, and they were more bloodshot now. Her mouth was agape.

"Theresa," he asked suddenly, "where's the knife?"

She seemed hesitant, but closed her eyes to see her memories. "It was on the tray, with the apple. And then, the apple is red . . . there's red everywhere," she continued slowly. "Damn it, why is everything so blurry?"

"Take your time," he reassured her. "It will come to you." Yet, something told him that it might be better if it didn't.

"Wait," she continued, "I see the knife. It's red too." She opened her eyes quickly. "Leo, is it blood? Am I seeing blood?" She was becoming frantic. "Leo, what the hell is going on? What am I remembering?"

His heart was beating in his throat. She had to stop before it was too late. But he couldn't stop her. He needed to know for sure. It was as if he could see it himself, because he knew what had happened that night. She had no idea. In her own mind, she wasn't even there. But he knew. She was there. She had been there all along. And the story Millie had told him had been another lie.

Her eyes closed again. "Okay, wait, it's becoming more clear now. . ."

He had to stop her. He couldn't let her continue. These memories had been forgotten for a good reason. He couldn't let her remember. He could almost hear the voice in his head, telling him to stop her, before it was too late.

"Leo, the knife. . ." Theresa said, ". . . there's blood on it . . . oh, my God, it's in—"

He reached out and grabbed her forearm forcefully, and she jolted back from his touch, exclaiming, "Jesus, you scared me!"

His heartbeat was echoing in his ears. He was flushed, his mind was racing. He had seen what she was remembering, had heard what she had not said. He had to stop her. "I'm sorry," he muttered. He breathed slowly to calm himself. "You were getting pretty upset there."

"That's because none of it makes any sense! Why would I be seeing—"

"Your memories are all screwed up," he said quickly, cutting her off. It sounded so foolish. "Think about it," he went on, desperate to come up with something, anything, to distract her. "You already said that you can't remember things from the past. You know you confronted Millie about the whole pregnancy and abortion, but it's all a blur."

"But you don't understand," she said in disbelief. "The knife with the blood was in my hand!"

She had said it. He had tried to stop her, but now it was too late. It was what he did not want her to say, but now it was out, and he knew it could mean only one thing. It was Theresa, not Millie, who had killed Jack.

He had so many questions now. Why would she have killed him? She had said she had loved him. She had insisted that he had loved her back. It didn't make sense. And yet, he knew it had to be true. In the deepest part of his mind and soul, he knew it was true, because it was the one truth that Millie herself had been so desperate to hide that she had lied, not once, or even twice, but three times. She had even killed herself, in order to protect her daughter.

He looked at Theresa, with her bloodshot eyes and worn face staring at him in disbelief, uncertain of her own memories and feelings. And then suddenly in his mind he saw another Theresa, one who was fourteen years old, not much different from the photograph of the Pierce family he had seen in Harrigan's videotape. She had been a precious little girl with a sad, but angelic face. And now she flashed in his mind the memory that Theresa was trying to recall, one of herself screaming at her mother, blaming her for killing the baby. She would have been wild with rage, and in that rage she would have picked up the knife that lay beside the apple. She would have attacked. . .who? Did she try to kill Jack, angry that he was not defending her? Did she try to kill herself out of desperation? Or, with a cold shudder throughout his body, Leo realized what in truth must have happened. Theresa had picked up the knife and attacked her mother, wanting to kill her for ruining everything.

And maybe Jack, in a rare act of gallantry, or perhaps just involuntarily, had intervened to stop her from attacking her own mother, and in doing so he had inadvertently fallen victim to Theresa's blind rage. Perhaps he would have tried to get the knife away from her. It would seem he should have been able to fight back. But her rage might have been so severe that she was like an animal unable to stop herself as she stabbed uncontrollably at the figure whom she believed was her mother, but in fact was her father, the father of her now aborted child.

Jack would have fallen, landing in a heap with a loud thud. Millie might have stared in shock, her hands covering her mouth, her body shaking as she stared at the wan fourteen-year-old she had given birth to, who now stood before her as a murderer, a young girl with tears in her eyes that fell and blended with the spatters of blood that stained her white cheeks, her golden hair, and the clothing that barely covered her adolescent breasts. In her hands she would have held the knife, her stepfather's blood dripping from the blade onto the Oriental carpet that Millie would use to wrap up his body and dump him in the lake.

Perhaps in that same moment silent tears would have fallen down Millie's own cheeks. She would have reached out and taken the knife away from Theresa, ignoring the blood now on her own hands. She would have placed it where the apple lay. She would have opened her arms and stepped forward, reassuring her daughter that it was all right, that she would take care of everything. She would have been in shock and horror over what had transpired before her eyes, but she would have embraced her daughter anyway because she loved her, knowing only that she had failed to protect her daughter from the monster who had molested her, but that from now on she would do whatever she could to protect the remnants of innocence that still existed within her little girl. She would have held her daughter tightly and let her cry against her, knowing in that moment that she would have to do everything she could think of to protect her daughter, to block out all memory of what had happened to her and what she had done. She would protect her from the truth.

It was that same realization which now occurred to Leo. With the understanding of the truth had come the responsibility that accompanied it. He had to save the child from the truth. He had to lie to protect her, and in so doing, he had to save the woman in front of him before she fell victim to her own horrors that she would never fully understand or emotions that she could never have validated. He had to protect Theresa from the truth, as Millie had done all of these years.

Leo gathered up his strength as best he could, suppressing the agonizing pain in his stomach and heart. "It all probably means nothing," he muttered, trying to sound matter of fact.

"*What?*" she shouted.

He took a sharp breath. He had to be stronger. He had to protect her. "I mean," he said more firmly, "obviously, the knife means something to you, if you were holding it in your hand."

He wasn't sure what to say. How could he lie to her? How could he convince her of something that wasn't true? He thought again of the knife, the blood. It made him think suddenly of Matt, the blood everywhere, the knife slicing into skin, the night Leo had come home late and discovered him in the bathroom.

"Theresa," he said, leaning forward, his hand still on her forearm, squeezing it slightly, "did it ever occur to you that maybe you had been a cutter too?"

She furrowed her brows in thought. "What do you mean?"

"Just what I said. Matt and you both went through a lot as children. It wouldn't be too much of a surprise if you had been a cutter too."

He could see her mind playing with the idea. "But that doesn't make sense. I would remember. . ." Her voice trailed off. He eyed her suggestively, to encourage her doubts. "All right," she continued, "I can see what you're saying. My memory is terrible. But I think I would have had scars on my body like Matt did."

"Not if you knew what you were doing." He was feeling desperate himself, but he was amazed at how freely the words were flowing from his lips. He found himself relaxing as he spoke more words to her. He caressed her forearm now, to ease her with the idea. "When Matt was in therapy, we read some of the literature on the disease, and it said that girls often find ways to hide it more than boys, because they are more conscious of their physical appearance."

She pursed her lips, then nodded. "I guess it's possible."

"Besides," he added, "you have the scars on your wrists." He hesitated to suggest the connection between attempted suicide and cutting, but he knew it was a connection she would understand.

She pulled her arm away from his grip, moving almost involuntarily to look at the faint scars that suddenly now were visible again once they had been discussed. She turned her wrists away. She shifted in her seat. She lit another cigarette. She was nervous, agitated now. She puffed. "All right, so maybe I was a cutter too. But then why didn't Mother tell me, especially after the whole incident with Matt?"

He discovered he had a response for this as well, although it bothered and surprised him to say it. "Maybe it's because Matt had seen you do it. Maybe he learned it from you." He watched the words sink in. "Millie probably didn't want you to feel guilty for getting him started."

She had put the cigarette down in the ashtray. The smoke unfurled into the black-and-white space around them. She considered what he said, then sat up in her seat. "If that's true. . ." Her voice trailed off.

"That's the truth she's always kept from you. She knew how much it would bother you, and she didn't want you to suffer."

She scoffed. "Please don't make my mother sound like she was a saint."

He shrugged. "Okay, I'll agree that she wasn't a saint. But she was your mother, and all she wanted to do was protect you. Both of you."

Theresa looked away, then glanced back at him. "Did she tell you all that?"

He hesitated before replying. He wasn't sure how much more of this lying he could keep up. "No," he said, looking away, "she didn't tell me this. But it seems obvious, doesn't it?" he added, hoping it would be obvious to her.

There was a slight pause, then she nodded slowly. "Yes, in some odd way, it does make sense."

He found himself silently sighing in relief.

She wiped at her eyes. "I think I need some serious therapy," she said.

He looked back up at her, cautious, but calmer now. "Or," he replied, "maybe you should just leave things alone. You're fine now, right? If you did have this cutting problem, it was in the past. You've obviously moved on." She was listening to him. "You've got this amazing job ahead of you. You're done with George!" She grinned. "Reliving things from the past isn't going to help you. What's done is done."

She chuckled. "God, now you sound like my mother."

He smiled too, not realizing until then that he had said the words Millie herself had spoken numerous times through the years. It occurred to him then that all of it, in fact, had been her words. It was as if she had been speaking through him somehow, or had told him what to say, in order to protect her daughter from the truth, and to allow her to move on with her life.

Theresa jumped up suddenly, interrupting his thoughts. "You know what?" she exclaimed, extinguishing the cigarette for good. "You're right. What's done is done. There's nothing I can do about it now. I'm going to live my life for me now." She was elated, and determined to remain so. "And so should you," she continued, pointing toward Leo. "You've got yourself a new man there, Leo. Don't let him go. He's really cute, by the way."

Now Leo was embarrassed. He could feel himself flushing. He rose from his chair. "Did you want help with those boxes?" he asked, pointing to the remaining ones on the counter.

"Yes, that would be great, thank you."

He picked one that didn't look too heavy, but it still aggravated the pain in his chest and back from the fight earlier. He didn't complain though. Theresa picked up a box as well and they walked outside to her car. They loaded them into the trunk with other boxes, and he offered to help her with more, but she turned him down, saying she could handle the last two in the kitchen. She shut the trunk, and they faced each other.

"Will I see you again before you leave?" he asked.

She nodded. "I think your mother wants to have a little dinner party before I go." She came forward with her arms open and gave him a hug. He returned her embrace, and they hugged each other for a few seconds. When they separated, she was smiling. "My mother was crazy about you, you know that, right?"

"She was the best. I still think so. There will never be another woman like her."

Theresa nodded and chuckled. "In more ways than one."

Leo got into his own car and waved good-bye. As he left Queen's Manor, he felt weighted down with knowledge of the truth, but somehow he also felt relieved to know that he had managed to protect Theresa as Millie would have wanted, at least for now. He could only hope that her determination to move forward without looking into the past would sustain her for the rest of her life.

– TWENTY-FIVE –

Leo stepped out of his red Toyota. He strolled up to the front porch door with thoughts in his mind of what had happened that afternoon with Theresa. He wondered to himself whether he should tell Armando. He had been with him through so much of this. He had listened to him like no one ever before had, and he had given him his all to comfort him. He almost felt as if he owed it to Armando to tell him the end of the story.

There was no proof of anything, of course. Jack was long dead, and the police had declared his death an accident. Matt was dead. And now Millie was dead. Only Theresa was left, with faulty memories. And Leo felt relatively certain that he had given Theresa enough ideas about what her blurry memories meant that she probably would leave them alone.

He entered the screened porch and opened the front door of the house. He went to call Armando's name, when he stopped. Something was different. It had caught him off guard. It even made him wonder for an odd moment if this was his own house. He stepped back and looked at his porch again, realizing how foolish he was to question such a thing. Obviously he was in his own house. But something was different.

It was a smell, an intense, flavorful smell coming from inside. Leo could smell fresh herbs and spices. He smelled olive oil and could hear it crackling in the distance as he entered. He didn't recognize the fresh herbs and spices. It reminded him of the Italian cooking from his childhood when his mother used to make veal parmigiana or chicken cacciatore. But there was a difference. The spices were stronger, more intense. As he walked further into the house, he recognized the pungent scent of onions. He called out Armando's name as he headed to-

Pierce
© 2007 by The Haworth Press, Inc. All rights reserved.
doi:10.1300/5849_25

ward the kitchen, where he could hear louder crackling noises from the stove. He stood in the kitchen doorway and watched as Armando cooked.

"Hey, you're home! Good timing," Armando said. He was wearing a white apron over his shorts and T-shirt and stirring away at something in the large frying pan.

Leo was completely taken off guard. "What are you doing?" he asked ridiculously.

"Uh, cooking. Bistec de palomilla, plantains, rice, and black beans." He pointed at each of the pots or pans with their food in them. He smiled proudly, but his smile faded. "What? You don't like it?"

"No, it's nothing like that. I . . ."

"What?"

Leo didn't know what to say. He was so completely taken aback by seeing Armando cooking him dinner in his own house. Matt had never cooked. Ever. He was incapable of making even a piece of toast for himself. Leo had done all of the cooking. Much like so many other things Armando had done for him already, Leo coming home to dinner was completely unexpected and surprising. It was so different, and so much what he wanted. He loved it. He loved all of it. And he loved Armando for it.

He shook his head, coming forward. He gazed into the pots and pans and saw the most incredible array of dishes . . . brown steak slices popping in hot olive oil with white onions and spices smoking upward through the house, gorgeous pieces of yellow plantains simmering in a smaller frying pan, white rice steamed and ready for serving, and black beans about to bubble in their pot. He looked at Armando and kissed him.

"What's that for?"

"For everything. You amaze me." They kissed again, then Armando shooed him away. The dinner was almost ready.

Leo washed up, then went into the dining room where Armando had set the table for their dinner. There were even fresh flowers that replaced the ones Armando had given him last time. Armando mentioned to him about a bottle of Chilean white wine in the refrigerator.

He asked Leo to open it. He did so and poured it for them. Armando served their food and they sat to eat.

The food was delectable. Leo wondered if this was the best meal he had ever eaten. He knew that he was enjoying it more because Armando had prepared it. As they ate, Armando spoke to him about Leo's afternoon and Leo joked with him about the situation with his brother and Charlie.

"How is Theresa doing?" Armando asked.

Leo shrugged. He wasn't completely sure how to answer that question. "She's . . . holding up all right." He told him about her plans to move away.

"What did she want to talk to you about?"

Leo drank some of the cool, buttery wine. "She wanted to ask me about the teddy bear." He saw Armando stop eating. He told him about how Millie had asked Theresa in her note to check up on this. "We talked about. . .quite a lot actually."

"About Millie, I guess?"

Leo nodded. He looked up at Armando, and he decided that maybe he should tell him everything. "We talked about her abortion, and her stepfather molesting her."

"Wow, that's heavy conversation."

"And . . . we talked about how Jack died."

Armando drank some wine himself, eyeing him oddly. "What do you mean? Millie killed him."

"You and I know that, Armando. But Theresa doesn't. She thinks the story about the business partner is the truth."

"Oh," he replied with surprise. Armando put the glass down, then asked Leo hesitatingly, "So, did you tell her the truth?"

The irony of the situation was that, had Leo allowed her to continue working with her memories, or in fact if he had encouraged them and had not lied to her, Theresa probably might have discovered the truth for herself. The real truth, that is. And she also probably would have fallen apart completely, maybe irreparably. When he had sought to cover things up, lie to her, he knew Millie had spoken to him or through him, something esoteric like that. Somehow Millie had made him realize that he had to perpetuate the lie in order to protect her.

What was it that she had written in her suicide note to him? Something about truth. He thought for a moment, then remembered what she had written: "The truth is what you make it out to be. Truth is not fact, it's what you believe."

So what did Leo believe? That Theresa had accidentally killed her stepfather while attempting to take her mother's life in a blind adolescent rage, that she had blocked out the whole incident from her memory, and that Millie had covered up her daughter's crime. He believed that Matt had witnessed his father dying at some point during the night, and that had affected him for the rest of his life as well. He also believed that Millie had attempted to provide her children with a clean slate because she loved them and wanted to protect them. Subconsciously, though, they were haunted all their lives.

And what of Theresa? What did she believe? That Jack had been taken away by his partner and associates that night, that he had apparently been killed, and that her mother had been attempting to give Matt and her a better life with their grandmother because of her drinking problem. And what else did Theresa now believe to be the truth? That because of the sexual abuse, she had become a cutter, and maybe had somehow shown her brother the way to bleed pain out in order to survive. It was the best truth to explain away her faulty memories and help her realize why her mother had made up stories. Millie had been trying to protect her children in a way that wasn't the best or healthiest, perhaps, but it was the only way she knew how.

At least, this was the truth that he hoped Theresa now believed. Leo had a responsibility to perpetuate that same truth, as Millie had. He realized then that he could tell no one. Not even Armando. In fact, there was no point in telling anyone the real truth. "What's done is done," Millie had said many times. It was over now. All of it. What mattered now was the future. Theresa's future, Jacksonville and what lay beyond. And Leo's own future.

He looked down at his plate, and he saw freshly cooked food, then looked up and saw a glass of wine, beautiful flowers. Across from him sat his new boyfriend Armando, with his beautiful black hair, sexy goatee, and brown eyes, and a caring sensibility that had listened to him as he cried, helped him with his wounds, and done so many things so far because he loved Leo. This was what lay before him. This was his new truth, the beauty of what he believed in. None of the other stuff mattered anymore.

"Um, hello?" Armando said aloud, distracting him. "Earth to Leo?"

"What?"

"I asked you if you told Theresa the truth."

Leo shook his head slowly. "No, I decided that if Millie didn't want her to know, then it wasn't my business to tell her."

"Are you sure about that?"

Leo paused a moment, then nodded. "Positive." He ate another bite of steak, savoring the spices on his tongue, and quickly changed the subject. "This dinner is absolutely delicious, by the way. You can cook for me anytime." Armando smiled sheepishly.

They ate and talked about everyday things, like they were a couple who had been in a relationship for a long time. They cleaned dishes and watched television, until Armando yawned and wanted to go to sleep. Leo encouraged him to do so, wanting to finish his last glass of wine first. He sat outside rocking on his front porch swing in the darkness. It was muggy, the air thick with humidity. The cool taste of the wine relaxed and cooled him.

He wasn't sure how much time had passed, perhaps half an hour so, before he decided to go to sleep himself. He walked into the bedroom. Armando had left the bathroom light on, and it cast an angled beam into the room and lit up most of the bed. Armando lay asleep, his breathing slow and steady. He lay on his stomach, with his face toward the light and his hands beneath his head and pillow. He was naked but for his white briefs, his caramel complexion glowing from the light. He was Endymion-like, and Leo smiled warmly from the beauty before him, suddenly understanding how Selene fell instantly in love with the shepherd boy in that gorgeous, sensual moment.

He undressed quietly and tossed his clothes in the corner with other dirty clothes. He put on a pair of boxers, then walked across the creaking hardwood floor as silently as possible so as not to disturb him. He lay down on his back beside him. As he lay there, he realized he had forgotten to turn off the bathroom light. He looked at Armando again, his beautiful face staring with closed eyes back at him. Leo turned his head, as if to somehow magically make the light go out, when his eyes rested upon the photograph.

He picked it up and held it above him. The bathroom light provided enough illumination for Leo to see the photograph, but not clearly. His memory of what it was, Matt and he smiling back at the camera at some party he hardly remembered anymore, was more hazy than it had been even just a few days ago. He turned to look back at Endymion, whose visage stared clearly back at him with the slow, steady breath of life. He reached down and placed the framed photograph on the floor.

Leo rolled to his side to face Armando. With his left hand, he reached out and lightly brushed his hair, caressing the strands and waves with his palm. He ran a finger down his cheek, letting it fall delicately on the bristles of his goatee, then ran the back of his finger up the side again.

Armando stirred, as if having felt something like the wind brush up against him. His hand came out from under the pillow to move it away, when he felt the finger and the hand. His eyes fluttered, and he saw him. "Hey," he whispered.

"Hey," Leo replied.

He took hold of Armando's fingers and brought them to his lips. He kissed his fingers, then lay their hands down intertwined on the bed between them.

"You okay?" he whispered.

Leo nodded, his face rustling against the pillow. "I am now," he replied.

He moved forward and kissed him on his luscious lips. They kissed a single time, Armando's body sleepily responding. Leo kissed him again, and with each kiss that followed, Armando awoke, until he rolled on his side as well, and their hands reached for each other. They moved closer, and their torsos pressed. Their hands explored each other's arms, backs, chests, faces. Armando tried to be gentle so as not to irritate Leo's wounds from the fight. They kissed each time, their lips opening and their tongues exploring each other's mouth.

They pressed their hips closer together, and their hard cocks touched each other through the fabric of their underwear. Leo could feel the head of Armando's cock peeping out from the top of his underwear as it rubbed against his stomach. He reached down with his left hand and slid Armando's underwear off his hips so that his cock moved on its own and hardened more. Armando kicked off his underwear as Leo removed his boxers. His cock slapped against his stomach and their bodies touched each other, head to head. They moved sinuously as they were meant to.

Armando pulled his head away and looked at him. "Are you sure about this?" he asked, his eyes glowing with concern, making him even more attractive to Leo. He responded by moving his head down Armando's body, and using his tongue to play with his nipple. He used his finger to play with the other one, than ran his fingers through the patch of hair in the middle of his chest. He continued to move downward, swirling his tongue down his stomach, kissing his side, then moving further down so that he inhaled the sweet smell of his sex, kissed his hip, nibbled his thigh, and licked the inner most part of his leg.

He rolled Armando onto his back and positioned himself between his legs. He opened his mouth and for the first time rolled down the foreskin and wrapped his lips around his uncut cock. He tasted the sweetness of his precome, and moved his head up and down as he swirled his tongue around him with each sucking moment. He could feel Armando's hips moving down into the bed and up again, and he relaxed as he sucked and swirled while Armando fucked his mouth.

Armando was moaning, reaching down with his hands, running his fingers through Leo's hair, holding his head steady as his cock moved in and out of Leo's mouth. He pulled out after a few minutes, and brought Leo back up to him, sitting up himself. They kissed, sharing the sweetness of his sex on Leo's lips and tongue. "Oh, my God, I have wanted you for so long," Armando whispered in his ear. "*Te amo,* Leo." His voice sent a shiver down Leo's spine.

"*Ti amo,* Armando," he whispered back in Italian, feeling Armando's response in a gush of kisses. He pushed Leo back into the pillows, delicately but ferociously running his lips over Leo's face, neck, and chest. His goatee tickled Leo's skin, but his lips and tongue cooled the heat. It was an explosive combination of sensations, and

Leo knew it felt right. Leo laid back and relaxed as the kisses with his lips, goatee, and tongue continued, and he enjoyed the moment completely when he felt Armando's lips wrap around his cock. He moved his head up and down hard, his desire heightening his actions. Leo found himself moaning in a way he hadn't in so long. He never objected as he felt the sensations overcome him, and he completely relaxed as Armando reached down even further with his tongue, lifting his balls with his hand, kissing and swirling his tongue in the precious, vulnerable spot between his scrotum and his ass. Leo's hips jerked involuntarily, and he exclaimed aloud as he felt Armando's tongue licking, tickling at the tip of his ass, playing up and down and around his balls, rubbing his goatee in just the right moments so that Leo's entire lower body was on fire. Armando grabbed Leo's cock, and he yelled aloud as Armando jerked on it while licking and rubbing his vulnerable spot. Leo's body was shuddering. He stared down and watched Armando's face gazing up with such an intense stare as he swirled between his legs and jerked Leo off. Leo shouted aloud without warning as he felt the intensity of what had been an unbelievably and lonely long time, and an ever-heightening passion for Armando built up over these weeks. He shot his come out of his cock and onto his chest, then shot a second time past his shoulder and onto the pillows beside him, and followed this with four more intensely heated loads, until he rested his head back into the pillow and shouted aloud to help come down from one of the most intense moments of his life.

Armando moved fast and climbed on top of Leo while his body still shivered, and kissed Leo's face all over, adding to the heat. Leo could feel him sliding his cock on Leo's stomach, using his come to lube himself, then using his one free hand to jerk himself off at the same time. He sat up suddenly, and Leo watched in utter joy as Armando's face exploded in a shout of intensity, and he fired his hot come from his cock out onto Leo's cheek, neck, and chest. He collapsed on top of Leo, and they kissed each other, rolling in the sheets, catching their breath.

They lay intertwined in the sheets, kissing and caressing. They shared their love. They teased each other. They giggled. They fucked and made love again, and fell asleep with the light shining on them, enveloping their bodies for good.

When they awoke, it was after nine o'clock. They were still holding each other, and they kissed and wanted to make love again. The rumbling of their stomachs helped them decide to hold off for the moment and have breakfast instead. Armando volunteered to make it, but Leo stopped him, telling him that he would cook for him this time. Leo ushered him into the shower, watching from the bed as Armando shimmied his beautiful ass toward the bathroom, then turned around and winked at him. Leo laughed at him, but found himself getting turned on again very easily.

Left alone for the moment, he sat up and went to put his feet on the floor, when they landed on something. He moved them aside, and looked down to see the framed photo staring up at him. He reached down with his right hand and picked it up. He could see the photograph more clearly now as daylight peeked in from the window to his side and mixed with the bathroom light. He looked at their smiling faces in the photo, and found himself smiling again, not because he was reliving a moment with Matt, but because he was recalling something good that had happened in his past. He listened to Armando sing off-key in the shower, and he chuckled.

He walked naked into the office. He put the photograph on the desk, then opened the closet door and squatted. He flipped through the paintings his mother had done through the years, knowing instinctively where the one of Matt and him was. He pulled it out, admiring his mother's work, the symbolism and beauty before him, for it was beautiful to him now for some reason, more beautiful than he had ever imagined it before. He touched the arrow that pierced Matt's body, feeling the hardened oil paint against his finger. He stood up again and moved to the photograph. They were so different in their depictions, and yet somehow he realized now that they were both a part of who he had been and who he was today. He carried the photograph and painting back to the closet, put them both inside facing each other, then shut the closet door.

Rather than go into the kitchen, Leo walked back to his bedroom. He headed right for the bathroom and Armando's off-key singing.

Without any warning, he pulled back the shower curtain and startled Armando. He joined him under the water, pushing Armando back against the tile wall and pressing himself against his body. He reached up with his hands and brought Armando's face to his. They kissed hard.

"What happened to breakfast?" Armando asked with a chuckle as he broke free for a moment, gazing into Leo's eyes.

"This is breakfast," Leo said with a grin, then slid the shower curtain closed behind him.

– Acknowledgments –

This novel never would have come to be without the help of a few important people. To Jay Quinn, Donna Barnes, Tara Barnes, and everyone at Haworth Press who helped make publishing this novel possible, I express my eternal gratitude. To Steven Levenkron, my admiration for your work *Cutting: Understanding and Overcoming Self-Mutilation* (Norton 1998), which I encourage people to read for more information about the lives of cutters and the help available to them. To Sgt. Tom Hines, retired Supervisor of the Criminal Identification Unit of the Coral Springs Police Department in Florida, I wish to extend my thanks for his important assistance in forensics and legal information. My thanks also to his wife, Paula, for bringing us together, and to my friend Joy Hunter for first introducing me to Paula. And *mille grazie* to Lina, Sheila, Cristina, Mario, Gherardo, and all the staff at Hotel Mario's in Firenze, for making my stay so comfortable while I completed work on this novel.

To my dear friends Andrew P. Gessner, Amy Kornblau, and Stacey Van Hoy, I thank you so much for reading early drafts of chapters of the novel and for giving me excellent feedback, information, and support when I needed it. To Ursula, thank you for helping me realize the full potential of who I can be. To the Lady Dorothea Dannenfelser, thank you for the many years of our special friendship and for inspiring me. To my parents, my family, and the rest of my friends, thank you for always believing in me.

And to Nana, to whom I have fulfilled a promise and thus have dedicated this book. I will never be able to fully express how grateful I am to you for encouraging me to read and to write. I know you look down on me from above with pride.

Pierce
© 2007 by The Haworth Press, Inc. All rights reserved.
doi:10.1300/5849_26

ABOUT THE AUTHOR

Roberto C. Ferrari has been an adjunct professor, bird handler, disk jockey, fortune teller, pianist, receptionist, and most recently a university librarian. He holds degrees from the University of South Florida and is currently a graduate student in New York City. His articles have appeared in the *Journal of Library Administration*, *Journal of PreRaphaelite Studies*, and *Notes and Queries*, and his fiction in the *Louisiana Review*. This is his first novel.

Order a copy of this book with this form or online at:
http://www.haworthpress.com/store/product.asp?sku=5849

PIERCE

_____in softbound at $22.95 (ISBN-13: 978-1-56023-657-3; ISBN-10: 1-56023-657-4)

370 pages

Or order online and use special offer code HEC25 in the shopping cart.

COST OF BOOKS_____

☐ **BILL ME LATER:** (Bill-me option is good on US/Canada/Mexico orders only; not good to jobbers, wholesalers, or subscription agencies.)

☐ Check here if billing address is different from shipping address and attach purchase order and billing address information.

POSTAGE & HANDLING_____
(US: $4.00 for first book & $1.50 for each additional book)
(Outside US: $5.00 for first book & $2.00 for each additional book)

Signature_____

SUBTOTAL_____

☐ **PAYMENT ENCLOSED: $**_____

IN CANADA: ADD 6% GST_____

☐ **PLEASE CHARGE TO MY CREDIT CARD.**

STATE TAX_____
(NJ, NY, OH, MN, CA, IL, IN, PA, & SD residents, add appropriate local sales tax)

☐ Visa ☐ MasterCard ☐ AmEx ☐ Discover
☐ Diner's Club ☐ Eurocard ☐ JCB

Account # _____

FINAL TOTAL_____
(If paying in Canadian funds, convert using the current exchange rate, UNESCO coupons welcome)

Exp. Date_____

Signature_____

Prices in US dollars and subject to change without notice.

NAME_____
INSTITUTION_____
ADDRESS_____
CITY_____
STATE/ZIP_____
COUNTRY_____ COUNTY (NY residents only)_____
TEL_____ FAX_____
E-MAIL_____

May we use your e-mail address for confirmations and other types of information? ☐ Yes ☐ No
We appreciate receiving your e-mail address and fax number. Haworth would like to e-mail or fax special discount offers to you, as a preferred customer. **We will never share, rent, or exchange your e-mail address or fax number.** We regard such actions as an invasion of your privacy.

Order From Your Local Bookstore or Directly From
The Haworth Press, Inc.
10 Alice Street, Binghamton, New York 13904-1580 • USA
TELEPHONE: 1-800-HAWORTH (1-800-429-6784) / Outside US/Canada: (607) 722-5857
FAX: 1-800-895-0582 / Outside US/Canada: (607) 771-0012
E-mail to: orders@haworthpress.com

For orders outside US and Canada, you may wish to order through your local
sales representative, distributor, or bookseller.
For information, see http://haworthpress.com/distributors

(Discounts are available for individual orders in US and Canada only, not booksellers/distributors.)
PLEASE PHOTOCOPY THIS FORM FOR YOUR PERSONAL USE.
http://www.HaworthPress.com   BOF06

Dear Customer:

Please fill out & return this form to receive special deals & publishing opportunities for you! These include:
- availability of new books in your local bookstore or online
- one-time prepublication discounts
- free or heavily discounted related titles
- free samples of related Haworth Press periodicals
- publishing opportunities in our periodicals or Book Division

❏ OK! Please keep me on your regular mailing list and/or e-mailing list for new announcements!

Name _____

Address_____

_____

*E-mail address _____

*Your e-mail address will never be rented, shared, exchanged, sold, or divested. You may "opt-out" at any time. May we use your e-mail address for confirmations and other types of information? ❏ Yes ❏ No

Special needs:
Describe below any special information you would like:
- Forthcoming professional/textbooks
- New popular books
- Publishing opportunities in academic periodicals
- Free samples of periodicals in my area(s)

Special needs/Special areas of interest:

_____

_____

_____

_____

Please contact me as soon as possible. I have a special requirement/project:

_____

_____

_____

_____

PLEASE COMPLETE THE FORM ABOVE AND MAIL TO:
Donna Barnes, Marketing Dept., The Haworth Press, Inc.
10 Alice Street, Binghamton, NY 13904–1580 USA
Tel: 1–800–429–6784 • Outside US/Canada Tel: (607) 722–5857
Fax: 1–800–895–0582 • Outside US/Canada Fax: (607) 771–0012
E-mail: orders@HaworthPress.com

GBIC07

Visit our Web site: www.HaworthPress.com